What readers are saying about The Lost Soul

'The best book yet in the lighthouse series, by AJ Warren. The author fashions her characters with feeling and subtlety and weaves a plot on how their lives become entwined. Romance and intrigue keep the reader turning the pages to see what happens next. If you enjoyed the previous books, you will enjoy this one more.'

Julia O, Oxfordshire
★★★★★

'The Lost Soul is the eagerly anticipated fourth book in the Lighthouse series and has not disappointed. The characters developed as the plot took many twists and turns. There were many surprises as the plot moved swiftly to a conclusion.

Dear Cath,
Happy Reading!

(Andrea) X

The Lost Soul

The author showed a thorough and compassionate understanding of all human emotions. Another triumph for this exciting new author.'

Mrs B, Cheshire

'Just finished The Lost Soul. Wow! What a fab book, it's definitely my favourite. I was up until 2am so that I could find out how it ended!'

Denise H, Oxfordshire

The Lost Soul

AJ Warren worked as Head of an Early Years setting for 18 years. She lives in Oxfordshire with her husband, and her two grown children, their spouses and two grandchildren live nearby. She is eagerly awaiting the arrival of her third grandchild, due in late December 21.

This year (January 2021), Andrea took on the Volunteer Lead role for the Covid vaccination programme in her area. To date they have done over 45,000 jabs! In addition, she became a district councillor to continue supporting her local community, alongside organising her marshal team for mass flu jab clinics.

She writes from the heart and has an imagination that keeps her head full of weird and wonderful ideas. She has two young Romanian rescue dogs and enjoys swimming, writing, going to the theatre and talking! Her books, The Lamp-post Shakers, The Ghost Chaser and The Box are available on Amazon in both E-reader and book format. The books are part of The Lighthouse Series and can be read alone or as part of the series. The Lost Soul is the fourth instalment in the series.

A short word from the author:

'Hello, I'm Andrea, alias AJ Warren and I hope you enjoy The Lost Soul, which follows on from The Ghost Chaser storyline. I'm a fairly new author and this is my fourth book since I first

The Lost Soul

began writing in 2018. I enjoy writing and love the freedom and escapism of developing storylines and shaping characters. One of my favourite characters in The Lost Soul is a young four year old called Zoe, because she reminds me of my grandson, and my work in early years.

If you enjoy The Lost Soul, please let me know, share on social media or write a review on Amazon. Reviews are the key to pushing the AJ Warren books onto the next level. Many Thanks. Andrea x'

You can contact Andrea via her website:
https://ajwarrenauthor.wordpress.com

or via her Facebook page

Other books by AJ Warren

The Lamp-post Shakers (Book one - The Lighthouse Series)

The Ghost Chaser (Book two - The Lighthouse Series)

The Box (Book three – The Lighthouse Series)

The Lost Soul

The Lost Soul

The Lost Soul

The Lost Soul

This book is dedicated to those who know what it is like to struggle. For those who walk through the darkness and the mist and wonder if they will ever see the sunlight again. There is a little seed within each of us, that will grow if we nurture it.

The seed of hope.

The Lost Soul

Part 1: Jules

My name is Jules Walker, and I am a murderer.

If I say the words out loud, it makes the hairs on my arms stand up, and my heart thuds hard in my chest. But it's the truth. To look at, I'm just a normal person, tall, cropped dark hair, slim build. I don't look like a murderer, at least, I don't think I do. As far as I'm aware, I don't act like a person who has committed a heinous crime. Unless you count that oppressive cloud of doom that follows me around, trying to suck the life out of me.

My world is grey. Devoid of colour.

Six months ago, I looked into the face of a monster, stared into the abyss and touched the devil. Of course, he was no mythical creature, just an evil specimen of a human being who damaged everything he touched. Lured women in with his good looks, charmed them with his smart mouth, before he began to use his fists. In the end, he needed to be stopped.

And he was.

I had looked at him, stared into his face before battering his skull with a baseball bat. And then, to my annoyance, the bastard had managed to get up again, so I finished him with a shattering blow to the back of his head.

The Lost Soul

Cold water gushes from the tap, spraying against the ceramic basin in the cloakroom. I reach in to splash a handful of the cool liquid onto my face, trying to boost my flagging spirit. I wonder how long I can live like this, gloomily trekking across the West Yorkshire moors in the Bronte village of Haworth, like a forlorn Heathcliff, searching for the love of his life and a new start. But there is a price for my freedom. No redemption. No peace of mind. And, if my actions of six months ago are anything to go by, whatever good I had within me, has gone.

Lost forever.

You see, I'd made up my mind to give myself up to the police. I never wanted to be free. I just wanted to do my time and quietly move on. I needed to see my parents, to explain what I'd done for Belinda, my younger sister, who I affectionately called Blip, but I didn't have time. I wanted to see if they could move on with their lives, now the monster who hurt her no longer drew breath.

Moving forward is the hardest part of recovering from traumatic grief. Even though, I've accepted the loss of a loved one, and I know her death has been avenged, it doesn't change anything. Blip is still dead, and living is still bloody hard. God knows, I've tried. I need to find a way to live in this world without her, and it needs to be worthy and productive.

I rest wet hands on the basin and study my reflection in the bathroom mirror. Beneath the water droplets sitting on my chin a haunted, weary face stares back at me. Who is this stranger with the haunted face and the dead eyes? I don't recognise him.

The Lost Soul

From the extra notch I've made on my black leather belt, to keep my jeans from falling down, I know I've lost weight. Clearly, it looks as though I've given up. My blue eyes are dull with dark circles under them, not surprising as I don't get much sleep these days. The light went out of my eyes a long time ago. And it never came back.

Some days I feel so bloody tired of living a lie my bones ache.

There is a loud knock at the door.

'Nick, you in there? Russell is asking for you. Can you come?' my work colleague, Sasha's soft velvety voice calls from the other side of the door. I grab the green towel from the rail and wipe it across my wet face. *For heaven's sake, pull yourself together.*

'On my way,' I reply with as much enthusiasm as I can muster. I look at my reflection one last time, and force my grim lips into a smile, when all I really want to do is shout, '*My name's not bloody Nick!*'

***

'Nick,' Russell Cherwell croaks, 'tell them to leave me alone. I need to speak to you.' I look at the old man sitting in the dark green wing-back chair, next to his bed. He's a well-educated university don, who taught English Literature and History at Oxford's Exeter College for twenty-five years. I love hearing stories of his life in the vibrant city of Oxford and its county, it reminds me of my family home in Thame, and Richmond Court

The Lost Soul

in Abingdon, where I had worked as the Manager of a home for youngsters leaving care.

Bittersweet memories that torment my soul.

I have grown fond of Russell, despite his growing cantankerous nature, there is much I admire about him. His interest in reading and collecting antique and first edition books for example. There are so many bookcases in his apartment, filled to the brim, it's like walking into a library. He will reminisce for hours about celebrated authors such as Lord of the Rings writer J.R.R. Tolkien, and His Dark Materials writer, Sir Philip Pullman who had studied in the same rooms at Exeter.

When Russell retired, he moved to Torquay in Devon because, he'd explained one day as we had sipped hot cups of tea, that he had wished to live in the birthplace of Agatha Christie. Following that, he had lived in Harrogate for many years, before deciding to spend the latter part of his life at Greystones, Haworth where he could be cared for, whilst retaining some parts of his independence.

Each apartment has the same layout at Greystones, which also offers nursing care facilities. Spacious, one-bedroom apartments, with a large lounge, dining area and a kitchen alcove. Patio doors lead to small, enclosed outdoor seating areas, bringing natural light into the main living quarters.

Russell is as fussy as they come, but there is something about him that calls to me, makes me want to protect him and slay his demons.

The Lost Soul

Despite his eighty years, he has an aura of someone much younger about him, in both body and mind and even though he walks with a stick he sets quite a pace. Thinning white wispy hair straggles against pale skin that appears almost translucent in the July sunlight. His face reflects the age of a person who has lived a full life, with lines and wrinkles that shoulder a wealth of experience. He has a perpetual grimace, and constant face of stubble, even though he has a regular shave from our on-site barber and hairdresser.

Nurse Lauren Skelton stands next to Russell, she's a tall thin woman, with kind eyes and a mop of short dark hair. She has an aura of kindness but firmness about her. She takes her work seriously, and treats Sasha, despite her young age, as an equal. For that alone, she earns my respect. Lauren wears navy trousers and a pale blue nurse's collared top. Sasha is the Manager, and has just completed her nurse practitioner qualification, specialising in care for the elderly.

'Hey Russell, what's the problem?' I ask, looking at his panicked face. He's wearing a cotton brown and beige checked dressing gown, tied at the middle and just peeping out of the gown are his pale blue and white striped pyjamas.

Sasha stands beside me, dressed in navy trousers and a smart white top, her dark curly red hair is tied in a loose knot bun. I try to gauge her age, twenty? Twenty-one? I've just turned twenty-six and she looks much younger.

'Lauren was trying to give him his evening medication and, for some reason, he refused. He says he wants to speak to you,' Sasha's voice is deep and soft, but holds a note of frustration, as

The Lost Soul

her eyes catch mine, causing a warmth in my stomach. Lauren, like us, knows Russell well and shrugs her shoulders, causing Sasha to give a little smile.

'Nick, I need to tell you something.'

Standing in front of him, I drop to my knees, pat his leg and say to him, 'tell me. Then you need to take your medication.' His face is devoid of colour, his pale blue eyes pained.

'She needs to go,' Russell mutters.

'Who?' I ask, 'Nurse Lauren?'

'Yes,' he says.

'It's all right Nick,' Lauren's thick Scottish accent cuts into the conversation, 'I've got to see Mrs B in room five. I'll be back in about ten minutes.'

Sasha lowers her head and is about to follow Lauren from the room when Russell mutters, pointing to Sasha, 'She can stay. I like her.'

I can't help but smile softly at Sasha, it's as though we're in the inner circle, similar to being in the 'groovy gang' in an episode of the vintage TV show Only Fools and Horses. When we're alone with Russell, I stretch my long legs, before taking a step forward to sit on Russell's bed.

'Russell?' I ask.

'Do you remember when I told you that my grandson was a no-good son of a bitch? Only got in touch when he wanted money?' Russell bangs his chest with his fist.

16

The Lost Soul

'Yeah, didn't he live in London?'

'Look,' he leans across to his bed, his wrinkly hand reaching for, and pulling something from under his pillow. It is a folded piece of white paper. 'Read this,' he says, handing the letter to me.

I take it from him, my eyes quickly skimming the hand-written note.

Dear Grandad,

Hope you are well. I'm fine, but I've got myself into a bit of trouble. I need your help. There's a problem with the London house, the tenants are messing about with their rent and I'm picking up the slack.

Remember that first edition of Little Dorrit, by Charles Dickens? It's in your mahogany glass cabinet, it's next to your other first edition books. Can I come by and get it? If I can sell it for £2000 that will really help me out.

You're a gem.

Anthony x

Shit. This is not good. I look at Russell and note the tears glistening in his eyes ready to fall. Our gazes hold, 'can I?' I ask him, before nodding at Sasha. He dips his head low, as though in embarrassment, as I begin to read the letter out loud. I hear her sharp intake of breath as she listens to what Russell's grandson wants from him.

The Lost Soul

I feel an anger sizzling through my veins, I can't stand people who take advantage of others. I mean, for heaven's sake, this man Anthony is his own flesh and blood, his grandson, does that not count for anything these days? What happened to family, respect, and loyalty? When did people start believing that they were owed a living, or a life, that they deserved? when in actual fact, they'd done nothing to help themselves! If I could find this Anthony guy, I'd give him a piece of my mind, along with a smack around the ears to knock some sense into him.

I knew someone in my social care group at university, who often got himself into scrapes. He was always late for lectures and always had an excuse. Midway through the semester, our tall, thirty something, easy going lecturer, Jeremy had even begun to run his fingers through his short blonde hair and roll his eyes in frustration. God, what was his name? I think for a second and the lightbulb moment flashes, yes. It was Harry. Of course. Yes, he only talked of himself, his life and how things we discussed were related to him.

Harry wasn't even interested in anything but himself, so I was a little unsure why he would be doing a social care degree. Surely, I'd argued at the time, if he couldn't develop empathy and understanding towards others and theory of mind, how would he be able to understand people, their physical and mental health struggles and the situations they found themselves in? I shake my head in disgust, which, in turn brings me back to reality. I look across the room to find Sasha, and the first thing I notice is that her face is devoid of colour.

The Lost Soul

She is so stricken, she leans over to the agitated man and doesn't stop until her face is level with his, before reassuring him in a quiet but firm voice. 'He can't be allowed to do this, Russell. This book, Little Dorrit, is your property, you don't have to give it away to anyone.'

'I agree,' I say, patting the poor guy's shoulder. He must have been so worried, wondering if his grandson was going to come and strong-arm him into giving away his valuable possessions. 'We're not going to let this man come anywhere near you, unless you give us the go ahead.' I reassure him.

'Thank you both,' Russell wipes wet tears away from his cheeks with his sleeve. 'I'm sorry for making a fuss, but the letter panicked me.'

'We are a private retirement home,' Sasha speaks gently to Russell, 'but we're not like others, we have resources.' She stops suddenly and looks up at me. She knows I meet regularly with Stuart and Jack, but I'm pretty sure she doesn't know why. My eyes hold hers for a moment and there's that warmth from earlier again in the pit of my stomach. I offer a nod to answer her unasked question. She wants me to speak to Stuart and organise protection for Greystones.

'We can easily assign security for the building if we need to,' I reassure them, 'it won't be a problem.' Russell's face relaxes, and he lets out a deep sigh. I give him a moment to regain his composure before asking, 'you ready to have your medication now?' Sasha waits for his nod, and when he does so, she leaves the room to find Lauren.

The Lost Soul

On their return, Lauren is holding two miniature paper, medication cups and a clipboard, whilst Sasha supplies the glass of water. I step aside and lean against the heavy closed beige curtains. My eyes never leave Sasha, I watch her every movement, as if mesmerised. It's as though I'm seeing her for the first time.

Her petite frame only reaches to my shoulders, making me feel like the giant from Gulliver's Travels. A dark red curl escapes from her loose bun and, to my surprise, I get a sudden urge to reach out and tuck it behind her ear. I want to touch her skin and wonder what it would feel like beneath my fingers, as they softly grazed her cheek.

'Stop it, man. Pull yourself together,' I mutter quietly to myself. But I must have said it louder than I realise because her soft voice breaks my thoughts asking, 'did you want something?'

'Oh nothing,' I shrug my shoulders, 'just thinking out loud.'

Sasha raises an eyebrow, and a small smile as she hands Russell the glass of water and both she and Lauren watch him swallow his medication. The sprinkling of light brown freckles sitting under her dark brown eyes and across her nose only add to the natural beauty of her face.

'Buzz if you need me, Russell,' Lauren tells our grouchy resident as she takes a pen from her clipboard and completes the medication log. She glances to Sasha, 'I'll get this sorted, then take my break if that's all right?'

Sasha smiles, 'yes, of course, I'll be out in a moment.' We watch Lauren leave and stand in quiet silence, both in our own worlds.

The Lost Soul

She smiles at Russell, 'don't worry about a thing,' she says, 'we'll sort it out.'

Sasha leaves the room, and I look at Russell. He smirks, in a knowing way, before giving me a wink of the eye, 'she's a lovely girl, that Sasha.'

'I know,' I sigh.

It doesn't pay to be too candid, so I say no more. We chat a little more, but I find myself staring out of the window, not really listening. My mind won't let me rest.

Greystones is an old, converted building that used to be a primary school, complete with a lift, restaurant, games room, landscaped gardens and pool facilities. We are also lucky that this retirement facility is nestled on the edge of the West Yorkshire moors, because it means I can go for long walks to be alone with my thoughts.

Sasha lives on site in an apartment with her four-year-old daughter, Zoe, as I do, and for visitors, there are several rooms with bathroom facilities set aside. When Stuart offered me the job as the Deputy Manager here it was a chance for me to start afresh with a new life. A life where I was unable to use my social care degree and training, where Blip, Richmond House, Corinna James, and everything to do with my past, could be left behind as though they never existed.

I knew it wasn't going to be easy, reinventing myself in this new guise, no longer Jules Walker. More importantly, I knew it was time to stop looking back. The Deputy Manager position included

The Lost Soul

an onsite apartment and a new car. I'd have been a fool to turn it down, considering I had nowhere else to go.

I came to Greystones six months ago to start my new life. I left my name, what was left of my family, and my previous life behind. Six months ago, I became Nick Flannigan.

Hiding from those who wish to bring me to justice.

We all have secrets, don't we?

The Lost Soul

Part 2: Nancy

He sits there with his greying short curly hair, wearing a navy pinstriped suit, white shirt and navy tie. He's eating his Shreddies and slurping his cold full-fat milk. God, that slurp grates on me, like a leaking tap. Slurp, slurp. A two-year old child can eat cereal with less noise than that. He thinks he's so clever, so respected, in a world where his word is gospel and no one dares to defy him, but I know different.

Over the years he has managed to retain his slim figure and good looks, although he's begun to develop a bit of a tummy. Too much food, too much drink. His skin is still smooth, despite the odd wrinkle and he has a small brown facial mole on his chin.

Lewis, my husband. God, how I hate him.

I should have got out of the marriage a long time ago, before things got this bad.

If only I had been privy to the real person hidden under the façade, during our first meeting, I would have turned around and ran in the opposite direction. I was twenty-one and had been in my final, year at The Royal Veterinary College, based in London and had been enjoying a weekend break at home with my parents.

The Lost Soul

It was one of those pivotal moments in life, that pushes you in a direction you never expected to go. Our first meeting took place in a Tesco's car park in Abingdon, Oxfordshire. My shopping trolley, full of family food and toiletries, had accidentally rolled into the front of Lewis' blue VW as I had transferred my shopping into the boot of my little red Micra.

I close my eyes, as the memories of that poignant moment send a shiver down my spine, as I now battle a marriage that has given me immense pain and joy, in equal measures.

'Hey,' he had got out of his car, squeezed between the trolley and the point of contact on the front right side of his car, and studied the paintwork.

'Sorry' I told him, feeling all sorts of a fool, 'thought I'd locked the wheels, so it wouldn't move.'

He was tall and skinny and looked nice in his dark grey suit with a crisp, white shirt. His hair was a mop of black silk, hanging in short curls to the nape of his neck. I watched with interest as he took a white cotton handkerchief from his jacket pocket and began to rub it across the car where he thought the point of contact had been. I couldn't see a mark, so I wasn't sure how he knew where to rub.

'Don't worry,' he suddenly smiled, and his face lit up, 'there's nothing there.'

'Oh, thank goodness,' I was so relieved that he agreed there was no damage, and I certainly didn't want any more drama in my life.

The Lost Soul

'Can I take your number and we can meet for a coffee sometime?' he looked expectantly, holding out his hand, 'I'm Lewis by the way. Lewis Benson.'

'Nancy,' I replied, taking his firm, cold hand and staring into cool blue eyes.

And that handshake had sealed my fate.

My husband is a local Member of Parliament for Oxford West and Abingdon. He works hard and plays hard, that means to say he is busy socially most nights, with a constant stream of invitations to dinner and to open museums, art galleries and the like.

As our relationship has reached an impasse, it is with relief on my part, that he almost always attends these events on his own. Lewis thinks he's beyond reproach, that he is invincible. Of course, his arrogance will ultimately be his downfall. He has a celebrity-style status here in Abingdon, where we live in a four bedroomed detached house overlooking Abingdon Marina.

When I met Lewis, he had been working as an assistant campaign co-ordinator for a local MP, Freddy Mason, and spent many years working his way up the ladder, making contacts within the circles of people needed to get him where he is today. He loves his job, making speeches, talking to people, invitations to social events and gatherings and, of course, - the attention he gets as a minor celebrity.

Lewis rents an office near Abingdon town hall, and to everyone he knows, he is a kind, productive, forward-thinking MP. I've

25

The Lost Soul

heard that his constituents truly believe in him and trust him to listen to their concerns. More fool them.

Me. I was the one who was going to save the animal kingdom. My parents had wanted so much more for me, and I cannot help but feel that I let them down. From a toddler, I was interested in animals. We had a black cat whose name was Lucky, and he had such a lovely, calm personality. Lucky had one strange and potentially dangerous quirk, and that was that he was prone to climbing to the top of telegraph poles when he was frightened or being chased, which seemed to happen quite often.

Several times, we had to call the fire service to come and retrieve him from his precarious stooping position at the top of the telegraph pole, to the applause and delight of the residents in our little cul-de-sac, in Appleford, Oxfordshire. Suffice to say, every time he ran to the top of the telegraph pole in our street, it became a big community event.

By the age of eighteen, I knew I wanted to become a vet. Having passed all my A levels with A's and B's, I was pleased to have conditional offers for my top three university choices to do my degree in veterinary medicine, The Royal Veterinary College in London, Bristol and Cambridge universities. In the end, the RVC in London called to me, and I began studying vet medicine in earnest.

My parents were good, hard-working people. My dad was a railway engineer, who worked for British Rail and specialised in train engines. Mum is a secondary school teacher. They understood the value of a good education and working hard to

The Lost Soul

build a future for yourself. They instilled that ethos in me, to be productive and work hard.

I finished my five-year degree, where I attained my Bachelor of Veterinary Science, BVSc, surprisingly I got a first. My future was looking good.

And then I married and moved in with Lewis Benson.

My dad died three years ago following an accident at work, where some heavy machinery, that hadn't been secured properly, fell on him. I went to dad's funeral, but Lewis wouldn't let me go to the wake at the house. Therefore, even though my mum had needed me, and I wanted to be there for her, I had to leave her at the cemetery graveside, heartbroken. While I went home, threw myself on our bed and cried myself to sleep. I will never forgive him for that.

Marrying someone like Lewis does that to you. Shakes you up, until you're all over the place. Then systematically withdrawing my access to my family and friends, my support network, leaving me feeling alone and isolated.

Lewis' behaviour changed during our first month of marriage. It began with the roll of his eyes, when I spoke, the deep sigh or shaking of the head when I wore an outfit he disproved of. He questioned my movements and decisions, restricted my choices and options, and six months after our wedding, he hit me for the first time.

My hand gently strokes the right side of my face. I can still feel the sting of the slap, as he'd lashed out with surprising strength, simply because I'd picked up the wrong deodorant for him at the supermarket. After that slap, he told me I couldn't get anything right.

He increased his emotional hold on me, by telling me I was no good. Lewis was desperate to keep me under his thumb, brainwashing me to do whatever it took, to show the world that we were a successful couple with an enviable lifestyle. Eventually, there would be children he had told me, even making that sound like a threat. But, in his eyes, I couldn't even get that right, because our child wasn't the gender he wanted.

My mind floods back to the time when I found myself pregnant and we went for our twenty-week ultrasound scan. The grey-haired ultrasound technician gave us a wide smile and revealed that he thought I was carrying a girl. Lewis' face had dropped as though someone had told him he only had two weeks left to live. 'Shit,' he'd said, 'are you sure?' The man's face had paled, with that comment.

'Er,' the technician glanced at the floor, trying to hide his embarrassment before he studied the screen again. 'Yes, I think it's a girl.' His face had turned to me, worried and apologetic.

Tears pricked my eyes as I lay there with cold, wet gel on my growing bump and my hands fisted at my sides, to stop from bursting into tears. I'd been so happy, to finally have a child, something of my own to love, someone to love me unconditionally.

'A girl? Bloody hell Nancy, I don't want a puny little girl,' he gave me a look of despair. Before turning to the technician,

The Lost Soul

'maybe you're wrong,' Lewis told him sharply, before picking up his coat and leaving me alone in the sterile ultrasound room.

'Are you alright?' the kind technician had asked, handing me some tissue to wipe my tummy.

'Yeah,' I had said, when clearly, I wasn't. The saddest part was that I came from a family who thought Lewis was the best thing since sliced bread, they wouldn't believe me if I told them what he was really like. The situation was hopeless. I didn't want to be with Lewis anymore, but I couldn't return home. My marriage was for life, for better or for worse, till death do us part. I'd made my bed, and I had to lie in it.

Our beautiful red-headed daughter, Sasha, was born nearly twenty-two years ago. I'd found a purpose to my life, a reason for living. That was, until she was almost seventeen and it all fell apart. She left the house as a young mum, blood pouring from her nose and one eye bruised and swollen shut, with a baby of six months held tightly in her arms.

It felt like only yesterday.

***

It was a sunny Saturday morning, and I was ironing in the living room. At 11am, I had looked at the clock on the wall and gently rubbed my jaw, thinking how sore it always seemed to be of late. This time, it was sore from a slap that Lewis had given me the night before. I was, still absently, rubbing the side of my face and Zoe was sleeping in the wicker basket under the windowsill, when Sasha asked in a solemn voice:

29

The Lost Soul

'Why don't you leave him, Mum?' she was leaning against the kitchen door frame, blowing into a steaming hot mug of tea. She was almost seventeen, but looked much younger in her blue jeans, grey longline jumper decorated in white stars, and her fluffy grey snuggle slippers.

'Shhh…' I said quietly, my eyes flitting to the ceiling, hoping that Lewis hadn't heard what she'd said, hoping that he was still busy going through his gym routine, in the spare bedroom upstairs, which he had converted into a gym.

'When are you going to reach your limit? When is enough, enough?' she persisted, taking a sip of her tea. 'We can go away, disappear. When he's at work. We can start again.' Her voice was almost pleading.

'It's not that simple, Sasha.' I said, my words sounding very defensive. It's strange how we feel annoyed when people state the obvious. I wish it was that simple, I pulled the sleeves of my blue cardigan down, more out of nervous habit than because I was cold.

'It is mum, it's that simple,' she said, carefully placing her mug on the small pine table and folding her arms. 'Let's just do it.'

There was a movement by the living room door and in walked Lewis, with a towel around his neck, knee-length black shorts and a white sleeveless top.

'Do what?' he said, walking into the living room. He was rubbing the towel against the back of his head.

The Lost Soul

'Nothing,' we both said together, trying not to look at each other. Immediately, I felt the hairs rise on my arm, as a mask of coldness swept across his face. I swear, his eyes turned black, and he began changing into the real Lewis Benson, just like Dr Jekyll and Mr Hyde.

He stopped mid-step, his hands still holding the towel and looked at both of us in turn. I caught my breath, here we go. I put the iron on the metal stand and rested both hands on the blue ironing board. Waiting.

'Not nothing. Something you didn't want me to hear,' he snaps, turning to me. 'You never learn, do you? Always have to stir things, don't you? You never bloody learn.' He reached out, took a handful of my hair and dragged me across the room to Sasha. They say the cheetah is one of the fastest animals in the world, but Lewis – he was a good match, he moved quickly, and my automatic response was to howl and scream at his brutal touch.

Vaguely, I heard the thud of a mug as it hit the carpet. Pain fired throughout my skull and shot across my sore jaw. I was screaming, and the baby began to cry.

It felt as though he was ripping the hair from my head, but my first thought, as tears filled my eyes, was to protect my granddaughter.

With my head held up and my shoulders straight, I looked into Sasha's stricken face, and pleaded with her not to goad him.

The Lost Soul

'Let go of her, you bully,' she said defiantly, her voice was loud, her eyes wide. She couldn't help herself, as she tried to distract his attention from hurting me, 'We weren't talking about you.'

With the lack of attention, the baby's screams had grown louder. Lewis turned to the wicker basket. 'I can't hear myself think with that bloody baby howling all the time.'

'Leave her alone,' Sasha shouted, 'she's just a baby.'

And then, he let go of me, and faced the baby. My heart stopped. Surely not, he wouldn't hurt a baby, would he? At that moment, I faced the seriousness of the situation. It was all right for me to be hurt, but not Sasha and certainly not Zoe. Sasha reacted. Sasha struck first from behind, jumping on his shoulder and pulling at his head. 'Don't you fucking touch my baby,' she screamed.

She was so brave, so slight and petite, my daughter as she fought to protect her baby. But she was no match for a grown man like him. He shook her off like a rag doll and as she dropped to the carpeted floor, he dragged her upright by the shoulders and punched her hard in the stomach. She doubled over and fell to the ground, groaning and heaving.

I looked around the room, looking for something to hit him with. My eyes rested on the wooden base of a lamp on a nearby small table, and without thinking, I yanked it hard until the plug came out and held it tight as I aimed for the back of Lewis' head.

'Get off her!' I screamed bringing it down hard on his back of his skull. Stunned, he looked at me, his cold eyes trying to focus, as a trickle of blood made it's across his ear and slithered down his lobe. I stood in a trance, fascinated by Lewis' blood, and missed

The Lost Soul

the movement that warned me that a heavy hand was heading my way. He slapped me so hard across the face that I flew across the room and landed with a painful thud against the solid unyielding wall.

Sasha's frightened voice yelled my name, over and over, rousing me from my pain. This time, I was sure that I had more than bruised my lower back, there had been a snap as I'd hit the wall and my shoulder was burning.

Lewis, his face red, had pulled back and punched Sasha in the face. 'That'll teach you, you little whore!'

'Lewis! Enough!' I shouted, moving to him and grabbing his arm. 'Leave her alone.'

I looked at my beautiful, young daughter, crumpled on the ground, her long auburn hair tied back, red blood splattered across her grey jumper, and I felt such guilt for staying with this man, for not being strong enough to take her and Zoe away. For leaving them to experience this violence.

Sasha stood up and wiped her bloody nose. One eye was red, swollen and shut. Angry tears, red marks and swelling marked her beautiful face. With her back straight, she walked over to Zoe's bag, beside her wicker basket, picked it up and crossed it over her shoulder. Silently, she scooped up her crying daughter, blankets, and all, and walked to the front door.

'I can't stay here, Mum. Not like this. With him,' she sobbed, struggling to open the door.

The Lost Soul

'No!' I said, still holding Lewis back, 'No Sasha. Please!' I shouted to her. 'Please don't go.'

Lewis had calmed down, but his voice was as cold as steel. 'Go!' he growled, 'And, don't come back. You're not wanted here anymore.'

For the first time in our marriage, I turned to my husband, completed deflated and said tonelessly, 'I hate you.'

***

I will never forget watching her wipe angry, silent tears from her face as her own father turned against her and pushed her away from the only home she had ever known. I can never forgive myself for allowing that to happen. For allowing Lewis to be part of our lives.

The only good part of losing my daughter and granddaughter was that my husband began to distance himself from me and the physical abuse came to an end. He became cold and indifferent, and treated me as if I were a housekeeper, rather than his wife.

Each day though, I simmered, planned my revenge as my blood boiled a little more. Some days I thought I'd explode, the feeling was so strong, like a tornado trying to get out. Then, when my head began to clear, I started to make plans.

There is more than one way of making someone suffer. One doesn't have to use violence. I learnt that four years ago.

'I'm going to be late tonight,' Lewis states, pushing his overgrown black fringe from his line ridden forehead. From his actions and confidence, he still demonstrates an arrogance, that

The Lost Soul

comes with someone who believes that he is good looking and clever. I shiver, as I look at him, not in a nice way, but in a way that says, 'you make my skin crawl.' I can't believe he used to be someone I loved.

'I'll leave your dinner in the oven,' I tell him, pushing my unruly grey speckled auburn hair behind my ear and looking forward to my own dinner of steak and vegetables. It is interesting that we've come to this, after twenty-three years of marriage, after everything that's happened.

His insistence that I have no contact with my family, that I don't work or have friends, it's a form of abuse and I am well aware that this is not how a relationship should be, that we should be equal partners and build a life together. But Lewis, he has a problem with managing his expectations, they are usually too high, too intense. And, I always concede defeat, no matter what.

Lewis pushes his cereal bowl forward and I notice a flicker of pain shoot across his face, as he holds his hand to his tummy. 'Bloody hell,' he grimaces, 'I feel like my guts have exploded.' He pushes out of his chair and slowly stands. It appears to take a lot of effort.

'Perhaps you've caught a bug or something.' I suggest, watching the range of emotions flit across his face.

'Another bug?' he says harshly, walking through the kitchen and into the hallway. 'Bloody hell, I need the toilet,' he mutters.

In a world where domestic violence continues to hide behind the front door of many homes, where the vulnerable and frightened are not sure if they will live to see another sunrise, and they

35

The Lost Soul

struggle to keep themselves and their children safe, it is a wonder that people are able to access help, to make the decision to change their circumstances, to find their limit. That is the difference between staying or leaving.

I made the decision to stay, I let Lewis win. My life with him, left me socially, emotionally, and physically isolated, he tore my confidence to shreds and made me withdraw within myself. Hurting me, making remarks, that was the life I had chosen, and accepted, but when he punched Sasha, he crossed a line. She gave birth to our first grandchild at sixteen and he had pushed them both out of the house six months later. I made the decision to stay after Sasha and Zoe left, but not because I was afraid of him. No, that day marked something very different.

That was the day, I started to plan my revenge on Lewis Benson, and decided to take the first small steps to escape from my toxic husband and this miserable existence. My ultimate plan is to find Sasha and my granddaughter, Zoe, so that we can be a family again.

The first steps were small, so that Lewis didn't notice, I moved quietly around the house, kept my words to a minimum and began to make myself invisible. At the same time, I opened a separate bank account in my name and started to syphon off some of my monthly housekeeping money.

There's a bang as the front door closes, and I know he's left the house. Collecting beef and vegetables from the fridge I set about washing, dicing and dropping vegetables into the slow cooker. The stewing beef is mixed with seasoned flour and quickly fried

The Lost Soul

before adding to the mix. I make beef stock from oxo cubes and add more before adding my final ingredient.

I reach into the medicine box, that sits on a high shelf in the pull-out narrow unit, and secure my most treasured weapon, the Dulcolax. Yes, it's a laxative in liquid form. He can't go without his daily dose of that. The dose depends on my mood and his behaviour to me, so today I'm generous. I pour the whole bottle in the stew and place the lid firmly on top. Of course, he doesn't need it, the Dulcolax is for my pleasure only.

Revenge comes in all forms.

Now, I open the fridge door, *what shall I have for dinner?* My eyes locate the herby new potatoes, the packet of mixed vegetables and the juicy red steak. Yes, that will do nicely.

The Lost Soul

Part 3: Jules

The woman sits on a wooden stool in the corner of the room, leans over her guitar, strums the strings to perfection and sings the words to 'Imagine' by John Lennon in a soft sultry voice. Jazz and blues tones echo around the room as she sings wistfully imagining a world of peace and love.

I look around and count the number of people in the bistro pub. Ten. I am relieved that it's quiet, less people to see me. I need to live in the shadows now, need to keep myself to myself and away from other people's business. I look around and smile as people slowly stop talking and begin to listen to the woman's sultry voice.

The music reminds me of a blues club I used to visit during my university days, where I loved listening to the soul music of great artists, such as Muddy Waters and Billie Holiday. She's good. And, pretty too, with light brown hair, chopped stylishly into a long casual bob-shape, which flows effortlessly to her white open neck blouse and blue jeans, ripped at the knees.

I take a sip of my whiskey and shuffle on the bar stool to ease an ache in my lower back. A vision of Sasha smiling at me earlier, with her brown eyes and thick black lashes, flashes before my

The Lost Soul

eyes and I shake the vision away quickly. I don't deserve to be thinking of brown soulful eyes and pretty smiles.

A hand pats my shoulder pulling me from my thoughts, and a deep, now familiar, voice says, 'Hey.' It's Stuart Greyson.

Before I can answer, the door opens, and another newly acquired friend walks towards us. They come together to check on me once a month. The second man draws attention from the women as he walks through the bar. Like Stuart he's tall, and they're both good looking guys, but Jack Kinsey has a certain swagger, an air of confidence that draws attention. With his bald head, lean features and neat designer stubble he always manages to attract the ladies, and occasionally the men when we meet.

Jack wears grey jeans and a dark red shirt, open casually at the neck. In looks and physique, he's not unlike the movie star, Jason Statham.

'Mine's a pint,' Jack says, as Stuart leans on the bar, his grey shirt stretching over his muscled shoulders.

I look around the bar to find a table to sit at, and am thankful that it's a Wednesday night, and therefore not busy, so there are plenty of tables to choose from.

When we have our drinks, I lead them to an empty table at the far side of the room, away from the singer. I look at the two men. You would think we have been friends for years, but that's a misconception. We've only known each other six months. Well, I have known them for six months.

I think back to our first meeting.

The Lost Soul

I was in a bad way. I had been drinking heavily and feeling sorry for myself. And it was all because of that bastard, Ray Delossi. The man who had been dating my sixteen-year-old sister, Blip. The man who had also lost his temper and assaulted her. An assault that had left her in such a dark place in her head, that she'd withdrawn from the world and given up on living. Not long after Delossi assaulted Blip, she'd cut her wrists and bled out. Machines kept her alive for a day giving myself, and my distraught family, a chance to say goodbye. It was a very dark period for us all.

That man had destroyed my sister, my family, my life.

Several years later I came across Delossi again by chance and, after following him home, I waited for the opportunity to put an end to the man's miserable life. Once I'd found Delossi again, I couldn't concentrate, I was consumed with seeking revenge for Blip. As I'd waited for him one evening, I'd seen a young woman, bloody and upset running from his home. Any doubts I'd had about leaving him alone disappeared when I realised that he was still hurting women.

Crossing that line would lead to consequences, I'd known that. My degree, my work experience as a trainee social worker, it all fell apart and led to me eventually confessing to the police to the murder of Ray Delossi.

***

41

The Lost Soul

And that's why I am sitting forlornly in the back of the police car, waiting to take my punishment.

The car door beside me, creaks and opens slowly, I shake my head trying to clear the fog. I raise my handcuffed hands and push my matted blonde hair out of my face. Am I imagining this? What on earth is happening?

A boy with short dark hair, startling blue eyes, and a serious face, looks directly at me, as though he knows who I am. He whispers urgently, 'come with me. I'm breaking you out.' How can that be, he's nothing more than a child?

I stare at my feet, glad that the DS gave me time to slip on a pair of trainers. I turn my head to search for the police officers, wondering if this is a test or a joke. Nothing. Everyone is busy with police business, milling around. The DI and her Sergeant are talking with solemn faces to each other as they stand in the doorway of the complex.

'Now,' the boy whispers urgently, before reaching in and pulling my front cuffed hands out of the car. 'You stink of booze, mate,' he mutters as he pushes my head down low with one hand and pulls at my handcuffed hands with the other. I sniff at the stench of stale whiskey, and I'm surprised that it appears to be coming from me. Embarrassment and annoyance fills my heavy heart. How can I have allowed myself to get into this state?

With surprising strength, the boy drags me out of the car, and pushes me a short way along a pathway before he pulls me into a small gap in the tall hedges.

The Lost Soul

Jesus, let me catch my breath. What the hell is going on?

Spiky branches from overgrown bushes catch on my skin and drag at the blue short-sleeved top I'm wearing. With his hand still on my cuffs the boy shuffles me forward to a sleek black car, waiting on the side of the road. The door behind the driver opens, and the boy lets go and pushes me inside, 'Lie flat on the seat.'

I hear the driver's voice for the first time, it's deep and husky. Winding down his window, he says, 'Thanks,' and puts paper money into the boy's outstretched hand. Quickly, I catch sight of the back of his short mousey hair before forcing my body, cuffs and all, flat onto the seat. I have no idea who this person is and what he wants. Should I be scared? Should I be thankful? I mean, he's just rescued me. But I don't feel very thankful.

The window winds up automatically, the car purrs to life on ignition and pulls away from the curb. Oh my God, I'm lying on my side on the rear seat of a stranger's car. He's going to kill me and throw me in a ditch, where my body will never be found.

'Who are you?' I whisper.

He doesn't answer, just concentrates on the road as he masterfully changes gear and takes corners. I'm convinced he's not going to answer. So, I close my eyes, trying to block everything out.

'I'm Stuart,' his deep, comforting voice says, 'and, I'm here to help you.'

The purr of the engine dulls my senses as I turn his words over in my mind. He's here to help me. How? What the hell is he going to do? Kill me slowly?

The Lost Soul

'Why?' I ask, slurring slightly as I struggle to stay awake. The sunlight is strong, and the rhythmic sound of the engine are too much for my booze-filled, weary mind.

I'm asleep before he offers his answer.

'Jules, wake up,' a male voice rouses me from my slumber, 'we're almost there.'

I sit up and, rub my eyes and shake my head, hoping to kick my brain into gear. The car sways slightly as the man called Stuart disconnects his seatbelt and leaves the car. Jesus, where am I? My mind tries to calculate what time it could be. It feels like many hours have passed from the moment I opened the door to DI Rutland this morning. I had spent most of the night drinking Jack Daniels, writing my murder confession and working out the best way to ensure that Corinna James was no longer the prime suspect for Ray Delossi's murder.

The passenger door opens, and Stuart leans in. He's tall, and wears a dark burgundy jacket, black T-shirt and navy jeans, which compared to my dirty, smelly appearance, makes him look like a male model. The rain drizzles lightly onto his jacket as he bends forward, the water sinks into the material quickly like water to a sponge.

'This way, we're stopping here for a few hours,' he gestures with long, slender fingers as he takes my arm firmly and helps me out of the car. 'First thing we need to do,' he says, looking at my hands, 'is to get these cuffs off you.'

I nod and take in my surroundings. We appear to be in a farmyard surrounded by several outbuildings, with the smell of hay and

The Lost Soul

manure wafting through the air. In front of us is an old brownstone farmhouse, that looks as though it's seen better days and is tired of life. A brown door, with faded patches of paint, stands between two large net curtained windows.

Stuart reaches into his pocket and pulls out a keyring with three keys attached to it. Silently, he grabs the cold hard metal around my wrists, before taking one of the keys. He studies it for a moment before putting it into the key slot. There's a slight jiggle of the cuffs, before I feel the mechanism release and my sore wrists fall free. Stuart pockets the cuffs and turns to me.

'There, that'll do,' he says with smug satisfaction, before stooping to pick up a large black holdall that sits on the uneven concrete floor.

I rub my wrists, pushing the circulation around until the feeling begins to come back and mutter, 'thanks.' My voice sounds croaky, and my throat feels like sandpaper. Bloody hell, I would kill for something to drink, and the irony of that thought is not lost on me, as I stand next to the mysterious tall stranger in this unfamiliar place, with the drizzle of the rain getting heavier by the second.

Stuart holds out the keyring again and selects another key, he walks to the front door, 'come on,' his firm, no-nonsense voice orders.

I follow him into the farmhouse, 'where are we?' I ask, looking around and feeling pleasantly surprised. The walls are white, the furniture is solid oak and in keeping with the old house, there are some modern touches such as a comfortable looking brown velvet

The Lost Soul

chesterfield style sofa, a microwave, a tall white fridge and a built-in oven. Stuart puts the black holdall onto a dark oak kitchen table, pulls out a large drinking glass from a cupboard and fills it with water from the tap.

'Here,' he hands it to me, and I drink long and hard until the glass is empty. 'You must be thirsty, I'll put the kettle on in a minute. The bathroom is through there,' he points to the right of the door, 'help yourself.'

'Where are we?' I ask, placing the glass on the table.

'Near Stockport,' Stuart answers, refilling the glass and taking a drink himself. His eyes look tired, but there is a fire in his eyes, a determination that fills me with hope and confidence that he knows what he's doing.

'What are we doing here?' I ask, dragging a kitchen chair from under the table and sitting on it.

'There are things we need to do before we arrive at our destination,' Stuart pulls up a chair and sits, facing me. 'First, we need to clean you up, you're a mess,' he says briskly. No argument there, I've been a mess for a while, since my sister died even, but more so since I committed murder. 'Have a shower, I've got spare clothes in the bag and then we're going to cut your hair and dye it dark brown. Once we've had a bite to eat, we'll carry on with our journey.'

'Journey? Where are we going?' I ask, alarm in my voice. Are we leaving the country? Do I need a passport? My mind goes into overdrive.

The Lost Soul

There's a silence. I realise if I'm waiting for an explanation about what's happening to me I'll be waiting for a while. Eventually, Stuart's deep voice says clearly, 'come on, let's get to work.'

Three hours later, I'm stone cold sober and feeling better, despite the niggling feeling that I'm a stranger in my own skin. I've showered and shaved, and my long blonde hair has been cut short and dyed a much darker colour. My dirty black jeans and blue T-shirt have gone, and they've been replaced with dark grey jeans, a white T-shirt and denim coloured sweatshirt. The holdall seems to have a never-ending supply of strange and interesting supplies, from clean underwear and hair dye to scissors and men's grooming gear.

Stuart takes a couple of pepperoni pizzas from the freezer and throws them in the oven, while I make a pot of tea. The farmhouse seems remarkably well stocked of frozen, tinned and long-life produce to keep any passer-by, in need of sustenance, fed for a week or more.

Thankfully, my head is much clearer now that the remaining alcohol has been soaked up by the pizza. I sit like a lost soul in the passenger seat of Stuart's black Mazda 6 and stare out of the window.

Goodness knows where we are going, but I hope that there is something good waiting for me at the other end. My mind flits to Corinna James, I hope that they release her from custody soon and that DI Rutland can help her get back on her feet. The pang of guilt for what my actions have done to her, sits heavy in my

The Lost Soul

stomach and again I find myself cursing the now deceased Ray Delossi.

'Settle back and rest,' Stuart's deep voice breaks into my turbulent thoughts several moments later, as we take the slip road to the M60, 'we'll be there in about an hour and twenty.'

'Ok,' I mutter, leaning my head back against the headrest and closing my eyes. My brain is happy to shut down, it wants to forget the pressure for a while.

A tap on the shoulder and a deep voice wakes me from my reverie, 'Jules, we're here.'

I look across to Stuart's profile, his face remains impassive, concentrating and I am surprised when he quickly glances my way. Shuffling in my seat, I sit up and stretch, rub my eyes, and shake my head, hoping to kick my brain into gear.

A pair of black wrought iron gates open and we slowly drive through and begin to veer to the left, where we follow a brick pathway, which leads to a large, gravelled car park. I check my wrist for the time and realise that I forgot to put my watch on this morning. Was it only this morning that I had spoken to the DI and her DS, telling them the truth about what happened to Ray Delossi? God, it feels like days ago. Everything is so hazy, I remember drinking heavily, to give me courage to do the right thing. But mostly, to help me to forget.

'What time is it?' I ask Stuart.

The Lost Soul

He twists his wrist to look at his watch. 'It's 5.30pm,' he answers, using the indicator to turn right, where I feel the car bounce over a pebbled road. Bloody hell! Where the hell are we?

The building in front of us is sprawling. It's an old double height, grey stone school building, with several independent blocks surrounding it, the ground is sectioned into neat grass lawns, flowerbeds, seated arbours and benches.

A tall, muscular man with a bald head and light stubble stands in the doorway. He's good-looking and dressed casually in black jeans and a dark blue shirt. Stuart steps out of the car, I open my passenger door, scramble out, and slowly stand beside the man who literally kidnapped me from a police car.

The tall man smiles and walks towards us, holding his hand out to Stuart.

'Hey man, glad you're here,' he smiles at Stuart, as he takes the offered hand.

'We hit some traffic around Birmingham and Sheffield, but nothing major,' Stuart answers.

'And you must be Jules Walker,' the man looks at me, brown eyes studying as though I was an exciting discovery on an important archaeological dig.

'I'm Jack Kinsey,' he smiles. 'Welcome to Greystones, Haworth in Yorkshire,' Jack offers his hand, and I'm not sure why, but I take it without reservation. I feel his solid grasp holding mine with conviction, and vaguely in the background hear as Stuart begins to explain why I'm here.

49

The Lost Soul

'You're here under an alias. From this moment on your name is Nick Flannigan,' Stuart begins earnestly. 'This is a private retirement home for the elderly. You will be working here as the Deputy to the Manager, Sasha Berrington. She also lives here with Zoe, her four-year old daughter and their nanny, Viola, who stays over some days to help with childcare. I have arranged for a car to be delivered here tomorrow for your use, along with an iPhone and have set up a bank account in your name, for your wages. You will live on site in a self-contained flat. Let's go meet Sasha.'

I think I must have zoned out after the word Yorkshire. I can't believe I'm in bloody Yorkshire!

***

'Jenny sends her regards,' Stuart says, pulling open a packet of chicken crisps. 'God, I'm starving. It's a long drive from Chippenham. Good job Jen knows why we're here, or she'd be suspicious of our monthly visits to Yorkshire.'

Stuart lives with his wife, Jenny, in a small village called Ford, four miles west of the market town of Chippenham. I haven't met Jenny, but I've gathered from our monthly conversations with Stuart that Jenny is involved with the widely renowned Gloverman Corporation, who are wine and champagne merchants. I'm also aware that Jenny and Stuart started The Lighthouse charity thirteen years ago to help abused women and children find a safe place to live and to help them get back on their feet.

The Lost Soul

Jack shakes his head and gives Stuart a nudge. 'Jen knows you'd never be unfaithful to her, not after everything you've both been through.'

'She'd bloody kill me,' he said, crunching a half-eaten crisp.

'At least, she's aware of it,' Jack's eyes darken and his brow furrows as he looks at me. 'I still haven't told Steph what we did for you, although sometimes I get a strange feeling that she knows I'm involved with your disappearance.'

And just to complicate matters, Jack is engaged to Steph Rutland, the DI who used to work on the Delossi case. Sometimes it's hard to get my head around that. I know that Stuart and Jack know each other well, I also know that they are close to Jack's fiancé.

'You need to tell her,' I say, 'I'm not worth losing your family over.'

Stuart drops the crisp packet on the table and looks at me. His face is suddenly stern, there's a grimace on his lips. 'Never say that. You are a person who has suffered unimaginable sorrow in your life. Your written confession was instrumental in freeing Corinna James. Yes, you have committed a terrible crime, but in doing so you have saved many women, including Steph and her son, Ben.'

'The bastard had planned to kidnap Ben, let's not forget that.' Jack's voice is deep and harsh.

'Yes, when you put an end to that sadistic brute, you did the world a favour. When Jack texted me to say that Steph knew you were the one who had killed Ray Delossi, and that she was going

51

The Lost Soul

to see you the following morning, I spoke to Jenny,' he nods to Jack, who dips his head in acknowledgement. The man is so chilled, it's as though we're talking about what we're having for dinner. I stare at Stuart, waiting for him to continue. 'We both believed that you were worthy of a second chance. Still do.'

I am humbled that this man, whom I've only known for a short time, has made so many sacrifices to enable me to start a new life. I don't feel worthy. That's the problem, my morals, my sins and my failings, they sit heavily on my shoulders.

I take a sip of whiskey and enjoy the burn as the amber liquid hits my throat. I don't want to hurt anyone else, especially DI Steph Rutland, so I turn to Jack, 'I don't want to cause trouble between you and the DI, perhaps you should tell her.'

Jack looks at me solemnly, 'I've been toying with the idea of telling her, especially as we're due to be married in just over six weeks, but I am worried that if I do all hell will break loose. That she'll want to do the right thing and have you re-arrested. Not to mention the damage it'll do to our relationship.'

Stuart leans forward, rests his arms on the table and taps his fingers. 'Look Jack, Steph is like a daughter to us, she's been through a lot. You know that.'

Jack nods.

Stuart continues, 'I'm confident that Steph will forgive your part in Jules' escape, which is minuscule by the way. And I also think that she will let Jules stay right where he is.'

The Lost Soul

Listening to Stuart's words brings home to me the gravity of my situation. I want to be honourable, to do the right thing. I couldn't let Corinna go to prison for a crime I had committed, that was why I'd written a confession note for DI Rutland. I never planned to escape, I just wanted to be left alone and take my punishment. What I didn't want, was to leave more destruction in my wake. Like I said, I'm not a bad guy.

'Tell her,' I whisper quietly.

We sit for a moment, waiting for Jack's reply. I glance at Stuart and catch his eye. He simply shrugs his shoulders and takes another gulp of his lager.

'I'll tell her when I get home,' Jack says finally.

Heaving a sigh of relief, I hope he's listened to me and took on board my worries. One small victory and I feel almost normal again, forgetting about the cruel world we live in, where people like Ray Delossi stalk the earth looking for their next prey, looking for someone vulnerable, kind and gentle to hurt and control.

For the moment, I forget that I am the unassuming Nick Flannigan, for a moment I am simply me, Jules Walker. There's definitely nothing unassuming about Jules Walker, and what I've done in the past. I can't guarantee I won't stand up for the next person I see being hurt or taken advantage of. It's not in my nature to sit back and do nothing.

My life is built on a multitude of 'ifs'. If my sister hadn't met Ray Delossi. If I hadn't listened to her begging me not to go and sort it out with him. If I hadn't walked into that bar and seen

The Lost Soul

Delossi strutting around, without a care in the world. If I hadn't followed him home and decided to end his miserable life so that he couldn't hurt anyone ever again.

The list is endless. If I had never seen that arsehole Leon, mistreating his girlfriend. Sniping at her and pulling her like a naughty child along the street for all to see. If I hadn't punched the arsehole and warned him to treat his girlfriend with respect, things might have been different. Of course, it was a series of bad choices and decisions on my part, and the power of social media, that had left me here in West Yorkshire in this predicament. And all because some kid had filmed me punching Leon down a side street, the video went viral on Facebook and alerted Detective Inspector Rutland to me and my family history. The rest, as they say, is history.

A shadow falls across the table and we look up, to see a slim, pretty brunette with a heart shaped face, wearing a tight black dress, leaning over the table. She smells of roses and vanilla, and her dress is cut obscenely low at the front, so we can easily see the fullness of her creamy white breasts. I blink, forcing my eyes to her chin and away from her cleavage.

She pushes a business card along the veneer top of the table. 'Sorry to bother you,' her voice holds a high pitch that messes with my brain, and not in a nice way. The sound forces me to close my eyes. 'But my friend, Alison, and I want to leave our numbers with you, in case one, or all of you need some company tonight.'

The Lost Soul

A smile begins to pull at my cheeks. I've never been propositioned before, it is very flattering and feels good, lifting my confidence. Stuart looks at Jack and clears his throat.

'Sorry,' he says to the brunette, with an apologetic smile, 'but we're not interested, we're all taken.' He gives me a quick wink.

'Yes, sorry er.' I stumble, and then realise that we don't know her name.

'Kitty,' the woman says, 'short for Kathryn. No problem,' and with a warm smile she walks back to her friend, Alison.

And before we can help ourselves, we burst into laughter.

'Cheers,' I raise my whiskey glass. The smile stays on my face, a strange emotion, as though something inside me has just cracked, and leaves a warm feeling deep in the pit of my stomach. The stiffness between my shoulder blades begins to ease. Perhaps there is a way that I can move on in the world. I think of Sasha, the sprinkling of freckles across her beautiful face, and I get the yearning to touch her soft skin. But another pang quickly overshadows this, not one of regret, but of loneliness and isolation.

Maybe it's time. Time to start again. To forgive myself. How does the Lord's Prayer go? 'Forgive us our trespasses, as we forgive those who trespass against us.' Desires, love, hope, happiness. Am I not deserving? Should I not try to make my life worth something, if not for me, for Blip and my parents. A voice breaks into my thoughts, it's Stuart.

'How are things?' he asks.

The Lost Soul

I roll my shoulders and shake my head, before answering:

'I've joined the local Taekwondo group in Keighley, how exciting is that?' I tell him, before explaining, 'my parents enrolled me when I was seven. Did it until I was fifteen.'

Both look at each other with raised eyebrows. I can see they're surprised.

'Impressive,' Jack's deep drawl focuses on me, 'what belt?'

'Black,' I say, 'but it's been a while since I did anything.'

'Good for you,' Stuart's warm gaze holds mine as his heavy hand pats me on the back. 'Any other news?'

'Not really.' I begin, my monthly update. 'There's a problem with one of the residents. Sasha and I are going to help him out. His greedy grandson is trying to fleece some of his personal belongings.'

Stuart rests his hands on the table and leans in. A serious look on his face. 'Anything we can help with? Or is it something you can sort out?'

I nod, holding his worried look for a moment. From the little I know of Stuart Greyson, he is caring, passionate and protective about those close to him, and a good listener. Everything I wish my dad could have been to me. Thinking of my dad, sends a wave of sadness over me. My broken parents, living in their own private hell since my sister took her life. I close my eyes and inhale deeply. A hand rests on my arm, and I open them to see Jack's concerned face looking at me.

The Lost Soul

'You alright?' he asks.

'Yeah sorry,' I say, 'I had a sudden vision of my parents and how badly Blip's death has affected them.'

'Take your time,' Stuart says quietly.

'I'm fine,' I offer a weak smile. 'Going back to the problem with the resident, Russell. I think I'll be ok. Although, it would be great if you could step up security at the entrance of Greystones for a little while.'

Stuart takes his phone from his pocket and starts to type some notes. 'No problem, I'll call someone first thing in the morning and organise a twenty-four-hour cover rota. It should be in place by lunchtime tomorrow.'

'Thanks, I appreciate it,' I feel humbled that I just have to ask and he takes my concerns seriously and acts on them accordingly.

'How is Sasha? And Zoe?' Jack asks, taking a sip of his pint and looking me straight in the eye.

'They're both fine. Yep, Zoe says she can't wait to be five! She's into My Little Pony and Baby Annabell. Everything she has is pink and purple. Sasha says she chatters more than some of the residents at Greystones.' I hear their chuckles as I talk and can't help but feel shocked as a wave of protectiveness for Sasha and Zoe fills me, making me want to slay anyone and anything that means to harm them and protect them from the world. Jesus! Where did that come from?

I can't help but smile, when I think of Zoe, she's a little ball of cuteness and chaos. With her darkened honey skin and her big

The Lost Soul

brown eyes, she seems to look into your very soul. She so trusting to everyone she meets, offering a big smile and a wave. Susan, one of our youngest residents at Greystones, lost her earring and Zoe was helping her to find it. 'Don't worry,' Zoe had smiled at her, and gently patted Susan's arthritic knee, 'it'll be all right.'

And, not for the first time I wonder where her father is, and why he would leave Sasha and his beautiful baby daughter. To have such a lovely family, and to let it go, I'm baffled why anyone would do that.

Some people just don't know how lucky they are.

Due to Sasha's working hours, Viola, the nanny lives partly on site at Greystones. I must admit that we're a strange group of people. A young single mum with a four-year-old daughter, a live-in nanny and me, a man pretending to be someone I'm not.

We are indeed a random group of people, who have somehow become a family group, not unlike the Greyson's who extend their family members daily, as they support and welcome people regularly into their family. I should know. Surprisingly though, our little Greystones family seems to work.

'Look,' I tell them, raising the glass to my lips and enjoying the burn of whiskey as it trickles down my throat. 'I've booked a table at Luigi's for 8pm,' I turn my wrist and check my Apple watch. 7.45pm. 'Let's finish up here and get some food.'

Stuart nods and looks at Jack. I watch as they pick up their respective glasses and finish their drinks.

The Lost Soul

Apart from my budding friendship with Sasha, these two men are the only true friends I have.

Part 4: Sasha

Love. It's fleeting and it hurts like hell. I will never fall in love again. I've been there, done that and have the T-shirt to prove it. In reality, I have something more substantial than a T-shirt. I smile, thinking of the one good thing that has come from my singular experience of love.

The water in the bath has cooled and the bubbles from my favourite bath soak have disappeared, leaving my body exposed to the harsh ceiling light. I need to rinse the shampoo from my hair before the water chills too much. Moving my legs, I close my eyes and allow my body to slide down the length of the bath, so that my head dips completely under the water.

Viola, my part-time live-in nanny, is amazing. She is stunningly beautiful with dark hair that is styled into a chic bob, she has the figure of a prima ballerina and the grace and allure that comes with her paternal French heritage. I often joke that she can make any outfit look cool and fashionable.

Viola Danes has a laid-back, easy-going nature and loves young children. I will be eternally grateful for Stuart and Jenny who brought us together so that I am supported and can develop a friendship with someone of my own age, while I manage this place and look after my young daughter.

The Lost Soul

Zoe was just turning four years old when we moved into the brand-new luxury residential complex that is Greystones, last year. Jenny had introduced Zoe and me to Viola when we arrived, as part of the staff team to open this new complex, and we hit it off straightaway.

Luckily for us, Viola wasn't sure which career route she wanted to take after completing her degree in fashion and textiles, so Jenny thought she would be a good fit for Greystones. And, she was right. Viola, is also the daughter of the Gloverman Corporation UK finance director, and long-term friend of Jenny, Eliza Danes, who is married to a French accountant called Remy.

Viola stays here on Tuesday and Thursday each week, looking after Zoe. Viola loves messy play with materials, such as paint, goop and shaving foam, so I never know what state the apartment will be when I get home from work. Zoe absolutely loves her. Viola has her own room within our apartment.

'Is Viola staying tonight?' Zoe looks at me with her loving brown eyes, looking like a dishevelled angel, in her long-sleeved pink nightdress.

'Not tonight, sweetie,' I smile, because Zoe is very attached to her nanny.

'I'm going to play with my farm,' she says, leaving the room.

'Leave the door open,' I call, resting my head against the bath and closing my eyes.

Viola and I are very much like sisters, we both like watching romantic comedies, eating chocolate ice cream late at night and

The Lost Soul

cooking. My apartment has three bedrooms and ample space for us to move around without bumping into each other. Viola has a one-bedroomed apartment in the nearby market town of Hebden Bridge, it is a beautiful place, full of character, both the town and apartment. Sometimes I have to pinch myself when I think how lucky I am that Viola is flexible and able to stay over when I'm working on call twilight shifts.

It's not so much that the Duty Shift Manager, Reg Woodward, and the four-person twilight staff team are unable to cope, but that Nick and I are the buffer. We're the ones who they call when there is an emergency, or a member of staff is sick.

My mind drifts to Dylan, my previously mentioned singular experience of love, Zoe's father.

***

At just turned sixteen, Dylan is six months older than me, he is good-looking and confident, reminding me of Luke Pasqualino, from the TV soldier drama, Our Girl, with his easy smile and dark flowing hair.

It is no surprise that he is popular with teachers and students alike. To be honest, I have a big crush on him. To my annoyance, I soon realise that I am not the only one with designs on the new boy, who'd arrived at the beginning of the final GCSE school year, for most of the girls in the class appear to be in awe whenever he enters a room.

Dylan sits at the table directly behind me in my English class at secondary school, and we are assigned to each other as partners to complete several literature papers on two nineteenth century

The Lost Soul

novels. We are studying Jane Eyre and The Strange Case of Dr Jekyll and Mr Hyde. We have to analyse the language, form and structure used by Charlotte Brontë and Robert Louis Stevenson, to create effects and meanings. Jane Eyre's first line is simple, 'There was no possibility of taking a walk that day,' and creates a feeling of miserable acceptance.

The sentence immediately draws me in, Dylan not so much, but the intensity and the dull ache is there, the need that makes me want to read on. I think of the child who wants to be in the fresh air but is held prisoner in her aunt's house by the weather. It makes me sad.

Dylan doesn't get it. He doesn't get the language used by Charlotte Brontë to create drama and atmosphere. We argue constantly in class and in the dinner hall, until he raises his eyes to the grey ceiling, before bringing them back at me. Casually, he suggests that we meet at his house one day after school, to work through the Jekyll and Hyde book. I am not looking forward to it, because it isn't the genre I normally read, and therefore, I've convinced myself that I won't enjoy it.

I pout and raise my eyebrows, 'it's just not my thing,' I tell him, as we arrive at his brown brick house two days later after school. From the outside, the house looks well cared for, with its grey door and vibrant coloured petunias standing proudly in white ceramic pots either side. Dylan takes out his key.

'Parents aren't home,' he announces in a way of explanation, as he opens the door. 'They're at work. Mum will be back in about half an hour.'

The Lost Soul

I should have been afraid. But I'm not. It's as though I know Dylan won't hurt me. Slowly, I take a seat at his kitchen table, pushing my curly hair behind my ears to keep it out of the way as I stare at the front cover of the book. My eyes dance across the synopsis and slowly I begin to relent as I read about the intelligent and respected Dr Jekyll who wants to explore the darker side of his character, Mr Hyde.

'Maybe, it'll be ok,' I concede, placing the book onto the teak table and looking up to see Dylan staring over at me from the fridge, two ice-cold cans of Diet Coke in his hand. There is a strange look on his face, as though he is seeing me for the first time. I feel a shudder of excitement as he walks across the room and stops in front of me, I hold my breath as he slowly places the coke cans on the table.

Slowly, his olive-skinned hand reaches out and long fingers stroke my cheek. And, all the time, I sit still, my breath catches and our eyes lock. Big brown eyes refuse to look away, and there is nothing but a timeless moment which holds us together, like a band of steel. I am unable to move, even when his hand gently cups the side of my face, and my tummy begins to flutter.

I know that he is going to kiss me, his beautiful brown eyes question mine and I give the slightest of nods, whilst holding my breath and waiting for his head to lower to meet mine.

'Dylan,' I half-whisper, before his lips take mine.

I didn't know at this point that his parents had already set plans in motion to move to a remote Scottish Isle. Each day I fell deeper for Dylan, on dates to the cinema and zoo, during school lessons

The Lost Soul

and break-times, on walks home from school, each day I gave Dylan a little bit more of my heart.

Three months later we decided to become more intimate, and sex seemed the natural progression. I didn't know then that the dream would turn into a nightmare.

***

'Mummy? Hurry up!'

The sound of a child's voice echoes through the water, and I realise that my four-year-old year daughter has finished playing with her farm set in her room. I drag my hands through my hair and peer over the top of the bath, to see the top of Zoe's soft dark shoulder length curls, watching them bounce when she turns to look up at me. She is sitting on her knees beside the bath, with several of her My Little Ponies spread out around her, and her Baby Annabell sitting on top of the toilet seat.

I smile, cherishing her beautiful olive skin and full smiling lips. She reminds me so much of Dylan.

'I'm coming sweetheart,' I say softly, 'I was enjoying the water so much that I forgot about the time. I must look like a wrinkled prune,' I finish the latter part in more of a mumble. Of course, my bright four-year-old is listening to every word I say, because Zoe immediately questions me, her big brown eyes looking up at me.

'What's a wrinkled prune?' she wrinkles her nose.

Reaching to pull the plug, I try to answer as simply as I can, 'it's a saying,' I grab the chain and hear the hiss of the water as it empties out of the bathtub. Turning my hands over and showing

The Lost Soul

Zoe my fingertips, 'can you see how wrinkled my fingers are?' I ask her.

Zoe pushes off the floor to her feet, and her small hands touch my wet ones. 'Will they go away?' she asks, her eyes wide with curiosity.

'Yes, once I've dried my hands, the wrinkles will dry out and my fingers will slowly go back to normal.'

'Oh, they feel funny,' she says, with a serious face, and her little fingers flitter across my hand. I can't help but smile. Zoe is my rock. She keeps me going when dark clouds invade my mind. When my days seem long and never ending, it's my little girl who keeps me going.

I don't allow myself to think of my parents, particularly of my dad. One of life's misconceptions, is that your parents love you unconditionally. If love is punching and kicking your sixteen-year-old daughter who had recently had a baby, then he must absolutely adore me.

My dad was controlling and abusive, and my mum was too afraid to stand up to him. He used to hit her, in front of me, using his fists to slap her. Demonstrating, that this is what would happen if I disobeyed him. My dad, the monster. No one knows what goes on behind the front door of a home. No one wants to believe that people, children even, are being abused and mistreated.

Jenny and Stuart, Lottie and Jem, became my new family from the day my dad disowned me, and I arrived at the refuge home, Shore House, with my six-month baby, Zoe. I have a sudden vision of my Mum's face and for the first time in a while, I

The Lost Soul

wonder how she is. I've not spoken to her since the day I left the house, and walked with tears blinding my vision, my daughter in my arms, towards the nearest bus shelter.

I don't know what I would have done if my English teacher, Mrs Chapman, hadn't driven by at that moment and rescued me. She had taken me home and called the police, who transferred me to DS Leadbetter, who in turn, had referred me to the Lighthouse charity. To Jenny and Stuart. Thank goodness they did, because between them all, they had saved me, and my daughter. With the Greyson's help, I changed my surname from Benson to Berrington, and never looked back.

The door to the apartment buzzes, taking me out of my reverie.

'Mummy? Can I get the door?' Zoe asks, picking up Princess Starlight and brushing her fingers along her purple hair.

'No, it's all right, sweetie. For one, you can't reach and for two, even if you could, you aren't allowed to open the door,' I tell her, as I stand up and reach for my grey towel from the nearby towel rail.

'I'll get it.' I wrap myself quickly, rubbing the water into my skin as I grab a hand towel, to wrap my soaking unruly curls in. Padding across the soft blue and white striped carpet in the hallway, I peer through the safety spy hole to see who's at the door at 9am on a Sunday morning. A black jumper catches my gaze and I look up to see a muscular neck, followed by a square-shaped chin. Nick. A frisson of something unfamiliar flutters in my tummy.

The Lost Soul

'Just a minute, Nick.' I tell him, rushing to put on my floor length, velvety dark grey towelling robe, which was the first luxury item I'd treated myself to, with my first month's salary.

Opening the door, he stands there, phone in hand and blinks twice when he sees me.

'Sorry, I know it's early, but I wanted to catch you before I forget,' his voice is husky and apologetic.

'Not a problem,' I tell him, 'come through.' I open my palm and motion him into my apartment

'Hi Nick,' my daughter smiles at him.

'Hi Zoe, how are you?' he asks, as if she's a mini adult – but then surprises me by kneeling to talk to her.

'I'm fine, but Princess Starlight got wet when mummy got out of the bath, and mummy's got wrinkles.'

Laughing, I walk through the yellow painted, open plan alcove area to the kitchen, check the water gauge on the kettle and press the button to bring it to life.

'Thanks, for that Zoe!' I say, feeling a little embarrassed especially when Nick's deep chuckle echoes through from the large, pale-yellow walled living room come dining area. 'Coffee?' I glance his way, watch as he gracefully raises himself to his feet, and our eyes lock briefly. Nodding, his tall presence hovers by the white wood dining table and his face lights up, offering an unexpected smile, but his eyes close quickly and I can almost see his guard return; the smile is lost.

The Lost Soul

When he smiles like that, it makes my breath hitch, and I'm not sure why. We have known each other six months and work and live closely together. He's always been respectful and professional when we're together, but there's something about Nick that's not quite right, I just can't put my finger on it. It's as though he's being careful not to show any real feelings. It's as though he's holding something back. One thing is for sure, he should smile more often.

Nick stoops over Zoe, and gently pats her head, 'oh dear, I'm sure we all have wrinkles!'

'No. Mummy's got them all over her fingers. Show him, mummy,' Zoe walks up to me and pulls at my dressing gown. Her brown eyes willing me to do her bidding.

I smile, as the kettle boils in the background, and turn to stroke the soft ringlets in her shoulder-length dark hair.

'Mummy?' Zoe's voice sounds more urgent.

'It's fine, Zoe – I'm sure Nick has seen wrinkles before,' I tell her, adding a firmer tone to my voice to let her know that she needs to calm down.

I look at the floor and see his brown suede boots walking in my direction, 'Let's take a look.'

This is the first time we have made physical contact. And I won't lie, it scares me. Slowly, I hold out my hands, slightly raising them, allowing my gaze to travel slowly to the top of his burgundy jeans and then upwards, to his black jumper, until finally, my eyes rests on his full lips.

The Lost Soul

Warm hands reach out and take mine. The moment we touch, I raise my brown eyes to his blue ones, and they lock with the same question. What was that? Did you feel it? I didn't realise I was holding my breath, until he turns my hands over, studies my open palms and gently strokes the faded wrinkles on my fingers.

Oh, hell. I'm in trouble.

'See,' Zoe breaks the spell, 'I told you.' My treacherous daughter mutters, with a smug satisfaction and a big smile. 'She's full of wrinkles.'

'I think you're right, Zoe,' Nick's eyes widen as he looks at me, before gently releasing my hands. 'No need to call the doctor though, they seem to be going now.' And, then before I know what is happening, he offers me a wink and sits on the arm of the dark brown sofa.

'Now, I wanted to talk to you about the new security and Russell,' he says, but his voice fades as I move to the kitchen to make the hot drinks and listen to him chatting, with my daughter interrupting every so often, in the background. My cheeks feel warm, and I touch them absently. My heart is beating so loudly, I fear they can hear it over their chatter.

What the hell just happened?

Part 5: Zoe

It's hard being four. Everybody treats you like a child, but I'm a big girl now, bigger than when I was three.

Mummy keeps saying, 'when I was your age,' but I don't know what that means. I know lots of things though. I know that when she's sad her eyes go red. I hope I don't have red eyes when I'm as big and old as she is. I know I like peas, but I don't like broccoli, and I know that Viola likes doughnuts, just like me.

Told you I know lots of things.

And I got married on Friday! At my nursery school. One minute I'm running around, chasing Sapphire and Keiron and then Keiron says, 'Zoe, do you want to marry me?'

I smiled at him, and he went red. 'ok, but Mummy says I'm too young to go on an aeroplane, so we can't do a honeymoon,' I said, with my hands on my hips.

Keiron quickly kissed my arm, then punched me on the shoulder, which hurt - before he ran away, shouting 'catch me, you're it!'

I love being married. Keiron is the best husband in the whole wide world, and Sapphire asked if she could be our baby. We

The Lost Soul

both said yes, because we like her, she's got curly hair like me and Keiron says she can live in our house and play with us.

If only Mummy would marry, then I can have a Daddy. I've always wanted a Daddy. Maybe she will marry Nick. I like him, he's got a nice face, it's a circle shape and a bit whiskery. He's got whiskers on his head too. I think he will make a good Daddy.

I bounce Twilight Sparkle and Applejack on my knee in my bedroom. The carpet is pink, my bed is pink, everything is pink, because pink is my favourite colour.

'What do you think Applejack?' I put Applejack in front of me, and then to my ear, 'Yes, he likes chocolate ice cream too.'

I make Twilight Sparkle and Applejack kiss and rub noses, 'you're happy, you can get married too,' I smile and run around my room, in my pink dress and white tights, singing 'la la la la la, I'm married to Keiron, la, la, le, la, la.'

'Zoe! Dinner's ready!'

I smile at my Mummy's voice. I love her so much.

'Coming!' I shout, taking my ponies with me, and running through the open doorway.

It's fish fingers, chips and peas tonight. Yummy. It's hungry work being married.

Part 6: Jack

The small ivory coloured letter tiles look back at me, and my mind goes blank. I admit I'm not great at playing Scrabble, or Monopoly come to think of it, but I can't help but feel deflated as I look at my seven tiles, two of which are blank, four are e's and the remaining tile is a u. So, I don't have a great deal of good letters to work with.

I reach for the wine glass and take a long drink of my red wine.

'Come on Jack, yours and mum's wedding will be over and done with, if you take much longer,' Ben, my fiancé Steph's son, stifles a yawn and smiles at his mum. She returns Ben's smile, before she looks my way and gently rests her hand on my thigh. Her touch is like a drug, addictive in the very air that she breathes and creates a kaleidoscope of emotions within me. God, I love this woman. I can't wait to make her my wife.

Ben's eyes droop, and the yawn he's been trying to hold back, forces itself out. With arms stretching above his head, he mutters 'I'm beat,' before he collects his phone from the coffee table, stands, offering his mum a kiss on the cheek.

'Night both,' he says, as he leaves the room.

The Lost Soul

Steph leans forward to study my letter tiles and her shoulder-length blonde hair rests on my arm. She's become much more confident in our relationship, in the six months that we've been together, each day she blossoms and shows her love for me in many ways, from leaving notes to gentle touches.

Only yesterday, I needed to wear a shirt and tie for an early morning court appearance and, we'd stood facing each other in our bedroom, where Ben, who had just turned fifteen, had sprawled across our bed with an array of colourful ties in front of him. Ben had taken on the self-appointed role of choosing which tie I should wear for court.

'What about this one?' Ben had asked, handing me a navy and burgundy striped one. I turn up the collar to my shirt, and Steph had said softly, 'Here, let me', she gently placed it around my neck, before looping the fronts together. I watched mesmerised, via the full length, floor standing silver edged mirror, as she concentrated until the tie looked perfect.

'There,' she'd announced with a smile. 'All sorted.'

I smiled and put my hand on her shoulder, feeling the need to touch her, but always being careful around Ben.

'Urghhh cut it out, you two,' Ben said in a deep voice, jumping off the bed.

'Oh, Ben, you know you like seeing your mum happy!' I smiled, giving him a quick wink.

The Lost Soul

'Happy yes,' Ben moved his arms in an over exaggerated motion. 'Looking like a love-sick puppy, Dad. I don't think so,' he said leaving the room. 'I'm going to get ready for school.'

I looked at Steph, my eyes blurred for a moment. Her fingers stroked my neck. 'He called me Dad,' I whispered. He doesn't say it very often, so when he does, it means a lot.

'I know,' she whispered back, and kissed my lips briefly, before looking up and facing the doorway. 'Don't forget to take plasters in case your shoes rub your ankles,' she shouted to her teenage son. Our teenage son.

***

I look at my watch, it's 10.30pm, and seven days since Stuart and I were last in Yorkshire, checking up on Jules slash Nick.

'Do you mind if we put this game on hold,' I ask Steph. 'It's getting late, and I want to talk to you about something,' I say, wishing there was another way to say what I'm about to say.

Steph looks across at me, her beautiful face suddenly becoming serious. Our eyes lock, and it's clear I have to tell her about Jules Walker, but I don't want to see the look of disappointment on her face. This confession of mine could backfire on me like a firecracker on Bonfire Night. I sincerely hope that Stuart knows Steph as well as he thinks he does.

She's going to be pissed.

I wait patiently as Steph folds the Scrabble board in half and I wait patiently as Steph gently pours the letter tiles into a green silk drawstring bag. A few moments later, she sits back in her

77

The Lost Soul

chair, her fingers linked together. It's something she does when she's worried or wary of something.

'What is it?' she asks in a low voice, 'are you breaking up with me, with us?' She looks pale.

'Hell no!' I say roughly. Why would she think that? I thought she trusted me, trusted in us. Leaning closer, I take her fingers from her lap, unravel them, and cover her hands with my own, to reassure her, 'No, nothing like that,' I tell her firmly. 'Never. Never anything like that babe. I love you and Ben so much - nothing will ever change that.'

I promised myself, when I fell in love with Steph, that I would do everything I could to make her and Ben happy, and to protect them. They've both been through so much in their lives. Ray Delossi, her abusive ex-husband and Ben's father, had a lot to answer for. Thank God he is dead.

'It's Jules Walker,' I say, standing up, and staring at the flames in the old stone fireplace. Facing away from her, I stare into flames of the fire and rub my forehead, *just bloody tell her and stop mucking around.* I know why I'm reluctant to explain about Jules, it's because this is the first real test of our relationship. She might walk out of my life, taking Ben with her, or give Jules up to her colleagues in the police force.

Who knows what will happen when she knows what we did to help Jules to escape from custody? But one thing is for sure, I need to face the consequences of my actions, so that we can start married life with nothing but love and respect between us. I turn to face her, my face serious, and I look into her eyes and see the

78

The Lost Soul

exact moment when her eyes dilate, and she realises what I've just said.

'Jules Walker?' she stands, tall and lithe in her grey leisure trousers, black T-shirt and grey jersey hooded top. She looks as sexy in her chill out gear as she does in her white blouse and black trousers for work. Steph stands in front of me and takes my arm, 'what about Jules Walker?' the tone of her voice is sharp.

'Well, erm. Just remember Steph,' I take her by the shoulders, 'remember that you love me, no matter what.'

'Spit it out Kinsey. I want to hear you say it,' she says sharply, her big brown eyes fix on mine.

I don't know what she means by 'say it.' It's a strange thing to add on to a sentence. Taking my hands from her shoulders and holding them by my sides, I stare into her face to read her reaction. Her face is so bloody hard to read.

'Tell me what happened to Jules Walker,' she finishes. And that's when I know that she knows that something happened, and that I was involved in Walker's disappearance.

Fuck. Fuck.

'Sit down Steph,' I say quietly. 'Sit down and I'll tell you everything.'

For a moment, she doesn't move, simply stands and stares into the crackling red and orange flames of the fire, until finally, shaking her head, she moves to the armchair and takes a seat.

The Lost Soul

'Tell me.' She says quietly, tucking her feet underneath her. 'What happened?'

I move to the sofa and look across at her.

'That night, the one when we found out that Jules Walker had motive because of what Ray Delossi had done to his sister. I couldn't sleep that night. It was playing on my mind. I mean, I would have done the same to Delossi if he'd hurt someone I loved.'

Tears fill her eyes as she listens to me, and nods briefly. She moves to get up, but I stop her. I need to look her in the eye and explain what I've done and why I did it. 'No Steph, please stay there, let me explain what happened.'

Sitting rigidly on the sofa, I feel so wretched as Steph wipes her eyes with the sleeve of her sweatshirt and resigns herself to listening to my confession. 'I never meant to hurt you, baby,' I tell her quietly.

I rub the bristles on my face, this is a lot harder than I thought. 'When you went to bed, I called Stuart and told him what we had found out about Jules Walker,' I take a deep breath. 'I'm sorry Steph, but I told him what time you planned to be at Richmond House, and I told him you were going to arrest Jules.'

She burst into tears. 'I knew, deep down. I bloody knew,' she said getting up and turning towards me. She slumps beside me on the sofa, 'I knew, you'd helped him, but I wanted you to tell me yourself.'

The Lost Soul

To my surprise Steph reaches out and puts her hand over my heart. 'You have a good heart, Jack, but you should have told me what you were doing.'

'I wanted to,' I whisper, caressing her cheeks with the back of my knuckles, 'but I didn't want my actions to put you in a difficult position. You are a DI, and I was trying to protect you.'

'Baby,' she says softly, 'we're getting married in five weeks. I want our marriage to start off in the right way, with no secrets, no lies and definitely no secret monthly jaunts to Yorkshire.'

The full enormity of her revelation shocks me. 'You know that Stu and I go to Haworth for a few days each month?' I shake my head, and chuckle, 'I thought I'd covered my tracks by saying we were going fishing in Wales.'

'You would have,' she smiles at me, and leans in to kiss my cheek, 'but for two things. One, neither you or Stuart know how to fish, and two, I'm a Detective Inspector and can smell a load of bullshit a mile off.'

I laugh, a big belly laugh, one that fills me with warmth, relief and gratitude, and I cup the back of her head with my hand and bring her forward, until our eyes meet, 'I love you Steph Rutland, you never cease to amaze me.'

'I'm relieved you finally told me what's been going on,' her voice is low. 'I love the hell out of you, Jack,' she reaches over and kisses my neck, letting her forehead graze along my skin.

The Lost Soul

Closing my eyes, I enjoy the tender moments of our skin-on-skin contact. A moment later, she breaks away, 'Now, tell me the rest, so we can get on with our lives.'

The Lost Soul

Part 7: Anthony

I hate my life. Right now, it's a bloody mess. I hate the way I look, I'm a bit overweight and my dark hair, although short, seems to have a life of its own. I hate having to suck up to people I hardly know, including my boss, the MP, Lewis Benson. And, I especially hate having to visit this person, in this particular place, Her Majesty's Prison, Wandsworth.

It never used to be like this, my life I mean. I was born in Southwark, South London to loving parents, Tom and Mandy, who both taught at Secondary schools near Edgware Road. I was easy going, popular at school and kept consistently good grades. That was until I was nineteen years old, when everything went black, and the world stopped turning. On 7th July 2005, my parents were two of the fifty-two people who died following the terrorist attacks on the London Transport System. That's when things began to go wrong for me.

I was left with a big three-bedroomed mews house that held no warmth, or companionship, and nothing but the gaping chasm of a hole that losing my parents had left. The rooms were still and quiet and eating became a chore. One night after a microwavable pasta meal from Marks and Spencer, I was browsing the Amazon website for a new watering can and was shocked to see the pages of cans, which then evolved into a variety of novelty cans. I

The Lost Soul

bought a traditional-shaped, dark green one, and then became consumed with the need to buy more. I am ashamed to say that I didn't stop adding to my basket, until I'd purchased a menagerie of seven novelty animal-shaped watering cans.

Feeling silly even admitting this, the cans were given names. How strange is that? If anyone found out that I have a fetish for purchasing watering cans and giving them names as though they were real people, people would think I am completely insane and I would lose credibility with my friends and work colleagues.

Deep down, I realise I was lonely at the time and simply needed someone to talk to. A grief counsellor would have been the obvious choice, I'm not one to go for the obvious though, therefore in that cold, empty, mews house, the watering cans became my new family.

And that's how it all started. Tragic death. Grief. Empty house. Watering Cans. Thankfully, studying for my second year of my degree, in Politics and International Relations at the University of Greenwich, gave me something to focus on.

When I finished my degree, eleven years ago, I managed to get a job working as a Residential Housing officer in the council office in Abingdon, Oxfordshire. I made my base in the larger commuter town of Didcot, where there are great rail services, in forty-five minutes I can get the train straight through to London Paddington.

I put the important pieces of furniture and personal possessions from the Mews house into storage and I put the Southwark house out to rent. A young family with two children became my first

The Lost Soul

and only tenants, two weeks later, and look after the place well. With the rent money I live in a three bedroomed semi-detached house on the Ladygrove Estate in Didcot, near the Railway Station, and bought myself a green Skoda to commute to work. I've also discovered a short drive away, the remains of an Iron Age hillfort known as Wittenham Clumps, which was the scene of a kidnapping and a couple of murders, a few years back. It's one of my favourite places to visit.

At least for the foreseeable future, I do not have to worry about money. Receiving my parent's life insurance, and monthly rental payments for the mews house, counteract the shortfall on the small mortgage and a large part of the monthly rent on my Didcot house. It's sad to think that the only good thing coming from my parents' deaths, is that I now have financial security.

My thoughts turn to Lewis Benson. He is a strange character to work for. He is a charismatic and hard-working public figure in the political world, but there's a side to him that I've seen, which is not nice, in fact, it's very unpleasant.

The main problem started six months ago, when Lewis took me to an Oxford nightclub, under the pretence of meeting an old friend. That was the first time I'd taken drugs, I'd never even smoked a cigarette before, had no interest in it during my university days. I'd taken cocaine and I loved it. That little white powder gives me the biggest high and makes everything all right with the world.

Lewis's Benson's 'old friend', Scott, was a dealer and soon got me hooked on the stuff. By month two, I couldn't get up in the morning without snorting a line. It was a way of coping, of

The Lost Soul

finding that bliss that could lift me up, even if only for a short time.

'You're using this every day,' Scott had said one day in November, 'It's costing you a small fortune to keep your supply coming. Maybe we could come to some arrangement?'

'Some arrangement?' I'd asked, thinking that this must be too good to be true, I mean it sounds suspicious, looking back, doesn't it? What was I thinking? I should have got off the drug, but my greed got the better of me.

'There's someone I want you to meet. You can do him a little favour.'

Enter Dave Delossi.

***

The prison visiting room is stark white, with circular aged off-white tables spread sporadically around the room. Tucked against each clean but grubby looking table are two blue plastic chairs with black metal legs. I've left my belongings in a metal locker and been searched on my way in –I think I'd feel safer if I could carry a knife with me when I'm in here. But then, where would I hide it?

I hear the creaking, opening of doors, busy shuffling of feet and scraping of chair legs as visitors find a table and take their seats. The metal door leading to the prisoners area, is suddenly pushed open by one of the guards, and several inmates stroll through, wearing grey T-shirts or sweatshirts, and dark grey jogging

The Lost Soul

bottoms. There are two guards in the room, standing against the wall and taking in everything that is happening.

My hands are clasped together tightly as the inmates push through the door and walk into the room to find their visitors, offer greetings and drag chairs from under tables to sit down and chat quietly. Someone begins to cry quietly, and I scan the room quickly, it's a young woman who sits hugging a young child closely to her.

The room fills with silence, as the door opens and in walks the person I'm waiting for.

He's tall and thin with harsh features, the front of his limp, mousy hair is tucked around one ear and he's wearing the standard grey sweatshirt and dark grey jogging bottoms. There's a long angry red slash that sits along his cheekbone to his nose, and another along his neck, as though someone has tried to slit his throat. I wonder about his age, there is no hint of youth about him, so the only conclusion is that he's got to be at least fifty. He's in here for dealing Class A drugs and is halfway through his fifteen-year sentence.

Dave Delossi.

He's Top Dog in here by all accounts. Well, he's been here long enough.

The man sits down.

'Tony,' he says, through black and broken teeth.

'Dave,' I say, 'You all right?'

The Lost Soul

'Yeah,' he says. 'You got the stuff?'

'No, but I'm working on it,' I say loudly, trying to sound confident, I can't help but glance quickly to the guards – thank goodness, his movements are being monitored. I don't like this man one bit. I wish I'd never got involved with him.

'I need it now, Tony,' Dave leans forward, his piercing blue-eyed gaze sends shivers down my spine. My fear of this man is so strong that I cross my legs to stop myself from urinating. I can't tell him that I used his money for my cocaine. Which in turn, means I can't buy the gear for him that he's paid for.

If I told him this, I'd be a dead man.

'I know, Dave,' I say in a low voice, trying to make my words sound confident. 'There's been a problem with delivery. I'll have it to you by Saturday.'

'You'd better fucking do, or I'll set Little Tim on you and by the time he's finished with you, you'll be eating through a straw.'

Shit.

The last time I'd seen Little Tim, he'd been over six feet tall and almost the same size around his middle, as he was tall. He's Dave's henchman on the outside and does all of his dirty work for him. He's not a nice man, in fact, Little Tim is a bloody psycho. Not unlike the man sitting in front of me.

'Understood, Dave,' I shuffle back in my chair slightly, because I'm struggling to breathe the same air as this man. 'Thanks.'

The Lost Soul

The man wipes his nose across the arm of his sweatshirt, rests his forearms on the table and leans forward. 'I need you to do something for me,' he states in a no-nonsense manner.

'What?' I ask, almost rolling my eyes. As if I haven't got enough stuff on my plate right now.

'I want you to find someone,' his voice is low, and his eyes hold mine. He doesn't blink and it makes me feel like we're in some sort of pissing contest.

'I'm looking for a man called Jules Walker.'

A frisson of recognition raises a red flag in my brain. The name sounds familiar. 'Jules Walker? I've heard that name somewhere before,' but for the life of me, I can't think where I've heard it.

'He was in the news a few months ago. Killed someone and then disappeared from the back of a police car,' he tells me.

'Jesus. Why? What's he done to you?' I ask, dreading his response. I don't want to be responsible for someone getting hurt.

'He's done nothing to me. But he did something to what was left of my family,' Dave looks at me, there is a coldness that leaves me shaking. His eyes are hard as stone.

'That bastard killed my brother!'

Part 8: Jules

'Fucking bitch. I'll get her for this.' The man is crouching, his head is face down, staring at the floor. He leans on the wall holding his groin, using the cold surface to help him to stand upright. There is a wooden baseball bat resting against the armchair, near the fireplace.

'No, you won't!' I tell him, picking up the baseball bat and walking over to him. What a poor excuse for a human being! He looks pitiful. For someone who likes inflicting pain on others, he is not one for tolerating it. Why doesn't that surprise me?

Taking my hood off, I allow him to see me for the first time. 'You!' he whispers, recognising my face, as my dead eyes stare back at him.

I lift the bat and haul it hard into the front of his skull. The contact sounds hard and hollow, the crunch of his skull vibrates through the bat and into the handle, but I ignore it. I am here to do a job and that needs me to focus. His eyes meet mine, shock in his, hate in mine, before his body begins to crumble, and he falls to the floor. I heave a sigh of relief, this is it, he's finally dead.

But then the bugger starts to move, and a pained sound shatters the silence in the room. He sounds like a wounded animal. I walk behind him and wait patiently. Bloody well, why the hell won't

The Lost Soul

he die? When Delossi finally stands, I swing the bat for a second time, this time aiming for the back of his head. There is the sound of bone cracking and a squelching in and around the wound.

This time he stays down. I wait a while for a sign of life, a sign that he'll get up again. But this time, he stays still, and the only sound is the eerie silence.

Bloody hell! I just killed a man.

The sweat gathers on my brow and I wake up with a start. I had the dream again, although it wasn't a dream, it was a flash back from the night I killed the woman beater, Ray Delossi. I wipe my brow with my bare arms and throw the duvet back. Even in shorts and a top I'm too hot. Bloody hell.

I can't breathe, I feel like I'm suffocating, fuck. I need some air. Jumping out of bed, I open the window and put my head into the cool breeze of the dark night. I close my eyes and count to ten, taking deep breaths to steady myself.

**

'I want to fall in love, one day. You know, find that special someone who loves me, no matter what,' Blip, my sister, declares as she pushes a slice of cheese and ham pizza into her mouth. I am home from university for the weekend because Blip was fifteen yesterday, and our parents had booked a family meal at a local pasta restaurant.

Tonight, I'm treating just the two of us to food at Pizza Express. Her medium-brown straight hair falls in a sleek bob along her neck, resting on the top of her longline pale pink jumper. Her neat

The Lost Soul

fringe frames her oval face, reminding me of a young version of the Hollywood actress, Anne Hathaway. She is beautiful, both inside and out.

'C'mon Jules, you must want that too. Eventually,' she says, finishing her mouthful of food. She's trying hard to persuade me to divulge dating information, but I'm not obliging. She'll have me married, with children, before my next birthday. Blip is a romantic through and through.

I smile, my younger sister is the only one who can make me forget about exams and university assignments. 'Blip,' I warn her firmly, raising my eyebrows. It's hard to be mad at her, when she looks at me with her clear blue eyes.

Deciding that distraction is a better tactic than interrogation, I feel around in my jeans pocket for the small square box containing the piece of jewellery that I'd acquired a few weeks ago.

I pick up my glass of ice-cold Coke Zero and take a quick sip before I say anything.

'I've got something for you,' I say, smiling at her.

'For me?' she lifts her eyebrows in query. 'Jules, you've already given me chocolates and a voucher.'

I take out the blue box, decorated with a white ribbon, lay it on the table and push it across the brown, wooden table to her. 'This is your real present. I saw it and immediately thought of you.'

The Lost Soul

She smiles at me, shuffles from her seat and walks to my side. 'I love it,' she tells me, throwing her arms around my neck and putting her lips to my cheek.

'You haven't seen what it is yet,' I put my hand over hers. 'Go on, open it.'

Blip smiles, tilts her head slightly and whispers, 'I'll love it no matter what it is.' I watch with bated breath as she returns to her seat, picks up the box, unties the white ribbon and carefully lifts open the box. Inside is a large silver butterfly pendant on a stainless-steel chain. Her eyes light up and she looks my way, as she takes the necklace from the box with slim fingers.

'I love it, Jules!' she exclaims, and I watch her fingers swiftly detach the clasp, take both ends of the chain, place it either side of her neck and reconnect the piece of jewellery under her hair.

'Need a hand?' I ask, as she fidgets slightly. I take a slice of pepperoni pizza and bite off a mouthful, enjoying the tangy taste of the cheese and the subtle hint of spice from the meat.

'Nope, done it,' she declares, with a smile. 'What do you think?' she strokes the cold metal.

Heaving a sigh of relief, I take my phone from the table to capture the moment. She looks so happy.

'Looks good on you, little Sis,' I tell her, as I turn the phone on to photo mode and snap a couple of shots of her smiling face and slender fingers, as they brush across the indentations decorating the wings on the pendant.

The Lost Soul

'It's so beautiful,' she beams, 'I'm never going to take it off.'
Blip reaches across the table to take another slice of pizza, and I
watch with interest as cheese and tomato pulp dribbles down the
side of her mouth. I know she can feel it, because she shrugs her
shoulders uses her index finger to slide across the excess sauce
and pushes it to the corner of her mouth, where her tongue dips
out to clean up the mess.

I shake my head and reach for a white serviette that sits on the
table and hold it out to her. She acts as though she doesn't have a
care in the world, when she takes the paper towel to dab her
mouth. If only life would always be this simple. When you're
young, everything seems exciting, and you feel invincible. The
world is full of clear, vivid colours, and you are looking forward
to a lifetime of new adventures.

 I didn't know then that the clock was ticking for Blip, and that
she would be buried in the cold dark earth by the following year.
Dead at sixteen, it seems so unfair, unjust. My world closed in on
itself, my parents struggled to understand what had happened, and
for our family – the sun never shone again.

***

I take my phone from the park bench in Haworth's Central Park,
and wonder, lazily if this park had been around when Emily
Brontë had written Wuthering Heights. Above me, clouds gather
and shadow the landscape. I check my watch and realise it's 2pm
already. I made a flask of homemade coffee when I decided, as
there was no sign of rain, I'd get a bit of fresh air and take a walk.

The Lost Soul

The village of Haworth, which is three miles southwest of Keighley, is undoubtably growing on me. With its rich history and wide selection of unique shops, not to mention the fact that it's surrounded by rugged moorland, what's not to like.

Of course, there are tourists who want to know and see every little thing to do with the celebrated literary sisters, and their family. They flock to the Brontë Parsonage Museum, and church in the summer, where the family lived from 1820 and wrote their famous novels.

The village at the time was a crowded industrial town with a child mortality rate of over forty per cent and the average lifespan was twenty-four years. A well-known fact, I learnt when visiting the parsonage last month is that the sisters, Anne, Emily and Charlotte, had written Agnes Grey, Wuthering Heights and Jane Eyre, whilst walking around the table in the dining room until 11 o'clock at night, discussing their ideas and plans, and reading their works to each other.

Tourists also like to take a drink at the Black Bull, which was their brother's, Branwell Brontë, favourite drinking haunt. He had quite a sad life, battling with drink and drug addiction and despite being an accomplished painter himself, he struggled to find his place in life, where he fitted in. I can empathise with that. I know what it feels like to be on the outside looking in. It's no joke. I'm already living a lie, having to remember my backstory every day, of where I'm from and my new name. Constantly looking over my shoulder and trying to ignore the dark shadows that seem to follow me.

The Lost Soul

It's hard work.

I battle my demons every morning when I wake up, look in the mirror and see Ray Delossi's face staring blankly back at me. And, all the while, I become frustrated and demoralised because I can't tell anyone why I have these feelings, because they may call the police. Sometimes, I think that would be the lesser of the two evils, at least I could be honest with people and form some sort of friendship.

I select photos on my phone and scroll down until I find the photo that has been playing on my mind. The one around her fifteenth birthday, when I gave her the butterfly necklace. Blip looks happy, with her innocent smile, wearing her favourite soft pink jumper and her brown hair cut into a shoulder-length bob. My eyes blur for a moment, and I force the tears back, as I whisper her name.

Some days it feels like only yesterday that she left us, on other days – it feels like forever.

***

'It's Nick!' a child's voice calls. The voice is familiar, and I turn my head to the right and see a bundle of pink heading my way on a pink and white scooter.

'Hi!' she says, pushing the scooter harder as she speeds past the rockery garden. I'm convinced she's going to crash into the bench, or my legs. 'Mummy, look. It's Nick,' her face beams with excitement.

The Lost Soul

'Sorry,' Sasha smiles apologetically as she draws to a standstill in front of me. She's wearing a dark red top over light grey jeans, and a short black padded jacket. Dark red hair hangs in curls at her shoulders and her brown eyes catch mine. I'm unable to move, to look away or even breathe. There it is again, that frisson of electricity and contact I felt earlier this morning in her apartment. I don't understand what's going on. Or maybe, I'm in denial.

Turning my head slightly in a bid to control these new feelings, and to hide the affect she is having on me, Sasha sits on the bench, and I can almost feel the heat coming from her. 'Want to sit down sweetie?' she asks Zoe.

'No, I want to keep playing with my scooter.' Zoe states, her confidence building with her speed.

'That's fine, but you need to come here first,' Sasha orders her daughter.

Zoe scoots to her mum and I love how Sasha reaches out and gently pulls the zip on her daughter's pink padded coat a little higher to keep out the cool air. 'That's better, we need to keep you warm.'

Sasha leans forward and pats Zoe's arm, as a warm feeling sears through my body, making me wonder what kind of parent I would make, if I were lucky enough to have children. Would I be over-protective? Or would I push my children to explore, have a go and learn through supervised risk-taking?

Watching their affection for each other pulls my emotions in all directions, forcing me to confront things in my life that I thought I

The Lost Soul

wasn't worthy or deserving of. The full force of these emotions brings unease to my already weary mind, and more questioning thoughts than answers.

Sasha pulls her daughter's head forward and drops a sweet kiss on her forehead, before she says in a soft voice, 'be careful, sweetie.'

Unable to look away, if feels as though I'm watching a film in slow motion. The caring way that Sasha tends to her young daughter has hit a nerve and I feel a strong need to connect. The urge to kiss her, to place my hands on her hips and feel the warmth of her hands on my skin, is so intense that I squeeze the hand that isn't holding my phone into a fist.

I can't remember the last time I held somebody close or felt the need to touch someone. If I'm honest, the colour had disappeared from my world the day I found my bloodied sister in the bath four years earlier, her wrists slashed as the life ebbed away from her. It feels like a lifetime ago.

Searching my brain, I try to remember the last time I'd had contact with another person. Suddenly a memory floods my mind, as I think of the day that Blip's life support was switched off, and our family broke into fragments so tiny that it couldn't be fixed. I'd held my mother's hand and tried to be strong, tried to hide the fact that I was full of pain, sadness and anger.

'You all right?' Sasha's husky voice breaks into my thoughts. Her eyes shift to my thigh, where I'm holding on to my phone with white knuckles.

99

The Lost Soul

'Yes, of course,' I answer, in a tone sharper than I'd intended. 'Why?'

'You just have this sad look about you,' she replies, 'as though something bad has happened to you.'

She doesn't know the half of it, and if I ever tell her, which will surely piss off Stuart and Jack, she'll run for the hills and never look back.

'I don't know what you mean,' I mumble.

'Look Nick,' she turns to face me, and all I see is her full pink lips.

I can't take my eyes from them. God, I'm like a schoolboy with his first crush.

'I know,' she moves slightly closer, until I can feel her warm breath on my cheek, 'that something isn't quite right. I've been there, to dark places, I mean, and I know the signs of guilt and pain. I also know that Stuart and Jack, would not have brought you to Greystones unless you needed their help. I know the signs.'

I sit quietly, realising for the first time just how astute Sasha is. My head is reeling that she recognised why I am here. That I needed help. Her mind is sharp as a razor blade, and she doesn't seem to miss a thing when studying people and their characteristics.

How weird is it, that this is the most we've said to each other outside of work? But the little red devil sits on my shoulder,

The Lost Soul

telling me that I don't deserve to be happy or settled after what I've done. Perhaps he's right.

Looking down at my brown boots, I fixate on the scuffs that show their everyday wear and tear on the suede. It feels much like my mood today, scuffed and worn, with such a feeling of misery wearing me down, that I want to crawl into the nearest hole and lie there until I die.

A warm hand covers both of mine as I hold my phone. I turn my head and study Sasha's face, she must have seen the shock on mine, because her dark brown eyes dilate, as though she's just found the answer to a puzzle. I watch in wonder as her face relaxes, and she gives me the biggest smile.

'Sasha,' I struggle with the words, a little unsure of what is happening to me, to us. Her smile lifts me, dissipating the misery that is rooted deep within my soul. Jesus, how does she do that? No one and nothing, has had this effect on me for a long time.

'It's all right, Nick,' she says in a husky voice, and without consciously thinking about it, one of my hands turns upwards, and I slowly thread my fingers through hers.

'Mummy! Nick!' A child's voice screeches, shaking us back to reality when we see Zoe slumped on the damp grass, about fifty yards away, with the scooter laying across her legs. We quickly pull ourselves together, leave the bench and rush over to her, watching as she holds her hands upwards, silently seeking help.

The Lost Soul

'Come on, sweetie, let's get you up,' Sasha soothes, about to take her daughter's outstretched hands.

'Not you, Mummy, Nick. I want Nick,' the little scamp pouts, and I'm shocked for a moment, because she reminds me so much of Blip when she was her age. My eyes meet Sasha's, and her easy smile is replaced with shock. I drop my gaze to the floor, feeling awkward that I've been chosen over her, and wish that the earth will swallow me up.

I've done nothing wrong, but the child seems to have singled me out, grown fond of me even. I'm hazarding a guess that this is the first time that Sasha has had to face this dilemma.

'It's fine, Nick,' Sasha's husky voice reassures me. I thrust my phone in my brown jacket pocket and reach out to take Zoe's hands. Tiny cold hands hold on to mine as I pull to her to a standing position, muddy knees and all and give her a quick hug.

'I'm ok Mummy,' Zoe says with tears in her eyes, glancing quickly at her mother, 'I didn't cry.'

The sun shines through the trees and glistens across Zoe's rosy cheeks, as she brushes a pink padded arm across her face, catching and rubbing the wetness from her nose. Sasha reaches down and scoops the small child up and into her arms. 'You are one brave little girl,' she tells her, kissing her cheek. 'Are you hurt anywhere?' Sasha is already checking out Zoe's pink leggings and knees, gently touching and patting her thighs.

'My hands are sore,' Zoe turns her hands upwards to show her mum. 'Look,' she shows the pale red grazes that appear on her hands. Sasha inspects the upturned hands and gently kisses them

The Lost Soul

better. To my surprise, Zoe turns to me, thrusts her hands my way and says, 'Look Nick, Mummy kissed them better.'

A sound interrupts us. It's a musical ringtone, as Adele begins to sing 'Hello,' in a deep, sultry voice that flows hauntingly through the crisp April air. Sasha places Zoe onto her feet, watches her as she walks to her scooter, grabs the handle-bars and sets the wheeled apparatus upright. Sasha fumbles inside both of her jacket pockets for her phone. 'Sorry,' she mumbles to me, as she rushes to take the call.

'Hello, who is this?' she waits and listens. Her eyes flit to me, worry shows on her face.

'Hello,' she repeats, in a softer voice. She's watching Zoe all of the time. When there is no answer, Sasha shakes her head, disconnects the line and pushes her phone back into her jacket pocket.

'Someone bothering you?' I ask, trying not to dig too hard, but failing miserably.

'It's nothing,' her eyes don't leave Zoe. I know she wants me to drop the subject, but I can't.

'Like, it's nothing when you worry that I'm not all right,' I mutter, shoving my hands in my jacket pockets.

'Something like that,' she says softly, shifting her gaze to the floor.

The Lost Soul

I look at her profile; slender figure, dark red hair hanging forward as it follows the shape of her head, hiding her face. I want to reach out to her, to touch her. I need to touch her.

'Sasha,' I say quietly, slowly taking my hand from my pocket and placing it lightly on top of hers as it rests on the bench between us. Her fingers move against mine and I am surprised as she threads her cold fingers through my own.

A silence fills the air, and I wait patiently for her to speak. It feels like we sit like this forever, my mind whirls with an array of memories, and thoughts, patience doesn't come easily to me.

'Five days, they've been bothering me for five days,' her voice has a flatness to it.

'The phone calls?' I ask her. Bloody hell! She's being stalked! My blood boils at the very thought, and I want to go and find this person who is making Sasha's life miserable and pummel them in the face until they need hospital treatment.

'Yes, they never say anything, just call and wait for me to answer the phone.'

'Jesus! Do you have any idea who it is?' I ask, trying to keep the anger from my voice.

She shakes her head in a silent no as Zoe heads our way – momentarily taking the focus from our conversation.

'Look how fast I can go Mummy!' Zoe shouts, even though she's almost upon us. Determination shows on her little face as she pushes on the ground faster and faster.

The Lost Soul

'Careful Zoe!' Warns Sasha, and I remove my hand from hers, 'remember what happened last time.' Zoe's smile stops, as she stops the scooter just in front of her mother's knee:

'Gotcha,' Zoe says with confidence, 'I knew I could stop.'

Sasha smiles and strokes her fingers through her daughter's dark curly hair. 'You sure did,' she tells Zoe, as she watches her daughter scoot around the circular shape of the flower garden again.

'That girl's going to be the death of me, one day,' Sasha turns to me, brown eyes glowing with love.

'The calls,' I push gently, 'is it someone from your past?' I hold her gaze.

Her brow creases and a solitary tear falls down her cheek. She closes her eyes and nods.

As I look at her, I realise two things. One, I'm going to put my arm around her. Two, that I'm going to help find out who is making the phone calls and put a stop to it. I raise my right arm and slide it gently around her shoulder. I'm about to draw her close when she turns to me, grabs my black jumper inside my open jacket and dips her head against my chest. I hear her sigh deeply, and something deep inside me breaks, forcing out an emotion I haven't felt since Blip died.

I stroke her hair gently, inhale the smell of rose petals and hold her close.

The Lost Soul

And just like that, without even understanding what is happening, my heart starts beating again.

The Lost Soul

Part 9: Dave

Mops are the bane of my life. Every day. Wet, slosh, slide. Wet, slosh, slide. Pick up the wooden handle, dip the mop and slosh it in the cold, dirty water. Rinse the mop, slosh and slide across the old grey concrete corridor floor. Repeat.

Day in, day out.

What a fucking nightmare!

If this is my life from now on, I might as well fucking overdose. Leaning against the grey walls of the canteen at Belmarsh, I think of that bastard, Jules Walker who is walking as free as a bird, when he has murdered my brother. While I get fifteen bloody years for dealing the likes of coke, heroin, and LSD. Bloody bastard.

'Oi! What are you looking at?' the familiar hard Irish brogue of Bomber O'Neal shouts from behind me. 'If you want some, you just gotta say, and I'll give it to you, long and hard!'

Bomber is a psychotic fool, who will, if what the papers say is true, throttle a person if they look at him the wrong way. Bomber is otherwise known as Sean O'Neal, motor mouth, and hard nut, he's always in your face. He's hard to miss, with his bald head, tattooed arms and big hulking body stretching his prison greys. It

The Lost Soul

is just my luck that he is here, on remand. I heard he had done some work a while back, for the left-wing Irish republican political party, Sinn Fein.

Keep your head down, Davey boy. I tell myself. Keep out of it. Mop the fucking floor.

'Nothing,' a petrified voice says. There are a handful of unwritten rules in here. Such as you don't grass on anyone, and you don't press the emergency buzzer. You don't take other people's stuff, and finally, if you're lucky. You get out of here alive.

Then there are the Bomber rules. Do what he says. Always. Never answer him back.

I can almost feel them getting closer to me. Keep the fuck away. I don't want to be involved. I just want to do my time and get out.

Something crashes behind me, causing me to stop and take a deep breath. I guess it's the newbie being smashed into the wall. What the fuck! My blood boils, like many people in here, keeping your temper when you live in close proximity to others, is difficult.

I am many things; cruel, greedy, self-reliant. But one thing I'm not is a bully. I can't stand people like Bomber O'Neal, who prey on the weak. At least do it for a reason and not just because you can.

My dad was an arsehole, he was always in trouble with the police for stealing stuff. The problem was, he wasn't a good thief, he always got caught and spent most of his time in a low security prison because of his repeat offending. That was until he got stabbed, by an inmate while inside, a couple of years ago.

108

The Lost Soul

There's a thud, as something hits the floor and even as I tell myself to block out the sound of one man beating another, I turn around and shake my head. Fuck.

I slowly rinse the mop head. Check the security camera and move it so that it doesn't face the corridor. Grasping the heavy wooden pole, I lift it and stick it hard into Bomber's side, just under his kidneys as he leans over the bleeding newbie. The swift movement of the pole pushes the big hulk across the corridor,

'Leave him alone, you fucker,' I growl, through gritted teeth, as I haul the young dark-haired man to his feet. 'Get yourself back to your cell. Tell everyone, you are now under the protection of Dave Delossi.'

The man mumbles a thanks, wipes his bloody nose with the sleeve of his grey sweatshirt and limps away.

Turning to Bomber, I watch closely as he gets to feet, one hand holding his back. I note the way he winces when he breathes, and the free hand that wipes his sweaty brow. He's not such a big man now.

'Why?' He asks, defensively, 'why did you get involved?'

Walking over to him, I get up close and personal and stare into his cold, jet black eyes.

'Because I can,' I hiss. 'Leave him the fuck alone,' I say, waiting for his reaction. It could go either way, so I hold the mop handle in a tight grip, ready to move – to immobilise him. A long moment later, and much to my relief, he shrugs and saunters down the corridor.

The Lost Soul

'This isn't over, Delossi,' he mutters, still holding his side as he turns out of sight.

Of course, it isn't, but I don't give a toss what he thinks, because he's just a bully. I knock the security camera back into place, dip my mop and clear up the blood from the floor.

There were two things that my dad was good at. One, was repeat offending, and the other, was his connections – he knew everyone. Commonly known in the area as Jim Can, because most of the time he couldn't, he was a popular rogue who couldn't support his wife or his children.

Growing up I had been angry with him, for letting us down and making my mum work four jobs to make ends meet. I was angry because he let the family down. When he should have been providing for us, putting money on the table to pay for food and bills, he pulled stunts that saw him bungling a job, getting caught, and being sent back to prison. Some days we had to have free school meals, because there was not enough cash to pay for dinner money for us both.

If only he could have pulled himself together and given me and my brother a fighting chance. Despite my anger at him, he was the only dad I had known. No matter what he did, deep down, he was just my Dad.

At home, watching my mother struggle on a daily basis was hard, it wasn't for me. I wanted more, so I started dealing drugs, let myself go a bit. My younger brother, Ray, had been a good lad, mum's favourite, he couldn't do any wrong in her eyes. But I saw

The Lost Soul

the darkness in him, he stood up to me, even when he wasn't tall enough to meet my eyes. He stood his ground and put me right.

Once, he caught me tormenting a cat in the field, and challenged me to stop. No one ever challenged me, because I had a short temper and was quick to intimidate people. That kept them at a distance, made people fear me. And fear is power. Until you meet someone like my brother, he will hold you accountable. Like that day in the field when Ray punched me in the face, because of the cat. I was proud of him.

Jules Walker. Where the fuck is he? He could be anywhere. My mind wanders to Anthony Cherwell and I wonder if he has found anything out yet. I don't trust Tony, I particularly don't trust junkies. When I get back to my cell, I'll get Little Tim to follow him and see what he comes up with. It may come in handy.

One thing is for sure, I'm not spending the next seven years sloshing a bloody mop around in dirty water.

Things are going to change around here.

The Lost Soul

Part 10: Nancy

I look at my phone, now silent in my hand. Why the hell didn't I speak to her? What's the point of calling if I don't have the courage to talk to her? *Silly, silly woman,* I chastise myself, *you are only going to have so many chances to make things right.* On the other hand, I am so happy to hear her voice, even for the briefest time, it gives me such pleasure and warmth, making me feel almost normal again. A vision of Sasha wearing an emerald-green velvet dress jolts me back to her fifteenth birthday.

***

My daughter is growing into a beautiful young woman, I muse as I plump up the green velvet cushion that rests on the black wingback chair that is my husband's favourite. I count my blessings each morning, that I am lucky to have Sasha as my daughter. With her graceful movements, her kind heart and a maturity of mind, she acts much older than her fifteen years.

Sasha is petite and slender with a cascade of natural dark red curly hair that reaches down her back, past her shoulders. With her looks and gentle nature, I know I'll have to give her the 'talk' soon, to warn her about boys and their hormones, before people begin taking advantage of her.

The Lost Soul

The dress she is wearing is emerald-green velvet with spaghetti straps and falls to just above her knees.

'Happy birthday darling,' I say, giving her a hug while we are waiting for Lewis to finish getting ready. We have celebratory dinner plans booked at a local Italian restaurant, which I'm looking forward to as I haven't been out in a while. This is due to being on the receiving end of Lewis' displeasure, which simply means that I had not mashed the potatoes enough to his liking and his rage escalated into a heavy punch to my face. Luckily, he didn't break my jaw, not this time, but there was bruising and swelling to one side of my face. At the time, it had hurt like a bitch, whenever I had blinked or tried to talk.

I hear footsteps, immediately my heart begins to race, and my brow starts to sweat. A feeling of panic flows through every pore, and I stand frozen in the moment. Ironically, I can't help but wonder in what universe can this reaction to my husband, the one who is supposed to love and protect me unconditionally, be classed as normal.

As my senses dull, the panic subsides, and I slowly pull away from Sasha and push my hands down the front of my black lace dress to wipe out any creases.

As he walks into the living room I can tell by his sour face and grim smile that the night is not going to be a good one. Poor Sasha. She deserves better, so much better.

'What the hell are you wearing, Sasha?' he snorts in a harsh way, his cruelty knows no bounds.

The Lost Soul

Sasha turns to look at me, shock making her pale skin appear almost milk white. 'What do you mean, what am I wearing?'

'You're dressed like a slut!' His voice is clipped and unrepentant, even when Sasha's sharp intake of breath stills the whole room. 'Go upstairs and put something decent on!' he looks at me, daring me to intervene. I am ashamed of him, for the person he turns into when he enters this house. I cannot call it a home, because the only warmth contained within its concrete foundations, is between my daughter and myself.

The Lewis we know, within the walls of this house is a bullish, cruel person, who will not hesitate to hurt me just because he can. The Lewis we know, is highly strung and very watchful of our actions, waiting for a reason to raise his hand to me. I lower my head and look at the blue carpet, shame overwhelms me. How can I allow him to treat me and my daughter in this appalling way?

'Lewis,' I say in a quiet voice, stepping protectively in front of Sasha, 'please leave her alone.'

Deep down, I know what will happen if I challenge his order, but I am not worried for myself. My concern is for my daughter and the effect that my husband's bullish and cruel behaviour is having on her mental and physical well-being. This worries me and takes priority every time. It's what gives me the strength to question him. Lewis' face contorts into a false smile, and the tell-tale tick flickers in his upper jaw as he steps closer to me, hands forming in fists by his sides.

'Mum,' Sasha pleads, 'it's all right, I'll go and change.'

The Lost Soul

'No, stay there!' Lewis growls as he reaches me, his eyes never leave mine. I don't look away, whatever he does, I never look away. That's my 'Fuck you' to him. We are so close that I can feel his warm breath on my face, as though he's imprinting his soul onto my skin. My husband's eyes roam over my body, assessing me from head to toe, trying to push down my spirit.

His fist comes hard and fast, I don't see it coming. The force propels me backwards onto the wingback chair, the shock and pain of his assault leaves me breathless and sobbing.

Sasha screams and rushes to my side, tears falling down her face. 'I'm ok,' I reassure her in a quiet voice.

'Why Dad? Why would you do this?' Sasha looks to her father for answers, that I've never been able to find.

'Shut up you little cow,' he replies, combing his hands through his dark, greying hair. 'This is between your mum and me. It's none of your damned business.'

'Leave her alone,' I repeat, holding onto the back of the chair, and gently rubbing my cheekbone. God, it smarts, shockwaves of pain move along the side of my face.

'You dare stand up for her?' he stalks forward, hands falling to his hips. 'I must be the unluckiest bloke in the world. A wife who dresses as though she's going to a fucking funeral and a daughter who dresses like a whore.'

Without another word he turns and storms through the front door, slamming it shut with a bang.

The Lost Soul

***

The painful memory of Sasha's fifteenth birthday lingers, and I can't help but feel resentful to Lewis, that he had ruined that night for her, just like he'd ruined most things. The anger eats away at me, but also keeps me strong. Sometimes in the dark recess of my mind, I allow myself to think about the 'what ifs.' What if, I'd met someone decent who had been kind and caring? What would my life have been like if I'd been happy? What if Sasha had never left?

So, here I am, facing reality and angry with myself for keeping silent on the phone. Ok, so it would have been weird. I mean, I haven't seen her in four years. What could I have said?

'Hi Sasha, it's mum. How are you? How's Zoe?'

That conversation is not something I think either of us are ready for. Yet.

One thing is for sure though. For the first time in four years, I have something to live for.

I have hope.

Last week began like any other week. The same routines, same indifferent comments to Lewis. Putting laxatives in his food. Finally, I had a breakthrough to help me find my daughter, a lightbulb moment, you might say. I remembered Sasha's friend, Tracy, from high school, they had been close since primary school and were inseparable for a while. Tracy was easy to find on Facebook, she hadn't changed in looks or surname, which was lucky because people can change a lot in four years.

117

The Lost Soul

I found myself scrolling through Tracy's friends and found someone who looked vaguely familiar, called Sasha Berrington. She wore large sunglasses and a sun hat, but there was no mistaking her dark reddish curls and the shape of her face, it was her.

Bingo. I'd found her. My daughter.

There are times when you have to take the plunge, a leap of faith to bring about the best outcome. This was one of those times. I had messaged Tracy explaining that I'd fallen out with Sasha, a while back now, and wanted to get back in touch, and she was only too happy to help reunite me with my daughter. I wasn't sure what, if anything, Sasha had told Tracy about what had happened, but Tracy never mentioned anything.

Which left me wondering, was Sasha still trying to stay under the radar?

A week later, I received a message from Tracy giving me Sasha's number.

And that's how I find myself standing with the phone in my hand, staring and wondering. I made the leap of faith by contacting Tracy. That was the hardest part, now I'm determined to follow this through, or life will not be worth living. One thing is for sure, the next time I call Sasha, I *will* be speaking to her. It's time to put the past and the hurt behind us, we need to move forward. It's time to rebuild my relationship with my daughter and granddaughter.

I wait twenty-four hours before I decide to call Sasha again.

The Lost Soul

It is 1 o'clock on Monday afternoon when I look at my watch and take the plunge, my need to hear her voice overwhelms my fear that she'll not want to speak to me. I find her name and press the call button. After a few moments the ringing tone connects and Sasha's voice slides over me like a warm blanket. I can't speak. She's asking if it's me or her father? I can hear her panicked breath and I can't help myself, as I whisper, 'It's Mum.'

There's a sob on the other end of the line, and I am about to tell her how sorry I am, that I should have listened to her, and left her father, when my head turns at the sound of a keys jingling and turning downstairs. A moment later the front door opens.

I put my hand over my mouth, to limit any sound I might make, but panicked words slip through my fingers. 'It's him,' I whisper, 'he's home early.' Sasha's worried voice becomes shaky, 'Mum are you okay?'

There are footsteps in the hall.

'Nancy!' Lewis shouts. 'Where the hell are you?'

'Upstairs,' I shout, disconnecting the call and quickly hiding the secret phone in the red fluffy Christmas sock I've worn for years. I need to hide it with its counterpart, inside my Christmas slippers, in the divan drawer of our bed.

'Putting laundry away,' I call back in a slightly breathless tone, 'I'll be down in a minute.'

I didn't hear his footsteps but as I stand in our bedroom, holding a pair of old Christmas socks limply in my hands, Lewis appears in the doorway.

The Lost Soul

'What have you got there?' he asks, his voice sounds intrigued and clipped at the same time.

'Nothing,' I say, feeling my hands begin to shake. I focus on the purple cushions, that rest against the white cotton pillowcases that match the duvet cover. 'Just putting stuff away.'

'Christmas socks, it's bloody April, silly woman.' He holds out his hand, 'hand them over!'

I take a step back, horrified and holding the Christmas socks tightly in my hands. I've become complacent in the past year. Confident in my ability to outwit him.

And now as I look at his outstretched hand, reality starts to hit me. This is my downfall.

'It's nothing!' I shout, as my body comes to a standstill against the hard bedroom wall, 'leave me alone.'

He walks with purpose until he's standing in front of me, swiftly his hand reaches out and seizes my hair in a vice-like grip. He wraps it around his hand and pulls hard. A searing pain burns through my scalp, it feels as though he's pulling the hair from my head. I scream and drop the socks, vaguely catching the dull thud of the phone as it hits the grey carpet. Scrunching my eyes together, hot tears falling down my face, I know what's coming next. But I'm determined to make one last stand.

'You bastard!' I grind out through the pain, as I reach up to try to dislodge his grip from my hair. But he's too strong. I think of the socks, remembering that the stakes are high. If Lewis picks up the phone, it won't be long before he finds out about Sasha and where

120

The Lost Soul

she is. I don't know what he'll do with that information, or how he feels about Sasha. He never speaks of her.

But I do know one thing, and that is I can't take the chance that he'll want to find her. Somehow, I need to distract him from finding the phone. 'Tell me one thing,' I say, wincing through the pain in my head, while using my foot to feel for the phone, 'why are you such a bloody coward?'

My foot hits something hard, and I slide it across the floor, as he pulls my head backwards sharply.

'You're asking for it, Nancy,' he snaps, his face inches from mine, 'you're fucking asking for it.'

The last thought going through my mind as he drags me by my hair across the room, and slams his fist into my temple, is that I have let my daughter down.

Again.

The Lost Soul

Part 11: Jules

There are three things I miss most about being Jules Walker.
Apart from the obvious loss of my own identity, which leaves me
feeling like a shadow in my own body, part of the walking dead.
Of course, I know I'm a real, physical person. I can see my
footprints in the rain and my fingerprints on the shower screen.

Back to missing Jules. Number one; I miss not seeing myself in
the mirror, the real me, with the face I've grown up with and the
life that I've lived. My long natural blonde hair is dyed brown,
cut close to my head, and a vision of the young boy I used to be,
growing up in Stoke-on-Trent with his heartbroken father, waiting
patiently for his mum to return home, fills me with sadness.

As a boy of three, I had tormented myself, that it was my fault
that my mother had left me, especially as she had used the
weakest of explanations pretending to visit her sick mother for
two days. We didn't know that granny wasn't sick, we didn't
think to question that my mother was lying, until she didn't return
home and dad had to call granny to see where she was. Sue, my
mother, with her pretty, blue eyes, petite figure and soft blonde
hair, had disappeared off the face of the earth, never to be seen
again.

The Lost Soul

A year later, we met Kerry and my dad fell in love for the second time in his life. She was like a golden-haired angel sent to look after us, to make us whole again. She was everything I wanted in a mum, kind and supportive. She loved me, unconditionally, and I realised for the first time in my life, that I wasn't bad at all, and was worthy of being loved.

Number two; I miss having a career and a focus. Training to become a social worker was rewarding and enabled me to use my degree to support vulnerable people in our society, particularly adolescents. Working also kept my mind busy, which in turn, enabled me to move on with my life.

Number three; I miss the freedom of simply being me and not having to watch my back all the time. Old friendships, from university and my social care work, were an important part of supporting me with life after Blip. They were a small group, but that's all I needed.

But now. Here. No one knows who I am.

'Nick?'

I walk past Jed and Leo, the new security guys who stand inside the main entrance of Greystones, in their smart black suits. I didn't mean to ignore them, but my mind is too busy and leaves little space to interact with others and make small talk. The elegant oak staircase stands central in the foyer near to the reception desk. Along the corridor, to the right, is The Bistro which is where I'm heading, to grab some lunch. The Bistro is our onsite restaurant. I wrap my hand around the shiny brass

The Lost Soul

handle of the heavy oak door, when I hear a familiar voice coming from behind me.

'Nick?'

I feel a hand on my arm and stop abruptly. 'Sasha?' There's a huskiness to my voice, and my eyes can't help but sweep up and down her body. Today she's wearing a light grey blouse, black trousers and low shoes.

'Nick, I was calling you and you didn't hear me. Are you all right?' she asks.

Bloody hell! My brain was racing around in circles, thinking about the things I'd missed about being Jules Walker, and worrying about Russell, which had left me preoccupied. Which, in turn had led me to not hearing or answering to my new name, Nick Flannagan. Jesus! It's a harsh reminder for me to be careful. I can't risk anyone finding out who I really am.

'Sorry. I was miles away,' I smile apologetically, and feel ridiculously happy when I notice that her hand is still on my arm. I am beyond embarrassed at not responding to my 'name' that the first words to come out of my mouth are, 'Sorry, I was thinking of ways to help you.' I can feel a warm sensation in my cheeks. *Now look what you've done!* I silently chastise myself.

Sasha's face softens, her eyes drop momentarily, as though unused to hearing such words of support. 'Don't worry about me, Nick. I'll be fine,' she reassures me, letting go of her grip on my arm and turning in the direction of the bistro. She falls into step beside me with an ease that makes our connection very comfortable and familiar. My mind knows that something has

The Lost Soul

changed between us, there's a heightened awareness of each other, for a start. We keep gravitating to one another.

I raise my eyebrows in challenge to her comment. She's so fiercely independent with her red curly hair tied loosely back with a large clip, and it makes me wonder when she last had someone to lean on and look out for her. To protect her.

'I've had Anthony on the phone, Russell's grandson. He wants to visit this Friday at 10am,' she tells me.

I stop walking and she comes to a halt beside me. We look at each other and I have the strangest feeling, it's exciting and intoxicating at the same time. I raise my eyebrow, stroke my chin and look at her, 'The game is afoot, Doctor Watson. Let's set the scene.'

She looks surprised at my joviality and, to be honest, I'm surprised myself. Only a few days ago I was struggling to live this new life and face each day as Nick Flannagan, and now – would you believe it, I'm making jokes!

Sasha clears her throat, there's a slight giggle as she struggles to hold herself in check. A pink tongue slips out and sweeps across her bottom lip, I feel a tightening in my groin. Jesus, what is this woman doing to me? When a simple innocent action from her, results in a physical and emotional response from me?

Unable to control herself any longer, Sasha lets out a deep, sexy laugh which is both infectious and charming. And, like a boy with his first crush, I feel such joy that I smile until my face aches. Her laugh is music to my ears, and something I want to hear more often. Watching her brown eyes light up when she laughs, it's

The Lost Soul

something I can get used to, and it makes my heart beat faster in my chest.

'What do we need to do, Sherlock?' her voice is full of mirth.

I'm enjoying this game.

'In the first instance, Watson,' I continue the banter, 'we need to tell Russell that his grandson is coming to see him this week and make sure that Russell's all right with that. Secondly, we let Jed and Leo know about the visit, and Anthony's proposed arrival time. Once on the premises, the loving grandson will need to be monitored closely.'

'Thirdly,' I stroke my chin, in an exaggerated Sherlock Holmes motion, 'I suggest we make up an excuse for the visit to take place in the lounge or Sun Room, a neutral place, where we can monitor them more closely. We can make it into a maintenance issue, damp, rot – anything.'

'Good thinking, Sherlock,' she giggles, 'I'll also ask Russell if we can set up a Nest camera in his room, in case Anthony accidentally wanders into Russell's apartment searching for the book!'

'Watson,' Sir Arthur Conan Doyle would be so impressed with us right now, 'there is nothing more deceptive than an obvious fact,' I quote, rather impressed with myself. All right, so I love the books, the films, and the TV series, and maybe one or two quotes have stuck in my mind. I see Sasha's eyes shine with excitement, 'so, let us retrieve Little Dorrit from Russell's safe keeping and, with his permission, put it in the safe in your office.'

The Lost Soul

With a smile, Sasha pats my shoulder and tilts her face upwards. 'The game is indeed afoot, Sherlock. I'll start putting the props into play, and inform Russell of our plans,' she says, turning away from me.

My heart drops into my stomach when she begins to move away, and I struggle to understand what is happening to me. I never expected to feel like this, but there's something about Sasha that is changing me, making me feel things.

'Sasha,' I whisper, touching her hand. 'Have dinner with me one night?'

Bloody hell, I can't believe those words just came out of my mouth. Immediately, I start berating myself for not taking things slowly. I shouldn't be thinking about romance and dinner dates. Expectations and hope should be kept for people who deserve it, such as Sasha, Stuart and Jack. For Jenny and Steph who live a good life, but definitely not for me, not with my history.

'Wednesday?' Sasha's voice is quiet but firm. 'I know you're on call, but it's usually quiet.'

I stand motionless, she wants to have dinner with me.

'I can cook, how about 7pm at my apartment?' she offers, holding her breath.

Adele's deep voice cuts in before I can reply, making Sasha glance briefly at me before fumbling around in her black trouser pocket for her phone. Silently, not checking the screen, she just accepts the call.

The Lost Soul

'Hello,' she says, as I wait patiently and wonder if it's the same person as yesterday.

Sasha stares at the ceiling and closes her eyes, waiting for someone to speak.

'Is that you Mum? Dad?' she whispers into the phone, 'say something, for God's sake, don't just call and say nothing,' her voice holds a note of anger.

'It's Mum,' Sasha looks my way, tears falling down her cheek.

'Mum are you ok?' the colour drains from her face as she holds the phone against her ear, waiting for a response. 'Mum, tell me you're all right!' She demands fiercely, looking at the phone in her hand, as though she's lost something precious.

'It was my mum, she hung up. I could hear another voice, I think it belonged to my father.' she tells me, using her hand to wipe unwanted tears from her eyes.

'Bloody hell!' I say, watching Sasha's shoulders slump. 'What is going on, Sasha?'

'I don't know, but he'll hurt her. Really hurt her if he finds out she's been phoning me,' her eyes suddenly lift and find mine. 'She could be in danger!' her voice sounds heavy and panicked, and her face is almost white.

'Don't worry, we'll sort it out,' I reassure her, knowing that even as I scold myself for getting involved with Sasha's problems, that I'll help her. There's no choice. And yet again I find myself drawn into something that really isn't my problem. Just like that idiot Leon, disrespecting his girlfriend in the high street. I

129

couldn't walk away then and pretend everything was fine, it's not in my nature. I'll be damned if I'll walk away from Sasha now.

She studies the carpet-covered floor, before she raises her face to look at me, with brown eyes that look defeated and full of fear, my heart stops. In that moment, I make a decision that changes everything. I reach out and take her cool hand firmly. Leading her back to the reception, I ask Susie, our Head Receptionist, to put a call out to Lauren and tell her that we'll be taking a thirty-minute lunch break, and to call us if needed.

Sasha walks silently beside me, her hand still in mine as I push through the walnut doors with my free hand and into the white-walled staff area, where we take the stairs to the first floor and walk towards my apartment. Taking the key from my trouser pocket, I place it into the lock and turn clockwise, before pushing down the brass handle and putting my weight behind the door until it opens.

As I pull Sasha in behind me, I realise that her hand is now warm inside mine, and I feel the pressure from her fingers as we silently walk along the grey carpeted hallway of my apartment. I open the door to the lounge, and panic momentarily. *Did I tidy the living room before I left for work this morning? Did I leave anything around the room that might be related to Jules Walker? Bloody hell, what is the matter with me? Does any of it really matter?*

The off-white colour of the walls and light grey carpet look good against the deep blue sofa and matching chair and give a sense of space and cosiness to the room. I let go of her hand, and hastily pick up a red coffee mug from the small oak table that sits in front

The Lost Soul

of the sofa. Leaning over the sofa, I grab the crumpled discarded blue jumper I was thinking of wearing two days ago.

Taking out my phone, I gesture to the sofa to ask Sasha to take a seat and focus on finding Stuart's name and pressing the call button. When I look up, she's still standing, but uses one hand to lean against the sofa.

'Stuart,' I sigh with relief when he answers, 'we've got a potential problem.'

'Nick, can you give me a minute,' Stuart's voice sounds serious. 'I've just got to the office.' Stuart works for the Gloverman Corporation Charity division, which enables him to work flexibly, so that he can manage the Lighthouse Charity's three women's refuge homes, and the support programmes that are involved with rehabilitation.

'Yes, of course. No problem.' I remain silent for a short while, until he begins to speak again.

'All done,' Stuart says, 'Fill me in.'

I glimpse Sasha's worried face. 'I'll put you on speaker if that's all right?' I briefly outline what has happened. He listens intently, without interruption. There's a short silence and I pat Sasha's arm.

'Sasha?' Are you all right?' Stuart asks, his voice softening.

'I'm fine, Stuart,' her eyes dart to mine. 'But I'm worried about my mum.'

The Lost Soul

'I know,' Stuart replies in a calming, tender voice. Clearly, he's very fond of Sasha, and I get that, now that I've been privy to his kindness and ability to help those in need. Stuart saved me from prison, and from myself when I had given up on myself and the world. Somehow, he had managed to right the world's axis for me, giving me a chance at redemption.

Stuart's voice crackles slightly, 'We've got your records on file, you lived in Abingdon, Oxfordshire, didn't you?'

'Yes,' she answers quietly.

'I'll see if Jack or Steph can pop over and check on her, they are nearer. Is it Nettie?'

'Nancy,' Sasha corrects him, 'her name is Nancy.'

I listen to the exchange, not dissimilar to a father talking to his daughter. It feels good having someone to rely on, who you can call when the going gets tough.

'Jul..shit..Nick, are you there?' I look at the phone and curse silently under my breath, as Stuart almost uses my real name. I hardly dare look at Sasha, and when I do, there's a question in her eyes, a raising of an eyebrow.

I shake my head, slowly. This isn't the time, maybe one day, but not today.

'Yes, I'm here,' I answer Stuart, watching Sasha's quizzical look.

'Keep an eye on Sasha and Zoe, keep them close. And whatever you do, try to keep a low profile.'

The Lost Soul

'We will,' we said at the same time, and I couldn't help the smirk that started to form at the side of my face.

'Thanks, Stuart,' Sasha replies, her eyes catching mine briefly.

'No worries,' he answers before disconnecting the line. Silence settles over us, as we think about the things that have been left unsaid and the questions that remain unanswered, and a flutter in my chest tells me that I've taken on the role of guarding this woman and her child. The flutter comes again when I think of Sasha, and Zoe. Bloody hell, this can only end badly.

I walk to the small, square-shaped alcove kitchen and fill the kettle.

'Tea or coffee?' I call out and her soft reply of 'tea' motivates me to collect what I need for our drinks. I want to help her, but I don't want to sound bossy and arrogant, and I don't want Sasha to think I'm meddling. Whether she likes it or not, she needs my help, if not for her, for her daughter.

I finish the drinks and take them through to the lounge, hearing her cushioned footsteps behind me, as I place the hot mugs on to the small table and motion for her to sit on the sofa. I mirror her movements and perch on the end of the sofa, like a bird ready to take flight.

Waiting patiently, I give her time to explain what is going on.

When she doesn't speak, I realise it needs to be me who makes the first move. Eventually, I speak:

'Sasha?' my voice is deep and there's an exasperation to my tone.

The Lost Soul

In slow motion, I watch her slump forward, lean her elbows on her knees and cradle the top of her face with her hands. With her eyes closed, she drops her head, so I am unable to see her expression. The hairs on my arms prickle my skin, surely it can't be that bad.

'Talk,' I ask, with a firmness that reflects the worry in the pit of my stomach. Softening, my voice, I follow with, 'please.'

She removes her hands from her head and looks at me with red eyes and wet cheeks. I reach for a tissue from the box on the table and step forward, holding it out to her. She mumbles a thanks. Finally, in a soft dull voice, unlike her own, she begins to talk.

'I thought the phone calls were from my dad,' she says, wiping her eyes and face.

I listen with bated breath as Sasha recalls the miserable story of her earlier life, of how she met Dylan and when she found out she was pregnant. The fragile home environment, where she lived with her parents, the place where she dreaded when the kitchen clock reached 6.30pm and her father would come purposefully through the front door, ready for a fight. Eventually, when the baby was six months old, her father had attacked her, and Sasha had left home with Zoe in her arms. She was seventeen years old.

Listening to her story was hard, my hands fisted at my sides and my heart raced. Anger bubbled within me, causing me to become rigid. And, all the time, I tried not to show her how angry I was, because if there's one thing I can't stand, it's a bully.

The Lost Soul

'That's how I ended up at the refuge home, Shore House run by the Lighthouse charity. I don't know what would have happened to Zoe and me, if I hadn't been introduced to Jenny and Stuart.'

I look at her, waiting for her to continue, as she rubs her hands along her black trousers. She seems so fragile, that the feeling to protect her against all odds, is overwhelming.

'I changed my surname to Berrington when we moved here,' she explains as a solitary tear escapes down her cheek, 'I wanted to start living again without worrying about my dad.'

'I get it,' I say, moving slowly to sit beside her, 'I do.' I wish I could slay her demons for her, find her dad and return the favour he did for his daughter four years ago. Instead, I put my arm around her slender shoulders and hold her close.

A moment later, I loosen my hold on her and gently turn her face to look at me, 'but, it wasn't him looking for you, was it?' I say in a quiet voice, watching her closely as she wipes her eyes again and begins to shake her head.

'No, it was my Mum. I was so angry with her during the first year on my own. So bloody angry,' she looks at me, her lips in a grim line, 'I was seventeen and I had a baby to look after, she should have fought harder for me.'

'She should have,' I agree sadly. 'She was supposed to look after you and keep you safe.' My blood boils and I know from my own experience what it feels like to be let down by a parent, particularly the woman who gave birth to you. Your own mother, not wanting you, it sounds crazy, but it happens. God, this is getting deep, it is opening feelings that I thought I'd dealt with years ago.

Somehow, while working through our own heartache, we've found each other, we weren't looking for it, we didn't want it, but we found it. Warm fingers reach up and trace my cheek, and I can't help but close my eyes and cherish her touch. A touch that jolts my senses to the point where I can only think of the here and now. Nothing else matters. Just me, Sasha and this moment.

Sasha's hand continues to skim lightly across my face, and my heart skips a beat at the contact. If only I can bottle this memory, keep it safe, away from harm, and my dark thoughts. I don't want to taint it with my demons and the lies that I've been living with for the past six months.

Her hand continues travelling across my shoulder, moving slowly upwards until it reaches my neck and finally rests on the back of my neck. Her touch wakens my senses, makes me realise how much I've missed human contact. Tilting my head to her neck, I whisper her name.

She pulls away slowly and stands with her hand out for me to follow her actions, without hesitation, I take her hand, rise to my feet and face her. Dilated brown eyes search mine, full of emotion, panic, passion, sadness. I wonder if she sees the same in mine, the wonder, the need, the panic. As the silence stretches on, I pull our connected hands to my lips and kiss her knuckles watching her swallow in return. For all the wrong reasons, we shouldn't be doing this, but for all the right reasons – it seems impossible to stop.

The Lost Soul

I lower my head so that our eyes meet, part my lips and take hers in a slow, tender movement, that feels new and exciting. Sasha pulls me to her with both hands and holds on as if the world is about to end. As her soft lips open, I explore her mouth and finally let the tip of my tongue touch hers. I give the deepest sigh of contentment, as though I've come home. I can't get enough. I want to stay like this forever.

I should have stopped the kiss there and then, but my brain is finding it hard to focus.

Instantly, my mind calms, and the storm that usually whirls inside me, the guilt of killing another human being, the grief and loss of losing my sister and family and the fear of living a life that isn't my own, comes to a standstill.

How can this be? How can Sasha calm my demons? A flash of acknowledgement hits me, and the realisation encases my soul like a warm glove. This is meant to be, everything I've been through and done has led me to this moment, here with Sasha.

Sasha's fingers curl into my neck for what seems like an eternity before she loosens them to break our kiss. 'Nick?' she says softly in the form of a question, as her fingers glide across the skin of my neck. Our eyes connect, and I can see that we're both finding it hard to look away. We don't want to return to reality quite yet.

And, deep down as I look into those beautiful brown eyes, I realise that it's too late to save myself. My heart thuds loudly in my chest.

'Nick?' she looks concerned.

The Lost Soul

'Not Nick,' I say bluntly, forcing myself to be honest and tell her to her face. *No, don't say it!* I tell myself. *Don't tell her a bloody thing.*

'Sorry?' she replies, trying to understand what I'm saying.

'I'm not Nick,' I say flatly, letting my hands fall from her hips to hang limply by my side. I push them into my trouser pockets.

'I'm Jules. Jules Walker.'

Fuck. What have I done? Why couldn't I have kept my mouth shut?

She looks at me with a strange expression, I can almost hear her mind ticking as my real name registers with her. Her face pales as she connects my name to a memory. Brushing a frustrated hand through her hair, she stares at me, with eyes that are wary and fearful. An icy chill fills the air, I can see that she is struggling, and I see the very moment when she begins to withdraw from me. She thinks I'm a monster. Well, she's right, I am.

Too late for redemption. The secret is out.

Sasha stands, her hands form small fists by her side. Bloody hell, she is looking at me differently. It's started already. She will be wary of me, and she should be wary of me:

'Jules Walker? How can you be Jules Walker? He was on the news, admitting to killing another man.' Her voice rises as she becomes more agitated.

'Ray Delossi,' I say flatly. 'I'm sorry Sasha, I wasn't supposed to tell you. Stuart and Jack asked me not to.'

138

The Lost Soul

'Stuart and Jack? What have they got to do with it?' Her brows crease and I can tell that she's putting two and two together to make five. 'They should have told me.' She mutters, more to herself, than to me, before staring into my face. I will never forget that look, her eyes wide with fear, mouth open. She thinks I'm a monster.

'Oh my God! You've been around my daughter!' Her voice rises, in her panic.

'You and Zoe have nothing to be frightened of,' I try to reassure her. 'I'd never hurt a young woman and her child,' I say with a clipped tone. 'I'm not bloody Marilyn Manson, for God's sake!' I almost shout. 'Just calm down and listen to me.' I talk to her as though she's got no right to be frightened of me. I need to calm the hell down and stop shouting.

I inhale deeply, close my eyes and count to ten.

'I can't have you around her,' Sasha's voice cuts in, and I cautiously open my eyes. I need to give her time to come to terms with my revelation, stop being so defensive, just take what she has to offer.

'Please Sasha,' I say, quietly. I know what she is thinking. I totally get where her head is. I've been there myself. She will be worried for Zoe, worried about what this means for us too.

'Something happened, a long time ago,' I begin, wondering if Sasha will ever look at me the same way again. I'm pretty sure I've lost her trust, and that's a big thing for her, for both of us. 'If you give me a chance, I'll explain what happened.'

The Lost Soul

'I don't know,' she says, shaking her head sadly. Please give me a chance to explain, I silently plead. I'm just beginning to find myself again, feel comfortable in this new life. Even feel happy. 'I don't know if I can Nick, er, Jules, I don't even know what to call you.'

'Just call me Nick,' I tell her, 'I'm the same person I was half an hour ago.'

As we stand facing each other, I see a solitary tear fall down her soft cheek, and it makes me feel like a bastard for hurting her, that's the last thing I wanted to do. I push my hands in to the pockets of my jeans, to stop me from reaching out and pulling her close.

In life we make decisions every day. I don't know what is going through Sasha's mind. My decision to tell her the truth about me, leaves me vulnerable. She could call the police and they'd be here within the hour, or she could listen to what I have to say. I hold my breath, desperate to reach out to Sasha, wanting to offer her comfort and reassurance and hoping to receive the same.

She's at a crossroads, will she turn left, take a chance on me, let me explain the events that led to me being here, with her? Or will she face right and use her phone to call the police?

Sasha takes a step to me. I take a step closer to her.

'Tell me,' she orders softly, her hand reaches for mine, touching my fingers gently. 'Tell me everything.'

The Lost Soul

Part 12: Anthony

'Where the hell have you been?' I hear Lewis Benson's angry voice before I see him. He's pacing by the door of his office, which is situated on the ground floor of a Victorian terraced house near the Fire Station in Abingdon. He's holding his usual mug from the American TV series, The Office, with a picture of Steve Carell smiling smugly in one hand. I notice the red raw marks on his knuckles and several scratches across his hand, and I feel the hairs rise on my arms.

'I've been calling you,' he says accusingly, waving his mobile at me.

'I'm sorry,' I begin carefully, something doesn't feel right, and I don't want to make him angry. Part of me is rattled, it's only two minutes past 8.30am on Tuesday morning, and Lewis should take a bloody chill pill, but as I say, something doesn't feel right about him today. 'I am late because of the roadworks on the A34,' I tell him.

'Bloody hell!' Lewis exclaims, clutching his stomach. 'I need the bathroom, again,' his voice sounds pained as he rushes along the length of the room, drops his mug on my desk before he reaches the partition wall that separates his desk area from mine. Picking up speed, he disappears through an open doorway to the

141

The Lost Soul

modernised bathroom and kitchen that are situated at the back of the building.

I dip my head and take my black cross-over bag from my shoulder so that I can place it on the oak wood desk, that was assigned to me twelve months ago – careful not to knock over his precious mug.

Dropping my brown jacket over the back of the black leather swivel chair, before taking a seat, I take out my phone and google Jules Walker. He's been on my mind since I visited Dave Delossi at the weekend, and I need to do some homework. When am I going to find the time to visit Grandad in Haworth to get Little Dorrit, I don't know, but I promised Delossi that I'd get him his bloody money, and I will.

Lewis returns, his pale face looks strained and there is perspiration dripping from his forehead, in fact, if he wasn't such a dick, I'd have felt sorry for him. I place my phone on the desk and turn on my computer screen to see what we're doing today.

Dragging fingers through his curly black greying hair, I glimpse another angry red scratch, and begin to worry. These marks I keep noticing on him, are really unnerving me, What the hell has he been up to? I try to keep my face impassive as I watch him staring out of the window at the passing traffic, before lowering himself into the black leather chair that faces my desk.

Lewis looks at me. 'Right, what have we got lined up for today?' he asks sounding tired.

I check the online calendar for the week. 'You've got an interview with BBC Radio Oxford at 11am, re housing growth in

The Lost Soul

Abingdon and surrounding areas. We'll need to be there by 10.30am and speak to the manager, Lesley Wickerman. This afternoon at two you have a call from Alex Hastings, the Minister of State, at the Ministry of Housing, Community and Local Government.'

'Right, get the kettle on,' thankfully, the colour has come back into Lewis' cheeks, and he appears focused again, 'I've got a report to write and things to do. Can you book a table for lunch at Mal Maison, Oxford for 12.30pm?' he stands up and walks to his office.

'Can you also forward me the paperwork for Mr Anderson, I need to follow through on his wife's immigration status?' It wasn't a question, more of a statement.

'Sure,' I reply, grabbing my phone and taking it into the kitchen with me. As the kettle boils, I google Jules Walker. Immediately a photo comes up of a good -looking man, with shoulder length blonde hair and blue eyes. He's not at all what I was expecting. To my surprise I come across a You Tube video, which has a ton of likes, and I'm intrigued to see what this man, that Delossi wants, is like. I turn the volume down low on my phone and play the video.

It's the strangest thing. Jules Walker, with his hair pulled back in a ponytail, holds a man firmly by the neck, against a brick wall in a quiet street. The man is black and wears a blue suede jacket, he also looks frightened, especially when Jules Walker swings back an arm and punches him hard in the nose. His voice is calm, and he has a slight northern accent.

The Lost Soul

'You need to reassess how you treat women and people who are physically weaker than yourself,' he tells the man. 'If you have to pick on someone, try doing it to someone your own size. Or someone who will fight back. Otherwise, I'm coming back for you.'

I watch mesmerised, ignoring that the kettle has reached boiling point and stopped, and continue to watch the video as Jules moves his face directly in front of the man, before saying clearly, 'And, next time, you won't live to call the police.'

Shit, I mutter. I kind of like him. But he's a bit of a psycho. How the hell am I going to find him? He could be anywhere. He might even be dead. I put the coffee and stuff in the mugs, add the milk and go and place one on Lewis' desk.

An hour later, I've called Mal Maison, caught up on some emails, and sent the Anderson immigration document to Lewis. A vision of my grandad comes to mind, reminding me that I need to get that book, so I can get the money to buy the cocaine for Delossi.

'Just need to make a quick call,' I tell Lewis, as I move to the kitchen for some privacy. By way of an explanation, I call back, 'my grandad isn't well.'

'Ok,' he says, 'don't be too long.'

I scroll through my contacts until I find Greystones, press call and wait for someone to pick up. After several seconds of listening to the ring tone, someone answers:

'Hello, Greystones, Miss Berrington speaking. How may I help you?'

The Lost Soul

I clear my throat. 'Hello, it's Anthony Cherwell. My grandfather is Russell Cherwell, he doesn't have a phone and I'd like to make an appointment to visit him this Friday, at 10 o'clock.' I close my eyes and rub the top of my head. I don't like taking advantage of grandad, but I'm out of options. This is the only way I can see that will sort Delossi out.

'Of course,' said the young woman, 'I've put it in the book. I will check that Russell is happy for you to visit and confirm. Would I be able to call you back on this number, once I've spoken to him?' she asks in a deep soft voice. Damn, I want to confirm now! Instead, I force a smile to soften my frustration before telling her, 'That's fine. As soon as you can please.'

I disconnect the phone and head back to my desk to get things ready before we need to leave for Oxford. I hope the woman gets back to me soon, but I'll continue to work on the assumption that Friday is a go.

'How is he?' Lewis' voice sounds concerned.

'Who?' I ask, stopping in front of him and raising my eyebrows.

'Your grandad.'

'Oh, he's fine. He's just got a sore throat, that's all,' I tell him sitting down and pulling my swivel chair closer to my desk. I don't know how this week will pan out, but I do know one thing. And that is as soon as I get the money from grandad, I can collect the coke from Simon, and then arrange to have the stuff delivered to Dave Delossi on Saturday. When this is done, I have made a promise to myself to lay off the drugs for a while.

The Lost Soul

I make sure that the front door is locked, it's one of my things, I have to pull the door handle down at least three time, before we are able to leave for the radio interview in Oxford. Lewis' phone rings as we walk to his blue BMW which is parked roadside. He throws me the keys, as usual preferring me to drive, it makes him feel important, as though I'm his chauffeur.

'I haven't got time for this, Nancy,' he says quietly. 'I'm busy,' his voice rises as he sits in the passenger seat, 'Under no circumstances do you call for help, do you hear me? You'll be fine, just a couple of bumps and bruises. Lie down and sleep it off.' He listens for a while as I turn the engine on and move the car into the traffic, 'now stop being such a bloody nuisance,' he finishes before pushing the phone in the pocket of his navy pin-striped jacket.

'Trouble?' I ask, wondering why he is always such a prick when he speaks to his wife. He treats her like shit, no one deserves to be spoken to like that.

'No, just my wife, she's been drinking a bit lately. Fell down the stairs,' he mutters.

I say nothing, sometimes it's better that way.

As I negotiate the traffic leading onto the Banbury Road, Oxford, my thoughts turn to devising an excuse to take the day off on Friday, so I can visit Grandad.

Parking in the nearby car park, we walk through the main door of the yellow brick BBC Oxford radio station and my eyes focus immediately on the strange looking chap standing next to the reception desk. What an eye sore! He is dressed in a yellow and

The Lost Soul

black, checked suit, a black shirt and yellow tie. His hair is black and drapes in a shaggy style to his neck. I'm not a betting man, but I'm pretty sure he's wearing a toupee and his thick rimmed black glasses seem to cover his entire face.

'Mr Benson?' The man swoops across the reception to us. 'I'm Lesley Wickerman,'

Lewis offers his hand to Lesley. 'Lovely to meet you, Mr Wickerman,' he tells him offering one of his dazzling smiles. 'Lead the way.' As an afterthought, he turns to me, 'Tony, get yourself a coffee, will you. I'll call you when I'm done.'

I nod, 'No problem, Mr Benson,' heading out of the doorway to find a coffee shop. I walk along the Banbury Road and come across a small bakery with a small café sitting area. Pushing the door open, my phone comes to life, and 'Don't Stop Me Now,' by Queen, breaks the silence of the café. The name Greystones flags up, 'Hello,' I say, accepting the call.

'Hello, is that Anthony Cherwell, Russell's grandson?' A woman's Yorkshire dialect asks.

'Yes,' I say, my heart quickening.

'This is Kate from Greystones,' she says, 'I'm just calling to confirm your visit with your grandad for this Friday at 10 o'clock.'

'That's great,' I tell her, relief evident in my voice. 'Thanks, see you Friday,' I tell her, disconnecting the number.

There's a bay window seating area, that overlooks the street where I sit with a chocolate sprinkled cappuccino and a pain au

The Lost Soul

raisin, in front of me. Picking up my phone from the table I feel a need to watch the Jules Walker video again. I listen to his voice several times, memorising it, in case I come into contact with him.

The big question is what will happen to Walker when I find him? If I find him. He could be anywhere. Do I tell Delossi? And, more crucially, will Delossi want me to hurt him? Fuck. That's not my thing, I don't hurt people.

My phone comes to life in my hands and the feeling of apprehension increases when I see Dave Delossi's name come up on the screen. For a moment, I wonder whether to accept his call or not, before finally sliding the button to the right and putting the phone to my ear.

'Dave?' I query.

'Tony. Have you had any joy with Jules Walker?' he asks.

'Jesus, Dave. You only asked me to find him two days ago?' I begin. 'Give me a break. He could be anywhere.'

'Shut up, Tony and listen to me,' Dave's voice spits back at me. 'I've been thinking about Ray and what happened to him. I think you should start by checking out that girl he was supposed to have hurt, and the police officers involved in his arrest.'

'But' I protest, staring out of the window and seeing a young woman dragging a reluctant toddler along the pavement.

'Don't interrupt me!' he snaps. 'Just do it, shake the tree and see what falls,' are his last words before he disconnects the phone.

The Lost Soul

Bloody hell. How on earth did I get myself into this mess?

Later in the day, I think of Delossi's words as I pull in the block paving driveway of my Didcot home. Dave Delossi is not someone you want to cross, he has an army of people to do his bidding on the outside, including Little Tim. Reaching to the passenger seat, I grab my work bag and jacket, and push open the car door, it's 6 o'clock and I need food. My stomach rumbles, reminding me that sustenance should be the first thing I do when I get inside the house.

Something furry and soft begins to weave in and out of my legs as soon I begin shutting the car door. Not that bloody cat again! I don't know who it belongs to, but every night this week it has greeted me from work. Usually, I ignore the attention the cat is desperate for, but today I make the fatal mistake of leaning down to pet the brown and white short-haired bundle of fur. It is no surprise, when I am rewarded with a loud purr that vibrates as the small animal strokes it's head up along my calves.

Bending down, I feel for a collar, hoping to find a tag attached to it that will offer a name or telephone number. I see the glint of blue leather, but there is nothing dangling, no metal or fabric.

I stand up, close the car door and with my jacket and bag under my arm, walk to the door. Digging deep into my trouser pocket, I find my keyring and pick out the front door key. The cat continues to follow at my heels, yellow eyes watch me with curiosity.

The Lost Soul

'Where's your owner?' I ask, opening the front door, stepping inside, and throwing my keys with a heavy thud, into the bowl which sits on the narrow console table in the hall.

'Well, if you're going to stay,' I tell the cat, making a decision, 'then we had better find out if you're a boy or a girl,' I reach down, scoop up the warm bundle. The cat is lean in body, and clearly undernourished, because I can feel it's ribs. A surge of sadness and anger courses through me, how can anyone treat an animal like this?

Honestly, I don't know why I've made the decision to keep it, it's not like me to be impulsive. And yet, here I am, holding onto the warm body of this affectionate little mite, allowing it to bring back memories of being loved. Of caring for someone and that affection being reciprocated.

I check the underside of the cat and it is clearly a boy. Upon closer inspection, it appears to be in remarkably good health, apart from a little matted fur and being underweight. Nothing that a few good meals, a warm home and some TLC won't sort out. And, all of a sudden, I have a purpose in life, someone to care for.

It feels good.

'Let's get you some milk and some food,' I say, carrying him to the kitchen. 'My name's Anthony by the way,' I tell him, placing him on the floor, so that I can pour milk into a bowl and root out a tin of tuna from the cupboard. 'Now, what shall we call you?'

The Lost Soul

My day just got a little brighter, as I look at the novelty watering cans on my dining table and realise that nothing can take the place of real-life company.

Now, to name my new pet.

The Lost Soul

Part 13: Jules

Bloody idiot! Why did I go and tell her who I really am? I silently curse myself as I sit in the onsite restaurant, holding a steaming hot latte. My fingers are smarting from the heat of the large ceramic mug, but I dismiss it, because I have far more serious things to be worrying about.

I think back to two hours earlier, and my conversation with Sasha in my apartment.

***

She had been sitting upright on the sofa, as I'd slumped on the far side and began retelling the shortened version of what happened to Blip, my family and Ray Delossi. I left out anything to do with Corinna James, because I wanted to take ownership of what I'd done to that bastard, Delossi. Every now and again, throughout my story, I'd hear Sasha's soft sigh or gasp. I didn't dare to look at her face though, couldn't bear to see the disappointment written across it.

As I uttered the words that had been playing on my mind it had felt as though I was talking about another person or reading an article in a newspaper that had no correlation to my own life. When I'd finished, I had felt emotionally drained, as though saying it aloud and facing the grief of losing my sister, the

The Lost Soul

remorse of my actions against Ray Delossi and the depression that seemed to follow me throughout, had simply wiped me out.

I'd felt bone-tired and weary. There was a short pause, when Sasha had looked at me, swiped the back of her hand against her nose and stood up.

'Sasha,' I said, with a pleading note to my voice, 'please say something.'

Her eyes were blank, defeated. If I expected her to understand, I was mistaken. 'What do you want me to say? Tell you it's ok that you murdered a person, and we carry on as if nothing has happened? That, what you did, didn't matter?'

I'd kept quiet, this was the reaction I'd expected. It was the reaction I deserved.

No more words were spoken. I'd stood there in my own private hell, as she'd left the apartment. I guess that meant our dinner date was going to be put on the back burner. Bugger.

***

I finish my still warm latte and head to the supply room to pick up a cardboard box to store Russell's collections, before making my way to his apartment. As I ring the doorbell, there is a grunting coming from inside, and I panic.

'Russell? You there?' I call.

'Come in,' his voice sounds stressed, and I hope that he's not been overdoing it. As I walk along the hall, the door to the bedroom is open and the first thing I see, is a long, wiry figure

154

The Lost Soul

dressed in black elasticated trousers and a grey jumper. Russell is half kneeling, half-lying on the floor in front of a dark wood glass display cabinet, his wooden walking stick lies abandoned on the floor beside him.

'I'm looking for my first editions and other valuable objects,' he states, coughing through his outstretched hand.

'Right,' I say, dropping the box to the floor and kneeling beside him. 'Let's get you off the floor and you can direct me, on what we need to pack,' I take his arm and gently pull him upright. 'I'll call someone from reception to make a note of what we're removing and give you a receipt.'

Once Russell is standing and steady, I reach down, grab his walking stick and place it in his hand, so that we can walk across the floor to the wooden padded chair tucked under the table, by the window. I don't rest until Russell is seated and I've called Kate from reception to come and take notes. With her long, dark hair pulled into a bun, her tall frame dressed in the reception colours of navy trousers or skirt and a white shirt or blouse, she smiles and utters a warm 'hello' to us, before taking a seat at the small table, next to Russell and placing her receipt book and pen quietly on the hard surface.

'How's that young lady of yours?' he suddenly asks me, making my cheeks burn, I turn to face him, ignoring flaming cheeks.

'What young lady?' I ask, trying hard not to make eye contact with Kate. Gossip can travel quickly in this place, only six months ago, when I arrived here there was lots of rumours floating around the complex, from staff and tenants about me – all untrue, I hasten to add. Some said I was a British spy, working on a top-secret undercover mission, another rumour described me as being an undercover millionaire, looking around the building for ways to improve the business and give millions to the residents of Greystones.

'You know exactly who I'm talking about. Sasha, the one in charge,' Russell mutters from his chair, and points a long thin finger in my direction. 'If I was fifty years younger,' his eyes light up, I'd be giving you a run for your money.'

'Stop right there!' I raise my eyebrows, 'I don't want to hear another word!' my words come out clipped, and I feel a protectiveness towards Sasha that I can't explain. Deep down, I know he's only teasing me, trying to get a rise out of me, it's just his way.

Russell waves his hands and looks at Kate, 'told you,' he says to her. Bloody gossip. Kate simply keeps a straight face, shrugs a shoulder, and begins to write a list of items on the invoice receipt.

Thirty minutes later, my box is full of first edition books, including the one that Russell's grandson wants, Little Dorrit, and Kate has handed over the paperwork of the goods that we're putting in the office safe.

I am about to pick up the box of goodies when my phone starts to ring, Jack's name flashes up on the screen.

I press the green button to accept the call.

The Lost Soul

'Hey Jack, how are things?' I ask, wiping an itch from my chin and watching Russell. He raises a white eyebrow in question, and I shrug my shoulders at him.

Jack's deep voice replies:

'All good. Apart from this problem with Sasha's parents. Is she there?' he asks.

'No, she's around somewhere. Is her mum all right?' I ask.

'When I got here, Nancy was conscious but on the living room floor. She was in a bad way, covered in blood, with one eye shut and a boot print on one side of her face.'

I inhaled sharply. For fuck's sake, what kind of man does that? 'Jesus, Jack – what a bastard!'

'She told me that she'd called Lewis, told him she needed the hospital, but he warned her not to contact them.'

'What a fucker!' I mutter in response, 'I can't believe he's still out there, walking free,' I shake my head in disbelief.

'I called the police and an ambulance,' Jack continues, 'then Nancy lost consciousness.'

Oh no, what I am I going to tell Sasha, she's hardly speaking to me as it is?

'Fuck! If I tell Sasha, she'll want to see her mum,' I say quietly.

'You can't let her. She should stay there with you, Nick. You need to keep her and Zoe safe until Lewis Benson has been arrested.'

The Lost Soul

'Understood, do you think he knows where she is?' I ask.

'I don't know,' Jack takes a deep breath. 'Don't think so at the moment, unless he forced Nancy to tell him.'

I hope for Nancy's sake that she didn't disclose her daughter's whereabouts. What a bloody mess. 'Keep me in the loop. Where is Stuart?'

'He's at the hospital, with Nancy.'

'I'll speak to you later,' I tell him, disconnecting the call.

'Trouble?' Russell's voice cuts into my troubled thoughts. I need to find Sasha and tell her about her mum.

'Nothing I can't handle,' I tell him, taking the box and weaving my way to the door of the apartment.

'They say it never rains, don't they?' I say absently, as Russell follows at a slower pace behind me.

'Unless it pours,' he finishes.

Part 14: Anthony

I call again, put the phone to my ear and wait for the dial tone to kick in. Again, it kicks into a message that states that the phone is not in use. There is still no sign of him. Where the bloody hell is Lewis Benson? It's Thursday and I haven't spoken to the man in forty-eight hours. I stare at the phone in my hand, as I stand outside the office in Abingdon. What the hell is going on? No message, no call. Nothing.

The morning traffic in the centre of town is heavy. There is the occasional beeping of a car horn and an emergency siren is blaring in the distance. I turn to head back to my car, and the phone rings.

I don't recognise the number – but I answer it anyway.

'Hello,' I say.

'Hello, is that Anthony Cherwell?' a woman's voice asks.

'Yes,' my heart begins to thud. 'Speaking.' My mind races, is this something to do with Dave Delossi? Crap, are they monitoring his visitors?'

The woman clears her throat, 'this is Detective Inspector Steph Rutland, from Thames Valley Police, I'm trying to locate Lewis

The Lost Soul

Benson.' At the mention of my boss's name, I breathe a sigh of relief.

I walk slowly along Ock street and in the direction of where I've parked the car in West St Helen car park. 'He's not turned up for work, and his phone is switched off,' I tell the DI, wondering what on earth is going on. 'Is there anything I can help with?'

'Well, actually, you might,' the DI's voice brightens up. 'Are you still in Abingdon? Perhaps we could meet for a coffee? Perhaps at Costa, in the centre of town? I can be there in fifteen minutes?'

Bugger! I can't turn around and say no, can I? Raking my hands through my hair, 'Yes, I'll meet you there.'

'Thank you, Mr Cherwell, I appreciate it,' the DI says, 'I'll see you there in a short while.'

I walk slowly in the direction of the coffee shop where we are meeting. The noise as I push the door open is almost deafening, goodness knows how we'll be able to have a conversation in here. I order and pay for my cappuccino and find a small quiet nook to wait for the DI.

While I have a moment, I decide to take out my phone and google Corinna James. The young woman who was initially arrested for killing Ray Delossi, flashes up on my screen. She looks fragile, not like someone who could take on a Delossi and win.

According to reports, Corinna sustained a number of serious injuries, following an attack from Ray, her then boyfriend, at his home. At some point she was able to make her escape, and this was when Jules Walker took his opportunity to enter the house

The Lost Soul

and kill Ray Delossi. Oh God. Delossi was a woman beater, the report said, with various women coming forward to testify that that he had assaulted them too. By all accounts, Corinna James was lucky to get out of the house alive.

Above everything one thing was clear to see, and that was that Jules Walker had done the world a huge favour by killing Delossi, because he could no longer hurt the women, he brought into his life.

Shit. Shit. I can't do this. I can't give this man up to Dave Delossi. My mind races, as I try to think of a way out of this mess, which keeps me and Jules Walker still standing. I skim through the rest of the report, there is no indication where Corinna James is now. I focus on a familiar name, as I read the printed article. My heart picks up pace, and my palms turn clammy. The police detective involved in the case is none other than DI Steph Rutland.

Bloody hell! What a small world we live in. A rush of excitement courses through me.

'Mr Cherwell? I'm DI Steph Rutland,' a sultry female voice breaks into my thoughts. Talk about falling into the lap of the Gods.

DI Rutland is a slim, tall blonde-haired woman, dressed in black trousers, a white blouse and a smart navy raincoat. In one hand, she holds a tall latte glass and, in the other, her work warrant card and badge.

The Lost Soul

She smiles, and her face lights up. What a beauty. I wonder if she's married and glance quickly at her hand to look for a ring.

I return her smile. It is hard not to. 'Hi, Anthony,' I tell her, gesturing with my hand to the seat opposite me, 'please take a seat.'

'Thank you for meeting me,' she says quietly, placing her hot drink on the table, hanging her coat behind the empty chair opposite me and sitting down.

She looks at me with clear hazel eyes, her hair is tied back in a messy bun. I sip my cappuccino and watch her take a small notepad and black pen from her coat pocket. I'm worried that I'm going to say something incriminating that will link me to Dave Delossi.

'So,' she smiles, 'how long have you worked for Lewis Benson?'

'About twelve months,' I take another sip of my cappuccino. *Pace yourself and don't give anything away.*

She scribbles a couple of things on her pad, and continues, without looking up, 'What is he like to work for? Is he a good boss?'

Pausing for a moment to think, I don't want to say anything too negative, but I saw his bloody knuckles two days ago, and there was no mistaking the ugly way he talked to his wife on the phone and about her afterward.

'Yes,' I consider. 'He works hard, he's very well-liked by his constituents.'

The Lost Soul

I watch the pen furiously move across the small page, 'But as a person? What is he like?' she asks, putting her pen down to study my face.

He's a nice bloke with a dark side, I am tempted to say. 'He's good to work for…'

'Why do I sense a but in that sentence?' she asks.

I shuffle uncomfortably. Why is it so bloody hard to tell the truth? Taking a deep breath, my hands sit snugly around the lukewarm coffee cup, I look at her. I don't owe Benson anything.

'He, Lewis. He isn't very nice to his wife,' there, I've said it now, no going back.

'In what way, Anthony?' she asks quietly, unfazed by my comment.

'Well, when I arrived at the office on Tuesday, I noticed a scratch on his neck and his knuckles were red and bloody,' I curse myself for talking, but it feels like the right thing to do.

'Ok,' she begins to scribble again, 'Can you tell me about the last time you saw him? Start from when you arrived at work.'

I tell her about Tuesday morning, what I heard when Lewis' wife called, how he told her to take paracetamol and rest, but not to get medical help. Although I'd forgotten about it, the words were as clear as day, as I recalled them to the DI, 'he told me that she'd been drunk and fell down the stairs.'

'Did you believe him?' she asks straightaway, her interest piqued. Now, we were on to something.

163

The Lost Soul

'Not really, but he's my boss. I can't accuse him of anything, can I?' my voice sounds angry, I am defensive and need to get my point across.

'When did you last see Lewis?'

I look at my watch. '3.30pm on Tuesday, he said he had to run an errand, and that he'd see me the next day, meaning Wednesday. He told me to pull the door shut when I left.'

'And that is the last time you saw him or spoke to him?' She writes down the information in her notebook, before glancing my way, 'how did he seem to you?'

'Yes, that was the last time I saw or heard from him,' I'm beginning to feel like this is an interrogation. 'He was a bit agitated and said his stomach was hurting again. That happens a lot, with the stomach, I mean.'

'He suffers from stomach problems?' she looks up, her eyebrow raises in query and brings her latte to her lips, closing her eyes as she takes a sip.

'Yes, but I don't know if he has ever done anything about it,' I mutter, thinking that Benson and I were not so close that we would discuss personal problems. He could be prickly sometimes.

'Right. So, he didn't turn up for work yesterday, Wednesday?' she looks at me, her eyebrows raised. 'Did that not seem odd to you? Has he done this before?'

I shrug, 'No, not really. One time, he suddenly left the office at lunchtime, walked past me, clutching his stomach – didn't say a word. But then he texted me to say he'd be in at lunch time the next day.'

The DI tilts her neck as she scribes the information, and I can almost feel the softness of her skin. I clench my hands tightly together on the table, forcing myself to focus on the here and now.

'When you arrived at the office yesterday, was the door locked?' she asks, looking straight at me.

'Yes, but I don't have a key, so I called him and texted him to see where he was. The phone went to a message that stated it wasn't in use. I gave it twenty minutes and then went home.' I admit, wondering if I should have left it longer. Something isn't right. I can feel it. 'Can I ask you something, DI Rutland?'

'Yes, of course,' she says in between gulps of her latte.

'Has something happened? Is Lewis in trouble?' I ask, as my questions tumble out.

'I'm not allowed to discuss that at the moment. Suffice to say that I would like to talk to him in connection with an assault on a woman, in the early hours of Monday evening.'

My hackles rise. Tuesday, he had bloody knuckles. Oh no! Not, his wife, surely not his wife. 'His wife?' I ask quietly.

She doesn't say anything, simply shakes her head slightly, I wait for her to stop writing, and the sound of her pen dropping to the table. The detective picks up her hot drink and I almost hear the cogs turning inside her brain.

The Lost Soul

'Thanks for this. It's been really helpful,' she says in between sips, 'would it be all right if we talked again? I'd like to hear more about Lewis Benson.'

'Yes,' I smile, pleased with myself that I've help them as much as I can. 'I won't be available tomorrow, though,' I mention, kicking myself mentally in the shin.

'Why is that?' she asks casually.

'I need to see my grandad, and he lives a long way from here,' I say, looking for a ring on her finger. There seems to be an engagement ring, but no wedding band.

'Where is he?' she asks.

'He's in a nursing come residential home, based in Yorkshire,' I explain.

Her eyes hold mine. Dilated pupils draw me in, 'Haworth?' she asks, casually.

'Yes, how did you know? It's a place called Greystones,' I explain.

A shadow falls across her face. Something has happened, but I don't know what.

'I have to go,' she says, pulling on her coat. 'Sorry, Anthony. I will be in contact again very soon,' she says, then stops as if she's thought of something. She reaches into her coat pocket, takes out a small white card, and puts it on the table, 'please call me if Mr Benson makes contact.'

The Lost Soul

Not sure what that is about, I muse, as the pretty woman DI rushes out of the door. I pick up the contact card and skim the details. 'Detective Inspector Steph Rutland,' I read, taking out my wallet and inserting the card securely, just in front of my driving license. I get the strange impression that Steph Rutland has just put two and two together and got five.

Bugger.

The Lost Soul

Part 15: Sasha

When I was little, my mum used to take me shopping after school, to make the most of the time we had before he came home. We would sometimes go for a cup of coffee and a cake. It was a little ritual, our thing, something he could never spoil. My violent, unpredictable father.

One day when we were having afternoon tea at the Randolph in Oxford, we'd had the best time; Pretending that our lives were different. I was a normal twelve-year-old girl with a normal family, but we had money, so we'd have these brilliant family adventures together. We'd take a cruise around the world, or first class on the Euro Tunnel to Paris where we'd pick up the Orient Express and travel to Istanbul. All imagined, of course.

But that is what we did to escape our family life and the reality of my father's temper.

'Sasha?' I vaguely hear my name as I sit at the desk in my white walled office with its rich walnut furniture, working on the monthly staff rota. I look up and Kate is standing in the open doorway.

'Your mobile is ringing,' she smiles, looking at the phone on my desk.

169

The Lost Soul

'Sorry, didn't hear it,' I explain, feeling a little foolish. 'My mind was elsewhere. Monthly staff rota,' I tell her, surprised at how easily the lie slips off my tongue.

I look at my phone, in its red rubber case, and pick it up. 'Hello?' I ask, absently. The number looks a little familiar.

Then the world closes in on me, as the sound of a voice I haven't heard in four years, begins to talk down the line. A voice, I had hoped, never to hear again.

'Sasha, it's your father.' The voice is deep, harsh and clipped.

My palms begin to sweat, I feel like I'm sixteen again, with a new baby. Vulnerable and living in fear. My head begins to spin, I shake it hard and roll my neck to clear my senses. He has no control over me anymore. No control. Fuck!

'What do you want?' I ask in a flat voice.

'That's no way to talk to your father,' his voice changes into a growl as he becomes the animal, I know he is. Vaguely, I hear a tap at the door, and it slowly opens, as Nick takes one look at me and walks to my side.

My shoulders are stiff, my heart is beating fast. I feel like I'm about to hyperventilate.

'It's all your fault,' my father's voice sneers.

A chill goes down my spine.

'What do you mean, my fault?' I ask with a dry mouth.

The Lost Soul

'If you'd kept away from her, I wouldn't have had to hurt her,' he answers in a flat, detached tone.

'What are you talking about?' my eyes blur with tears. What has he done? Has he hurt my mum?

The silence lasts for an eternity, before I speak again.

'What have you done?' I ask in a low voice, feeling an ice-cold shiver creep down my spine. Nick puts his hand on my shoulder, and I'm surprised by how much his touch calms me. I take a deep breath and wait for my father's reply.

'Your mother has gone and it's all your fault!' my father grinds out furiously, before he disconnects the phone.

I can't believe it. He has the nerve to accuse me, when the very reason I moved away from my mum and home, was because of him.

Bastard.

I am not going to let him bully me again.

As I stare at the phone in my hands, tears blur my vision and, like other hard times in my life, I find myself wishing that my father was dead.

Strong arms pull me from my seat and into a warm, hard chest. How can I be mad at this man? For the lies and the truths that keep him hostage and for forcing me to make decisions about his past, that I'm not yet ready to make.

Because right now, he is the rock that keeps me standing.

The Lost Soul

The Lost Soul

Part 16: Zoe

Mrs Keaton, my teacher looks at me, with a sad face.

'Do you think that pinching Sapphire on her arm, is a very kind thing to do, Zoe?' she bends down so that her face is close to mine. I shuffle my black shiny shoes, on the carpet floor, and look at Sapphire.

Her eyes are red, they remind me of the time when Mummy twisted her ankle when she fell off my scooter. Mummy cried, and I gave her a big hug and kissed her better. Sapphire stands next to my teacher.

'Zoe, it is not a very nice thing to do, is it?' she pushes her white hair off her face.

'No,' I say quietly. 'But.'

'No buts, Zoe. Violence is never the answer,' Mrs Keaton says in a cross voice. She points to Sapphire, who has blonde hair and pretty blue eyes, and wiggles her finger at the girl who used to be my best friend. Sapphire walks over to me. 'Zoe, do you have something to say to Sapphire?'

I shake my head from side to side. I'm going to cry and its Sapphire's fault.

The Lost Soul

'Zoe, you need to apologise to Sapphire, for hurting her,' my teacher says.

Tears burst from my eyes and my nose runs, I use my hands to wipe it all away. 'Sorry,' I shout before running off to the toilet, and shutting the door. I cry loudly.

Keiron says he doesn't want to be married to me anymore. He has married Sapphire, and now they are in love and smile at each other. They dance on the outdoor stage together and tell everyone that they are married and love each other. To make things worse, they want me to be their baby! They want to call me Zack, and I'm not a boy, and Sapphire says mean things to me, like:

'Go to your room Zack, you've been a naughty boy.' And 'Zack, you haven't eaten all your lunch, so go to your room.'

I don't want to be a boy, I don't want to be called Zack and I don't want to go to my room, which is the crate at the bottom of the nursery playground. I told Sapphire to stop bossing me around, and I was so mad at her, I grabbed her arm and pinched her.

Then Sapphire started crying, and Keiron ran to fetch Mrs Keaton and she took me and Sapphire into the classroom and looked at her arm. There was a little red mark there. Mrs Keaton used to be my favourite teacher, but now I don't like her. Because she told me off.

I'm sick of Sapphire and Keiron, so I'm not playing with them again. Ever. I am never being best friends with them again.

The Lost Soul

Mummy sometimes tells me when she's had a hard day at work, 'When life gives you lemons, you make lemonade,' and then she gives me a big hug and we eat ice cream.

I don't know what she means, but I don't like lemonade, and I'm fed up of school. Fed up of being married and being a child and of the crate at the bottom of the nursery playground.

It sure is hard work being a little girl.

The Lost Soul

Part 17: Jack

 I have had this song in my brain all day, and I cannot shift it.

'Alexa,' I wait for the smart speaker that sits on the built-in bookcases, either side of the fireplace in the living room, to respond, before I give my instruction, 'play Heroes by David Bowie.' I really need this on high volume, there's no other way. I walk through to the kitchen to make myself a coffee and I shout – 'Alexa…. Volume eight.'

Oh yes, this is what I need.

It is 4pm and Steph is still at work. I'm hoping she'll be home before 7 o'clock, because I've got a chicken roasting in the oven, which smells delicious. I have even got vegetables sitting in water in their pans, ready to boil. I cannot believe how domesticated I've become. I feel like a different person now.

I spent this morning at the hospital with Stuart and Jenny. Steph popped in, to see how Nancy was doing. She has got some internal bleeding and there was a knock to the head, which is worrying the Consultant. The CT scan should let them know clearly what's going on. Alongside the broken ribs, one eye is swollen shut and they're worried that she'll lose the sight in that

The Lost Soul

eye. Jesus. How could someone stamp on another person's face. He must have done it hard because the imprint is still showing.

Ben is due back home from school any time now and I have something important to discuss with him.

It is just under seven weeks before I marry Steph, and I cannot wait.

I unbutton the top three buttons of my thick navy shirt and pull it over my head. My dark green, short-sleeved top, cools me instantly as I continue singing along to the song, 'We can be heroes, just for one day.' This is something else, this is new for me. Singing along to loud music.

'I, I will be king, and you, you will be queen,' my voice sounds gravelly, even to my own ears, but not totally unpleasant. Swaying to the music, I fold my shirt and drape it over the top of the sofa, 'Though nothing will drive them away,' I sing, staring at the double silver photo on the mantlepiece, one of me and Steph and one of us, including Ben. I can't help but smile. My heart is full.

'Jack!'

'We can be heroes, just for one day,' I'm pulled from my reverie by a hand on my shoulder and turn suddenly, to find myself facing Ben, my fifteen-year-old soon to be stepson, in his school uniform.

'Hey Ben,' I smile and pat his shoulder, before walking to Alexa and directing her to stop playing the music. I walk to the deep wine coloured, modern sofa, and sit down.

The Lost Soul

'Come and sit down, Ben,' I say in a husky voice, 'I want to ask you something.'

Ben's face becomes serious, and the colour drains from his skin, his eyebrows lift in question, 'has something happened? Is it Mum?'

'Don't worry Ben,' I reassure him, with a big smile. 'Everything is fine, your mum is fine.' I put out my hand, and gesture to the sofa, 'take a seat.'

Ben's face relaxes, and his shoulders slump a little as his tall, lean frame, walks my way. I feel a drop in the seat as he sits beside me. It's been six months since Steph and Ben moved in with me and it has been the best six months of my life. We have all had to make some adjustments to family life and shared living, and it was decided very early on to have regular family meetings, to iron out any worries or problems. I wanted to make sure that they were both happy.

One time, not long after they moved in, I took Ben out in the Aston Martin to buy some new stuff for his bedroom. We had spent the day at the shopping centre in Oxford, browsing through shops, for lamps and rugs. Then I had taken him to lunch at Nandos in the Westgate Shopping Centre.

***

'I love this place,' Ben says through a mouthful of chicken burger. 'Jack, this is so cool.'

I laugh, pushing the arms of my navy long sleeved T-Shirt up to my elbows. 'I'm glad, you're enjoying it.' I tell him, as I tip Piri

179

The Lost Soul

Piri sauce onto my half roasted medium spiced chicken and fries. 'So, tell me. How are you settling in at the house?'

He finishes chewing and looks at me seriously, his brown eyes searching mine.

'You make Mum happy, Jack. If she's happy, then I'm happy.'

What can I say to that? The boy floors me with his words. My heart is so full of love for this young man and his mum. From the first time I met them, it had felt so easy to be part of their life. They accepted me and I accepted them. It was meant to be.

'But what about you?' I persist, resting my forearms on the table. 'Are you coping all right? It's a big change to move into someone else's house, and for your mum to be with someone else.'

He looks across at me for a few seconds, before licking his fingertips, it's important that he has time to process what has happened in a relatively short period of time. 'It was a bit odd, at first,' he says, his voice serious. 'I mean, getting used to my new room, and going to school from a new home, but after a week or so, it just felt natural. Mum keeps asking if I'm ok.'

I smile, reaching out to pat his shoulder, 'that's what mum's do Ben, they fuss and make sure you're all right. She loves you, and I love you too. You know that, right?'

Our eyes catch and I see his glisten, at fourteen he's still young, but so very grown up. A hand lifts and sits heavily on my forearm, with a lump in his throat he tells me, 'it feels like you've always been here, Jack. I love you too.' And, then he does an

The Lost Soul

about turn, pulling his arm away and unapologetically wipes an eye, before regaining his composure.

'But, do you want to know the best thing about all this?' Ben states before collecting a couple of fries from his plate and dipping them into tomato ketchup.

'Yes?' I ask. 'Tell me,' I smile, bringing a glass of diet coke to my lips.

'I get to ride in the Aston Martin!' he says, as he stuffs his mouth with fries.

***

'Jack,' Ben's fist bumps my shoulder, 'you've gone into a bit of a daze.'

'Sorry, I've got something on my mind, something I want to ask you. Maybe I should make a coffee first.'

Ben takes a deep breath and gives an exaggerated shrug of his shoulders. 'Jack!'

I turn to him:

'You know, your mum and I are getting married in six weeks time,' I begin, worrying what his response will be to my, as yet, unasked question. I really need Ben on board for this to work.

'Duh,' he shrugs, moving his hands up and down in flamboyant gestures. 'Tell me something I don't know. Mum never stops talking about it. What colour dress should she wear? Flat shoes or heels? Hair up or down? It's driving me mad.'

The Lost Soul

'She's excited,' I smile, thinking of black heeled shoes and stockings. 'Anyway, I wanted to ask you if you will…'

'If I will, what?' he jumps in quickly before I finish my sentence. Bloody hell, this is becoming a nightmare. 'Will you hurry up, because I need sugar and a Diet Coke.'

I half smile at his flippant comments, he is a typical teen. I've picked up a lot from Steph and Ben over the past few months, to work out the dynamics of bringing up and negotiating with a teenager. 'If you will be my… you know?'

Why is it so hard for me to ask him?

'For goodness sake, Jack,' he smiles in a happy way, putting an arm around me. 'Of course, I would love to be your best man,' he brings me into a bear hug. I hug him back and hold him close. He feels like my own son, and after his dead biological father, the one who beat and tortured his mother, I want to be the father that he deserves.

'Good,' I say, patting his back. 'Glad that's settled.'

We stand and he looks seriously at me. 'You are the dad I always wanted, Jack.'

I bring him close again, and whisper – 'And, you are the son, I always wanted, Ben.'

Part 18: Nancy

There is a buzzing in my head, it never stops. I can also hear a bleeping. Bleep. Bleep. Bleep. Buzz. Buzz. Buzz. I try to open my eyes, but they won't move. I want to see the sunlight. I don't want to be in here anymore. I don't want to be in the dark, a prisoner in my mind, in the darkness. I need to get out, to get to Sasha.

I struggle to remember what happened after Lewis grabbed my hair and pulled me across the bedroom. Then an image flashes into my mind, of Lewis reaching the bedroom door, of him slamming it shut and smashing my face into the hard wood. I cry out as pain sears across my forehead, my nose, mouth and chin. Every inch of my face burns as though it's on fire, and a hollow sob escapes from my throat.

Closing my eyes, I quietly sob, whilst keeping my face on the door. I know I'm bleeding, because I can feel sticky blood trickling down my skin.

'You sneaky bitch, I try my best to be a good husband, and this is how you repay me,' he snarls, over my tears. I almost laugh at the absurdity of his words. Can he hear what he is saying? It's utter rubbish. Good husband? He's delusional.

The Lost Soul

Lewis' face falls into a sour smirk, and he mutters, 'let's see what you've been up to.'

Watching helplessly, the man who believes he is a good husband moves across the room and stands, with his hands on his hips, looking at the red and white fluffy socks on the floor.

I turn to face him, and the sudden movement causes an agonizing pain in my shoulders, the pain is so bad, that I want to retch. My head hurts and I feel disorientated. Trying desperately to calm myself, I touch the soft skin of my throat and stroke it gently.

Lewis bends down to pick up the folded socks from the floor. 'Now, what do we have here?' he asks.

'It's nothing. Lewis. Please, just leave it alone,' I step forward, hold out my hands, silently begging him to give me the socks. Then he realises that there's something hidden inside.

Mortified, I watch him feel around the sock material, until he touches something hard. 'Ah, curiouser and curiouser,' he says, taking the phone out of the folded socks.

He holds the phone out, taunting me, 'now, why would you want a secret phone? What on earth would you need another phone for?'

He steps closer, a wild look on his face:

'Are you having an affair?' he asks.

'What! No. Of course not,' I shout, and my throat hurts with each syllable.

The Lost Soul

He runs a hand through his hair, in frustration, 'I don't believe you, why else would you have a phone?'

I scrunch my eyes shut, trying to pretend I am somewhere else. Anywhere, but in this room, with this man. *Please God, let this be over. Let him finish me and let that be the end of it.*

'Nancy, answer me!' he shouts, slipping the phone into his trouser pocket.

I open my eyes. 'No man, no affair. You must be mad,' I shout back. 'You are enough to put me off all men.' At that moment, I realise I've gone too far, by shouting back at him. His eyes are hard, his face is a deep red colour, and his shoulders begin to shake with anger.

'You bitch!' He spits at me. 'Who the fuck do you think you are? Talking to me like that!' He reaches out and grabs another handful of my shoulder length dark hair and uses this leverage to pull me away from the door. Reaching for the door handle, I am swiftly pushed aside, as strong fingers burn into the hair directly attached to my scalp.

I am forced into the old pine chest of drawers, the hard circular handle catches on my hip bone and makes me howl loudly. There is pain everywhere from my head to my arms, down to my hips and I scream at him, 'Stop, Lewis! No!'

Before I know what's happening, I am being dragged bodily along the landing to the top of the stairs, like a sack of potatoes. My ankles catch on the carpeted steps and twist as he forces me backwards. Lewis is pulling me, twisting me, and all I can do is sob and grit my teeth as my husband stops halfway down the

The Lost Soul

stairs and punches me in the face. One eye immediately begins to swell.

The punch knocks the wind out of me, and I forget to breathe through the pain, until finally – by the time we reach the bottom of the stairs, I'm flailing like a rag doll. All I can think of is that I want to die, want this attack to stop, to never experience one second of violence, at his hands again.

He drags me into the living room and throws me with brute force onto the floor. Standing over me, he takes the phone out of his pocket, and looks at me. He taunts me with the device, as though he wants me to fight for it.

Unfortunately for me, the phone is old. It doesn't have a password, and he easily unlocks it. 'So, who is this person on your outgoing list?' he asks, as he gives me a swift kick to the stomach. I howl in pain but say nothing. I need to keep my daughter and granddaughter safe.

'Tell me!' he orders as he kicks me in the ribs.

I taste blood, but I'm not sure where it's coming from.

'Tell me, Nancy!' he says, his voice deeper, harsher. He kicks me again.

Managing to roll on to my back, I look up at him. This monster of a husband. The man who has ruined my life, lost me my daughter and granddaughter and left me a shadow of my former self. I look up at him, at his hateful face and his stone hard eyes and say:

'Fuck you!

The Lost Soul

He shakes his head, and the last thing I remember is the heel of his shoe heading toward my face.

***

The buzzing in my head continues, I want to open my eyes and say, 'I'm here, I'm all right.'

But my eyes won't open.

The Lost Soul

Part 19: Anthony

I pull my dark green Skoda into the car park at Greystones and finally put on the handbrake, I give a huge sigh of relief. It's been a long four hour journey, which wasn't helped by slow moving traffic on the M6 motorway. I started out at 6am and the landscape before me has changed from hard hitting rain as I bypassed Birmingham and Wolverhampton, to bright sunshine as I drove across the outskirts of Stoke-on-Trent.

Meatloaf's, Bat Out of Hell has come and gone, the radio has done the same and I finished the last leg with the Best of The Who, the volume turned up and singing along to the words. By the time I'd reached the A629 around Halifax, the sun had broken through, and brightened the skyline as I drove through Denholme, a village approximately four miles from Haworth, I am exhausted and in dire need of the toilet and a cup of tea.

I've had plenty of time to think on the way down here. At least with Benson missing, I didn't need permission to take time off work. I look at the box of Milk Tray sitting on the passenger seat, thought I'd better bring a token treat for my grandad if he's going to give me that book.

Not sure what I'm going to do with this Jules Walker business? I just need to find something to levy, to get Dave Delossi off my

The Lost Soul

back. Once I've sorted this mess out, I'm going to pull back from the prison drug running. It's time to grow up and start getting my act together. The money I could save instead of snorting cocaine, could probably buy me a villa in the South of France.

I grab the chocolates and my brown corduroy jacket, lock the car and pop the car keys in my jeans pocket. My phone says it's 10.05am, and I can't help but feel relieved that I've made good time. The gravel driveway crunches beneath my feet as I walk towards the entrance of the building.

The heavy oak doors are closed, and I press the entry button on the grey panel next to the door, to speak to reception.

'Hello, can I help you?' A female voice asks, over the intercom.

'Yes, it's Anthony Cherwell, I've come to visit my grandad, Russell Cherwell. I'm booked in at 10am.'

'Yes, Mr Cherwell, please come in,' the woman replies as she unlocks the door and I push my body into the hard wood to open it. I'm met by two tall men wearing black suits, white shirts and black ties, which is unusual as they weren't here three months ago, when I last visited my grandad.

'Mr Cherwell,' a man walks up to me, he's tall with short cropped dark hair. He is wearing black chinos and a white shirt, open slightly at the neck. His shoes match his trousers. The man smiles and holds out his hand. 'Hi, I'm Nick Flannigan, the Deputy Manager.'

Our eyes make contact briefly, his are blue, and they startle me, I'm not sure why. A tingle goes across my arm under my dark

The Lost Soul

green jumper. Those eyes look familiar. I've seen them somewhere before.

'Mr Flannigan,' I acknowledge, taking his hand in mine. His hand is warm and strong. 'I've come along way, been driving for four hours, can I use the bathroom, please?'

'Yes, of course,' the man smiles, 'it's along the corridor and to your left.' I murmur my thanks. The voice sounds familiar, and I can't shake the niggling feeling within my brain, that I'm missing something, as I walk to the bathroom. The sound of the chocolates moving in the box, and my swishing jacket are quickly tucked under my arm as I reach the door to the bathroom.

When I return to reception, Nick Flannigan is waiting. 'I'm afraid your visit with your grandad will have to take place in the Sun Room this morning,' he glances at one of the men in suits, and they give the briefest nod. It's strange, but I don't remember seeing security when I have been here before. Very odd 'We need to do maintenance work in his apartment.'

His words hit me like a bulldozer, hitting a brick wall. Shit! Double shit! I need to get that bloody book today, and I can't even get into his apartment. Jesus, I've driven four bloody hours for nothing! My whole body is rigid with anger and disappointment, and I can feel a pain building at the bridge of my nose and working its way just above my right eye. I flinch at the spasm of pain, as it sits just above my eye.

'You all right?' he asks.

The Lost Soul

'Yeah, just a bit of a headache,' I tell him, rubbing my fingers gently across my forehead to ease the pressure. 'It's probably the driving.'

He nods, watching me closely.

I think I was born unlucky. In my despair, my shoulders slump, and wonder if I should simply jump back into my car, and head back home.

'I'll take you to the Sun Room,' says Nick Flannigan's deep voice. There it goes again. That familiarity. I have heard that voice somewhere before. But where the bloody hell was it? Bugger. Now, I'm getting annoyed with myself.

I walk behind Nick.

The sharp pain turns into a dull ache as I am led along a series of corridors, until we're stood in front of an open door. 'Here you go,' he says gesturing for me to walk into the room first.

I walk into the room, it's bright with pale yellow walls and a feature wall that contains a subtle array of wildflowers printed onto paper. Heavy velvet beige curtains adorn the French doors which lead out on to a terrace of casual furniture, closed parasols and thick shrubbery.

There are a variety of tables, sofas and chairs dotted around the room. With some highbacked chairs and a circular oak table in a corner of the room, for communal sitting. Grandad sits on a highbacked chair by the window beside the French doors, looking out at the gardens. I recognise the top of his head and the wooden scorched Derby cane walking stick, I got him for Christmas.

The Lost Soul

'Russell,' Nick says, standing beside grandad and patting him gently on the shoulder. 'Your grandson is here.'

'I'll leave you to it. Unless you'd like a coffee or tea?' he asks, looking at both of us. Grandad is wearing a pair of brown corduroy trousers and a brown knitted jumper over a black and white striped shirt, which sits open at the neck.

'That would be good, tea for me. White no sugar,' I answer the Deputy Manager. 'Do you want some tea, Grandad?' I ask my frail looking grandfather.

He nods, and looks up to Nick, 'Please, son,' he says, and the use of the word son to a person who is not his relative, isn't lost on me.

I sit in the empty chair beside the old man and lean in quickly to give him a peck on the cheek, 'Hi Grandad, how are you?'

Carefully, I place the chocolates and my jacket on the floor and study my maternal grandfather.

He looks pale today and a bit pre-occupied, and I couldn't help but notice that when Nick Flannigan had patted grandad on the shoulder, grandad had reached up and briefly patted Nick's hand, there is some sort of connection there.

'Tony.' This is the first time he's spoken to me. It takes me back to my childhood when he would travel to London to stay with us, during the summer holidays. He used to be an Oxford Don and told us tales about life at Oxford University. He loved English Literature and History and would quote from CS Lewis, Byron and Shelley all the time.

The Lost Soul

When I was ten, I remember walking along London's South Bank with grandad Russell waving his hands in his flamboyant way, and mum and dad smiling and chattering behind us.

'The Tower of London,' he said with a voice full of bravado, 'or to give it it's full name Her Majesty's Palace and Fortress, was built nearly 1000 years ago, as a royal palace and defence system.'

'Grandad,' I listened with bated breath and a smile, in awe of his knowledge. He wasn't one for affection, but he would pat my head with a heavy hand, as we walked around. To me, it meant the world. But the death of my parents sixteen years ago changed him. It changed us both. And now we are all that is left of our family. My paternal grandparents are dead and I'm not aware of any other living relatives.

***

'Your dad would never have asked for my things, no matter how much he needed the money,' he says in a sad tone with a bitter note to it. He turns to study me fully in the face. 'You make me ashamed.'

'I'm sorry, but I had no one else to turn to,' I feel like I'm ten years old again.

'True, but this isn't the way, lad.' He shakes his head. 'It's never the way. Tell me.' he orders, in a gruff voice.

'Tell you?' I query, not sure what he wants me to say.

The Lost Soul

'Do not play games with me, Tony,' he looks down at the green carpet on the floor. 'Tell me what happened.'

'It's a long story, Grandad. I've done things I'm not proud of,' I tell him, feeling such shame.

'I'm not going anywhere, son,' he says, his endearment sends a shock of warmth through my veins.

If I tell him he'll never look at me the same way again. I'm not sure if that is something that I want to risk. But what is the alternative, I don't want to take his prized possessions from him, he's worked hard all his life for everything that he has. Who am I to lie to him and cheat my way into his good graces? All for a measly three thousand pounds.

Time to grow a pair, I think.

'Well, it started...' I begin, turning to face him.

I tell him everything, as Nick brings us mugs of hot tea and a small plate of biscuits, without saying a word, allowing us privacy. It feels cathartic, as though a heavy weight has been lifted from my shoulders. At the end of the day, I just needed to be reminded that grandad is my flesh and blood, all I have left in the world, and that's all I need to bring me to my senses.

When I finish telling him about what a mess I've made of my life and what a fool I've been, he simply sits next to me in silence. In front of us, through the French doors, tall green conifers blow gently in the wind, shaping the grey slate pathway that winds its way through the flowery gardens. Small wooden seating areas and tables are sporadically set around and are easily accessible.'

195

The Lost Soul

'I'll give you the money,' his gravelly voice says.

'What?' I wasn't sure I'd heard him correctly. Silently, I rub my sweaty palms across my jean-clad thighs, trying not to get my hopes up.

'You heard what I said,' he looks across at me, 'I'll give you the money.'

The first thing that comes to mind is the relief that has justified my driving to Yorkshire to see my grandad, and I'm glad that it hasn't been a wasted journey. But more than the relief, is the feeling of a weight falling from my shoulders, by talking honestly to my grandfather and apologising. And now the old guy has offered to pay my debts.

'Thank you, it is really appreciated,' I lean slightly and put my arm around my grandad's frail shoulders.

'Don't mess it up son, get yourself together,' his eyes are sad, and his eyes shine with unshed tears, before he adds in a quiet voice, 'you're all I have left of your mum.'

'I won't. This time, I'm going to sort myself out and get away from these idiots,' I say with conviction. 'I don't ever want to be in this position again.'

'Good boy,' he pats my head again in a fatherly way, and realisation hits. I'm not alone. I had shut myself down and wouldn't let anyone in, following my parent's deaths. Visiting grandad three times a year won't develop our relationship, won't make us any closer. It is mostly just completing my grandson duties and keeping in touch.

The Lost Soul

I need to work through some hard questions. Do I want a relationship with my grandad? If I do, I have to work at it. Am I prepared to do that? The answer comes quickly. Yes. I want a proper relationship with him and yes, I am willing to work at it.

There is a shuffling behind us, as Nick comes into the room carrying a tray with two mugs on it. The tall, dark haired Deputy Manager carefully places the tray on a nearby side table, which he picks up as though it weighs nothing and deposits it carefully in front of us.

'Here you go,' he says, smiling.

'Anthony and I have had a good chat,' my grandad gestures to Nick with his hands. 'My grandson needs my help. I would like your help to transfer funds into his account.'

The Deputy's face scans my grandad's face. 'Are you sure? Do we need to talk privately?'

Grandad smiles, a knowing smile. That smile is reminiscent of days gone by, when I was younger, before I distanced myself from him and only visited a couple of times a year.

'Yes,' he says, 'I'm sure. He and I have come to an understanding. Family is blood, when it bleeds, we need to stitch it back together.'

Nick's face slackens and he nods, 'of course, Russell. Glad you've sorted that out.'

The Lost Soul

An hour later, as I leave grandad, Nick walks me to the entrance, and I can't help but feel grateful for the people here who are looking after my grandad.

'Thanks Nick,' I say, because I have a sneaky feeling that he's been looking out for my grandad and making sure he isn't taken advantage of in his later years. Which is just as it should be, we all need someone to be in our corner.

As Nick nods and our eyes meet as we smile, something hits me, like a bolt out of the blue. I know where I know him from.

It's the video. The YouTube video. The man who stood up for that girl in the street.

It's him.

It's Jules Walker.

The voice, the face, it all comes together.

Bloody hell, how can this happen when I'm one step closer to sorting my life out?

I make up my mind that I won't tell Dave Delossi that I've found Jules Walker. I need to start afresh, and that doesn't involve giving up a man who is trying to build a new life. If his brother was anything like Dave, Jules Walker will have done us all a favour.

What I don't see as I make my way out of the car park in my Skoda, is the old black BMW parked in the far corner of the car park. I don't see that psycho, Little Tim, get out of the car, dressed in dirty denim jeans and a navy sweatshirt, take his phone

198

The Lost Soul

from his pocket and make a call. I certainly don't hear his conversation and see him get back into his car to wait.

Nope, I'm oblivious to that. I'm just so pleased that I've reconnected with my grandad, and that he and Nick have transferred three thousand pounds into my bank account, so that I can pay off Dave Delossi.

I am nearly free of them.

Nearly free to start my life.

Almost there.

Part 20: Jules

I had another nightmare last night.

Again, I found myself walking into the bathroom at the family home in Thame, and all I could see was deep red, splattered blood. It was everywhere. Seeing my sister's lifeless body lying in the bathtub, next to the serrated kitchen knife, blood pouring from her wrists and her eyes shut.

Time stood still, I was frozen to the spot, unable to move, and then, adrenalin kicked in as I rushed to Blip's side, pushed her hair to one side, to find a pulse on the side of her neck. At first, in my panic, I couldn't find a thing, and then when I concentrated, there was a faint pulse.

I grabbed a couple of towels and held them tight, against her wrists, trying to stop the blood. Panicking, I replaced my right hand with my knee, pushing down hard on the wounds, as I took out my phone and called an ambulance. Damn, I should have got the towels first, as I berated myself and screamed at her to hold on. Then I called my parents.

How the hell is a person supposed to recover from that?

From finding your younger sister, alone and in such despair that she would attempt to take her own life?

The Lost Soul

As though a heavy shadow was hanging over me, I had slowly dragged myself out of bed this morning, and after several cups of strong coffee and a harsh word with myself, I'd pulled myself together ready to face the day.

***

'Nick!' Sasha's husky voice calls, 'how did it go?' I look up from signing some documents on the reception desk. The feeling of relief that Russell and Anthony are back on track is good. Russell simply needed to be frank with his grandson and talk some sense into him.

I stare at Sasha and my heart misses a beat. Feelings and emotions are breaking down my barriers, making me face the world and real life, despite the worry and fear that I'm not good enough.

When I had gone to find Sasha, following Jack's call about her mum, I had watched her face intently as she talked to that beast of a father, my only thoughts had been to protect her, and hold her close. I was pleased and humbled that she had allowed me to do that.

I updated her with the news of her mum, being in the John Radcliffe hospital, often referred to as the JR. Immediately, she had wanted to go to Oxford and see her, but we both knew that it wasn't the right time. Benson was on the loose somewhere and Stuart and Jenny were keeping an eye on her unconscious mum.

'It went well,' I smile. 'Russell and his grandson have started to build bridges and Russell has given Anthony the money he owes.

The Lost Soul

He wants to take more of an interest in the lad, keep an eye on him.'

'That's really good, I'm pleased for them both,' she smiles, stepping closer and patting my arm with slender fingers.

Can there be a chance that she is willing to put my past behind her? That she is processing what I have told her about my past? Zoe should be her first priority and, of course, I understand the need to keep her daughter safe. I would do the same, if I were in her shoes, but I also hope that she can see beyond my past.

As a parent and a person, I cannot fault her. She is passionate, kind and very protective of Zoe. It's what parents are supposed to do for their children, isn't it?

'Sasha, about what I said?' I begin, quietly trying to gauge her reaction.

'Not now, Nick,' she says quietly, leaning into me and looking up into my face. Our eyes meet as I look down at her. 'We will talk about it, but not now.'

'I was just going to say,' I tell her, putting a hand lightly onto her lower back, 'that I understand your need to protect Zoe. It's the right thing to do.'

She takes a deep breath and looks at me solemnly, 'how do you do that?

'Do what?' I ask, unsure of what she is saying.

'You always know what to say. You always say the right thing,' she smiles shyly.

The Lost Soul

'I don't,' I smile, 'in fact, you'd be surprised how much trouble I can get in to.' I wink, thinking of the YouTube video of me having words with Leon against the wall in a little side road. I add a little pressure to her back, feeling the warmth of her skin through her white blouse. Pleasure ripples through me as Sasha leans back slightly, into my touch.

My phone begins to sing Bat out of Hell, and immediately the 'moment' between us is lost. It's Jack:

'Hey Jack, how are you?' I ask, still smiling as Sasha uses her hands to signal that she's got things to attend to. I nod, and wink at her. Wow! Now, I know there is definitely something wrong with me if I'm winking at people.

'Good,' his husky voice replies. 'How are things there?'

'Looking good,' I smile down the phone. For the first time in a while, it feels like everything is falling into place, that I don't have to look over my shoulder and be cautious.

'Did Russell give his grandson that book?'

'No,' I reply, explaining to him what had happened and how things were left.

'That sounds like a promising start to rebuilding their relationship,' he sounds genuinely pleased. He pauses. 'I've got something to tell you and I'm not sure if it's linked or not, but you need to know.'

Hairs stand up on the back of my neck. I should have downplayed the optimism.

The Lost Soul

'Ok,' I draw out the words slowly, not sure if I'm going to like what I'm about to hear. 'What is it?'

There is a brief silence on the line, before Jack continues, 'Steph spoke to Russell's grandson, Anthony Cherwell.'

'What? After he spoke to his grandad?' I ask.

'No,' he continues, 'in Abingdon, before he went to Haworth.'

'Oh, and …?' I'm not sure where this conversation is going.

'And,' he sounds annoyed, 'Anthony is a Publicity Manager for an Abingdon Member of Parliament. The man's name is Lewis Benson.'

'Lewis Benson,' I repeat the name, but it doesn't sound familiar. 'Who is Lewis Benson?'

'Lewis Benson is Sasha's father,' he says finally.

The world begins to go in slow motion before me, as people go about their business, and I feel as though someone has pressed pause on the remote control. 'No shit!' I mutter, without thinking.

'I'm sorry Nick. I know you've got enough stuff to deal with. But where there is a connection, there's always trouble.'

'Thanks for the heads up.' He's got the phone that Nancy used. Does he know that Anthony's grandad lives here? That his daughter and granddaughter live here? If he finds out, I fear he may be already heading this way. Benson is spiteful, he is cunning, and he is violent.

The Lost Soul

'I'll keep them both close,' I tell him. 'And I'll update Jared and Leo.'

'Good, if you need anything else, or you see him, let me know,' he tells me before disconnecting the line.

I go to the bathroom and lock myself in a cubicle. Jesus. Fuck. Fuck. How does this all tie in together? A little while ago, I felt as though everything was coming together, that I had found a place and purpose for living. That I belonged. Now, I feel like I'm being punished. Again. I can't bear for anything to happen to Sasha or Zoe. I would rather die or give myself up. This is like history repeating itself. Corinna or me. Sasha and Zoe or me.

Right, pull yourself together and start planning. I need to collect some bits from my car, I need to update security, to get Zoe home from nursery. Keep Sasha safe.

At the sink, I wash my face. Letting the cool water revive me, I pat my wet skin dry with a paper towel, before slapping both cheeks, to spur myself on. You can do this. Keep them safe and save the world.

When I reach the reception, I look for Sasha.

'Have you seen Sasha?' I ask Kate, looking along the corridor for the petite dark-haired manager. Kate shakes her head, to tell me no. 'Want me to call her?'

'Please, I just need to get some things from my car. Then I need to speak to Sasha, Jared and Leo privately in the office.'

The Lost Soul

'No problem,' she says. 'I'll tell her to wait here,' she smiles, picking up the phone and calling Sasha.

I pass the security guards, explaining that I need to collect something from my car and will return soon. As I push open the main door, the crisp air hits me and chills my face. I march across the gravel and to the right of the building, where the car park is situated. Walking to my blue Fiesta, I take the car keys from my trouser pocket, and release the door locks. I open the passenger side door, lean in and reach over to access the glove compartment. Right at the back of the small dark recess, I feel the handle of a Swiss army knife and next to it, a small flat headed, red-handled screwdriver.

I take the objects and push them deep into my trouser pockets. I feel safer, now I have a couple of weapons. Grabbing a black jacket from the passenger seat, I hear the slight crunch of gravel, but it doesn't seem to register in my brain, what it is.

'Jules Walker?' A rough Geordie voice asks, from over my shoulder.

As I turn toward the voice, I face an obese male, around thirty, with a toothless grin, baggy old stale jeans, a grey dirty sweat top. What little hair he has, is mousy and strays across his head and face.

'Dave Delossi says hello,' he says, swinging a baseball bat, long and hard.

The Lost Soul

My final thoughts, as the bat makes contact with my head, is, to wonder what the hell is going on. Recognition of Delossi's name, hits me like a freight train, knocking the wind out of me.

Then the world goes black.

The Lost Soul

Part 21: Sasha

'I'm on my way,' I tell Kate, balancing my phone precariously against my ear, while one hand pats Esther on the arm, and the other hand, flicks quickly through her small black handbag. 'Just looking for Esther's purse, she thinks it may have fallen from her handbag on the way from her apartment.' I disconnect the call.

I look at the older woman's face, with her greying, shoulder-length hair. She wipes threatening tears from her eyes, with a wrinkled hand, and sits proudly upright in her high back chair. Her nearby, blue-haired friend, Jess tugs her wig slightly, before patting Esther's hand.

'We'll find it, Esther dear, don't you worry.' Jess soothes, moving her mouth up and down as though she's playing with her false lower teeth.

Esther is seventy-eight years old, and fiercely independent. Something like this is hard for her to grasp, losing her possessions and asking people for help. She pulls a white, cotton handkerchief, from her mauve dress pocket and uses it to dab at her eyes.

'Don't worry Esther, we'll find it,' I reassure her. It's not in her handbag, it's not on the floor near her chair. Where the hell is it? I return my phone to my trouser pocket, and all of a sudden, the picture of my mother's face flashes into my mind, making me wonder how she is doing.

I know Stuart will let me know if she deteriorates, but despite everything, the pain of my childhood, the worry of my father's volatile moods and behaviour, I know that she loves me. There is no denying that mum had put her life in danger by contacting me but is that more out of stupidity, than her feelings for me?

'But, what if you don't?' Esther sniffles into her handkerchief. 'What if I never find it? I am such an old fool.'

Patting her shoulder, I smile reassuringly. 'Of course, you're not Esther. We all lose things now and again.'

There are several people in the Sun Room, Robert and Charlie are playing bridge at the table. Clara and Edna are knitting on the dark green sofa in the far corner of the room, chatting and putting the world to rights. Their needles clicking, as their respective balls of wool become smaller. Jared, one of the new security guys walks into the room, scans the area until he finds me.

'Sasha, Kate just found a brown purse on the reception desk, it could belong to Esther,' he explains, walking to stand in front of me. He holds out a large rectangular dark brown purse with gold zips decorating it.

I heave a sigh of relief and offer a smile and thanks to Jared. Thank goodness we found it. 'Here you go, lovely,' I say, giving it to Esther, who let's out a sigh of relief, before bursting into tears.

The Lost Soul

'Thank you,' she says in between sobs, her bony fingers stroke the purse as though it is a long-lost artefact from a bygone era. 'Thank you.'

'I need to go, Esther. Need to take a call,' I tell her. 'Push that purse right to the bottom of your bag, that should keep it safe.'

I rush to the reception and mouth the word 'sorry' to Kate. 'Someone on the line, it's for Nick. Can you take it? He's collecting some things from his car. He needs to speak to you, Jared and Leo.'

'Sure, who is it?' I ask, taking the phone.

'Anthony Cherwell, Russell's grandson. He said it is urgent.' Kate explains solemnly as she hands me the phone.

'Hello, Mr Cherwell, it's Sasha Berrington here,' I say into the receiver, 'Nick is busy at the moment, can I give him a message?'

'It's awkward,' his voice sounds rushed, panicked even. 'But I wanted to give him a heads up. Someone called Dave Delossi has asked me to find a guy. The person he wants me to find is Jules Walker.'

My brain freezes, and an icy shiver builds up along my spine and grows in intensity until it reaches my shoulder blades. *Bloody hell! Jules Walker. I can't think straight. For goodness sake woman, get a grip.*

'I'm sorry, Mr Cherwell. Can you repeat that?' I ask quietly, walking into my office, I kick the door shut behind me.

The Lost Soul

'I said, I've been asked by this low life Dave Delossi to find Jules Walker. It was in part payment for a debt. Which I've now cleared. Walker murdered his brother, Ray.'

No. No. No. This can't be happening. Forcing myself to keep calm, I inhale slowly before asking:

'Why are you telling me this? Have you told Delossi that you've seen Jules Walker?'

Bugger, in my panic, I'm being careless with my words. Shaking my head, I clear enough space to focus on the conversation.

'Just tell him, will you,' he says. 'Tell him, that I won't say anything, but Delossi is snide and has a henchman they call, Little Tim, to do his dirty work for him. Tell him to watch his back.'

The line disconnects before I can say another word. What a bloody mess. Needing a minute before I speak to Nick, I sink into the seat of my black leather chair. I pull the clip from my loose knot and let my hair fall to my shoulders, taking solace in the way it frames me when I let my head slump forward. My hands massage my scalp, backwards and forwards. Nick could be in danger. If this man called Little Tim finds him, he'll probably kill him, and that has got to be Delossi's endgame. To silence Nick.

An eye for an eye.

I push out of the chair and rush to Kate at reception, 'is Nick back from his car yet?'

Disregarding the fact that Kate is talking to Jared, I put my hands on my hips and stand waiting for an answer. She excuses herself from her conversation, before she turns to me to answer my

The Lost Soul

question. 'No,' she says. 'Perhaps he can't find what he's looking for.'

A frisson of panic goes through my whole body. A warning that something isn't right. 'I'm going to the car park,' I look across at Leo the blonde-haired, black suited security guard, 'Leo, can you come with me please.'

He nods and follows as I pick up the pace across the gravel and glance around for Nick's blue Fiesta. The first sign that something is wrong, is when I see that the passenger door is wide open.

The second, is Nick's black jacket on the ground, near the door.

The third sign is the drag marks and blood splatters on the gravel.

Bloody hell!

I hear myself screaming, as Leo begins to run around the car park following the dragging marks in the gravel and calling Nick's name. 'Over here!' he calls. I make my way to where he is standing.

'You see these tyre tracks, the drag marks?' he points to the ground and clear signs.

'There's blood,' I whisper, my breath hitches and I begin to feel nauseous. My extreme reaction to Nick's disappearance and his potential injury, surprises me. Floors me, even. I didn't know I felt this strongly about him. We haven't had time to talk about his past properly. Fear and anger suddenly engulf me, there are so many bloody obstacles between us.

The Lost Soul

Life keeps getting in the way, and that makes me mad. Why can't things be simple? I don't ask for much, to be able to look after my daughter, and possibly find a decent man.

I think Nick is that man. No, my brain is addled. I know Nick is that man.

'We need to call the police,' Leo says, taking his phone from his jacket pocket.

Above all else, Nick needs to be safe. Stuart saved him for a reason. I think that reason was because Nick's story hasn't finished yet, that he is about to embark on another chapter, right here, right now. The only thing I know for certain as I process Leo's words, is that there is no way we can involve the police for the possible attack and abduction of a wanted murderer.

Who could have done this? And, then I remember Anthony's phone call. Is it possible that Little Tim was following him?

'No,' I say firmly. 'I need to make a few phone calls first.' I take photos of Nick's jacket as it lay on the rough ground, I snapshot the blood and drag marks too. 'Can you stay outside and keep the area clear?' I ask Leo, 'I'll get Jared to bring the car park CCTV up and find out who our extra visitor was this morning.'

Leo nods, making his way back to Nick's car and I make a mental note of what I need to do and in what order. Walking into the building, I locate Jared and ask him to check the CCTV cameras over the past three hours.

Alone, with my thoughts, I decide to call Nick. I'm disheartened by the dialling tone and answerphone that kicks in. Once I'm in

The Lost Soul

the office, I make sure that the door is shut, before taking a seat in the leather chair behind the desk. I speak into the phone, trying to keep the panic out of my voice.

'Hi, it's Nick, leave a message and I'll get back to you.' I'm comforted at the sound of his voice.

'Nick, it's me. Sasha,' I say, in a rush. 'Call me back, I'm worried about you.' Well, that's that. My options have just run out.

It is time to call Stuart.

I stare at Stuart's name before pressing the call button. It seems to take forever, until an automated message speaks the words, 'I'm sorry, but this number is currently unavailable.

Damn. There is a specific protocol for emergency situations, such as this.

Stuart has a plan for every eventuality, if we have been compromised, and Stuart is unable, or can't answer, I need to text four people and type the words, 'Code Red, SB.'

The four people are Stuart Greyson. Jenny Greyson, Jack Kinsey and Steph Rutland.

I put a group text together, with the four necessary names and send my code sign. It's all very cloak and dagger, but we have to adhere to it, in emergency situations. The first person to answer, then follows up the case and updates the others.

Swivelling my wheeled chair forward, I rest my head on my arms. What a mess. Looking up, I check the time on my watch, it's 12.45pm. Zoe finishes nursery in Hebden Bridge at 2.50pm, and

The Lost Soul

Viola said this morning that they are going to get a milkshake before heading back home.

Two minutes later, my phone jumps to life with the sultry tones of Adele. Jack's name appears on the screen. Thank goodness. I feel like a nervous wreck. Not just because of Nick's disappearance, but that it has happened where I live. With my daughter.

'Jack?' my voice is shaky, and I push my finger through a speck of dust on the corner of my desk, to calm my nerves.

'Sasha? What's happened?' Jack's deep voice asks.

I tell him, first about the phone call from Anthony Cherwell, and then what we've recently found in the carpark at Greystones, including the blood and the connection between Dave Delossi and Little Tim. I finish, by telling him that Nick isn't answering his phone.

I hadn't realised that I'd left my chair and am pacing the room, until I catch sight of my pale reflection in the mirror that sits above a mahogany cupboard unit. Bloody hell, I look like a ghost, and my eyes have that deer in headlights look about them.

'I'm worried Jack, he could be hurt,' I say in a flat, defeated tone.

'I know, look Steph's here, I'm driving. We were on our way to lunch. I've got you on speaker and Steph is bringing up the tracking app, to locate Nick's phone.'

'Tracking app?' I query, Nick won't be happy when he finds out. 'You can track his phone?'

The Lost Soul

'Yes,' Jack replies, his voice sounds unapologetic. 'We had them downloaded into new phones twelve months ago, Nick's was a spare.'

'He's not going to like that, Jack,' I say, quietly – a picture of Nick's annoyed face comes to mind, and I hold back a smile. Well, needs must.

'Right now, I don't give a flying fuck what Nick likes or dislikes,' Jack curses, reminding me why I like him so much. He says what needs to be said and doesn't dress it up with fancy words. 'The app was set up for exactly this reason, to protect us.'

'I'm glad,' I tell him, all that matters is that we get Nick back safely.

'It sounds as though you've grown attached to our Nick,' he says, to distract me from my worries.

'Don't go there, Jack. He's got a load of stuff going on in his head, with Ray Delossi and his sister.'

'Wow, you must have made a big impact on him, for him to tell you about his sister and what happened,' Jack's tone is suddenly serious. 'Hang in there, Sasha. Despite everything, he's one of the good guys.'

Tears blur my vision and I say quietly, 'I know.' There is a conversation on the line, which I can't quite hear, before Jack's voice sounds louder and clearer when he speaks:

'Right, Sasha. According to the tracker, he's on the A629 heading toward Huddersfield. If the blood is anything to go by, he's been

217

The Lost Soul

taken on Delossi's orders by Little Tim, so we can assume that he's been incapacitated somehow, injury, drugs, chloroform.'

There's an urgency to my voice, 'Oh no! We need to get him back,' There's a knock at the door and it's Jared, he's holding a piece of paper.

'Jack, I'm going to put you on speaker? Jared has just arrived, with more information.' I don't wait for the reply, just press the speaker icon.

'What have you got?' I beckon to Jared to come closer. He leans forward, his blonde hair is dishevelled, he holds the paper in front of himself, reading from handwritten notes.

'CCTV shows a black BMW, registration AR53 OLE, it arrives a couple of minutes after one of our visitors, Anthony Cherwell. Possible link? Following him?' Jared looks at me. I raise my eyebrows in question, my mind is working overtime as I think of the BMW. How did we not notice this? Do we need security in the car park?

'We've got the whole thing on tape,' Jared continues, 'the big guy waits in the car park, mostly in his car. As soon as he leaves, the thug gets out and makes a quick phone call, before reaching into the car boot to take out a baseball bat.

'When Nick comes out, the man says something to him, before knocking him unconscious over the head with the bat and dragging him to the BMW – where he puts him in the boot.'

'Fuck!' Jack spits out. 'A baseball bat, you say?'

218

The Lost Soul

'Yes,' Jared glances at me, as he answers. 'Why?'

'It's very apt, that he should use the same weapon, that Nick used to kill Delossi's brother.'

'That's awful,' my whole body begins to shake at the thought of Nick lying in a ditch injured after being attacked in the car park. 'Thanks Jared,' I say, as he gives me a quick nod, before leaving the room.

'We'll intercept him and get Nick back,' Jack says, with a confidence I don't feel. Bloody hell, what a mess! I lower my head and rub the pain that sits just over my right eye.

'Did Nick tell you about Anthony Cherwell?' Jack's question surprises me, are we going down another rabbit hole? I place my hands on my cheeks, wishing this day would end.

'No, what? What is he supposed to have told me?'

'Ok, and you're not going to like this. But.' Jack is procrastinating.

'Just tell me, Jack!' I order him, let's get this over and done with. What more can go wrong today?

'It appears that Anthony Cherwell works as the Publicity Manager for your father in Abingdon.' Jack says quietly.

At first, I think I've misheard him. In fact, I blink several times before I acknowledge Jack's words.

'Shit!' I say eventually, feeling my body go completely limp, as though I am about to melt into a puddle on the floor. How the hell did that happen? I've come all this way to make a new life for myself, when all the time, Russell's grandson is working for my dad.

'Does he know? My dad?' I ask in a quiet voice, silently holding my breath. Following my dad's phone call to me a few days ago about my mum, my nerves have been shot.

'About you working at Greystones?' Jack asks. 'No, I don't think so.'

I exhale slowly, feeling thankful that my dad does not know where I am. 'You seem quite sure,' I say with relief.

'Did the grandson give you any indication that he knew who you were?'

'No,' I answer slowly. 'He never said anything, even when I spoke to him on the phone.'

'There you go, but it will only be a matter of time before your dad finds you and Zoe. Stay alert, Stuart is watching over your mum.'

'How is she?' I ask, thinking about the pain she has suffered in her life, and hoping that she will one day find a life without violence and pain, like I have. It's taken a little while, but the first steps are the hardest, learning to trust your own decisions and not feeling guilty.

At least I have my daughter, what did she have, after I'd left? Nothing. Still, I can't let myself become too involved and feel responsible for my mum, I have to protect myself and Zoe, and I don't have the time or energy to get involved with her at the moment. We all have to find a way to survive, don't we?

The Lost Soul

'Is there any improvement?' I ask.

'No, but the consultants are hopeful, that she will come around. The swelling on her face is going down.'

'That's good, I'm pleased,' and I really am.

'Do you want to come and see her one day?' that's Steph's voice, asking and probing.

'I don't know,' I say dully, 'at first, when I found out that he had attacked her, my instinct was to rush to be with her. But.'

'But?' Steph isn't giving up so easily.

'But now I know that Stuart is there, and that she is being looked after, I don't feel the need to run to her bedside, particularly after everything that has happened. The feeling of protecting myself and Zoe, is much stronger than I realised.'

'I understand,' Steph says, 'she let you down, she should have been the strong one, she should have left your dad.'

'Yes,' I say quietly, that about sums it up. 'Maybe one day, I will visit when she's better. But a part of me has to forgive her first.'

'It's your call, take your time. There's no pressure,' Steph says softly.

'I know,'

'Steph and I are going to make our way to Huddersfield,' Jack cuts in. 'We'll continue tracking Nick's phone, follow him. Hopefully, he will stop, which will give us a chance to get to the car and check the boot. You keep calling his phone. Let me know if you hear from him.'

'Thanks Jack,' I finish, disconnecting the phone.

I call Nick one more time, 'C'mon Nick, answer the bloody phone,' I mutter in frustration as the answer phone clicks on.

Well, that's different. At least it's not turned off this time.

The Lost Soul

Part 22: Dave

Holy Cow! He found him! He fucking found him. I take the sim card from my phone, kneel on the cold concrete floor and push the phone through the slit of my mattress, I'd made by fashioning a sharp point from my toothpaste tube and rubbing vigorously. Feeling the springs and padding of my shallow, hard mattress, I push the small oblong object as far as I dare into the bed. The sim, I slide inside the lace flaps of my trainers.

In a sort of daze, I slump onto the edge of my bed, my fingers curling into the thin blankets either side of me.

I can't believe Little Tim found him.

Staring at the grey walls facing me in my cell, it is dismal and cold. White shelves and an old silver toilet, a sink, nothing to offer any comfort or give you a reason to keep going. I know we're not in prison for a holiday, but they could make a bit of an effort. At least do the odd repair or repaint the cells.

I go over the earlier conversation with Little Tim:

'I think I've found him, Boss,' his Geordie voice had held the excitement of a child.

The Lost Soul

'No shit!' I wasn't expecting that and couldn't hide my surprise. 'Jules Walker?'

'Yeah, I'd recognise his face anywhere,' the big man had confirmed.

Wait a minute, I'd paced backwards and forwards across the tiny space of my cell. This was more than I could have hoped for. Vengeance for killing my brother, even though we weren't close, is near – I can almost taste it.

Ray didn't deserve to die like an injured pig in his own home. I thought of Ray's car and the cars from the sales business that I'd had Little Tim steal, re-condition and sell on. Thought of the money, sitting in my offshore bank account. Did I really want to do anything to jeopardise the last seven years of my sentence?

'Boss?' Little Tim's voice woke me from my head conversation. 'What do you want me to do?'

There was a pause. Shit. The decision is easy when it comes down to it.

Family is family.

'You still got that baseball bat on the back seat of your car?' I ask.

'Yeah, want me to do a bit of damage?' he asks, as though he's asking me to pick up a bunch of bananas from Sainsbury's.

'Yeah, I think so. Tell him Dave Delossi says hello.'

'Ok, Boss.'

The Lost Soul

My neck cricks as I roll it around and push my shoulders, backwards and forwards.

'Oh, and bring him to me,' I smile, as a plan forms in my mind. I stare at the mirror, at the man looking back at me. Sometimes, I feel that the years haven't been too kind to me. With my long, greasy brown hair and the reddish scars across my cheek and neck, I look older than my forty years.

'Boss?'

'You heard me,' my stiff shoulders ache with lack of exercise. 'Bring him to me.'

'You got a plan, Boss?' he asks, with confidence. He likes it when I have a plan.

'Yeah, I got a plan, bring him to Anthony Cherwell's house. The one in Didcot,' I order him. 'Then, I'll be in touch.'

'Fuck yeah! I like that.'

So, here I am. My plan is simple.

Get the fuck out.

Kill Walker.

Disappear.

I go in search of Bomber. He's got a grudge and it won't take much to push him over the edge.

Let the party begin.

The Lost Soul

Part 23: Jules

The thud of a sharp dip and quick rise wakes me, forcing me out of my unconscious state. It is dark and I am moving at speed. My body is scrunched up. I don't know where I am. My head hurts when I attempt to move, so I stay as rigid as possible. Motionless.

I am in a car, I think. Bugger. The boot of a car. Holy shit.

I try to open my eyes, but the moment I begin to focus, a pain sears across my head, like hot metal rods being inserted into my skull. The front side of my head has a dull ache, and I lift my hand to touch it, immediately, my fingers find tender, broken skin and my hair is wet and sticky. Great. I'm bleeding.

Keeping my eyes closed, I concentrate on the sounds I can hear. A male voice shouts obscenities and pounds at the steering wheel. 'Shit. Shit. Shit.'

What the hell happened? My memory is still hazy. Think, goddammit, concentrate. What is the last thing I remember? I was at Greystones. I needed to speak to Sasha. I went to get some things from my car.

Then what? As I massage my temple gently, the car suddenly swerves, jarring my whole body, the pain shoots up my shoulder and neck and explodes in my head.

227

The Lost Soul

Fuck! I take a deep breath and slowly count to ten. I need to open my eyes, so I force myself to keep breathing as I do so, working through the pain, until my eyes are open and adjusting to the darkness. Bloody hell. How long have I been in here? I have no idea.

Disjointed visions jog my memory. There is a male voice calling my name. My real name. I remember turning automatically, to face the person, forgetting that I am Nick Flannigan. Then the man said something that made my blood freeze, 'Dave Delossi says hello,' before he swung a long piece of wood at my head and the world went black.

Shit! I'm totally screwed.

Dave Delossi. Dad, brother, cousin? It could be anyone. Why now? How did he find me?

So many bloody questions. I shuffle slightly, there is a hard rectangular object digging into my hip. What on earth is that? It isn't my phone, is it? I swivel slightly, so that I'm almost lying on my back, giving access to my trouser pocket. I reach in and my fingers wrap around a cold, hard surface. My phone. Carefully, I put in my security code and unlock it, and with a huge sigh of relief, I realise that there is a signal, and battery.

There are several missed calls from Sasha, in addition to a voicemail from her, and one from Jack. Sasha must be worried sick. I find Jack in my call history and call him first. It seems to take forever to connect and begin dialling his number.

The Lost Soul

Jack answers, his husky voice hard, 'Hello? Jules?'

'It's me,' I say quietly, not wanting to attract any attention.

'Jesus! Thank God, I was genuinely thinking the worst for a moment. Steph and I are on the M6, going around Birmingham. We're heading your way.'

'Don't know where I am,' I say quietly, 'I'm in the boot of a car. I got hit on the head, I've only just come round, must have been out for a couple of hours.'

'Bloody hell, we know,' Jack almost shouts with emotion. 'We've got it all on the car park CCTV. Someone hit you with a baseball bat and dragged you to his car, locking you in the boot.'

'It's something to do with Ray Delossi. I think it's a relative. Just before the man hit me, he said, 'Dave Delossi says hello.''

'Right first thing, can you see the emergency boot release? It should be lit up somewhere near the boot clasp.'

'No,' I say, looking around. 'I can't see it.' I wriggle around, but I'm a tall man, scrunched up, with very little room to move around.

'Keep looking, it's there somewhere,' Jack says.

Steph Rutland's soft voice comes through the phone. 'Don't give up Jules, we're on our way.'

Guilt and despondency overwhelm me, these good people are trying to help me again. I don't feel worthy of their commitment. Steph is now in a precarious position with her job, all because of me. I don't want to have that responsibility for ruining people's lives and careers.

I think of my time at Richmond Court, my social work placement. The moment when young Corinna James was arrested for something I had done. I did the right thing, but now I'm here, in Yorkshire, or wherever I am at this very moment.

'I'm sorry DI Rutland,' I say quietly, so damned sorry. 'Sorry for causing more trouble.'

'This isn't your fault, it's Dave Delossi and his henchman,' she says with a harshness to her voice, but then softens it considerably, 'And, you need to call me Steph, we're way past the DI stage now.'

As the car changes lanes, I roll on to my side. There's a small square sign, it's bright green. It's near the boot mechanism. A surge of excitement and relief, makes my eyes blur and I use a finger to wipe the wetness from my vision. 'I found it,' I say quietly, 'found the boot release button.'

'That's great,' Steph says. 'If he stops somewhere, you'll have a chance to get out and hide.'

'Let's hope he's got a weak bladder,' Jack mutters.

'Yeah,' I agree, 'but what happens if he doesn't stop until he gets to his destination? We don't know where he's taking me.'

'Don't worry about that, we're tracking your phone so we can follow you,' Jack says.

The Lost Soul

Wait a minute, did he say he's tracking me? How the hell is he tracking me? Has he put a tracker on my phone, and I never noticed?

'Jack?' I begin slowly, 'did you put a tracker on my phone?'

There was a silence, and then he spoke, 'Sorry, Jules. We've all got trackers installed, just in case. The phone you had is one of Stuart's spare ones, he'd put it on the phone before he gave it to you.'

'Fucking crazy,' I mutter, in anger, 'Where am I?'

'You're on the M1 probably somewhere near Barnsley by now,' Steph answers, it sounds like she's driving.

'Well, that's great then. When I get home, we're going to talk about this tracking business.' I hear a chuckling sound. 'But for now, can you let Sasha know I'm all right. I'm going to go now, save on the phone life.'

I switch off the phone and try to stay awake over the humming of the car engine. A loud dialling tone vibrates from the front of the car and for a moment I panic, believing that it's my mobile. Through the back speakers I hear someone talking:

'You got him?' An unfamiliar voice asks.

'Yeah, he's in the boot,' the car driver replies, in a loud Geordie accent. 'He's a big fella, had to clock him one and drag him to my car.'

Clock him one? What am I, a dog?

'Bring him to the house, after 6pm tonight, as agreed.'

The Lost Soul

'Ok, Boss,' the Geordie agrees.

'Oh, and no stopping on the way,' the boss orders.

'Got it,' the driver replies, and the line goes dead. My mind whirls, as I try to imagine where he might be taking me? Where is the house? I move my right leg slightly, the muscles cramp instantly sending shockwaves of pain throughout my side, I wince careful not to let any noise become too loud in the silence of the dark confined space.

The driver bangs hard on the steering wheel. 'Bloody idiot,' he shouts. 'Now I need fucking petrol. Delossi, can take a flying leap. I'll get there when I get there.'

The radio begins to play, and the volume is turned up. I breathe a sigh of relief that the music will hide any noise I make. Painfully, I manoeuvre myself to get comfortable. He's got to stop, I tell myself. He needs petrol.

That's got to be a good thing. My chance to escape. So, I wait in the darkness for the car to stop, comforted by the memory of a pair of dark brown eyes.

Part 24: Nancy

'Mummy? Mummy? I can't find you,' Sasha's voice ricochets through the stillness of the kitchen. She is five years old, and we're playing hide and seek. I am crouching in the kitchen, beside the large white fridge freezer, hoping that she will find me before my knees become so stiff, they lock into place.

Sandalled feet clip clap, using small steps, across the laminated wooden kitchen floor. I can't resist calling out a reassuring hint, 'you're getting closer, sweetheart.' I can hear the lightness in my voice, and a bubble of laughter threatens to escape my lips. I slap a hand over my mouth. 'See if you can find me,' I almost sing, 'Perhaps, I'm near the door.'

My daughter, Sasha, is such a sweet little girl. Her speech is good for her age, she demonstrates a caring and thoughtful personality, and she is the reason that I wake up every morning. She gives me a reason to live.

I peek around the corner of the fridge, and spy a flash of her bright pink dress, with matching tights. Quickly, I shuffle backwards, out of sight.

The Lost Soul

'Mummy? Where are you?' She bends, as though she thinks I am very small, and pops her head around the side of the fridge freezer.

Curling up in a ball, isn't as easy as you think, but when I venture to look up, we find that we are almost nose to nose. We both squeal with fright and then burst into laughter simultaneously. Her curly shoulder length auburn hair dances across her shoulders as she jiggles on her feet with excitement, arms waving madly. She chatters with delight at securing her find.

'Mummy, I found you!' She smiles, throwing her arms around me.

'Yes!' I smile, slowly straightening my aching bones to my full height, and taking her little body with me. 'Yes, you have sweetheart! Well done.'

'I love you Sasha,' I smile into her ear. 'I love you so much.'

***

A bright light, sears across my face and comes to a stop over my eyelids. Warmth, like a hot sun on a clear day, heats the skin of my injured face. It must be daylight. My eyes open of their own accord, taking in the sun that reflects across the white walls.

Am I in heaven? If so, it's very clinical.

I move my head to the side, and focus on the blurred half-open door, I'm relieved when my vision gradually becomes clearer. My face feels tight, as though it is covered in a giant elastic band, and part of it has a burning sensation. I slowly raise my right hand, noticing that it has a cannula with a tube attached to it. This is not

The Lost Soul

a good sign. I continue to explore the damage to my face; feeling thick dressings, mostly on one side, a split lip and wound closure strips on one cheekbone and across my nose.

Further exploration reveals a heavy adhesive pad over my left eye. Panic begins to set in. Holy Mother of God, I am in a big mess. Amid the panic, the machinery next to me begins to bleep. My throat feels dry.

Lewis really hurt me this time.

The door opens fully and a stout nurse, wearing a pale blue cotton top and matching trousers marches to my bedside. She has a pretty face and short dark hair.

'Good to see you're awake, Nancy,' she says knowingly, as though I have woken from a short nap. She picks up a blood pressure monitor and wraps it around my arm. 'You had us worried for a little while. My name is Emma, I'm your nurse, and I'll be looking after you today,' she explains with a smile.

'I'm thirsty,' I whisper, catching her concerned gaze. She nods and steps to the trolley, where she pours water from the jug into a small glass.

'Take small sips,' she advises, holding the glass and tilting it slightly so that it dribbles into my mouth. The cool liquid refreshes my throat. Bliss. I nod to her when I've had enough.

'Let's check your bloody pressure,' she says, pressing the buttons on the wheeled monitoring machine.

The Lost Soul

The machine whirls to life, and the cuff begins to tighten on my arm. 'What is the sight like in your right eye?' She looks around, finds a printed sheet and hands it to me, 'can you read that?

'Seems good.' The writing on the sheet is easy to see, 'Keep safe and sanitise your hands.'

'Good,' she says. 'We will wait for the swelling to come down on your left eye, and then send you to x-ray and for a CT scan, to make sure there are no broken or detached sockets. The ophthalmologist will go from there.'

Emma picks up a clipboard from the end of the bed and records my blood pressure. She moves to the trolley in the corner of the room and reaches into a cardboard container, she retrieves a digital ear thermometer and a packet which she unwraps, takes out an earpiece and slips it onto the thermometer. She sticks the cold hard instrument into one of my ears, and reassures me, 'I'm going to take your temperature.'

She looks at the temperature gauge and records the result on her iPad, before flicking the used earpiece into the clinical waste bin. She looks up, 'all good.'

'Will I be able to see from my left eye?' I ask.

'I can't say Nancy,' she stops to look at me, giving my arm a pat and reassures me, 'Mr Evans, the Consultant Ophthalmologist is due to come and chat with you today. Let's not worry about that at the moment, we'll know more when the swelling goes down.'

A tear comes to my good eye and sits waiting to drop onto my cheek. It wasn't supposed to be me, in the hospital, it was

The Lost Soul

supposed to be Lewis. He was the one who was going to develop a stomach ulcer and hopefully die. It wasn't supposed to be this way. My heart aches for my bad fortune.

'By the way, your brother has gone to get a coffee. He's been here watching over you since you came in.'

'Brother?' I ask, my blood freezes. 'I don't have a brother!' My head is beginning to thud. Who the hell is this man? What is going on?

'You don't?' Emma asks, immediately turning to face me. 'The man who found you and called for the ambulance, and who has stayed with you since you got here. He told us, he's your brother.'

I shake my head, slowly.

'I'll contact security when I leave,' she reassures me. 'Are you in any pain?' She studies.

'My head hurts and I feel as though I've done a few rounds with Mike Tyson,' I mutter, trying to ignore pain in my stomach, hips and ribs. I'm still thinking about the man posing as my 'brother,' and praying that it isn't Lewis, or I'm going to be a dead woman, when I get home.

'I'm not surprised, you've taken quite a battering,' Emma straightens my pillow and uses the remote control to raise the head on the bed slowly. 'You have a couple of broken ribs so, take it very easy, and I'll organise a top up of painkillers.'

She helps me to shuffle upward onto my pillow. 'Would you like a cup of tea?'

The Lost Soul

'Please,' I say, and lie staring at the storage unit.

'Milk and sugar?' Emma bustles, folding my bedclothes and flattening the cool cotton.

'Yes,' I nod, watching her busy figure leave the room. 'One more thing. How long have I been in here?'

'Three days. You came in on Tuesday afternoon. I'll be back soon with your medication, and there is the emergency buzzer if you need me,'' she looks over her shoulder and points to a white rectangular control with a big button in the middle.

Three days! I've been in here for three days! What the hell!

Through the open doorway, there are voices, and a male voice is talking and softly laughing.

Meanwhile, amid the dull thud of the pain in my head, I try to make sense about what has happened to me, and where I go from here.

Out of the corner of my eye, I catch a movement in the doorway, and to my horror, there standing in front of me, hands deep in his black trouser pockets and wearing a smart, white shirt is my husband. And, by the sour look on his face, he doesn't look happy. My fingers creep across the bed to the emergency button.

'I wouldn't do that if I were you,' he says softly, shutting the door as he walks into the room.

'What are you doing here?' I hiss. 'You've come to see your handiwork, is that it?'

The Lost Soul

'Don't start that, Nancy,' I can see he's trying to hold his temper in check, but the blood vessel on his neck is pulsing, as though it's about burst. 'It was your fault. You shouldn't have been hiding things from me.'

'Leave,' I shake my head, even though it feels as though it is about to split in two. 'Now!' I sob.

Ignoring me, he strolls casually to the side of my bed, 'Just a warning, dear wife,' he says leaning down and speaking in a low, menacing tone, 'don't even think of pressing charges and leaving me.'

I press the emergency button and pray that it is silent.

A vice-like grip snakes around my wrist, burning my skin and making me wince.

'You shouldn't have done that!' he snaps, suddenly pulling away. At that moment there is a gasp from Emma, as the door is thrust fully open, and she rushes into the room. Behind her is a tall, good-looking man with short mousy hair, who takes one look at my husband and steps forward:

'Let go of her!' the tall man shouts, pulling Lewis away and dragging him across the room to the door.

Emma fusses over me, pulling my blankets and sheets across me, asking if I am all right.

'Get your bloody hands off me! Do you know who I am?' Lewis' loud arrogant voice echoes through the room. The tall man continues to ignore him, as he keeps pushing him through the

The Lost Soul

door and into the hallway where their bodies collide with a young nurse, as she walks innocently past the door of my room.

In the commotion, Lewis manages to free himself and drapes his arm around the young blonde-haired nurse's neck, before tightening his grip. The nurse screams, feet shuffle and there is much movement, as Lewis pulls the woman backwards.

'Back off, or I'll hurt her,' I hear Lewis warn, his grey-brown curls sweating around his face and his skin is flushed.

The tall man answers, 'I can't do that, Lewis. You need to let the woman go.'

Scrunching my eye shut, I shallow breathe because of my broken ribs, trying to calm myself, and in the hope of blocking out the nurse's screams. Every syllable hurts my head, as though one hundred drawing pins are being pushed into my scalp.

I want the noise to stop, and I want my husband gone. I don't want to even utter his name, because then I will have to admit that he's here in the hospital. I will have to admit to myself that he has threatened me, and he is now threatening someone else. I don't want to think of the nurse, I just want to sleep, to block it all out.

The noises quieten, as though they're further away. Footsteps. Running. Keeping my eye shut, it helps me to calm me, staying in the darkness.

'Who on earth was that?' Emma asks, raising her eyebrows while she gently lifts my wrist and checks it out.

'My husband,' I say sullenly, opening my eye.

The Lost Soul

Her eyes widen with shock. 'Your husband?' she says with disbelief. 'He did this to you?'

I nod. What can I say? I am unlucky. There is one thing I know for certain, and that is I'm not going back to that home, not while he lives. I would rather let him have it all, than risk being his punchbag again.

'We need to call the police, Nancy,' she looks at me seriously.

'No need, I've done it. Benson is being held by security staff in their office, until they arrive, 'the tall man says, striding back into the room, his cheeks are flushed.

'It's a good thing you were here,' Emma acknowledges him with a wry smile. 'You were able to get him off her.' Emma turns to me, gestures with her hand and points to the tall man. 'Security have checked your visitor out and he has been given permission to continue to support you, if you choose to accept it. I'll leave it to you,' she looks at him, 'to explain who you are and why you're here,' and I watch as he nods, with his hands settled deep in his trouser pockets. 'I'll be back with tea and medication as soon as I can.'

We watch in silence as Emma leaves the room. I'm not nervous, but I am wondering who this man is, who has so far been sitting with me, and chasing my abusive husband away.

'The name is Stuart Greyson, by the way,' he holds out his hand, and waits for me to move my hand to his.

'My fictitious brother,' I answer, carefully touching his hand.

The Lost Soul

'I'm a friend of your daughter, Sasha,' he explains.

'Sasha?' I try to move, agitated. How does he know Sasha? What is she to him?

'My wife and I run a charity for abused wives and children. Sasha was referred to us, not long after she walked out of your home.'

'How? Why? When?' so many questions, I don't know where to begin, and I'm feeling so very tired.

'When she left home, with Zoe, she was found near a local bus stop by one of her teachers. The teacher took Sasha and Zoe home and contacted Thames Valley Police. They put her in contact with a police officer called, DS Leadbetter who talked her through the referral process, for the Lighthouse Charity.'

'Are you saying that you looked after my daughter and my granddaughter? That they weren't on the streets?' I couldn't keep the relief from my voice. My imagination had been working overtime, wondering about those first few months, and how Sasha was coping, homeless and with a young baby.

He leans forward, with his hands on his knees. 'Not me, per se, but my wife and I would check in with staff at the refuge home where Sasha and Zoe were homed, until they could be independent. My wife and I would speak to Sasha regularly and monitor Zoe to see how they were both doing. We became her support base and watched over her.'

Words fail me, it sounded like they had taken on the role of parents to Sasha, the role that should have been mine and Lewis'. The role that we had failed to do.

The Lost Soul

'Thank you.' I say simply, for words are not enough. My heart welled and tears misted my eye. 'Thank you.'

Stuart's face didn't show any condemnation or accusatory signs, his face lights up as his mouth forms a big smile. 'It was my pleasure. Sasha is a bright, hard-working young woman, and an amazing mum to Zoe.'

His eyes close momentarily, as though he is remembering happy moments. He touches my arm briefly. 'Here's the thing, Nancy. Sasha and Zoe are part of our family, part of the increasing Lighthouse family, and as such, that makes you part of that family too.'

'I've not been part of a family for a long time, Stuart,' I tell him, with a lump in my throat. 'Lewis took that away from me.'

'I know, Nancy,' he says softly, looking into my face. 'I can see that.'

Telling myself not to cry, is getting me nowhere. I can feel the tremble of my shoulders, tears making their way along my throat, bubbling away, choking me. I have been on my own for so long, with no one to look after me, to defend me or to help me stand up to Lewis. There had only been Sasha, she had stood up for me, as I had for her. But that wasn't her role to be supporting me, she shouldn't have been put in that situation.

'Following your phone call to Sasha, she thought you were in danger. She contacted me. I found you at your house, do you remember? I called the ambulance.'

The Lost Soul

Memories come and go as I try to remember what happened after I blacked out. 'I'm sorry, it's a bit vague.'

Part of me wishes that Stuart had never found me, that I had been left on that floor to die. Quietly, and in the dark shadows in which I lived.

There's a knock on the open door and two people stand in the doorway. A man and a woman. The woman is tall, with long blonde straight hair. She is wearing jeans and a long pale pink, expensive-looking jumper, she carries a large tan leather handbag. The man is of similar height, dark blonde hair, a white shirt and, dark grey trousers.

'Hi,' the woman smiles, as she walks into the room, 'I'm Jenny Greyson, Stuart's wife, and this is DS Chris Jackson.'

Stuart looks up at the woman, and the smile he gives her is dazzling. I watch mesmerised, when she puts an elegant hand on his shoulder, see the moment that he covers her hand with his. This is how love is supposed to be, not with fists and split lips or punches and kicks.

I try to smile, but my face hurts too much. I'm finding it hard to keep my eyes open.

'Sorry,' I say quietly, 'I'm feeling very tired.'

My nurse walks in with two cups of tea, she glances at the growing group of people around my bed, 'here is your tea,' she puts it on the wheeled table. She looks at me, and my eye, that is struggling to stay open. 'You look tired Nancy, perhaps your visitors can give you some privacy while you take a nap.'

The Lost Soul

The world stops and I am comforted that my daughter and granddaughter are safe, before I allow sleep to finally claim me.

The Lost Soul

Part 25: Jack

'He'll be ok, won't he?' Sasha sounds worried.

'Yes,' I reassure her for the hundredth time, 'he should be fine.'

'Shall I call him?' desperation in her voice.

'No, he needs to save his battery. No incoming calls, or Little Tim might hear it. He's risking a lot, just by talking to us.'

'But I need to do something,' she mutters flatly, 'or, I'll go mad.'

'You are doing something,' I lighten my words to give her a much-needed boost. 'You're keeping thIf ings going at Greystones. You're also on the end of the phone if we need you.'

I glance across at Steph, who is driving. We're in her blue Fiesta. Ben is at school, and Stuart and Jenny are staying with us, while they help Nancy. Steph briefly glances my way, before clearing her throat and attempting to reassure Sasha, 'we're pretty sure he'll be fine, Sasha. I'd rather not involve the police, because of Jules' identity and my job, but I won't risk his life.'

'Good,' Sasha gives a heavy sigh. 'Keep me updated, will you?'

'Of course, Sasha,' I say, wanting to reassure her. I feel protective about Sasha, she is young, bright and a great mum to Zoe. I don't know much about her history, apart from the fact that she arrived

The Lost Soul

at Shore House, bleeding, bruised and carrying a small baby. It doesn't take a lot to work out what happened, especially in light of her hospitalised mother. 'Don't worry, we'll speak later.'

Disconnecting the call, I look briefly at Steph, there are no words to describe how we feel, so we sit in silence, trying to make sense of what is happening. We need to wait and see how this situation plays out, and we have to be very careful about what we do today. How do we rescue Jules? If we have the opportunity to rescue him – are the worries that stick foremost in my mind.

There is also a strong feeling to protect Steph and limit her involvement with the kidnapper and Jules. The fewer times she uses her identity badge, the better chance she has to protect her job.

My hand reaches for her thigh, and I let it rest there, enjoying the warmth of her leg through her jeans, and feeling her muscles, when she uses the clutch control. I need the physical contact from her, it calms me and puts things into perspective. Steph's hand rests on mine.

I speak first, my voice is husky with emotion, 'I want you to step back from this, where you can.'

'Jack,' Steph's voice is poised, ready to counter-argue.

'I know what you're going to say,' I turn my hand from her thigh, and thread my fingers through hers. 'But this is my mess, Stuart's and mine. We dragged you into it.'

'Doesn't matter,' she shakes her head, adding pressure to my fingers. 'We are in this together, no matter what.'

The Lost Soul

'You might regret saying that.' I glance across at her and hate myself for causing her such stress.

'No matter what,' she repeats, solemnly.

The car phone comes to life, interrupting our tender moment, and I watch with disappointment as Steph lifts her hand from mine, and presses the answer button on the car.

'Hi Chris, I'm in the car and Jack is with me,' she says, with conviction.

'Hey Jack,' Chris' soft voice comes through the speaker, 'how are things?'

'Good, Chris. Good.' I answer, giving nothing away. 'How is Sasha's mum?'

'She says she feels better, now Stuart and I are here with her. But there are a couple of problems.'

'Of course, there are, 'I mutter quietly, under my breath, 'nothing is ever straight forward.'

'Problems?' Steph's voice deepens. 'What kind of problems?' She looks at me, before shaking her head in annoyance. I can feel my blood pressure rising.

We hear the deep intake of breath along the line and wait patiently for Chris to explain what has happened. 'Benson managed to persuade one of the security guys to allow him to use the bathroom, before we got here.'

'Bloody hell, Chris!' Step says harshly, 'Please tell me, you have Benson in custody.'

The Lost Soul

'No, we don't,' Chris replies harshly, he sounds as frustrated as Steph. 'He managed to get out of a window in the communal bathroom,' Chris admits, 'I've read the officer the riot act, for allowing him to go into the bathroom without checking for exit points. Anyway,' he halts the conversation briefly, 'I've put an alert out for his car and registration number.'

'I want him, Chris,' Steph says quietly. 'I want him to pay for what he's done to Nancy Benson.'

'I know,' Chris comes back, 'and I want him arrested just as much as you. But there's another issue. Steph, I've just had a call from a friend of mine who works at Belmarsh Prison.

'Belmarsh?' I repeat, as something flags up in my mind, causing hairs to stand up on my arms and my heart to thud loudly.

'Chris?' Steph's voice is slightly higher, as she stares at the Sat Nav screen, we're on the M1 driving around Nottingham.

'It's Dave Delossi, he was injured in the arm, by an inmate, allegedly stabbed with a makeshift knife. Twice. They took him to St Mary's, London. And you won't believe this.'

Bugger, and there is it. As the memory clears, I remember Steph telling me that her now deceased, ex-husband's brother, is in Belmarsh.

'No!' she says angrily. 'What the fuck is going on?'

'I know, Steph. I know,' Chris says, frustration, evident in his voice. 'He was in a cubicle waiting to be stitched, apparently his police guards never heard a thing,' Chris explains bluntly.

The Lost Soul

'Was he not handcuffed?' I was about to ask this, but Steph gets in first.

'Yes, they put one on his non-wounded hand, but Delossi had managed somehow to pick the lock. He must have smuggled something out with him, or the cuff hadn't clicked properly.'

The explanation seems so pitiful when you hear it out loud.

'Fuck! Have you got eyes on him?' I ask, a frisson of unease settles in my stomach. How the hell has this happened?

'No, he's gone. No trace,' Chris states flatly.

It's not Chris' fault, he had nothing to do with it, but there is no one else to vent our frustration on.

'Bloody hell,' I mutter.

'Check all his known contacts, places of business, friends, friends of friends, places that he lived, shopped, visited. I want him bloody found, Chris.'

'I'm already on it, Steph. I'll get one of the team to stay with Nancy, while I help co-ordinate trying to find Delossi.'

'Also,' I add, 'check out any prison visitors or officers he's been close to? Particularly, the officers who took him to the hospital.'

'Sure, no problem,' Chris says, 'I wish I had better news, Boss.'

'It's not your fault, Chris. I should be back onsite tomorrow, I'm on my way to visit a friend and her daughter, in Yorkshire, as we speak,' she explains. I am impressed how easily she seems to have her back story up and running. 'I want to know if you hear

251

The Lost Soul

anything on Delossi, Lewis Benson or Sasha's mum. Thanks Chris.'

'You got it, Boss,' Chris replies before disconnecting the call.

'That's very convenient,' I begin, 'Jules is attacked and kidnapped, and Delossi is injured, taken to hospital and manages to escape. He's somewhere out there. Loose.'

'Too convenient, maybe this is Delossi's endgame,' Steph muses. To avenge his brother's death. I never met his brother, the only things I know about him, were from Ray, and all he said was that Dave had spent most of his life in prison.'

She shivers, I know she's going to be worrying, for herself and Ben, but I'm here now and if he comes anywhere near us, he will find himself six feet under.

'I'm afraid, Jack,' Steph says quietly, and adds in a mixture of accusation and plea, 'why can't that family leave us alone?'

I look across at her profile, see a stray tear threatening to drop on to her nearside cheek, and wish that Dave Delossi had been involved in a fatal stabbing, like his father before him, and not given the chance of going to the hospital.

But wishes aren't reality, reality is helping this beautiful woman, my bride to be, to move on with her life.

'I know, babe,' I reach out to stroke the soft skin of her cheek with my knuckles. 'But if it's any consolation, he's not coming for you, he's coming for Jules Walker.'

The Lost Soul

It sounds lame, even as I say the words, it's the Delossi name that she is struggling with. She has suffered enough at the hands of Ray Delossi. She needs to be able to sleep at nights without the nightmares of a knife piercing her skin, or a hard fist punching her stomach.

I have never suffered brutality at the hands of another, but I can imagine the suffering. When I see survivors like Steph, with her physical and psychological pain, the scars on her body that some days she wears like a warrior, and other days like a victim. Steph is the first person to tell herself to move on and live life the best way she can, but not everyone can do that. And there are triggers, such as the abuser's brother escaping from prison, which can bring all the panic and fear rushing back, like a tornado.

'It doesn't really help, Jack,' she whispers, her hands gripping the wheel and her focus firmly on the road ahead. 'I don't want any reminders of him, nothing, apart from Ben. He is the only good thing that came from my life with Ray.'

The sadness in her voice is almost unbearable, how this woman bears her scars, and terrible memories, is beyond me. One of the reasons I became interested in the Lighthouse charity, was because I wanted to help others, to make a difference.

Working with the charity shows the worst and best of human nature, where committed, genuine people put themselves out and tirelessly work to help others, to help them build a better future. It shows the importance of what we do and that our actions have serious consequences. I'm not exaggerating when I say that I

The Lost Soul

would give my life to spare Steph and Ben what they have been through at the hands of Ray Delossi.

My role now, as I see it my main responsibility, is to spend a lifetime making new memories for Steph and Ben. I want to get them out of the darkness and into the light, where we can bask in the sun together.

As we drive, I catch sight of a services sign. 'Pull into the services,' I tell her.

'What? We haven't time,' she argues, brushing a wisp of hair from her cheek.

'Just pull into the next service station,' I repeat firmly, and feel relieved when she indicates into the left-hand lane and begins to follow the slip road to the services. I focus on the road ahead and say nothing, until she parks the car.

When the car is stationary, I twist towards Steph and depress the buttons on our seat belts, spending a little longer with Steph's until the clasp releases. When we're both free, I open the car door and walk around the bonnet, not stopping until I open the driver door, take her hand, and pull her to stand in front of me.

Cupping her face, I say her name, 'Steph,' and hear my voice is husky with emotion. My hands move to her shoulders softly and with reverence, as though she is a cherished jewel, 'I love you. I love Ben. I promise, I won't let anything happen to either of you.'

Her blue eyes hold mine, glistening. She leans in until her lips are touching mine and I am lost in her touch, with my hands exploring the softness of her pink cardigan to rest on her lower

The Lost Soul

back. Our mouths move in unison, not with passion, but with a need to connect and comfort.

I roll my tongue against hers and hear her moan of satisfaction. For a while, we stand with our mouths connected, drawing strength from one another. I want to link us to the here and now, because this woman means everything to me, and I need her to know that. Eventually, she relaxes, and we pull away, the only part of us still touching are our joined hands and our foreheads.

'Thank you, I needed that,' she smiles.

'So, we know that there is going to be a meet,' Steph says, deep in thought, 'but we don't know where, and we don't know when.'

'Yeah, that about sums it up,' I mutter. 'Do you want a coffee or something to eat, or are you happy to carry on?'

'I'm fine for food and drink, but I might use the Ladies room quickly,' she says, grabbing her bag from the car. 'I'll be back soon,' she calls rushing off towards the entrance.

Shaking my head, I return to the passenger seat and take my laptop from the rear passenger area, before returning to my seat. I boot it up and follow Jules' phone tracker. The curser shows he's moving in a straight line on the A629, getting closer to Stocksbridge, making his way to Sheffield.

All the time, I'm wondering if the car that Jules is travelling in will stop at some point. And, if it does, will he be able to get out? I pull out my phone and look at the screen. Nothing. We will be in real trouble if we can't get to Jules Walker before Dave Delossi does. Because, if he's anything like his brother, all hell will break loose.

Part 26: Jules

I hold the cold glass front of my phone to my ear and listen to the ringing tone, waiting for it to connect. Come on, pick up, pick up. I need to speak to you. I mutter quietly, trying to will the phone to connect at the other end. Somewhere in the back of my mind, I hope no one answers, but I need to do this, need to tell them that I'm ok, even though, deep down, I know I'm not.

Raking long fingers through my cropped hair, is just another reminder that things are not the same now. That I am not the same.

A clicking sound comes on the line, and a man's familiar, deep northern twang answers, 'Hello.'

For a few seconds my mouth won't work, words fail me, and I close my eyes, rubbing my temple. Shit. Just leave it, disconnect the call, and leave things alone.

'Dad?' I whisper, into the silence. 'It's me.' My whole body and mind, turn into that small, unsure child again, the one who wants nothing but warmth and reassurance from his mum and dad.

There is a deep sigh before my dad speaks again, 'Jules, thank goodness. Are you all right?'

The Lost Soul

'Yes, Dad, I'm fine,' I tell him, picking at a piece of fluff on my dark green Tee shirt, and flicking it onto the floor.

'How are things with you and Mum?' It feels awkward asking, because I know deep down, that there's something he desperately wants to know. He wants to know if I killed Ray Delossi.

'A bit better,' he says in a flat tone, 'we keep going, you know.'

'I know,' I agree, taking a seat on the blue sofa in my new apartment.

'Did you do it son? Did you kill that man?'

Strangely, the first thing I notice, is that he can't say Delossi's name. How to answer such a question. I can't take it back, once I've admitted what I've done. My index finger makes circular marks on my black jeans, and for some reason, I find the pattern comforting.

Still, I can't pretend that it didn't happen, either. My parents are going to be so disappointed in me.

'Where's Mum?' I try diverting the topic.

'Son?' he admonishes, his voice becoming stern. 'Son, did you? Kill him?'

Taking a deep breath, I answer him slowly so that he can process my actions. 'Yes.'

'Oh lad, what a mess,' his voice sounds flat.

The Lost Soul

'I know, I know,' tears blur my eyes. 'I came across him in Oxford, then followed him home…the rest you already know. I'm sorry, Dad,' I sob, 'sorry for making things worse.'

My Dad has always been my hero, but he became withdrawn following the death of my sister. It took him and my mum a long time to come to terms with what had happened to my sister. The dark days following her death, we each walked our own path of grief and misery, trying to reason why Blip would take her own life, knowing how much it would hurt us.

But experiencing traumatic events, such as a physical attack, doesn't allow you to put things into perspective, it swallows you whole and consumes you, so you can't see anything but the struggle to get through each day. Finally, I understand why Blip did what she did.

From a young age, my dad taught me the difference between right and wrong. But look where that had got me? Doing what was wrong, but for the right reasons.

'Oh Son, you didn't… make things worse, you made things better,' Dad has a strength to his voice, that I hadn't heard in a long time.

'Better?' I query.

'Yes, better. Your Mum and I can sleep at night now, knowing he no longer draws breath, that he can't hurt anyone else.' He stops for a moment, so that I can fully understand what he is saying.

'I don't understand,' I was not expecting this.

The Lost Soul

'Son, the papers said he had hurt his ex-wife and a string of other people, including the young woman they originally arrested.'

'Yes, he did,' I agree, 'But I thought you and Mum would be mad at me.'

'We are grateful Son, grateful that the person who hurt Blip, is no longer alive. But we are sad,' his voice is husky, 'sad, that we can't be there for you.'

I sob quietly. My dad is grateful that I killed a man. How can he be? But I can't help but feel surprised and comforted by his words.

This is more than I can take.

***

The sudden movement of the car jerks me to reality, and I find myself propelled forwards into the dark abyss. The dream of my conversation with my dad two weeks ago, is quickly forgotten as the searing pain in my head, is a stark reminder that I have a head wound and that it needs attention. Pushing the nagging pain to the far recess of my mind, I begin to focus on making my escape.

The car begins to slow down, and I try to contain my excitement, and stay calm. I need to wait for the right moment, and then hopefully I can get out of this hell. My gaze falls on the illuminated boot release button, and stays there, until my eyes blur. Not too long now.

We turn right and then left, before coming to a stop. I hear the passenger door open, and footsteps walk around the car, before the petrol cap opens, and I hear the sound of liquid coursing

The Lost Soul

through the pipes of the car. All goes quiet before the cap is secured back into place and the person's footsteps fade into the distance.

This is my chance. I move closer to the boot release latch and grab the cold plastic lever. Pulling hard, one, two three, pull. It doesn't budge. Bugger. I wince as the throbbing at my temple increases. I pull harder. Come on, you fucker. Open.

In the distance, a siren wails and I pause for a moment, before bracing both feet against the roof of the car, as my fingers pulled the lever. Bugger. Bugger. Why the hell is it not opening? In my frustration I kick at the hard metal, ignoring the pain that shoots through my legs in a kaleidoscope of painful colours. Gritting my teeth, to stop me from moaning, I kick a few more times until my ankles are sore and throbbing.

'Life is full of misery, loneliness and suffering – and it's all over much too soon,' Woody Allen once famously quoted, and I can't help but mull his words over in my head. Misery and frustration envelopes me like a heavy cloak, as the unmistakable thud of heavy footsteps move closer to the car. The click of the door release system, the slight shake as the driver side door is pulled open, confirms that my attacker and kidnapper is back.

As I lie here wearing my cloak of despair, the heaviness sitting in the pit of my stomach, matches the heavy dip of the man, as he drops into his seat. The engine is switched on and I take my silent phone, from my trouser pocket, and text Jack.

'We stopped. Couldn't get out. The lever is stuck,' I type and wait as bubbles appear on the screen, he is writing a reply.

The Lost Soul

'We know, we saw on the tracker. Don't worry. He might stop again,' Jack types back. He's trying to reassure me. Maybe he can hear the despair in my words.

'Where the hell is he taking me?' my fingers fly over the letters.

'I don't know, but we'll get closer to you in a little while. We'll find a way to get you out.'

I'm not usually a pessimist, but this idea is the most ludicrous idea I have ever heard. I don't believe for a second that they will be able to find me. What happens if the car doesn't stop again? How will Jack and Steph be able to catch up with us? They are coming towards us, in the opposite direction. How will they know to turn? I want to tell them these things, but I don't want to waste my battery life, arguing the point.

'Ok,' I finally type, 'but I'm running out of steam here.'

'We know,' Jack answers, adding a sad face and a muscled arm, 'hang in there.'

My phone flashes, and I remember that there is voice message from Sasha, so I press 1571 and listen.

'Nick, it's me. Sasha. Where are you? Call me back, I'm worried about you.' Her soft tones soothe my fractious mind, and I replay the message, just to hear her voice again.

When I get back, if I get back, I am going to make the most of my time with Sasha and Zoe. I don't know how long I'll have at Greystones before I have to move on. It is only a matter of time

The Lost Soul

before someone recognises me or finds out my secret and then I'll need to go on the run.

At some point I want a new life, one where I don't have to look over my shoulder every five minutes, one where I can start to think of making roots, having a job, a family, maybe even children. A sudden vision comes to mind of Sasha wearing a green sun dress, Zoe in a pink dress, carrying a bunny, and walking towards me, smiling and happy on a lovely sunny afternoon.

It doesn't hurt to dream. Maybe one day.

Looking at the phone in my hand, encased in a red rubber case, I decide to text Sasha.

'Hi Sasha, it's me. I'm all right but I'm locked in the boot of the car. I'll text you when I manage to get out.' I leave a gap, intending to disconnect, but then write solemnly, 'I'm sorry for everything, and I wish I could take it all back.'

I check that the phone is still on silent and push it deep into my trouser pocket.

The car continues its journey, and all I can do is wait and hope that I get another opportunity to escape. I must have fallen sleep because when I open my eyes, my head throbs and both legs are cramped. I wake to the smell of screeching tyres, and a huge plop sound, as one side of the car drops slightly.

Bloody hell, I think we've got a puncture. The car slows, moves to the left and I'm sure we're moving into the slow lane. There's a hollow sound from one of the wheels.

The Lost Soul

'Fuck! Fuck!' the driver shouts, banging the steering wheel hard. 'I haven't got a fucking spare.'

Here's my chance, I think as the distant sound of the signal indicator clicks in the front of the car.

We're stopping.

He calls the recovery truck from the car, before opening the door and walking away. I wait, concentrating hard, until I can no longer hear his footsteps.

Right. Let's get out of this bugger.

I flex my hands, my ankles and I tense the muscles in my legs. Grabbing the boot release handle with both hands and taking a deep breath. One. Two. Three. I force the biggest push through my legs and ankles and pull with everything I have.

To my surprise the boot door lifts. 'Gotcha, you bastard,' I whisper to the door with a grim smile. I use my legs to push it wide enough for me to heave myself over the lip and onto the hard concrete floor.

Bloody hell! I did it! I check my phone is still on me, quietly push the boot shut and keep low. My legs and ankles are sore and cramped after being bent for so long, but I push through that and focus on hiding between the cars, moving as far away from the Geordie and his vehicle as possible.

Stooping as low as possible, I make my way across to a group of buildings. I look at the signage to find out where I am, Jesus! I'm at the Welcome Break, Keele, Southbound. Quickly assessing the area I'm in, I see a Starbucks drive-thru, with an exit road nearby,

The Lost Soul

which is flanked by a woodland of tall, bushy trees, ideal for someone trying to take cover and hide.

Casually, I slip my hands in my pockets and walk towards the drive-thru, my heart is beating fast, and I expect someone to grab my arm, or at the very least, to call in a thick Geordie accent. But there is nothing. I keep walking. Keep my head down. Checking the road carefully and keeping my pace. I keep walking, until I reach the trees and disappear from sight.

I keep walking for about fifty yards, stumbling occasionally over fallen branches, and thick undergrowth, as I push through the trees.

Finally, when I think I'm safe, I take out my phone and call Jack.

The Lost Soul

Part 27: Sasha

I put the phone down, after speaking to Jack, and immediately burst into tears.

'Mummy?' Zoe looks across at me from her seat at the dining table, where she sits with her colouring pens colouring in a picture of Pinkie Pie in her My Little Pony magazine. Her face is full of worry. 'What's wrong?'

Wiping away tears of relief with my hands, 'I'm fine honey,' I reassure her. I open my arms and lean in to reassure her with a hug. I take a seat and look fondly at my beautiful daughter, Zoe is wearing her favourite pink dress, the one with white spots, her legs and feet are bare. It's 6pm. We had our dinner thirty minutes ago, one of our favourites, home-made cottage pie with broccoli and hidden cauliflower in the mash.

Zoe is going to be five in six days, and I am so excited for her. Even though the world around me seems to be falling apart, I have Zoe. Despite my dad threatening me, or my mum being in hospital or the kidnapping of someone I care about, Zoe is always here. Always my one constant.

The Lost Soul

There's a fumbling at the door lock to the apartment, and footsteps rush through the hall. My heart almost beats through my chest. Is it Nick? Did he escape?

'It's only me,' Viola shouts, as she rushes, with purpose, into the living room, wearing a navy woollen coat, with a wine-coloured long skirt swooping out from under it. In her hand is her favourite large, cane handled, circle-shaped brown handbag. With dark hair, which falls elegantly into a long, sleek bob, allowing its delicate tips to frame her slender, neck.

Zoe's eyes light up when she sees Vi, and smiling brightly, she rushes over to give Vi a hug.

'Hello, angel,' Vi's endearment is soft, she bends to scoop Zoe into a big hug. The bond between the nanny and her charge, is very strong and I wouldn't want it any other way. As I've said before, it was a blessing the day Viola became part of our lives.

Viola looks over at me. 'Thought I'd pop in to see how you are holding up,' she says, disentangling herself from Zoe's grasp, and dropping her handbag onto the dining table. I watch Vi with affection, she is strong, passionate about things she cares about and full of life.

I sniffle and force a smile on my face. 'I'm okay,' my voice sounds flat. Who am I kidding? I'm not bloody okay.

My friend looks at me, her face is serious and there is concern in her eyes, she can see straight through my bravado and shakes her head. Unapologetically, she looks me up and down, before stating, 'you're not okay, are you? I mean your eyes are all red and…'

'Vi…' I direct my glance to Zoe. 'Enough, I'm fine,' I tell her, standing and watching my beautiful daughter take Vi's hand and lead her to the large dark brown, velvet sofa.

'So, angel,' Vi snuggles into the sofa and loosely puts her arm around my daughter, threading her fingers through her long curly hair. 'Have you decided what you would like for your birthday?'

'I'll pop the kettle on, coffee?' I ask her, listening to their banter.

'Please,' Vi's voice trails into the kitchen.

'Well,' Zoe's face lights up with excitement, she quickly shuffles to her knees until she's close to Vi's face, 'I want a pram for my Baby Annabell. A pink one to match my room.' Vi smiles, and Zoe catches a twirl of Vi's hair in her small fingers.

I walk behind the sofa, lean over and put my arms loosely around Zoe's neck, I love this child so much. My hands gently pull her face upwards, and I lean in to kiss her forehead. 'That's quite a big request, Zoe. Let's see what happens on the day.'

Zoe reaches up and catches my face in her hands, 'Yes! I'm going to get a pram. I'm going to get a pram!' she screeches into my face.

'Calm down, Zoe,' Vi laughs, patting the little girl's arm, 'you'll internally combust, if you carry on.'

The Lost Soul

I laugh, thankful to not be thinking about Nick for the moment. Zoe removes her hands from my face, and looks at her nanny, 'what does interly comvust mean?'

Laughing, I make my way around the brown sofa and stop in front of my daughter, 'Well,' I begin, tapping her gently on the nose, and looking to Vi, before answering softly.

'It's just something people say, when someone becomes very excited.'

'Oh, okay,' she's already forgotten what we are talking about. 'Mummy, can I have one more thing, for my birthday?' she asks, her big brown eyes pleading with mine.

'We will see, darling!' I ask, 'what is it you want?' Ready to make mental adjustments to her birthday gifts.

Zoe smiles, her cheeks are rose pink with excitement and anticipation, and by the look of concentration on her face and the way her small eyebrows furrow, it suggests that there is a cauldron of brainstorming going on inside that head of hers:

'Can I have a husband? One like Keiron, but different,' she says sweetly, her smile disappearing for a moment.

Vi and I look at each other and try hard not to laugh, but we can't help the smiles that form on our faces. My daughter is such a character, and typical of many young children, the things she says as she makes sense of the world, force to me giggle out loud.

The Lost Soul

'Husbands can be very hard to find,' Vi half laughs, hugging Zoe's little body with delight. 'I know, I've tried, but I will definitely look out for one for you, angel.'

'Can you ask Nick if he can find me one?' Zoe asks earnestly, sitting up, she grabs my large hands in her small ones, her brown eyes pleading with me.

At the mention of Nick's name, reality hits me, and the moment of joyful respite is over, as a sob forms in my throat, and I feel my eyes begin to burn. I feel pathetic, unable to control my own tears, which is not the strong person I have become since leaving home. This just isn't me.

'I will ask him when I see him. He should be back soon, hopefully,' I tell her quietly.

Vi and I exchange glances, hopefully is a word I use more often than I should these days. Vi jumps off the sofa and takes Zoe's hand, 'C'mon Zoe, why don't you show me your magazine.'

My small daughter follows Vi eagerly to the dining table and they both take a seat. 'My Little Pony,' Zoe says proudly, pointing to the magazine. 'I'm counting here. One, two, three,' her little fingers point to the three pony figures, 'this is Pinkie Pie.'

'Can I colour that one in?' Vi asks her, as I head to the kitchen to finish making the hot drinks.

'Applejack? Sure?' she looks at Vi, picking up an orange felt tip pen and handing it to her.

There are moments in my life, when everything seems to fall into place, when I don't have to fight to make it through each day.

271

The Lost Soul

Moments like this, when I know that Zoe is safe and happy, with the easy banter and love that flows freely between the three of us, is something that soothes me and settles me. Zoe and I are so lucky to have Viola in our life.

'Mummy?' Zoe asks, as I place the coffees and a glass of orange squash onto the dining table.

'Yes, sweetheart?' I answer, sitting down near to her.

'Where is my daddy?' she asks, putting down a red felt tip pen.

My heart almost stops and an icy chill seeps through my veins. Unable to move anything, apart from my eyes, I glance at Vi's shocked face, before turning to the questioning face of my young daughter.

I clear my throat and lean in to face her, 'your daddy?' I stroke my fingers through her curly hair, 'do you remember, I told you his name is Dylan and he moved away, a long way away.'

She puts soft little hands either side of my neck. 'He lives far away, so he can't see me?'

Her question brings tears to my eyes.

Throughout my pregnancy I had sent several letters to the address that Dylan had given me. As my tummy grew bigger with Zoe, my hopes of a romantic reunion between her father and myself, dwindled – until my feelings were left in tatters, splintered with bitterness and anger.

***

The Lost Soul

Did you know that there are more than sixty lighthouses dotted around the UK? I know because, I've been googling it. I am sitting crossed legged, my back is pressed against the side of my bed and, and I'm intermittently picking up fluff from my purple carpeted bedroom floor. Alexa is playing Motown classics quietly in the background. Shivering, I pull my thick blue cardigan around my torso, holding it close.

My eyes flit to the white plastic pregnancy test sitting in front of me, next to my phone.

Taking a deep breath, I close my eyes and listen to the music. Diana Ross sings, 'Baby, baby. Where did our love go?'

'Alexa?' I wait for her to answer.

'Volume five.' I tell her and wait for the volume to increase. The sound dulls my senses, distracts me from worrying. Keep calm. Keep calm. Keep... I open my eyes and stare hard at the oblong object.

Two blue lines.

No way.

Fuck.

I'm pregnant.

Bursting into tears, the stark reality of how my life will now change, hits me hard. No college or university. No chance to earn my own money and make my own way in the world. I so desperately wanted to leave home and get away from my father, but now my chances are limited. Dylan and I only had sex a

The Lost Soul

couple of times before he moved away and we had used protection, but clearly, something hadn't worked right.

And now I'm sitting in my bedroom staring at a positive pregnancy test. Which changes everything. I am dreading telling my parents. How will my dad react? Will he kick me out? Will he hurt me?

As the weeks went by and my tummy became bigger, I found it harder to disguise my morning sickness, and eventually, my mum walked into my bedroom, sat down on the bed next me, and asked me the dreaded question.

'Sasha, are you pregnant?' She asks, nervously tucking strands of wavy auburn hair around one ear.

Raising my eyes to meet hers, I give her a weak smile and shrug my shoulders. 'I am so sorry, Mum.'

'Oh Sasha,' she says, pulling me into her arms. I snuggle into her warmth and allow the softness of her pink cashmere jumper to rest against my cheek. Tears fall down my cheeks and I hadn't realised how much worry I had been holding on to, until I hear myself sob. But the quiet sobbing is nothing compared to the turmoil of emotions that are gathering in the pit of my tummy.

Part of me feels as though the world is about to end, that things will never be the same. Guilt pours through me, that I have let myself and my family down. Sitting with my mum on the bed, I can feel her sadness and disappointment. I totally get her - I feel that way myself, who knows how my life would have turned out if I hadn't got pregnant.

274

The Lost Soul

'It'll be all right,' she mutters quietly into my ear.

And, then a strange thing happened. At around four months along, I woke one morning to feel a fluttering kind of movement in my tummy, and I knew that no matter what happened in the future, that my baby would be loved and cherished, always.

The day I told my dad about the baby still makes goosebumps creep along my arms. It was the weekend, and we were eating breakfast at the kitchen table. My tummy had grown rounder and harder, then I felt an odd fluttering, not unlike a small wave struggling on to the shore.

At first, I'd felt queasy, and thought I'd eaten something that hadn't agreed with me. Two minutes later, it happened again. I put down my cereal spoon and lay both hands, gently over my tummy. This time, the fluttering seemed to move across my tummy. Wow! This is real. I smiled to myself, and Mum had looked across the table at me, worry evident in her brown eyes. With a yellow coffee mug in mid-air, our eyes had locked as she asked me a silent question.

I smiled and nodded, and as she placed her coffee cup on the wooden table, I knew that we had done the right thing. To my surprise, Mum got up from her seat, brushed her hands down her navy jersey dress, came over to me and hugged me tight.

'What going on with you two?' My dad asked in a clipped tone, as he slurped his hot tea and folded his newspaper in half, before laying it down on the table. 'You're always in a corner chatting. Obviously, it's not something I'm important enough to be privy too.'

The Lost Soul

Mum stroked my shoulder length curly hair, 'Sasha…' she pushed. I felt my eyes tear up with desperation, this is the moment I've been dreading. Having to tell my abusive father that I am pregnant.

'Dad,' I said quietly, laying my hands on the hard surface of the oak table. I glanced at the half-eaten bowl of Cheerios in their white breakfast bowl, soaking in the honey-coloured cold milk and silently counted to ten, to calm my nerves.

'I'm pregnant,' I said, staring into his cold face. He was a good-looking man in many ways, with an angular face and straight nose, but when he smiled, which wasn't often, it was a real disappointment, because the smile never reached his blue eyes. His dark curly, hair had silver grey sprinkled through to the crown. I wondered for a moment, how long it would be until he went completely grey.

Eyebrows dropped and met in the middle as he processed my words.

'You're what?' his words were low, and far more impactful than an aggressive roar, which sent an icy chill down my spine. And, my first thought was to protect my tummy, protect the baby growing inside me. Quickly, I held my right hand over my small baby bump, as though instead of flesh, the hand was a band of steel that could ward off any demon.

Still, I knew my father, and I knew the storm was coming.

The Lost Soul

His fist hit the table hard, making me jump – crockery and cutlery jumped from their places on the table and banged on to the hard surface on their return. Shit. I'm in trouble.

'You bloody whore!' he pushed out of his seat with such force that the heavy wooden chair, fell backwards with an almighty thud. I left my chair quickly and sought shelter by walking behind it and gripping the back tightly.

'Don't!' was the first word that came from my mouth. 'Don't you dare touch me.'

My mother covered a scream with her hand, her eyes were wide with horror as she stood up and watched the angry scene unfold.

Dad turned to her, 'how the hell did you let this happen?' he ranted, taking a step closer to her, and grabbing her blue linen dress near the neckline. I watched, unable to move, as her arms flailed, trying to push his hand off her dress, and all the time, he was pulling her closer to his red face. The colour of his anger.

'Dad!' I pleaded, 'stop. It's not Mum's fault.'

Briefly he turned to look at me, with lips that turned into a snarl. He was disgusted, I could tell, and he didn't even try to hide it. That was the day that did it for me. Made me realise just what a monster my dad was.

He suddenly let go of mum's dress and I breathed a sigh of relief. Thank God. It was almost over. Then, before I knew what was happening, he swiftly raised his hand and hit her so hard across the face that she stumbled into the yellow curtains that framed the windowsill.

The Lost Soul

'No!' I screamed, rushing to mum, who was holding her hip and keening quietly like a baby.

Dad stormed out of the room, yanking the door open until it slammed into the sideboard.

I held mum tightly in my arms, whispering, 'are you alright? I'm so sorry.'

And, then she said the strangest thing, in a low voice, against my ear. 'Well, that went better than I expected.

***

My phone rings, breaking the almost stifling air of resolution that has befallen us, and I reach into my jeans pocket to retrieve it. I stare in disbelief as Nick's name flashes across the screen.

'Who is it?' Vi asks, quietly, she knows how much I've grown to like Nick. She knows that I am very careful when introducing new people into my family, to Zoe.

I can't answer her, my throat is suddenly dry. I depress the call button to answer the phone. 'Hey,' I sit up and force out the word. It sounds cracked and whispery.

'Hey. It's me.' His familiar, husky voice answers.

Thank God. I look up at the ceiling, offering a silent prayer.

'Nick,' heaving a huge sigh of relief, I rub my thumb and forefinger across my temples. 'How are you?'

'I'm fine,' he answers, quietly, he doesn't sound fine. 'I'm in the car with Jack and Steph. On my way home.'

The Lost Soul

The word 'home' warms me, and every essence of worry I've been holding within me, as I waited for news of him, starts to ease. I feel settled.

'I'm glad you're okay. I'll see you soon,' I tell him, my voice is husky with emotion.

'Yes,' comes his reply. 'Oh, and Sasha?'

'Yes?' I answer breathlessly, absently making finger zig zag shapes on the arm of the sofa.

His voice is low, almost a strangled whisper, as the words, 'I love you,' echo down the line. Then he disconnects the call, and my heart skips a beat. I cannot believe he's just told me that.

Slumping back in the dining chair, I can't help the smile that spreads across my face.

Vi takes a sip of coffee, holds the mug to her lips and waits.

'Well?' She asks, her eyes peeping over the top of the mug.

'He's on his way home,' I answer brightly, reaching out to stroke Zoe's hair.

Zoe holds the colouring pen still between her small fingers and looks up at me. 'Who's on his way home?'

'Nick,' I smile, 'he went to visit someone and now he's on his way back.'

Vi moves from her chair and wraps me in her arms, a well of emotion brings a lump to my throat.

'I'm so pleased for you,' Vi says quietly.

The Lost Soul

Zoe joins in, 'yippee, Nick's coming home!'

The Lost Soul

Part 28: Anthony

'Hi, what can I get for you?' An eager female voice asks from behind the serving counter.

I scan the menu, I'm holding in my hand, once more. 'A lounge burger, with cheese, and a bottle of Peroni please,' I tell her, waiting for her to put it through the till. I pay with my phone, holding it carefully over the card machine until I hear a faint ping. The joy of a cash free society.

Following my visit with grandad in Haworth this morning, I'd headed straight back home – determined to return to Oxfordshire at the earliest opportunity. Despite my best intentions, the car had run low on diesel, needing a top up, plus I needed a toilet break, so I had made a quick stop just outside Wolverhampton. The stress of the past few weeks, owing money to Delossi, and asking Grandad for money, is disappearing from my shoulders, and I roll my neck slowly from side to side easing it. My fingers fly over the access codes to my phone, and I quickly scan my emails. Nothing from Lewis Benson.

If I'd known that it would feel this good to clear the air with grandad, I would have done it much earlier, and I curse myself for not being honest with him right from the start. Making decisions that ultimately changed how I reacted and responded to family,

The Lost Soul

didn't work out for me. I believed that I could pick up a relationship with my grandad, as and when I wanted. Mainly when I wanted something from him. Clearly, it shouldn't be that way. And, thankfully, there are fault on both sides. My grandad was an academic, with social skills that would make a grown man cry. He was hard, unapologetic and had spent most of his life teaching in Oxford. He had made me feel as though I wasn't good enough, when my parents and I visited him at the weekends. Unfortunately, he became withdrawn following my dad's death, and we grew apart.

But now, I find that I want to be the bigger person and reach out to him. I want to build trust between us, so that we have something solid to start from. After all, he and I are all that are left of our family.

I was starving by the time I came off the A34, ad I decided to visit one of my favourite eating places, a bistro bar in the Orchard Centre, Didcot.

'Thanks,' the dark-haired woman replies, and I catch a wave of blue sweeping through her hair. It looks good. Taking my Peroni, I make my way back to my table and sit down. Taking a sip of the cool lager, I savour the liquid and close my eyes for a moment. What I wouldn't give for a line of snow right now. Something to just take the edge off everything that is wrong with my life.

But after talking to grandad, I know I have to change. I need to straighten myself out, sort my priorities and start taking the blame for things that happen, instead of blaming others. If I can become less dependent on the snow, it will be a huge step forward. I can

The Lost Soul

start to get my finances under control, which will give me a chance to think about building a future.

A picture comes into my head; a pretty, blonde-haired woman smiling, carefully holding a baby, wrapped in a white blanket, with me standing beside her, my arm around her shoulders. Protecting them both. Grandad sits in a nearby chair, chatting away as the woman gently moves away from me and walks across to Grandad. His delight as she gently hands him the baby.

The future. A wife. A child. Family.

The food arrives and after my good deed of calling Greystones to warn Jules Walker, my upbeat mood continues. I bite into the burger with a hunger I haven't felt for a while. My phone says it's 6pm. Where has the day gone? Mostly driving to and from Haworth, I suspect. It's a long and tiring journey and it doesn't get any easier, however many times I do it.

A vision of a brown and white four-legged creature, my new cat Oscar comes to mind, and I realise that I need to go home to feed him.

I had no idea, what was waiting for me at home. If I had known, I would have run in the opposite direction, as fast as I could.

Twenty minutes later, I park the car in the drive and take the house key from my wallet. As soon as I turn the key into the lock and push the door open, I know something is wrong. Hairs stand up on my arms and my heart begins to pound. There is movement in the house. I look around for a weapon. There is nothing apart from the hall lamp and my car keys.

283

The Lost Soul

A figure walks towards me from the kitchen, he's wearing my clothes, the scent of my own shower gel lingers in the air, and, as he stands in front of me, the second thing I notice, is that he's holding my cat.

Dave Delossi.

Shit.

I'm in trouble.

'I've been waiting for you, thought you'd never come home,' he says in a dramatic voice, stroking the cat. He had better not hurt him. 'I've made pasta.'

'I've eaten,' I tell him in a wary tone, I don't want him to see how afraid I am. So, I stand to my full height and push my shoulders back, trying to appear taller, more confident. I walk to my cat, smile and stroke him.

'Hello Oscar, sorry I'm a bit late.'

The jagged scar across Dave Delossi's face reminds me that this man is trouble, with a capital T. Bloody hell, panic sets in when I remember that this man, standing in front of me, is capable of many things, including murder. The stringy hair has been brushed back and he's wearing my jeans and blue zipper hoodie, zipped to the middle where I can see that he's also wearing one of my favourite grey T-shirts. I note a largish stain on the forearm of my hoodie. Bloody hell, is he bleeding?

I knew from the first moment I met Dave Delossi that he was as unstable as a dinosaur balancing on eggshells. He has several personality traits, unpleasant traits – from violent and

284

unpredictable to manipulative and threatening. He was simply a ticking time bomb, waiting to explode.

And now, he is in my house, cooking pasta and holding my cat.

'What the hell are you doing here?' I ask him quietly.

'Don't stress, or you'll worry the cat. What do you feed him on, anyway? He's like, really thin.' he says as his fingers grasp the short brown fur at the back of Oscar's neck, yanking his head up. The cat growls.

'Hey! Be careful with him,' I say, in defence. Who the hell is he to question me? He's just trying to provoke me, and although I try not to rise to his accusations, I find myself muttering, 'I've not had him long, the vet said to build his food intake up gradually.'

A wave of displeasure passes across Delossi's face as he holds Oscar aloft and looks him in the eyes, for a long moment, before shaking his head. Suddenly the cat is thrown to the floor with such venom, as if he'd grown devil horns.

'I fucking hate cats,' he hisses, making the long red scar across his face become more transparent.

Oscar lands with a soft thud on to the hardwood floor, thankfully landing on his feet, and misses Delossi's outstretched boot by a fraction of a second, as he retreats upstairs, to my bed. *Good boy. You stay up there, away from this cruel, deranged man.* I say, silently.

The Lost Soul

'I'm sure I've got room for pasta,' I say, walking past him, into the kitchen. If I keep calm, I might be able to leave this house in one piece. 'Smells good.'

Delossi follows me into the kitchen.

'Sit,' the deranged man orders and I drag a chair from the small kitchen table and watch his movements carefully. 'It's been years since I've cooked anything.'

Looking around, I see shattered glass sprinkled across the floor and jagged parts of the glass jut out from the upper part of back door. He must have smashed the glass panel, to enter before reaching inside to twist the key and unlock it.

Bloody hell. I am all sorts of a fool for leaving the bloody key sitting in the lock, I should be more careful. I must be mindful of making it too easy for someone to break into my house. Although, if that someone is Dave Delossi, determined, brutal and violent – then he would have found another way to get into my house.

He drains the pasta, using the lid and returns it to the pan, before adding a knob of butter and giving it a stir. I wonder when he learned to cook like this. There can't be much opportunity to cook in prison. Maybe, he works in the kitchen and likes to experiment.

Delossi picks up a handful of cooked chicken and scatters it through the cooked pasta in the saucepan, before taking a dessert spoon from the kitchen drawer, dipping it into tomato pesto and coating the pasta and chicken.

I'm impressed with how quickly Delossi has managed to familiarise himself with the food in my fridge, and cupboards and

The Lost Soul

utensils in my kitchen. He seems at home, amidst the mayhem of utensils and cooked food. What I am not impressed about, is how he got into the house.

'Have you got beer?' he asks, pouring the pasta mixture into bowls, collecting two forks from the drawer and placing them on the table. I walk to the fridge, pull the heavy door open and reach across to the wine rack and take out two cold bottles of Corona, kick the door shut with my foot and delve into a drawer for the bottle opener. A quick flick of the opener against the metal tops, and I take them to the table to resume my seat. Delossi is already chomping noisily through his pasta.

Careful to stay sober, I take a long gulp, rather than drinking the lot in one go.

'I hated my brother, he was a right knob,' he announces in between mouthfuls of pasta that can be seen through his open mouth and the red pesto that coats his thin lips The sight makes my stomach roll and I have to put my hand over my mouth, to stop the threatening bile, from exploding from my throat. *Close your mouth when you're eating, you bastard,* I mutter under my breath.

'You say something?' He looks at me, and I cringe because I realise that I have said the words out loud.

'You weren't close, then?' I ask, using the fork to push the chicken and pasta around the bowl.

The Lost Soul

'No, but that's irrelevant, he was still my brother,' he mutters, stuffing the fusilli pasta into a big heap on his spoon and shovelling it into his mouth.

When I can take the suspense no longer, I finally ask him the question that has been niggling at me since I got home. 'What's going on Dave?' I study his face, watching the feeding frenzy that illuminates his pale skin. I know that behind his actions, is a man with a devious mind.

'Little Tim,' he replies in between mouthfuls of pasta, 'he's been out and about today.'

My heart skips a beat. 'Out and about?' I repeat, spearing a piece of chicken from the pasta bowl and pushing it into my mouth. Bugger. Don't say anything. I warn myself. Don't say a bloody thing.

'Yeah,' he says, suddenly looking across at me, with stone cold brown eyes. 'He had a little drive up to Yorkshire.'

Fingers wrapped around my fork, stop in mid-air on their way to the pasta.

Shit. Keep it together, hold your nerve. But I can feel, deep in my bones, that he knew where I had been earlier today. Hold your bloody nerve.

'Actually, he followed you to the residential home.' Hell of course, he followed me. Now, I know I am in trouble.

'Why would he do that?' the fork clatters on the table as I put it down.

The Lost Soul

'The question is, why didn't you call me to say you'd seen Jules Walker?' he asks, resting his elbows on the table and looking directly at me. I hold his stony gaze, didn't want to give him the satisfaction of forcing me to look away, before my eyes rest on the back of his hand. There is bruising and some scratch marks, which lead to the blue sleeve of my hoodie, near the mark I noticed earlier.

This is a surreal situation. How the hell did this man escape from prison and know where I live? I'm done for, if he finds out I knew the man he'd asked me to look for, was in Yorkshire.

'I didn't see Jules Walkers,' I shake my head vigorously.

He slams his spoon in the bowl, brushes a hand through thin, greasy hair and I catch sight of a bloody wound on his hand. Something happened to this man, and now he's here, so I have to deal with him.

'Don't lie to me. Little Tim recognised him straight away,' he snaps.

'I'm not bloody lying, I told you I didn't see him,' I challenge his accusation, it's all I can do right now, feign ignorance and stick to my story.

'I don't believe you,' he says, picking up his fork and taking more pasta into his mouth. I take this as a good sign. If he was going to hurt me, he would have done it by now.

Reaching for my Corona, I take a gulp of the cold liquid, thinking of ways to keep calm. I decide the best approach is to appear

The Lost Soul

disinterested, with an air of confidence. 'You don't have to believe me, but it's the truth. I never saw Jules bloody Walker.'

I watch Delossi finish his pasta, noisily eating each mouthful as if it was his last meal. The sound of his chewing echoes through the kitchen, and his open mouth gives me a clear view of the mulched food. Revulsion hit me as he wipes the sleeve of my hoodie across his face. God, I'll never get rid of the vision of him doing that. I wait while he takes a drink.

'Doesn't matter. Little Tim sorted it,' he tells me, studying my face.

Bloody hell, what has he done?

'Sorted it out,' I repeat, 'what do you mean, sorted it out?' I sit back and stare at him. 'What's he done?' I tap my fingers on the table, trying to calm my mind. What the fuck is going on? What has Delossi done?

An unfamiliar ringtone fills the air, and he shuffles in his seat and takes a mobile out of my, now his, jeans' hip pocket.

'Where the fuck are you?' he snaps, looking at me. I stare back, trying to read his expressions, to work out who he is talking to. Little Tim?

'See you in twenty minutes,' Delossi disconnects the call and pushes out of the chair, the mobile still in his hand, and stands up. 'I need a piss,' he states, before leaving the room.

At the silence, I pick up the Corona bottle and take a long drink of the cold, bitter liquid. My phone vibrates in my back pocket, and I

The Lost Soul

quickly reach for it. It's from DCI Steph Rutland. I glance at the open doorway and bring the text up.

'Dave Delossi has escaped. Be careful and let me know if you hear anything.'

Escaped! Don't I bloody know it?

The flush of the toilet alerts me. Fuck. Why can't life be simple? I type quickly:

'He's here at my house,' check it's still in silent mode, before sending it, and return it to my pocket.

'So?' I ask, staring at the bread bin, where I keep some of my snow. What I wouldn't give right now, for a line. Just to take the edge off. But I made a promise today to make a new start, without the drugs. Obviously, that was before this madman forced his way into my home.

'So,' Delossi gives me a big smile. 'It's time for payback. They will be here in twenty minutes.'

Fuck.

Part 29: Zoe

I'm pretending to be asleep. It's hard, so I've got my eyes closed really tight. I can hear mummy and Vi talking in the background. Mummy was crying because she was worried about Nick, but I knew he'd come back. This is his home.

I feel excited and am going to make him some toast in the morning. I'm not allowed to use the toaster because I'm too little, but I'm going to use my brown pen to draw on the bread to make it look like it's been in the toaster. Sapphire says I should eat toast for breakfast, because she does, and her mummy says it will make her hair curly if she eats the crusts! I don't like the crusts and my hair is already curly.

Snuggling under the pink duvet with me, is my dolly, Baby Annabell. She likes pink too. I had her for my birthday last year. She is the best dolly in the whole wide world, and she reminds me of my mummy because she has dark curly hair and a pretty face.

I love mummy so much, and it hurts me when she cries. She must really like Nick, which means that she might marry him. If she does, I'm going to be a bridesmaid. Maybe I can be a princess.

Does that mean he'll be my new daddy?

The Lost Soul

Pulling the pink duvet around my ears, I let myself dream of wedding dresses and pink bridesmaid dresses. Happy things.

Because I want a daddy who will love me enough to live here with me and mummy.

Forever and ever.

Part 30: Jules

Life is different now.

It is strange how a serious event can change your outlook on the way you live. Before the attack, I was beginning to fall hard for Sasha, which is something I would never have predicted happening, even if I'd been to a fortune teller in a previous life. I thought my life was meant to be an atonement of sorts, for my sins, for murdering Ray Delossi. I thought that all I deserved was a solitary, half-living kind of existence.

But now, I'm beginning to feel as though there may be another road that I'm destined to take. One filled with hope and love and everything in between.

I can't explain it. It just feels different. I feel different. My heart beats faster and I feel heat in my groin when I'm with her. I also get an urge to touch and kiss her. A lot.

I feel alive.

I feel reborn.

For the first time in my life, I feel that my future could be bright. I would love to keep exploring my relationship with Sasha, and Zoe, I would love to marry her one day, and I love the possibility of having children, of being a father.

The Lost Soul

I am a new man, with dreams and hopes, and thoughts of a future.

Let this feeling never leave me, because I don't ever want to go back to the old Jules.

The Lost Soul

Part 31: Anthony

The clashing of the dishes, as I put them into the dishwasher, stops me from checking my watch. Twenty minutes goes annoyingly slow when you're waiting for each minute to pass. Rinsing the cutlery under the hot water, I throw it into the cutlery divider stopping briefly as Delossi's phone comes to life.

He sits casually, with his arm draped over the back of a chair, drinking his way through a second bottle of Corona, he picks up the phone and looks at it.

'They're here,' he says, finishing off the bottle and leaving it on the table. Pushing out of the chair, he looks at me, 'come on, let's go and check out the new arrival.'

I rinse my hands and dry them on a nearby tea towel before I reluctantly follow him to the front door. Oscar appears from nowhere and sweeps around my ankles. For heaven's sake, you need to be upstairs, out of sight. I can't be worrying about you, my furry friend, there are things I need to attend to, one being to get rid of this dangerous unwanted visitor in my home, and two, to somehow rescue the man, who I think has been kidnapped and brought here to die.

There is a dark BMW parked next to my car on the driveway. I watch in horror as Little Tim, wearing jeans and a sweatshirt that look as though they've never seen a washing machine, hauls himself from the car and stands in front of the boot.

'Well done! I knew I could rely on you,' Delossi reaches the car, patting the large man on the back. Delossi looks antsy, as if on edge. I stay quiet, assessing the situation. Looking around, I check to see if any of my neighbours are about, nope. All quiet. Thank goodness.

Loitering around the back of the car, I watch in silence as Little Tim reaches down to release the boot. 'Don't know what state he'll be in. He's been in there for a few hours.'

I'm holding my breath and think my heart is about to explode, as the boot slowly opens. I fully expect to see Jules Walker's bloody and trussed up body, possibly unconscious or worse, in the confined airless space.

Does anyone know he's been kidnapped? Are there people looking for him? How can I help him? How long before the police arrive? It can't be long now.

I put my hands on my hips, trying to ignore the guilt that lies heavy on my shoulders because, without meaning to, I had led Little Tim straight to Walker. If the henchman hadn't been following me. If I hadn't been to see my grandad. If I hadn't got into money trouble. So many ifs.

It's only now I realise that I need to take responsibility for the things I do, for things that go wrong in my life. It's been a long time coming but wanting to be a better person doesn't come easily or quickly. I look in the open boot.

The Lost Soul

'What the fuck! Is this some kind of joke?' Delossi says harshly, as we stare into the empty boot. He looks furiously at Little Tim.

'Shit! He was in there. I swear he was!' Little Tim's eyes focus on the space in the car where Jules Walker is supposed to be, the colour disappearing from his face. I slowly exhale, silently thanking God that the kidnappee has somehow managed to escape.

'Right, both of you,' Delossi snarls, 'in the fucking house now!' Little Tim closes the boot and locks the car.

How on earth did Jules Walker get out of that boot?

Little Tim must have stopped for a break on route, how else would there be an opportunity to break the lock and climb out of the boot? On one hand, I'm thoroughly relieved that Jules was able to escape, but on the other hand, I'm frustrated that this nightmare may never end.

There's no way that Delossi is going to leave my house now, and there's a feeling in the pit of my stomach that tells me that things are about to become very heated. Someone will have to pay.

How the hell can I walk into my home, knowing that I'm possibly signing my own death warrant, or being a witness to murder? I rub my forehead. This cannot be happening.

There's movement in my peripheral vision. Along the road, the other side of my two-foot green shrubbery, a dark blue van pulls up. Swiftly and in total silence, a group of people dressed in black police vests, some carrying firearms and others holding batons, begin leaping from the doors.

The Lost Soul

A tall man stands at the front of group with floppy dark-blond hair, wearing navy trousers, a white shirt and a police stab vest, he puts a finger to his lips, telling me to be quiet. I nod. Little Tim reaches the front door first and turns to face Delossi. He takes in the scene beyond his boss, as it unfolds, the police officers approaching, the shuffling of feet, and in that moment, Little Tim stands still, open mouthed, as if he can't believe what is happening. Then he says loudly, 'Holy Shit!

There's a sound, and Delossi looks over his shoulder, before pushing past me at speed, leaps over the small shrubs enclosing the front garden, and out onto the road, like an Olympic sprinter, about to get his first gold medal.

The tall man shouts, 'Delossi. Thames Valley Police. Stop.'

Bloody hell! It's like something out of a police crime drama, and if that isn't bad enough, if my stomach, full of pasta and burger, is now threatening to leave my stomach. I swallow deeply, forcing the food to settle, before I slowly put my hands up and behind my head.

Officers follow at speed, forcing me to step into the rambling rose near the front door. Recovering, I slowly walk to the driveway, I need to see what is happening further down the road, I take my hands from my head, stand by the car and watch in awe as officers give chase to Delossi along the road.

Police sirens emerge from the end of the street, a car comes to a standstill in the middle of the road in front of him, officers jump out of the car. There are police on both sides of him now,

The Lost Soul

cornered and with nowhere to go, he has no choice but to give himself up.

'Get the fuck off me,' Delossi snarls, as officers cuff him and bring him back to the officer with dark blonde hair, who seems to be in charge.

The tall officer strolls up to Delossi, and stares at him. 'Dave Delossi, I am DS Jackson. I am re-arresting you following your escape from St Mary's Hospital, whilst being detained at Her Majesty's Prison, Belmarsh. following an attack at the prison earlier today. In addition, I am charging you with breaking and entering and for intimidating a member of the public. Justine, read him his rights.'

DS Jackson walks away, leaving a pretty young woman, who is dressed in black jeans and a dark grey blouse, with a stab vest and short pixie-style haircut. Justine stands in front Delossi. 'Dave Delossi. You do not have to say anything, but it may harm your defence if you do not mention, when questioned, something which you later rely on in court. Anything you do say, may be given in evidence.'

Little Tim looks shiftily around, and decides to make a run for it, he makes his way through my open front door and into my house. Shit. 'Stop, police!' Voices call as several people rush in through the door.

Staying close to DS Jackson, I watch as Delossi is taken to a waiting police car, an officer holds his arm tightly. The man won't give up, I guess it's not in his nature, as he pulls against the restraints, making every step difficult. He stops in front of me and the DS, just as we are about to walk away, his dark eyes almost popping from their sockets.

'This had better not be your doing, Cherwell,' Delossi's voice is hard, menacing, 'if I find it is, you're a fucking dead man.'

I shake my head, I know I'm about to get myself in trouble, but I can't help it. 'You're nothing but a menace, Delossi. Breaking into my house, stealing my stuff.' I pull back my arm and punch him straight in the face, 'And, don't touch my fucking cat!'

'Hey!' DS Jackson says sharply, caught off guard, 'that's enough.'

I slip my sore hand into my pocket and nod to the DS. Do you know what, I'd rather be a dead man, doing the right thing, than a living man having to cower to the likes of Dave Delossi and Little Tim.

'Oi!' Little Tim shouts from the house, 'get the fuck off me!' There are sounds of furniture being thrown, of a short scuffle and a lot of moaning. Minutes later he is hauled outside by a couple of officers.

'Get them both booked in and Delossi transferred back to Belmarsh,' DS Jackson says, as Little Tim is put into another waiting car.

'It's Anthony, isn't it?' the senior officer asks, brushing a hand through his hair.

'Yeah,' I reply, 'he's a bloody nutter. Thought he'd never go.' Oscar saunters out of the door and gracefully walks across the

The Lost Soul

drive to where I'm standing. I stoop down and pick him up, check him over quickly, and stroke his soft silky coat.

'How's Nick?' I ask, not giving away Jules' real name. It makes me feel good inside, I think I can get used to this feeling of doing the right thing.

'He's good. I understand he's safe, and on his way back to Yorkshire, where he'll be checked over and hopefully given the all-clear. I'm afraid I'll need to get scene of crime down here to check the place over.' He looks at his watch. '7pm already, can you stay in a hotel for the night?'

'Sure,' I say stroking Oscar, 'I'll just need one who can take cats. Can I pack a small bag?'

'That shouldn't be a problem,' he says, smiling for the first time.

As we enter my house, an overwhelming tiredness falls on me, and I feel like I could drop right there on the spot and fall in the foetal position on the floor. My phone vibrates and I check the message.

'Glad you're all right. A serviced apartment has been booked for you tonight. Here is the address in Blewbury. Steph Rutland.'

'Anything important?' DS Jackson asks, as I lead the way to my bedroom.

'No,' I reply, feeling like there is someone looking over me, my parents even. 'Just a friend checking in,' I smile

.

The Lost Soul

Part 32: Sasha

'She's so beautiful,' Jem smiles, as she carefully holds on to Zoe's hand. My daughter is three years old now, and our life at Shore House in Lyme Regis has settled into a loving, family routine. We are walking along the sandy Front Beach in Lyme and staring out at the blue sea.

I smile, 'she's not when she's crying at 3am in the morning!'

Jem's deep laugh warms my heart as we brace ourselves against the late September early afternoon breeze.

'Mummy, can I get pebbles?' my daughter asks, her dark, curly windswept hair is getting longer and is held back using a pink elasticated headband sprinkled with tiny white stars. It matches her pink dress, and is accompanied by a white cardigan, short white socks and a pair of blue Mary Jane shoes.

I hand the green plastic bucket and spade which I am carrying to her, 'Here you go, but don't go too far!'

'Won't', she laughs, scurrying off along the beach, ahead of us.

'Have you had any thoughts of what you want to do when you leave Shore House?' Jem's question takes me by surprise. She moved out of Shore House last year, now that her paintings are selling well, she is financially independent and a much sought-after artist who paints under the name of Marnie Lake.

'No,' I link my arm through Jem's arm, snuggle into her long thick multicoloured woollen coat. 'What work can I do, with a three year old child in tow?' I ask, raising my eyebrows.

She bumps into my side, playfully and tells me firmly, 'there are loads of things you can do, Sasha. Don't use Zoe as an excuse.'

I stop, release my hand and we stand facing each other. She looks every inch a creative person, with her wild, curly hair and colourful knitted coat, worn over navy jeggings and a long silk grey top. She matches these with silver dangly flower earrings and a long silver necklace that contains a chunky silver lighthouse. Brown leather flat boots reach her calves.

'I'm not, using her as an excuse, Jem,' I look at her seriously. 'I just don't know where I'm going to go from here.'

Jem pulls me into a firm hug. 'Why don't you ask Jenny and Stuart, see if they've got any suggestions? They may be working on some projects or can advise you on training.'

'Good idea,' I hug her back. 'I miss not having you at Shore House. We all do.' I touch her curly hair affectionately. She has been such a dear friend to me, like a big sister. Jem, in turn reaches across and kisses my forehead.

'I miss you too. But I come to dinner twice a week, so I'm hardly a stranger,' she laughs.

'Mummy, Jem!' Zoe's voice calls out, 'come see what I found.'

The Lost Soul

This time, Jem links my arm. 'We're coming,' I call back to my lovely daughter.

'You never know,' she says, 'one day, we might even find Mr Right!'

***

'We're here, Sasha,' a voice wakes me from my memories of walks on the beach at Lyme. I must have dosed off. The music has an upbeat rhythm, I think it's the Jackson Five.

'Don't blame it on the sunshine, don't blame it on the moonlight, don't blame it on the good times. Blame it on the boogie.'

Stuart turns the car ignition off, and the music abruptly stops, leaving a sudden silence in the car. He looks across at me, smiling cheerfully, 'I used to love that song.'

'Mummy, can we play it again?' I swivel, and turn my head to look at Zoe, who sits behind me, wearing her prettiest pink dress, her unruly dark curly hair bouncing naturally on her shoulders.

'Perhaps later, darling. We are at the hospital now.' I tell her. Before we set off on our long journey this morning, I had explained to her that we were visiting my mum, her granny, who had fallen over in the kitchen, and was in hospital.

My thoughts stray to Nick and his return to Greystones. I am so relieved, but things are different now. I shove those thoughts to the back of my mind. Time to think about Nick, later.

'Ready?' Stuart asks quietly, his hand briefly resting on my arm. I nod. I am not ready. Not really. But this is the last chance I will

The Lost Soul

have to see mum before she is discharged and Jenny takes her to Shore House, to convalesce. Despite my reservations, it feels like the right thing to do. And, I have always prided myself on trying to do the right thing, no matter how hard that might be. It felt right to leave home with my baby, to get us out of that toxic environment before either of were damaged beyond repair.

Stuart puts the parking ticket in the car window, and collect our bags, before using my phone to re-touch my lipstick.

'What does granny look like?' Zoe asks innocently, taking my outstretched hand and jumping out of the car.

We set off a 7 o'clock this morning from Haworth in my green Peugeot and arrived at Stuart and Jenny's house in Chippenham at midday, because Zoe needed a toilet stop on the way. After a quick lunch, Stuart offered to drive us the forty minutes to our final destination, the hospital in Headington, Stuart calls the JR.

'I don't know, I haven't seen her for a few years,' I mutter, taking her hand and following Stuart across the car park. I have no idea what my mum will look like when we get inside, or what state she is in.

Stuart leads us through the main automatic doors, through several corridors to a lift and, after what seems like an age, we arrive at Level 5, the female short stay medical ward. In the reception area, we explain who we are to the dark-haired nurse, who I assume Stuart hasn't seen before. She nods her permission and my daughter and I, follow him along a corridor, to the two men talking quietly by a window.

The Lost Soul

'Hey,' Stuart addresses the shorter of two, the man has a serious face and brushes his hands through his jet-black floppy hair. He wears navy chinos and a white shirt. 'Any problems? How has she been?'

'No problems. She's had no visitors, apart from you. The Consultant says she's a bit down,' the man glances at me.

'This is Sasha, Nancy's daughter, and her daughter, Zoe,' I hold out my hand to offer a greeting to both men and am pleased when both take my hand in warm, firm handshakes. Zoe does a full twirl in her pink tutu ballet style dress. 'Look, I can twirl,' she smiles their way.

The unpredictable May weather has decided that it will bring some sunshine to this side of Oxfordshire. Inside the room the curtains are open, there is one bed within the room, and a half open door which may be an attached bathroom.

In the bed, my mother lies still, pale and attached to a tube. There is a dressing over one eye, marks on her face, and finger marks make her swollen face look as though she's been in a car crash. She lies still, her unbandaged eye is closed, as though she's sleeping. I put a hand over my mouth to stifle a gasp, the shock of seeing her in a hospital bed, like this, is too much.

I don't know what I was expecting, but it wasn't this.

Shaking my head in denial, hot, salty tears blur my vision and slip silently down my cheeks. That my father can treat my mother with such brutality and carelessness is beyond my understanding. How can one human being do that to another? I move closer to the bed without realising what I am doing. Each step feels heavy,

The Lost Soul

as though I'm wearing weighted shoes that are determined to keep me from reaching my destination.

Finally, I stand next to the bed and gently grasp mum's hand. Stroking the back of it with my fingers, I'm relieved to find that her skin is warm to the touch.

'Mum,' I whisper.

Behind me, I hear Stuart talking quietly to Zoe. 'Come on sweetheart, let's see if we can find the coffee shop.' I turn and give them both a quick smile. When the room is empty, apart from me and mum, I pull a green padded, wooden chair to the side of the bed and take a seat.

Reaching out, I take her hand again, and stroke the cold metal of her wedding ring, before gently adding pressure.

'Sasha?' a quiet voice asks.

I look up and see that mum is awake.

'Hey,' I say, holding back a sob. I am not prepared for the myriad of emotions that overwhelm me at the sound of her voice. My heart races so hard, I can feel it pounding in my chest, and I absently wipe stray tears away using my free hand. I feel anger, and a sense of hopelessness, that she didn't leave him after I went. Part of me wants to shout, 'this is your fault! You should have left him!' But where will that get us? Absolutely nowhere. Instead, I quell my anger, and don't speak until I have my emotions under control.

'How are you feeling?' I eventually ask, in a quiet voice.

The Lost Soul

'A bit sore,' she replies, attempting to move in the bed. 'Can you help me sit up?'

Standing, I move mum's pillows into a large V shape, gently taking her arm, I help her to shuffle backwards. Pain flickers across her face, 'broken ribs,' she winces as she moves herself into a comfortable position and I press the button to raise the headrest slightly.

Right now, I am so angry with my father, for doing this to her, to us. She doesn't deserve this.

As I look into her good eye, a brown one just like mine. I see nothing but a deep sadness.

A tear slides down the side of her face, and I can't help but reach out and gently wipe it away with my thumb.

'Don't cry, Mum, this is not your fault,' I tell her, and suddenly I feel like I am twelve years old again, in full protection mode, ready to jump in and protect us from the storm.

'I'm sorry, Sasha, so sorry,' she weeps openly.

Taking both her hands in mine, I look at this broken woman, the one who gave birth to me, who tried to protect me, but wasn't physically strong enough to match the strength of my father, or mentally strong enough to leave him.

'It's all right, Mum. Don't worry about the past,' I reassure her. 'Everything will be all right,' I repeat, again and again, as I stroke her hair.

The Lost Soul

'I should have left him,' she mutters as I take a tissue from my pocket and carefully wipe her face.

'Doesn't matter now,' I say, and my heart agrees. We've been through so much and there comes a time when you have to let go of the baggage and move on. 'We're only going to think of the future.'

The door opens and I turn to see Stuart and Zoe hovering over the threshold. I smile and wave, 'come in.' I beckon Zoe to my side. She frowns. 'Nothing to worry about sweetie,' I take Zoe by the hand and gently pull her to me.

'Zoe, sweetheart,' I put my arm around my daughter's pink shoulders. 'This is your granny.' My young daughter stands quietly, unsure what to do. 'It's ok, honey,' I encourage her to approach the bed.

'Mum,' I smile at Zoe, 'this is Zoe, my daughter.' Mum's fingers reach across the bedsheet to touch Zoe's dark curly hair.

'You've grown so big, Zoe,' Mum tells her, tears streaming down her cheek. 'You were only a baby when I last saw you.'

I look across the room to Stuart, he's leaning against the door frame quietly watching us, he nods and I give him a weak smile in return. He knows what I've been through, how vulnerable I was when I walked out of the house with Zoe.

The horror of not knowing where I was going, of the sky turning dark, and small spots of drizzle hitting my nose. I had reached the nearest bus stop and had planned to use it for shelter until the rain had subsided. I had been crying so hard, that Zoe had become

The Lost Soul

upset too, and neither of us had seen the green Fiesta pull up beside us, the window rolled down.

My English teacher, Mrs Chapman, had asked if I was all right, must have taken in my bloody nose and swollen eye and knew that everything was far from all right, even as I had shaken my head. I had watched in shock as Mrs Chapman had got out of the car, taken my bag, and carefully put me and Zoe in the back of the car. No baby seat, due to the circumstances, all I could do was carefully pull the seat belt around both of us.

Mrs Chapman saved us. I still send her a letter every three months to let her know how we are doing. Thank goodness she made a call to the police and was put through to a DS Leadbetter. The DS knew Jenny and Stuart Greyson, and the rest is history.

***

A short while later, we say goodbye to mum, and Stuart assures me that he and Jenny will look after mum, which makes me so relieved.

As Stuart drives us back to Chippenham, he calls Jenny and there is no denying that she is happy to have us here, when she laughingly tells us that she is preparing dinner and has made-up a room for us to stay in overnight. Nick texts to see if we are all right, and I reassure him that we are and that I will call him later.

Can there ever be the right time to start a relationship? Is this the right time to open my heart again? I have a four year old daughter, is this the right time for me to be distracted, when I should be putting her first? Of course, this is a no brainer, I always put her first.

Always.

'How is Nick?' Jenny offers me the salad bowl, as we sit at the modern oak table eating dinner, and I smile my thanks, taking the colourful array of salad ingredients, and adding a big scoop to my bowl of macaroni cheese, ham and egg bake, before adding a smaller scoop of salad to Zoe's.

Spearing a cherry tomato with my fork, I pop it into my mouth, enjoying the tangy taste. I chew slowly before I answer. 'He's good. It's been five days, since he returned and he still looks over his shoulder when he goes outside, but I think he's getting there,' I tell her honestly.

'Nick can be at my party now,' Zoe smiles, alternatively using her fork and fingers to eat her pasta. She's so excited for her birthday and party, which takes place this coming Saturday. I've hired the local hall next to the village church, for Zoe and twenty of her friends from her nursery. 'I can't wait to be five!'

I reach out and pat her little shoulders, as she picks up another mouthful of pasta with her fork and stuffs it into her small mouth.

Stuart rests his cutlery in his bowl and lifts a glass of water to his lips, before turning to Zoe to ask her if she knows what she's getting for her birthday.

'I might get a pram for Baby Annabel,' she looks at me and smiles.

The Lost Soul

I smile back and shrug. 'We'll see on the day, shall we?'

'We're looking forward to Saturday,' he gives her the dazzling smile of someone who cares deeply about her. 'I'm not sure if I can fit your present in the car, Zoe!' I watch Zoe's eyes light up and her mouth forms an O shape.

'What is it?' Zoe puts her fork down and her hands start gesticulating madly, 'What is it?'

Wiping his mouth with a serviette, Stuart chuckles. 'You'll have to wait and see. It's a surprise.' He looks across the table to Jenny, and winks. I am mesmerised as I watch their eye contact, before Jenny smiles and reaches across the table, taking Stuart's hand. I love watching their 'moments', when they connect, smile and seem so at ease with each other. I want that one day.

'And Nick?' Jenny asks, 'how is that going?'

I know what she wants to do, she's trying to draw me in, so that I'll make sweeping statements about my relationship with Nick.

Looking at her, she seems genuinely concerned, and for that I am grateful. To have someone worry about me, my life and my happiness, fills me with a warmth I have only experienced from my mother. I swallow before answering. 'It's very early days, and I have other things to worry about at the moment.'

'Like your mum?' Stuart answers. 'Jenny and I will make sure she is safe and recuperates at Shore House.'

Well, that's one thing. The other, I'm not sure I should be discussing when Zoe is here and sitting with us.

The Lost Soul

'And the fact that you didn't tell me about Nick's past, the one he had before he came to Greystones.'

An eerie silence fills the dining room. Everyone stares at me, including Zoe. 'What's up mummy?' she asks.

'Nothing,' I murmur, feeling like an ungrateful school child, who has been given new shoes and a blazer, but still isn't happy. I don't want to be mean, but I want to explain my feelings, because they're important to me, and I need them to know that.

Stuart looks across at Jenny and she nods. 'We apologise Sasha, it was never our intention to hurt or deceive you. We knew that Jules had a past, as we all have.'

Jenny reaches for Stuart's hand, 'I'm sorry Sasha. He did something wrong, something bad, but Stuart felt,' she looks at her husband and her face lights up. 'We felt that there were extenuating circumstances and that Jules deserved another chance.'

'Who's Jules?' Zoe asks innocently. 'Is she Nick's friend?'

I stroke her hair, 'no one for you to worry about, sweetheart.' I smile, kissing the top of her head.

'You were never in any danger from Jul..er Nick,' Stuart says, 'we wouldn't let anything happen to you or Zoe. He was about to give himself up, which wouldn't serve any purpose.'

Jenny pushes her chair away from the dining table, her face is etched in worry, lines that I hadn't noticed before, were beginning to show on her soft skin. From the first day I met Jenny Greyson, she has been nothing but supportive and caring towards me and

316

The Lost Soul

Zoe. She arranged for Zoe to go to childcare, while I started my nursing training. She checked on me at Shore House, checked with Lottie and Jem about my progress.

The first few weeks, I was utterly lost and I felt desperately alone, as if the weight of the world were on my shoulders. I missed my mum. I questioned whether I should have left her with my dad, knowing that she would take the brunt of his brutality.

Reaching my side, Jenny envelops me in the soft, strong warmth of her arms and holds me tight. 'I am so sorry for letting you down,' she says quietly. 'We'll try to do better.'

I throw my arms around her. Jenny is the woman I wish my mum had been. Strong and self-assured. Worthy of any child. It is sad that the very people who have helped so many, have no children of their own.

'It's all right,' I whisper into her blonde hair, holding on tightly, 'it's all right.'

And just like that, it is.

Three hours later, I walk into the bedroom I am sharing with Zoe. The room is bathed in soft light from the glass lamp that sits on the white French style side table. The bed is huge, probably kingsize, with a high padded velvet grey headboard and soft white bed linen. My daughter looks tiny as she lies sprawled amongst the thrown off duvet, her unruly dark curls spread across the pillow and her little legs peep out of her pink frilly pyjama shorts.

Leaning over, I softly kiss the top of her head. She smells of strawberries and cream, which immediately calms me and fills me

The Lost Soul

with warmth. Standing quietly, I watch her for a moment, making sure that I haven't woken her. I hold my breath, as she stirs briefly to slide an arm under her pillow, and then walk from the room.

On the way past the coat stand in the hall, I grab my black jacket, shrug into it, and silently walk through the house towards the garden. As I move through the rooms, I hear sounds coming from the kitchen, voices. Someone giggles. Jenny.

'Hey, watch it!' she says playfully, 'the suds are getting everywhere.'

'What?' Stuart's voice challenges innocently, 'like this.' There is a shuffling movement and murmurings.

I reach the kitchen door and find them both, faces covered in suds from the basin. This is a part of them that I have never seen. Goading each other, teasing and making flirtatious remarks. It's a good look on them, almost as though they are teenagers messing about in their parent's house. Jenny turns to face her husband, steps closer until they are nose to nose, and they both smile as she softly strokes the bubbles from Stuart's face, using her forefinger as a razor blade. He reaches up and does the same to her.

'God, how did I ever get so lucky as to find you?' Stuart's voice is husky.

Feelings of guilt, of intruding on a private moment, engulf me like a cape, but I can't move. Mesmerised, I watch as he curls his hand gently around Jenny's neck, and slowly moves in to kiss her.

Deliberately, I cough as I walk through the open doorway.

The Lost Soul

'Mmm… sorry,' I say, briefly looking at them both, before focusing on the floor.

Laughter fills the air and I look up at their faces. 'Caught red handed,' Stuart's husky voice never leaves his wife's face, even as he chuckles.

'Nothing to be sorry for,' Jenny says, stepping to the sink. 'You need anything?'

'No,' I say, digging for my phone in my jeans and showing her. 'Just thought I'd give Nick a quick call, see if he's still up.'

I walk to the kitchen door that leads to the garden and turn the handle. Something stops me in my tracks, as I'm about to leave, and I impulsively turn to face them. 'I want the fairy tale too, one day,' I mutter, quickly closing the door behind me.

It's cold outside, I search for the wooden bench, hidden in a quiet, secluded side of the garden by the trellis. There is a rambling clematis and chiminea next to it, and I plop down onto the cold, hard surface. There are fairy lights, dotted around the garden, giving it a magical look.

I feel discombobulated, uneasy. It's been a long day, and it's beginning to take its toll on me, but for some reason I can't go to bed until I've called Nick.

***

I remember that night he came home after his ordeal at the hands of Little Tim. It was nearly midnight, and he had been to the local Accident and Emergency with Jack and Steph. The five inch gash on his head had been glued together and a dressing added for protection. He had looked pale and tired as he rang my doorbell, standing there with Jack and Steph in tow, both looking equally tired.

Zoe had been in bed, and Vi was in her room. I had fallen asleep on the sofa, and rushed dishevelled to the door, on hearing the bell.

'Nick,' I had said breathlessly, my eyes drawn to his, as he strode into my apartment. There was something in his eyes that was new, determined. I didn't know what. But he looked different, despite his tired, injured state.

Jack and Steph followed me into the lounge.

'Sorry it's late, we wanted to reassure you that everything was all right.'

Nick looked at me, slightly raising his eyebrow. What was that?

'I'm fine,' were the first words he spoke, 'glad to be home.'

Steph patted my shoulder, 'he's a bit worse for wear, but nothing a good nights sleep won't cure. We'll leave you to it.' We're going to take visitor room five for the night, Ben is staying at a friend's house.'

'Thank you,' I said to them both, 'for everything.'

I walk them to the door as we say our goodbyes. 'Keep an eye on him for any headaches etc, will you?' Jack says, 'he should be fine though.'

Nodding briefly, I close the door behind them. There were going to be consequences to his ordeal, but right now, I am pleased just

The Lost Soul

to have him physically back home. Walking back to the lounge, I find Nick facing the open doorway, waiting for me.

Slowly, I walk up to him. When we are mere centimetres away, I reach up and put my hand over his heart. 'You frightened me today,' I say, as a sob finds its way to my throat. 'You really bloody frightened me.' Without thinking my hand has turned into a fist, and I start to pound his chest, hard. As I beat his chest, I sob hopelessly as though my whole being is on the verge of extinction and there is no tomorrow.

'Don't do that to me!' my voice is harsh as strong arms enfold me tightly. I can't stop the fat tears from rolling down my face as large warm hands reach to cup my face and stroke the tears from my cheeks. Within seconds he swoops down and kisses me long and hard, until the feeling that he is home has settled, and his lips soften. He breaks the connection and whispers in my ear, 'I'm sorry.'

***

I put the phone to my ear and listen to it ringing. Maybe he's gone to bed. He's on the early shift tomorrow.

The line connects:

'Sasha,' his voice is deep and husky, seductive even.

'Hi, sorry it's late,' I tell him, but there's no sincerity in my voice. I want to hear him, feel his closeness.

The Lost Soul

'I waited up for you. Couldn't sleep until I'd heard from you,' he sounds as though he's smiling. 'How was today with your mum?' he asks.

'She's getting better, and things are good.' I muse, 'better than I thought it would be. I'm glad I went.'

'I'm happy for you,' he says sincerely, 'but I want you back here, where you belong.'

I smile and jiggle my knees, because they're beginning to cramp in the cold. 'I want to be back home too,' I say, chiding him gently.

'Yeah?' he asks.

'Yeah, Zoe misses you,' I say lightly.

'Only Zoe?' he pushes.

The smile on my face is causing my jaw to ache but I know it's because I'm feeling so happy, right now. The silence stretches for a few moments, before I speak.

'No, I miss you too Nick. Of course, I bloody miss you.' I smile.

'Good, I can't tell you how relieved that makes me feel,' his husky voice replies, 'now do you want to know what Russell said to Lauren this afternoon?'

'No, I dare not think. He's such a character,' I laugh, as we talk for another twenty minutes until we are both so tired, we need our beds.

The Lost Soul

Part 33: Lewis

My parents are high achievers. From the moment I was born, a child to much older parents, they indoctrinated in me the need to focus on what I wanted in life, to form a pathway for my chosen career – whatever it was, and to never veer from my goal.

They both went to Cambridge and introduced me to the elite world of academia. I mean, they would do, wouldn't they? With names like Horatio and Cleopatra. By the time I was five, Harry and Cleo, as they were fondly known by their nearest and dearest, had engaged a tutor for me, Miss Kingston, who had the coldest face I had ever seen at that age, apart from my mother. It was hardly surprising that I thought all women were cold hearted, empty creatures by the time I was in my teens.

The stern tutor had a pale wrinkle free, sickly pallor to her face, which seemed to be stretched with effort like an awning attached to a house. Her cheekbones were high, her lips thin, and as noted, no laughter lines.

The fifty something year old woman, had brown beady eyes and greying black hair that she diligently scraped back into a severe bun. This woman, with her black, long dresses, was going to be the making of me, my parents had said. She was going to fill my young sponge-like brain with long and unusual words, alongside

The Lost Soul

an acute understanding of the wider world. The joys of arithmetic and the ability to begin writing sentences, were forced upon me, until they made my head hurt.

My parents were politicians, before they retired. We lived in a five bedroomed house in Harwell, Oxfordshire where we engaged in a rich and busy life of politics, canvassing, networking and agendas, both hidden and in plain sight. Mum had sat on the Harwell Parish Council and dad had been a special advisor to the Leader of the House of Commons. Life had been a game of chess in the Benson household, where you would spend every minute of every day, trying not to give your opponent a reason to defeat you.

Poor Nancy, she never stood a chance. I saw so much potential in that pretty, crazy haired woman in the car park in Abingdon. I thought, here's a woman I could potentially like and not feel constantly in awe of, like my mum and now long-term friend, former tutor Frenella Kingston. But in the end, I couldn't change, no matter how much I tried or wanted to, it was ingrained in my DNA that I couldn't fully trust, or be happy, unless I took charge and controlled the situation. That way, I could be me.

The first time I hit her floored me in a way, that had me rushing to the bathroom and staring at my reflection and my hands in the mirror, asking myself, is this really me? How can I do that to someone who has never shown an iota of disdain or disappointment in me?

We had been going out for an evening meal with friends, when I had walked into the kitchen and asked her if the neckline on her midi, deep v-neck navy dress was a little too low. I saw the light

The Lost Soul

in her eyes dim, and knew that I had done that to her, but I couldn't help myself. The grim line on her beautiful face, had told me that she was not happy with my comment. Her eyes took on an accusing tone, and without thinking she rolled her eyes and looked up at the ceiling.

'Did you just roll your eyes at me?' I had asked, feeling a rush of anger seep through my bones.

'No, of course not, 'she'd smiled.

I raised my hand, I don't know why, but I raised it high and slapped her hard across the face.

She had looked at me in horror, like a heroine in a slow-motion horror movie. She had whimpered like a cat in pain and put her hand to the smarting skin. Her eyes were full of tears.

'Lewis!' she had shouted, 'what the hell!' She began to claw at me, and I had stood in a daze as she began to beat my chest, with as much strength as she could muster.

'Shit!' was all I could say, panicked by her attack. But I was stronger than she was, so I grabbed her hands and pushed her away with such force that her back slammed into the kitchen units and she howled in pain and shock. In my frustration, I rushed into the hall, took the stairs two at a time, and didn't stop until I'd reached the family bathroom.

It is true what they say, sometimes you can be your own worst enemy.

***

The Lost Soul

The rain is beating down on me hard, I let my head fall back and embrace the early evening changeable weather. Warm bubbles soar around me in the hot tub, and the glass of Dom Perignon that sits in my right, outstretched hand, splashes like a waterfall as rainwater plummets into the cool liquid.

Closing my eyes, I think of the day when I finally give that so called daughter of mine, her comeuppance. She will get what she deserves, for the trouble she has caused me, and her mother. It's her fault that I hit Nancy so bad, that she is now hospitalised. If Nancy hadn't been trying to make contact with Sasha, this could have all been avoided.

It's Sasha's fault that I had to leave everything behind and disappear, to become invisible. All her fault of course, that she hadn't been born a boy, when I believe that things could have been very different. He would have been like me; strong, confident, hard-working, knows what he wants and goes for it.

Instead, I was lumbered with this little bitch of a daughter. A child who always seemed to look down her nose at me, as though I was never quite good enough. As though, I'd ruined her life.

I am staying at a hotel in Mytholmes Lane, Haworth. So, I am almost within touching distance of Greystones and my wayward daughter. My life would have been so different if I hadn't met Nancy, and she hadn't got pregnant, and I curse myself, again for giving in to my carnal pleasures, when I should have followed my path. I should have listened to my parents and focused on my career, who knows where I may have been without my wife and daughter holding me back.

326

The Lost Soul

Staring at the clouds hovering above me, I let the bubbles relax my tired body, and take a large sip of my now, diluted champagne. Once upon a time I would never have found the time to sit like this, but now there is a nothingness. I can't go back to Abingdon and the police are looking for me after I visited Nancy in the hospital. Why can't they bloody leave me alone? What goes on between a man and his wife is nobody's business but theirs.

So, I've been staying here, in Haworth.

Watching.

Waiting.

Checking movement patterns.

A week ago, I was living at the Cowley Premier Inn, near Oxford, trying to decide my next move. After the disaster at the hospital, I knew it was time to stay low for a while and let the dust settle. That bloody wife of mine is a nuisance, causing no end of problems.

The strange thing is that everything that has happened, feels like a dream. From the moment I left Nancy in that state on the living room floor, I had signed my own death certificate. One way or another. Knowing that I had never intended to go home early, which in turn, enabled me to find the phone she'd been hiding, didn't give me any comfort. I had packed a bag, with my laptop, chargers and a few clothes and took the phone she'd been hiding from me. Then, I found my passport and the five grand in cash,

The Lost Soul

that I kept stored in my morning suit pocket in the wardrobe, for a rainy day, and walked out the door.

I couldn't stay because there was blood all over the place where I'd hit her or dragged her across the house, so I'd booked into a nearby hotel. The following morning, Nancy had called when I was at the office and said that she needed an ambulance, but I was still mad at her. Deep down, I knew this assault had escalated more than the others. For a start, I hadn't hurt her since Sasha had left with the baby, maybe there was a remorse thing going on there. Maybe I had thought she'd been punished enough?

The phone was surprisingly easy to open, Nancy had used her year of birth as the passcode and as my fingers fell over the buttons, I was able to access her Facebook page, call list and contacts. From there it was easy to simply dial the last few numbers until Sasha had answered. Nancy had also been googling a place called Greystones, a retirement home in Haworth, Yorkshire. It took me less than two minutes to bring the place up on my laptop, study the staff information, and to make a quick call.

'Hi, can I speak to Sasha Benson please,' I had asked innocently.

'Do you mean Sasha Berrington, the Manager?' The helpful female voice had asked.

'Oh yes, sorry. Berrington.' I'd smiled down the phone. So, she had kept her first name but altered her surname? 'Look, I've got a call coming in, I need to take,' I muttered, before disconnecting the call. My name, it appears, isn't good enough for her anymore. No surprise there.

The Lost Soul

A few days ago, I called Sasha on the mobile, Nancy had been using. I told her that her mother was gone and that it was all her fault. Sasha had the nerve to be angry. Angry at me! For God's Sake, how conceited is she?

Someone hand delivered a large black box to me, this morning. Reception gave it to me when I went down for breakfast. There was a note on the top from an old friend called Chris, who owed me a favour. It was handwritten:

'For the attention of Mr L Benson. Fragile, handle with care. We are even now. Chris.'

I had made a call a couple of days ago to Chris, who knew a shady business guy called Gino Camprinelli. Apparently, if you know the right person and have a couple of grand going spare, - you can secure yourself a weapon. As I took the black Berretta from the box and laid the gun and its bullets on my bed, an excitement coursed through my veins, that I hadn't felt before, a feeling of power.

And power is a good thing. Especially, when you plan to do, what I am about to do.

I am getting my own back on that wretched daughter of mine, and that means, taking from her the most important thing in her life.

Her daughter. Zoe.

Whatever happens after that, is anyone's guess.

I am a man with nothing to lose, and no ties. But before I disappear for good, my daughter will see me again, and it won't

The Lost Soul

be a happy meeting. Finishing off my champagne in one mouthful, I leave the glass on the side and step out of the tub.

My time for revenge is getting closer.

Part 34: Sasha

'Happy birthday to you,' a chorus of voices sing in various harmonies, 'happy birthday to you, happy birthday dear Zoe, Happy birthday to you.' Holding the pink My Little Pony cake with five lit candles, in front of my beautiful daughter, I say quietly. 'Make a wish and blow out the candles, sweetie.'

The excited faces of twenty young children shuffle about on their chairs, facing each other, at the long trestle table. Amid an array of brightly coloured princesses and superheroes, a King sat with his crown around his wrist, a Batman with a red face had been persuaded by his mum to take off his mask, and a young boy called Jonah, would only dress up as a police officer.

Zoe's eyes are bright with joy as she tries to blow out the candles, I help a little. As the last of the flames die out, people cheer, take photos and clap. My little girl is growing up fast and it is all I can do to keep up with her and enjoy the ride. Her dress looks glorious on her. A fitted pink silk sleeveless bodice with delicate pale pink butterflies stitched along the neckline, and a matching full chiffon skirt, it looks fit for a princess.

Being a parent is never supposed to be easy, that's for sure. Being a single parent is additionally complicated. There is no one to share these memorable moments, or to take over when you're

The Lost Soul

exhausted, and your child can't sleep. There are so many different ways that having a partner to co-parent a child, can enhance early experiences. Some days, like today, I wish I'd told Dylan about Zoe, so he had the chance to be a father to Zoe. But sadly, it simply isn't to be.

My eyes search the room and rest on Nick. He's looking smart with a white linen shirt, rolled up at the sleeves, showing his muscular forearms and dark grey jeans.

I smile and give him a brief nod, watching fondly as he leaves the room with his mission. Jenny and Stuart are here, supplying drinks to the youngsters and replenishing the finger food on the trestle tables. These children are the majority of children from Zoe's nursery class, including the notorious former husband and parents, Keiron and Sapphire, and I am thankful, that any bad feelings have been lost amid the food and cake.

A short while later, as everyone is enjoying the birthday cake, Nick returns. He's stooping as he's pushing something that clearly has wheels and a handlebar. We've wrapped the top part of the present, but it's still very clear what the gift is.

'Baby Annabell! Baby Annabell pram! It's a pram!' Zoe jumps off her chair, with joy and beams the biggest smile, as she moves around the obstacles in her way. 'Can I open it, mummy?' she begs, stroking the handlebar, with love.

Nodding, 'yes,' I blow her a kiss and gesture for her to help herself to the unveiling of the clearly, badly wrapped gift.

The Lost Soul

It's hard not to be affected by her excitement, as she easily pulls the wrapping paper off the top of the pram. I take out my phone and capture the moment.

***

So many precious moments to remember, such as the day she was born. When the simple chore of hoovering the house resulted in my waters breaking, and I realised that those niggling pains I had been having all through the night, had been real labour pains and not Braxton Hicks. It was the day before my seventeenth birthday.

Mum had called The Spires birthing suite, the level seven suite at the John Radcliffe hospital and we had grabbed my hospital bag and rushed there in mum's battered old, but reliable, red Micra. Six long hours later and my beautiful daughter, born at just over six pounds, was laid in my arms. Mum had been brilliant, fussing and cooing over me and the baby. I spent the first night on the ward and woke up a seventeen-year-old, with a newborn baby.

I can't tell you how frightened I had been. I was barely more than a child myself. But I was one of the lucky ones, it came naturally, and Zoe was a contented baby.

***

'Mummy, I love it!' Zoe throws her arms around me, but her eyes never leave the pale pink Baby Annabell Roamer pram, with the tiny pink and blue sheep patterned hood. 'Nick, look what I got.' She surprises me by letting go and grabbing one of Nick's hands instead, 'my dolly is going to love it.'

The Lost Soul

I make my way to the refreshments table, where Jenny and Vi are chatting, and pour myself an orange squash. 'Someone is Mr Popular,' Jenny smiles, wearing navy tapered trousers and a pale pink blouse, draping her arm around my shoulders. I'm wearing a simple navy shift dress, with a soft grey cardigan, leggings and brown ankle boots. For ease, I put my curly hair up in a messy, loose bun. I've added a touch of lipstick and a quick layer of mascara.

'She likes him,' I murmur, watching Nick patiently listening to Zoe as she shows him the storage tray under the pram. 'A lot.'

Vi holds a plate of mini sausage rolls in front of me, 'it's going well. Take one.'

I take one and pop it into my mouth.

'How's Mum?' I ask Jenny.

'She's doing well,' she increases her voice over the chatter, 'really well. The Consultant thinks she'll be out within the next few days.'

I'm pleased, now that I've made my peace with her, I want her to start living her life the way she wants to, without my dad directing, or controlling her.

'Has she agreed to go to Shore House?' I ask, hoping that she will take advantage of Jenny's kindness.

'Yes,' Jenny answers, 'and she will file charges against your father. I'm sorry, Sasha.'

The Lost Soul

I smile, looking at the people around, and shrug. Does it matter that some of the most important people in my life are not my own flesh and blood? That some of the people standing in this very room are not my biological family? No, why should it? Families are made up of many different groups of people, different colours, nationalities and genders, as long as the adults take on the role of supportive caregivers, and offer their love unconditionally, they are a family.

In my mind, I see Jem's face again, as we walk along the beach at Lyme, with Zoe. God, I miss that woman. I must call her soon for a catch up, before the moment is gone, and it'll have been another six months before we speak.

'No need,' I reassure her, 'he deserves it.'

'He does, but he's still your father. Life can be so unfair,' Jenny states, looking wistfully across to the corner of the room, where Stuart is helping with the 'colouring table'.

I hear the disappointment in her voice, and she tucks stray hairs around an ear. 'We could never have children, you know. Stuart and I.'

My heart stops and restarts as a bone deep sadness hits my chest. This beautiful woman, who had inherited the CEO position of the Gloverman conglomerate empire at the age of twenty-one, and who had been through a terrible ordeal, of which I knew very few details, apart from what I found on google.

This woman who had started the domestic violence refuge charity, called The Lighthouse Charity, with her husband, Stuart.

The Lost Soul

So many people, like myself had benefitted from the charity and from being part of Jenny and Stuart Greyson's life.

'I'm so sorry, Jenny. I didn't know.' I cup her cheek, wiping a stray tear down her cheek. Stuart looks up, assesses the situation, and strides over to us. Immediately he takes Jenny in his arms.

'Can't leave you for a minute, can I?' he jokes, kissing her gently on the cheek.

'No,' she half laughs, regaining her composure and putting her hand on his shoulder.

'I'd better go and rescue Nick from Zoe,' I tell them, as I wave hello to Keiron and Sapphire's parents. Checking my watch, I realise that it's nearly time to finish up the party. I have hired two entertainers, Elsa and Sven from Frozen, to keep the children entertained. I search the room, and spy them by the door, waiting for direction, they look at me, I nod for them to come forward for the final two games, before handing out the goody bags.

Joining in with the final game, I allow myself to be young again, without responsibility. As we dance to the popular Frozen song, Let it Go, with most of the children, and some of their parents, we wait until the music stops and create various stances. Wiping hair from my eyes, I take Zoe's hand, and she turns and calls someone's name. Nick. Of course, I think I'm not the only one with a crush on him.

He shakes his head, and I see him roll his eyes and smile, before walking our way. He takes Zoe's outstretched hand, and we move to the music, making exaggerated animal shapes. I can't stop laughing, I feel drunk in the moment, I catch Nick's gaze and my

The Lost Soul

cheeks feel like they're on fire. My tummy flutters and I lick my suddenly dry lips, watching closely as he raises an eyebrow, and a devilish smile spreads across his face.

Oh hell, I can feel the blush gliding softly across my face like a silk handkerchief.

I'm so mortified that I let go of Zoe's hand and walk away. I desperately need fresh air, feel like I'm suffocating in the warm hall, with all of these little bodies running around. Walking briskly to the main door, I yank it open and step into the fresh, early May evening. Once I'm outside, I berate myself for blushing and becoming flustered when Nick pays me attention.

This is so new to me.

It begins to drizzle, and the door opens. 'Sasha?' Nick's familiar voice calls from behind me.

I turn and reply huskily, 'just needed some fresh air.' There is movement and he stands beside me. Fingers reach out and entwine mine, bind us together. In this moment I close my eyes briefly and inhale him, trying to memorise every last bit of him, for who knows what will happen in the future.

Nick smells of oranges and pine trees, sending a warmth and familiarity to my panicked thoughts. Where my deepest fear is that he won't stay, that he will leave, and my heart and Zoe's will be shattered into tiny pieces on the kitchen floor.

'I'm frightened,' I murmur, looking at the stone wall over the narrow pebbled lane.

The Lost Soul

'Of what?' he asks softly, and I can feel him turn my way.

How do I tell him? 'Of you, of life, of everything. Of everything falling apart,' I blurt out breathlessly.

He gently turns my shoulders, so that we face each other, and reaches for my free hand.

'It won't happen, I'm here to stay,' he tells me, his voice husky and his blue eyes searching mine.

'Promise?' I ask, earnestly.

'Promise,' he says quietly, kissing my forehead. His voice becomes lighter, sharper, 'now, let's make sure Zoe's party finishes as spectacularly as it started. I'll give her my present when we get back.'

We walk inside, our fingers detach as we walk through the door. My eyes catch Vi, then Jenny and both look worried, but I smile and nod, letting them know that everything is fine. Vi gestures to the dance floor, and I see Zoe, Sapphire and Keiron chasing each other. It looks like they're friends again.

Fifteen minutes later, the children are slowly leaving with their goody bags and I give an appreciative thank you to Elsa and Sven, for their hard work. Stuart and Jenny are staying over tonight and will stay for my birthday lunch tomorrow, because Jack and Steph are planning to join us too. Vi is collecting Zoe's presents and putting them in my car.

Nick is taking the pram home for me. If he can prise it away from Zoe, that is.

The Lost Soul

Jenny puts her arm around me. 'Why don't you take Zoe home, and we'll finish off here?' she says softly. 'She looks worn out.'

Smiling, I hug her back. 'Thanks, Jen,' I tell her, happy to call my daughter, grab our things and head home.

The car is parked down the side of the alley, as we walk along the pebbled path, we hold hands and softly sing, 'Let it go, let it go.'

'Did you have a good time, sweetie,' I ask, opening the car, throwing our things inside and letting her jump into her car seat behind the front passenger seat. I reach over, snapping her seat belt across her tummy.

She throws her arms around me, and kisses the side of my cheek with big, sloppy kisses. 'Yes, mummy. It was the best. I loved it!'

I kiss her back making sure she's secure in the seat, before closing the door and walking around the side of the car.

They say that things happen when you least expect it. That you can't predict what will happen at any given moment, because things are changing all of the time.

For the life of me, I didn't see the person lurking in the shadows. I wasn't paying attention. Until a cold, hard object is pushed into my temple, and although, I've never seen one in real life, I've seen enough crime dramas to know it might be a gun.

'Get in the car!' A voice from my past hisses. It's been four long years since I've been this close to him. The sound of his voice still makes my blood go cold, still makes me want to run for the hills.

The Lost Soul

'What do you think you're doing?' I hiss in a low voice to my father, feeling the pressure of the gun push harder into my skull. The pain was bad, but the shock of him covered it.

'Get in the fucking car!' he repeated in a snarl. I try to turn around, ready to beg him to let me go, because Zoe is in the back of the car.

'Mummy? Who's that man?' I vaguely hear Zoe's voice.

Desperate not to worry her, I reassure her as calmly as I can, 'it's all right, darling, it's just a friend.'

Before I can react, I'm pushed bodily into the car, and I watch in silence as he runs around the front of the car, opens the passenger door and jumps into the seat.

I get my first full glimpse of him. He's still slim, but has a bit of a pot belly now, and I'd forgotten how tall he is. His black hair, is still curly but he has a good deal more grey hair threaded through it than I remember. He is wearing black chinos, and a navy zipped up jacket. Worryingly, he's wearing black gloves.

He snaps his seat belt on, and all the time, all I can hear is my daughter whimpering mummy. Anger shoots through my veins, but I tamper it down, I know I need to keep calm. For Zoe's sake.

'What do you want?' I ask, staring at the gun sitting in his lap, I know my hands are shaking, because I can feel it, but I'm not sure if it's fear or rage. Whatever it is, it's working its way through my body.

The Lost Soul

He doesn't answer for minute. 'Drive. Straight on, I'll direct you as we go,' he brushes the back of his hand across his forehead. 'Just bloody drive.'

I turn on the engine. Look at Zoe's face in the rear-view mirror. 'It will be all right, baby,' I tell her, even though I'm not sure what the outcome will be. 'Be brave, angel.'

'One more word, and I will gag you,' my father snaps.

'Now, drive.'

Part 35: Jules

I know something is wrong when I can't see her grey Peugeot parked at Greystones.

A frisson of unease creeps across my skin as I call her phone. It begins to ring, before going to voicemail.

'Sasha, it's me. Where are you?' I ask, trying to keep the worry from my voice. But the niggling feeling is building, spreading through my body like a cancer. Something feels wrong. Very wrong. 'Call me as soon as you get this message, will you?'

I disconnect the call. Shit. Where the hell is she? She can't be far, they only left fifteen minutes before I did.

The voice of reason echoes in my mind, telling me to keep calm. Not everything that happens is bad, is it? Maybe she had another surprise for Zoe, and they've headed off to retrieve it? Perhaps she'll drive into the car park at any moment, and we'll laugh about my worries, when I chastise her for worrying me. It's a possibility, right?

But at the back of my mind, I think of Blip and how her life ended, because the relationship she had with Ray Delossi, and his brutal behaviour that had traumatised her so badly. So badly, that she didn't want to live anymore.

The Lost Soul

Don't even go there, Walker!

God, I'm even calling myself Walker.

When I'm inside Greystones' reception area, I question Jared to see if Sasha and Zoe have been seen. My heart races when I realise that my worries for them and their well-being are real, and now the only option I have left is to rush to my apartment, still carrying the Baby Annabell pram, and left-over birthday cake, and call Stuart and Jenny.

Pacing the lounge floor, my fisted hands at my sides, I try to make sense of what is happening. I can't think straight. The doorbell rings, and I rush to answer it, naively thinking that I'll find Sasha and Zoe standing there, smiling to each other and chattering away. Wishful thinking on my part, as Jenny and Stuart Greyson's worried faces look back at me, before hastily following me to the lounge.

'What's happened?' Jenny asks.

I gesture for them to sit down. Stuart doesn't, Jenny does. 'She didn't come home,' I state flatly. 'Where the hell are they?' I pace up and down, talking to myself.

'She didn't say that she needed to go somewhere?' asks Stuart.

I shake my head vigorously, 'no.'

'Then we need to find her, and Zoe,' he says quietly.

Jenny looks across at Stuart, and he shakes his head.

'What?' I ask, raising my eyebrow.

The Lost Soul

'Nothing,' he says.

I sit next to Jenny, put my hand on her lap briefly, encouraging her to speak. 'Tell me,'

They glance at each other again, and she clears her throat before she speaks, 'there's a possibility that her father may be here.'

'Her father? I thought he was in Oxfordshire?' I ask, my mind notching up a gear. God, give me strength,

'We lost him, after the hospital incident. We have no idea what he's driving, how he's moving around and where he is,' Jenny explains.

'And, if he can't get to Nancy, then he might be aiming for his daughter and granddaughter,' Stuart adds.

'Shit!' I brush my hands through my short hair. 'If there's any chance. Any chance at all, that he's here, then we're in trouble,' I say, more to myself than to anyone else.

I take out my phone and dial again. This time the phone goes dead after two rings.

Stuart looks at me, 'I'm going to call Steph and see if she can put an alert on her car.'

'What about tracking her phone?' I suggest. It worked for me, maybe it will help us find Sasha and Zoe. 'Can we do that?'

Jenny takes out her phone, and I wait patiently and watch, as her fingers fly across the screen. Silently, I pray for Sasha and Zoe to walk through the door and announce that they've been to the ice cream parlour.

The Lost Soul

Jenny looks up at her husband, her face is shockingly pale. I know there's a problem.

'Her phone is switched off, 'she says in a low voice. 'Last known location was the village hall.'

This is not the news I want to hear.

Where the hell are you, Sasha?

The Lost Soul

Part 36: Zoe

It's really dark. My eyes are open, but I can't see anything.

Mummy's arm pulls me closer, and I snuggle into her. She's asleep next to me on the bed, I don't know where we are, but the bad man put us in this room and locked us in.

I'm cold and start to shiver.

'You cold honey?' mummy's voice whispers in the darkness, her fingers rub my arms. I'm still wearing my party dress, but it doesn't feel like my birthday anymore.

'A bit,' I say in a low voice, so the man won't get angry and shout at me again.

'Come here,' mummy pulls the thin duvet over me and holds me with both arms. I smell her scent, and it makes me feel better.

'Mummy?' I whisper, hugging her close.

'Yes, sweetie,' she murmurs, half awake.

'Is the bad man going to hurt us,' I say into her neck.

My mummy opens her eyes, and in the dark, she lifts my chin, so that we are face to face, and looks into my eyes.

The Lost Soul

'Not as long as I still draw breath,' she says, kissing my cheek softly. 'It's me he's angry with, not you. Now, try to get some sleep, while we can.'

I close my eyes and start counting backwards from ten, thinking of my Baby Annabell and my new pram.

By the time I get to six, I'm fast asleep.

The Lost Soul

Part 37: Jack

'I don't bloody believe this!' I throw open the door of the office at Greystones and march in. I'm tired and annoyed, Steph and I were due to set out a little later to get here for lunch, as it's Sasha's birthday. But, following Stuart's call last night, we jumped in the car first thing this morning, with Ben and headed this way. It's 9 o'clock already, 'How the hell have they both managed to disappear off the face of the earth?'

Steph walks in, dressed in black trousers and a cream blouse under a black padded jacket, flat boots and a phone glued to her ear.

'Thanks Chris, let me know if anything flags up. I'm pretty sure Benson's behind this.' She shrugs out of her jacket and drops her large brown swing bag, unceremoniously onto the desk. The jacket is dropped onto a nearby chair, before disconnecting the call.

'Hey all,' she announces as she flops next to Jenny on the sofa and pulls her into a hug. Nick is leaning against the front of the desk, yesterday's stubble on his unshaved face, and dark circles under his eyes. Eyes that flick to each of us in turn, in a look I've seen before, the look of a man on the edge, with his furrowed

The Lost Soul

brows, solemn face and crossed arms. Stuart is seated behind the desk in Sasha's chair.

'Where's Ben?' Jenny asks.

'In reception, chatting to Jared,' I say. 'Jared's going to keep him busy for a while.'

'We should call the police,' Nick addresses the white elephant in the room. No one wants to acknowledge this because we know what calling the police means. If we call the police and they do enough probing, they will realise that he is not the person he claims to be. But, I know Nick, he's been down this route before, with Corinna James, and like Corinna, I'm pretty sure that he won't allow Sasha and Zoe to be put at risk.

'No,' Jenny and Stuart say together. 'That's not an option.'

'But,' Nick insists, unfolding his arms and pushing his hands into his jeans pocket

'I say we give it twenty-four hours, to see if we can locate and retrieve them, and if we don't hear anything, then we contact the police.' She looks at me for support, and I nod.

'Stuart?' I turn to him and watch him slowly dip his head, in the affirmative. 'Jenny?' I ask, knowing that this is probably hurting her more than anyone.

'Agreed,' she says quietly, pushing a stray strand of blonde hair out of her eyes, 'but we need a strategy to work out what happened and where she is.'

The Lost Soul

'Yes,' Steph smiles. 'I've got some ideas on that one, but we will have to break a few rules.'

'Nothing new there then,' Stuart, smiles for the first time.

'What are your thoughts?' Nick asks.

Steph pushes to her feet and collects her bag. The room is silent as we wait for her to speak. She reaches inside and pulls out an A4 notepad and pen.

'First, I've got Chris doing me a favour and checking CCTV to see if there are any sightings of Sasha's car.'

I slip the rucksack from my shoulder, place it on the desk and take out my laptop. I know what Steph is going to say, we've discussed it in the car. Walking around to the chair, I look at Stuart, 'can I?' I ask, motioning for him to move. He nods, pushing out of the chair to allow me access to the seat and desk. He strides across the room and perches on the edge of the sofa, next to his wife.

Steph continues, 'we need to retrace Sasha's steps. Jenny, Stuart can you go to the houses near the village hall, knock on a few doors and see if anyone saw anything out of the ordinary last night; whether out walking or in a car parked nearby, around the time Sasha was leaving. Jenny, when did you last see her?'

Jenny looks across at Steph, 'she took Zoe to the car around 6pm.'

The Lost Soul

'So, that's where we start,' Steph makes notes. 'Was anyone else there? Which direction did they go? Was there another car? Did Sasha leave in her own car, with Zoe?'

'Jack, you know what I'm going to ask you,' Steph looks at me, with that serious, sexy, I'm in charge look. 'Hack into Benson's bank accounts, I want to know if he's using a credit card and where he is staying. How is he able to move around without us knowing?'

'I'm pretty sure, Benson's the key. Does anyone have any other thoughts?' Steph asks, looking around the room at our faces, giving us the chance to make comments.

Nick offers a brief nod, before striding across the room and dropping into a chair. He rubs his hands along his thighs, before facing Steph. 'One thing. What if it isn't Benson? Could it be Delossi?'

'Why Delossi?' Stuart asks, and then he sighs as he realises what Nick is implying, 'ah... because of you, to get back at you.' He studies Nick, 'how would he know about your relationship with Sasha?'

Nick rests his forearms on his knees, and leans forward, 'I don't know. I just don't know anymore.'

Jenny's voice is firm, as she too stands, 'Let's not get too far ahead of ourselves. We know very little at this point, and Benson does make the most sense.'

The Lost Soul

Nick sighs visibly, rubbing his forehead. He looks like a distraught man. Sasha must have made quite an impression on him.

There's a knock at the door and Kate brings in a tray with tea and biscuits, 'here you go,' she announces, laying the tray on the desk. 'Sustenance, to keep you going,' she leaves the tray behind, as we utter our thanks.

My fingers move automatically across the keys of the laptop, as I attempt to get into Benson's accounts, but I need to access his password. I try the obvious numbers, the first being, his year of birth. No. That's much too easy. 'Can someone find out Nancy's date of birth?' I ask.

'I'll text Nancy,' Stuart volunteers, his phone ready in his hands.

Jenny looks at him. 'Don't tell her about Sasha and Zoe,' she says quietly. 'Not at the moment.'

Stuart presses a hand to her shoulder, in agreement, at some point we will find Lewis Benson and when I get my hands on him, there will be hell to pay. I don't like bullies and I particularly don't like bullies who prey on women and children.

It takes a great deal of time and patience to locate a person's personal details such as bank and phone accounts, so I zone out of the group conversation and focus on breaking the various passcodes. As my fingers fly over the keys trying to hack into accounts that will give me some indication of Lewis Benson and his whereabouts. If he's got access to cash, he will be near impossible to trace, but I'm mindful that in today's almost

The Lost Soul

cashless society most companies want a credit card as payment for hotel rooms and car hire.

Struggling to get into Benson's online bank accounts, I try his phone records.

A few moments later, Steph leans over my shoulder, and asks quietly, 'any luck?'

I shake my head slightly, 'can't get into his bank accounts,' I mutter, my eyes never leaving the screen. I press the numbers one, two, three, four and fully expect to keep putting in various numbers and letters. But, bloody hell, I'm shocked and a bit disgusted that those four numbers allow me access to Benson's phone accounts.

Why the hell would someone do that? Use the easiest password imaginable for the most important information in their life; bank accounts, phone records.

'I've got into his phone records!' I announce to the group, the sound of relief is evident in my voice. 'You got a printer in here?' I ask Nick, who nods to the filing cabinet behind me. Swivelling in my chair, I check the printer details before I link my laptop and the printer and press print. 'Nick, can you go through these, and see if anything turns up?'

We listen as the printer comes to life and without saying a word, Nick moves to the printer and waits for the paperwork to finish printing before grabbing the sheets and pulling a nearby chair to the side of the desk, he drops himself into it, reaches for a pen and eagerly begins scanning the printed papers.

The Lost Soul

God help us all, if we don't get some good luck soon

.

The Lost Soul

Part 38: Sasha

When I was thirteen years old, my English teacher introduced me
to a book by an author called RJ Minney. The book was called
Carve Her Name With Pride and is the true-story of a British
Special Operations Executive (SOE) agent called Violette Szabo,
one of the bravest women in British history and one of only four
women in history, to be posthumously awarded the George Cross.
Her father was British and her mother French.

This fascinating young woman was a young war widow, with a
small child, who transitioned from serving on the perfume
counter at Le Bon Marche in Brixton, London, to becoming a
secret agent in the Second World War. Violette was parachuted
into occupied France on her second mission and captured by the
Nazis before being tortured, interrogated and deported to
Ravensbrück concentration camp in Germany. Finally, she was
executed at the camp in 1946, aged only 23.

Violette's daughter, Tania, was only two years old in 1946 when
her mother died, and I often wondered why Violette would risk
her life in such a way, that would leave her daughter, growing up
without her one remaining parent, being brought up by her
grandparents.

The Lost Soul

Now, I'm a mum, I get it. I get why Violette needed to work against the Nazis, to help bring the war to an end, to make a better world for her daughter to grow up in. History is filled with people who gave their all, to make a difference, to make it a better place.

I get it now.

There is nothing stronger than a parent protecting their child.

***

I wake up with a start, it's cold and there's a dampness in the air. My arm is cramped, where I'm holding Zoe. We're huddled under a thin duvet. The duvet is white, with no cover. My daughter stirs, and I stare hard in the semi-dark room. There are curtains that are mostly closed, but daylight is trying to creep through.

With my free hand, I reach for my phone which lies in the pocket of my dress, and then realise with dismay that it was confiscated by my father yesterday. As I look up at the shadowed ceiling, I wonder how I am going to get Zoe and myself out of this situation unscathed. Getting the phone back would be my best option, but is nearly impossible. I know where it is, but the battle will be to get it back and to make a call, undetected.

I'm not sure what his plans are for us, but after we arrived here, we had been bundled upstairs to this old, jaded room where the only piece of furniture is the metal bed. My father had slammed the door shut behind us. The sound of a bolt being drawn had filled me with dread, as Zoe had sobbed in my arms.

But Lewis Benson has forgotten one thing.

358

The Lost Soul

I am my father's daughter. And, I won't go down without a fight. Whatever his plans I will give my life for my daughter.

'Mummy, I'm thirsty,' Zoe whispers in the semi daylight. My watch says it's 9am, so not too early.

'Sorry, sweetie,' I tell her, looking into her frightened face and stroking the curls from her forehead. 'I'll buy you a thousand chocolate milkshakes when we get home.'

'A thousand?' her lips turn up slightly, 'that's a lot of chocolate milkshake.'

I pull the duvet around us, and look at my daughter, as if for the first time. I don't want my ghosts to shadow her past, but they have already caught up with me, and I need her help to get us out of here.

'Listen Zoe,' I tell her quietly, 'the man that has taken us is, my dad.'

Her eyes widen, and her mouth forms an O shape, 'your dad?' she repeats. 'Aren't daddies supposed to love their children?' she asks, innocently.

'Yes,' I whisper, 'but not all people are good, my daddy used to hurt me and my mummy. Make us cry.'

To shatter a child's innocence is soul destroying. I don't want her to know these things about me, and the world we live in. Not yet, but I need to get her on board.

'We need to get away from him, but first, I need my phone back. I need to call for help,' I tell her.

359

The Lost Soul

She strokes my face, as if we have formed an elite army. A special task force to escape from our captor.

'I will keep him busy, when we get out of here, but if you get a chance, I want you to try and look in his jacket pocket to find my phone. If you can't, that's fine too. But, if you can, I can call for help.'

'If I get it, where can I put it, so he won't see?' she asks. I look at her, my mind flicking through various hiding places, that are easily accessible. Maybe this plan is stupid, but we can potentially succeed, if I annoy him enough, he'll hurt me, and forget about her.

'Put it in your panties, or pass it to me, if he's not looking.' I tell her. 'But first, we need to leave a clue that we've been here,' I reach for the neck of her sleeveless party dress, where it is decorated with delicate purple butterfly motifs. My fingers scoop around to the side of the neck. 'Sorry darling,' I tell her. 'But Nick and Stuart will know instantly that we've been here, when they see this. Do you trust me?'

She nods, giving me the most precious gift. Trust. 'Brace yourself,' I yank at the motif, and it comes away in my hand, with a little tear. 'Let's put this just next to the pillow,' I tell her, slipping the torn butterfly beside the flattened pillows.

'One more thing, my dad doesn't like babies or children. He doesn't like the noise. I'll need you to be a distraction, so I can make the call to Nick.'

The Lost Soul

'We have to be ready at any moment because my dad is unpredictable, so remember the plan. Look out for my phone,' I tell her, kissing her soft warm cheek.

We talk some more, until heavy footsteps echo up the stairs and stop at the bedroom door. I hold Zoe close as the bolt is lifted. My father stands there, dressed in black trousers and a black zip down sweat top. His face is devoid of emotion, maybe it has always been like that, and I just accepted him as he was. This man, my father, standing at the foot of the bed, with his hands on his hips, is nothing but a psychopath, a monster.

'You're awake,' he says. Neither of us answer him. He reaches into his trouser pocket and takes out two breakfast cereal bars and throws them carelessly onto the bed. 'Here, eat up.'

'Zoe is thirsty, do you have water?' I ask.

'No, she'll have to make do,' he says. 'Now eat your breakfast, we are leaving in five minutes.'

I scramble along the duvet, collect the bars and open them up. I hand Zoe hers, before I take a bite of mine. 'Eat up, sweetie,' I say quietly, 'we need to move. Remember what I said.'

'What was that?' My father asks, turning my way.

'Nothing. I was telling Zoe to eat it up quickly,' I tell him.

He stands in the doorway and waits for us to finish chewing. Leaving the wrappers on the bed, I feel Zoe take my hand as she follows my lead. We walk carefully down the steep steps, my father a few steps ahead. Waiting.

The Lost Soul

I search the room and my gaze wanders to the white duvet scrunched on the old-patterned sofa. So, he slept down here last night. That's interesting. There's a coffee cup on the floor by the sofa.

My father walks across the room, picks up the coffee cup and tilts its contents into his mouth. Jesus. I scan the room for his jacket, it's not there. Bugger.

'Right, time for us to leave,' he takes the gun that is tucked in the waistband of his trousers walks to the kitchen.

'We need to use the toilet,' I tell him, following him into the kitchen. Immediately, I see his navy jacket, sitting on the top of the blue and white kitchen unit.

'No!' he says, 'don't push me, Sasha.'

'Push you!' I say, 'we need the toilet, or would you rather my daughter and I soil the car.'

Zoe looks at me wide eyed. It's ok honey, I silently tell her.

'Go, quickly,' he jams the butt of the gun into my back.

I take Zoe's hand. 'Come on,' I walk us to the uninviting, windowless bathroom. 'Leave the door open,' he says.

'Pervert,' I spit back at him.

'Shut your fucking mouth!' he pushes me forward with the gun. Inside there is nothing to use as a weapon, so Zoe and I quickly relieve ourselves, and prepare to put our plan into action. My eyes motion to the jacket. She nods.

The Lost Soul

When we return to the kitchen, I stand by the jacket and lean on the counter, pushing it slightly towards the edge.

'You made a mess of my mother,' I suddenly say, watching his blank expression. I need to press a few buttons to give us time to find the phone. Zoe stands half beside me, half behind. 'I just want to know one thing,' I say, staring at this hateful person, who is my biological father.

His eyes look my way, now I've got his attention. I feel movement behind me. Zoe.

'Why do you do it? I mean, hurt my mother? Hurt me?' I know that's more than one question, but I need to provoke him, so that Zoe can find the phone.

'It's your mother's fault, she's always doing stupid things,' he sneers at me. 'She knows it makes me mad, and she continues to do it. She does it on purpose.'

'Oh, for pity's sake, listen to yourself.' I put my hands on my hips. 'You sound like a bloody stuck record,' and then I did something that I knew would ignite a fire within my father. I mimic him, feign his voice, use a whining, pathetic tone. 'She didn't cook the dinner right, or iron my shirt properly. Then she had the audacity to look at me in a funny way, she's such a...'

The slap comes quickly, giving me no time to prepare, as he hits me hard across the face. Pain sears my nose and cheeks, and I stumble sideways, holding my arm out, to keep Zoe behind me. God, that hurt. I think he broke my nose.

The Lost Soul

'Such a big man!' I splutter, as hot fat tears smart my eyes, but there is no way I'm going to give him the satisfaction of seeing them roll down my cheeks.

'Get the fuck in the car, before I finish you here and now,' he shouts, taking my car keys out of his trouser pocket and handing them to me. I use the sleeve of my grey cardigan to dab at my bloody nose, before taking my daughter's hand and pulling her towards the door.

When I've unlocked the car, I lean in to fasten Zoe's seatbelt. Studying her face, I raise my eyebrows, in a silent question. She winks. I didn't even know my young daughter could wink. Glancing quickly behind me, my father is pulling on his jacket. I gesture for the phone and watch in awe as she takes it from inside her pink panties. I wink back and stick it into the linen pocket of my dress.

I can't believe she managed to get it.

'Your nose is bleeding,' she says quietly.

'Don't worry, it's nothing. Looks worse than it is,' I reply. Clicking her seatbelt in place, I give her a peck on the cheek and move around to the driver's seat. The weight of the phone feels heavy in my pocket, as I settle behind the steering wheel, and check my mirrors.

Now I have a lifeline to call for help. Anyone will do, but Nick is the first person I think of.

Something hard bangs on my window, making me jump. It's him. I open the car door and look at him.

The Lost Soul

'Give me the keys, I'm locking you in. Need the bathroom before we go,' he says.

Handing him the car keys, he slams the door shut and I hear the car lock from the inside.

'Keep an eye out for him, Zoe,' I quickly turn to her, 'I'm going to call for help.'

As soon as he disappears into the cottage, I reach in and get my phone out. Quickly turning the power on, I sigh when I see that there is only half of the battery life left; but it should be enough for me to make a phone call or to call Nick and leave the line open. But I don't know where we're going, and I need him to follow us or meet us there. I choose option two. Calling Nick, I listen to it ring, hoping he'll pick up. 'Come on. Come on, I mutter. 'Pick up the bloody phone.' But there's no answer and all I can hope for now, is that if I leave the call open, that it will click onto his voice mail.

'Mummy, he's coming back,' Zoe's voice is urgent. Shit! Where the hell can I hide it? Do I put in my dress pocket, or in the side compartment of the car? Nick needs to hear where we are going.

I choose the dress pocket.

There is a click as the central locking system unlocks the car, my father drops into the passenger seat, and hands me the car keys.

'So, where are we going?' I ask casually, turning on the ignition. Where would he take us?

The Lost Soul

'Back to the main road, and turn right,' he says, holding the gun in his lap. 'Don't try anything, or you'll get another slap.'

I turn the steering wheel. 'You'll never get the father of the year award, you know,' I say conversationally. 'Not with that attitude.'

'Shut up and drive, you little bitch,' he snarls.

With pleasure, you sadistic pig.

With pleasure.

Part 39: Jack

We're in the office at Greystones, when Steph's phone starts to ring. I watch her walk slowly to the window and look out into the landscaped gardens beyond, before taking the call:

'Hi Anthony, it's DI Rutland. What can I do for you?' she asks, her voice serious. 'He did? What did you say?' She listens and the room suddenly goes silent, I hold my breath, this could be the breakthrough we're looking for. 'All right, Anthony calm down. No, you've done nothing wrong. In fact, you've done a good thing by calling me. Text me the address, will you? Thanks again.'

Bloody hell, this sounds like the good news we are looking for.

We all gather around Steph, waiting for her to tell us what Anthony said.

'Benson got in touch with Anthony a couple of days ago, asking him to book a cottage in Haworth for a week on his credit card and said he'd transfer the money.'

Holy fuck, it feels like we're getting really close.

Steph's phone pings to life. 'I've got the address. Jenny, can you stay here and keep checking those phone records,' she directs Jenny as though she is part of an investigation team. 'Look for

The Lost Soul

Sasha's number, Greystones number, anything that connects him to Anthony and Sasha to him.'

Jenny nods and reaches over to hand Steph her jacket. My fiancé smiles her thanks, touching Jenny's arm softly. I love the way these two interact, how Jenny watches over Steph and the others. Quietly in the background, Jenny and Stuart, are the glue that keep the family together.

'Right, Jack,' Steph looks at me, but I am already at her side. I will always be at her side, no matter what shit goes down. We are destined to be together, and I can't wait for the next few weeks until she becomes my wife. 'Stuart and Nick, you're with me. Let's get this son of a bitch.'

Steph forwards the address to us all. Nick and Stuart take Nick's car and follow me and Steph. Google maps says it's a cottage in Stanbury, the next village – not more than five minutes away.

'How do you want to play this?' I ask, as I drive along West Lane, following the Sat Nav.

'As near to the book as possible,' she smiles grimly. 'If they are there, our first priority is to get Sasha and Zoe to safety. Anything after that is a bonus.'

Her warm hand soothes my thigh. God, this is going to be a nightmare. I check my rear-view mirror and see Nick's blue Fiesta following us. Turning right onto a dirt track, we bounce over potholes, which will do the suspension on the car no good at all, until around three hundred yards on the left of the track, is a

The Lost Soul

tired old looking, two up two down cottage. There is no sign of life, or Sasha's grey Peugeot. Crap.

The first thing we notice when we get out, is that the windows are dirty and some of the nets and curtains are hanging from their poles. Jesus! It's in a terrible state. Hairs stand up on my arms, as I think of Sasha and Zoe being held here.

Who could rent this unloved place out and hope to make money from it? Clearly someone, but it looks unfit for human habitation. The brown wooden door is rotting and there is no garden to speak of. We knock on the door, and unsurprisingly, there's no answer.

'Stuart, Nick. You go around the other side and we'll meet you at the back. Call if you see anything.' They both nod and walk slowly around the far side of the small building.

We slowly move around to the back of the building, following Steph as we walk beside a mall stone wall that has fallen apart in big clumps, weeds grow along the wall, leading to an old black paint weathered door, with a latch.

'We've found another door,' I call to the others, and wait they step over the dilapidated stone wall and clumps of weeds, to reach us. Steph takes out a pair of disposable gloves from her coat pocket and slips them on her hands, before handing pairs to me, Stuart and Nick.

'When we get inside,' Steph orders, I'm on full alert, not if but when, 'don't touch anything unless you're wearing gloves.'

She carefully lifts the latch, it seems locked, but when she tugs again it squeaks in protest, but begins to move. Apart from the

The Lost Soul

squeak and the snap of us donning the gloves, there are no sounds
at all. We follow Steph through the open door into a dark, dank
room with a very basic kitchen of pale blue and white units. A
silver, whistle-top kettle, sits on one of the rings of the gas
cooker, I move forward and slowly put my hand onto it, it's
lukewarm.

'It's warm,' I tell them. Nick's face pales, but he keeps his cool.
Off the kitchen is a small simple bathroom; a bath, a sink and a
toilet.

We walk into the front room where we find the flight of stairs that
leads to the first floor. Again, the room is dark, the furniture
consists of a faded, patterned sofa and a wingback chair. A new
looking duvet and a cushion are strewn across the sofa. A black
mug sits on the floor, next to it.

'Stuart, stay here in case he comes back, will you?' she asks and
Stuart nods, still looking around the room.

As we climb the stairs, my hairs stand on end. What will we find?
I have no idea. At the top of the stairs there are two rooms, both
with closed doors. The room we choose first, is the one fitted with
a large silver bolt on the outside. I bend closer to the floor and see
shavings of wood. 'Look,' I point to the dirty patterned brown
carpet, 'that bolt has just recently been put on.'

Using her gloved hand, Steph opens the door slowly. I'm holding
my breath, as we walk into a bedroom, that is both dark and
dismal. The only piece of furniture in the room is a bed, which is
made up with a sheet, two new pillows and a new duvet. No
covers or cases. The bed isn't made, but the relief I feel when I

The Lost Soul

realise that it is empty is almost palpable. I turn to Nick and pat his shoulder:

'You okay?' I ask, but he just nods and closes his eyes, taking deep breaths.

'I think they were here,' Steph says, bending over the bed and looking at us. How does she know this for sure? She takes a photo of something inside the bed, near the pillow.

She picks up a pale pink butterfly. It looks like one from Zoe's dress and it sits alongside two empty breakfast cereal wrappers. Taking out two evidence bags from her trouser pocket, she puts the wrappers in one and the butterfly in the other, before sealing them and putting them back in her pocket.

'Fuck! We have got to call the police, Steph,' I tell her, there is no coming back from this, 'they need to get crime scene in here, right now.'

'I know, I know,' she mutters as we check the second upstairs room and find it completely empty. No furniture, carpet, nothing.

When we return to the living room, we tell Stuart what we have found and make the decision between us that, when we call the police, Nick will need to be kept away from Greystones, or ideally, he needs to disappear.

Of course, Nick doesn't hesitate, as he nods his agreement, with a grim look on his face, but that's the measure of a man who puts human life first. With an air of despair and frustration, we leave the cottage and head back to our cars.

The Lost Soul

Nick takes the keys to his car, and his phone from his trouser pocket. I watch as he presses the release button, to open his car door. He quickly scans his phone and his face pales.

'Shit!' he mutters.

'What?' I ask, hoping that it's something that will help us find Sasha. Steph, Stuart and I, step closer to Nick, waiting for him to answer.

'I've got a voice message,' Nick looks at Steph.

'From Sasha?' Steph asks.

'Not sure,' he says, as his fingers move effortlessly across the keypad. Nick puts the phone to his ear and begins to listen to the message. His shoulder is slump slightly, and his eyes find mine. 'It's her,' he says.

Steph touches Nick's shoulder, offering reassurance. 'Put it on speaker,' Steph tells him, before she turns to me. 'Can you bring up the tracker on Sasha's device?'

I nod, taking out my phone, we listen to the message. '*You'll never get the father of the year award, you know,*' Sasha says conversationally. *'Not with that attitude.'*

'Shut up and drive, you little bitch,' Benson's clipped, harsh voice can be heard in the background, along with Zoe's sobs.

Bloody hell.

'And keep that whore child of yours quiet, or I'll slap her.'

The Lost Soul

I look at Nick, and my fists curl at my sides. His knuckles are white against his phone. There's a queue for a piece of Mr Lewis Benson.

'Don't you dare touch my daughter! You bully.' Sasha warns.

There is the sound of a slap. I think he's hit Sasha.

'If you hadn't been born, your mother and I would have been happy.' Benson snarls.

'What kind of reality do you live in?' Sasha retorts, 'All you do is bully, belittle and hurt her. How the hell can that have made her happy?'

Another slap and Sasha winces loudly. Zoe's sobs grow louder.

'Mummy, I want to go home. I'm frightened.'

'I know baby,' Sasha reassures her, 'we will go home soon.'

'You'll never go back,' Benson shouts. 'You're both going somewhere cold, dark and wet where you'll meet your fucking maker.'

Fuck, I look at Steph. She reaches for my free hand, and I hold tight, trying to give a reassurance, I'm not feeling. I look at my phone, watch the tracker. I don't know the area at all well, but I can see that they're not that far in front of us. 'Got you!' I say, releasing Steph's hand.

'You're all talk, you wouldn't dare. The nearest water here is the reservoir. No!' Sasha shouts.

The Lost Soul

'Eyes on the road, keep going. Won't be long now.' Benson's chilling voice booms over the phone.

'Fuck,' mutters Nick taking the phone and jumping into the Fiesta, 'follow me, I know where they're heading.'

The Lost Soul

Part 40: Jules

'Whatever happens today, Jules, I want you to know that I don't regret saving you.'

I glance furtively across to Stuart as I put the car into third gear on the side road that leads to Ponden Reservoir. I know what he is saying.

'I'm glad you did, or I would never have met Sasha and Zoe,' I say solemnly, checking that Jack and Steph are following us. 'I would never have had the chance to rebuild my life and to fall in love.' I tell him honestly.

'But things might not go the way we want them to, today. You might have to disappear again, and I'm sorry for that,' Stuart's deep voice shows genuine concern.

'If it happens, it happens,' I say. 'As long as Sasha and Zoe are safe, I will do what needs to be done.'

The silence is almost too much. I focus my mind on finding them both.

'No, dad. We're not going in there!' Sasha's voice booms over the phone, she sounds terrified. And then the voicemail ends.

375

The Lost Soul

I just want to speak to her and reassure her that I'm coming for her, for them both. In all seriousness, they could be anywhere on this beautiful, but barren landscape. As we reach Scar Top Road, I let out a huge sigh of relief, I spot Sasha's green Peugeot, it's parked on the side of the narrow road. I know they're nearby.

I bring my car to a halt, beside hers and throw the door open. I'm on my feet and moving around the car within seconds. Leaving Stuart still unbuckling his seatbelt, I look around me and try to get my bearings. My heart is beating so fast, at the vast wilderness surrounding the reservoir, and it suddenly feels like I am looking for a needle in a haystack. There is no sign of life among the heather and barren land, for as far as I can see.

Just a big area of wasteland, and a scattering of morning breeze. Where the hell are they? Turning my gaze from the moorland to face the reservoir, my eyes focus on the wire fenced enclosure around the water, near to several wooden gated access points. As soon as I see the open gate about fifty meters away, my gut instinct kicks in.

Movement in the distance catches my eye, and I exhale with relief when I see the small group of people on the grass verge, moving slowly towards the reservoir and the deep, dark water. Without thinking, I give chase, vaguely I hear Stuart shouting my name behind me, but I ignore him as I focus on reaching Sasha and Zoe and getting them away from that monster

The tall figure of Lewis Benson becomes more recognisable, the closer I get to them. He is pulling Sasha and Zoe towards the unforgiving water. Fear is mixed with anger; I am going to bloody kill him. Footsteps follow in my wake, but I don't turn,

The Lost Soul

I'm guessing it's Stuart, Jack and Steph. All the while, my eyes never leave Benson.

He's pushing Sasha and a crying Zoe across rough, uneven grassland, towards the water's edge. I can hear Sasha's and Zoe's sobs, and my anger builds. I am so angry because I didn't protect them from this man, that I didn't try harder. How could I have foreseen this? No one knew where he was, or what he was planning. Clearly, after what he did to his wife, he is a man on the edge, with nothing to lose.

'Let them go, Benson!' I shout as I rush through the open gate.

'Never!' Benson shouts back, dressed dark clothes, with his arm firmly locked around Sasha's neck, and his free hand pulling her five-year-old daughter along harshly. That's when I notice the gun in his hand, the one attached to his arm around her neck. Holy shit! He's carrying a weapon.

Zoe is crying, 'Mummy! Mummy! Ow! He's hurting my arm.'

At the sound of Zoe's panicked sobs, I step closer to them, my adrenaline surging into hyper mode, I am ready to do battle, I will do anything to protect them. Benson stops and Sasha immediately pushes her head forwards and throws it back, into the bridge of his nose.

'Thames Valley Police!' Steph shouts. 'It's over, Benson. Give yourself up.'

There is nothing more powerful than watching a mother protecting her child, it's exhilarating to see the strength even the slightest person can have, when motivated. A warm feeling fills

The Lost Soul

my chest and I'm shocked by the raw, intense emotions I feel for this woman and her child.

Droplets of rain fall on my face and glancing briefly at the dark clouds that are looming overhead. Benson moans and inadvertently releases Zoe; stumbling back, he howls and covers his nose with his hands. I take the opportunity to shout to the little girl to run to me. As though watching a film in slow motion, Zoe hurries our way, still wearing her pale pink party dress, swishing across the uneven ground, her red blotchy face streaming with tears.

Steph steps forwards and grabs the little girl's tiny hands hauling her tightly into her warm body, all the time Zoe cries. 'I want my Mummy,' her little voice gulping in air amidst her sobs. 'I want my Mummy.'

I walk to Zoe and pat her long curly hair, kneeling to the ground I hug her briefly.

'I'm going to get your Mummy,' I say quietly. 'Close your eyes and count to ten very slowly.'

Benson recovers from the attack, and I can see that he still has the gun in his hand. I wonder why he hasn't used it yet. If he wanted them both dead surely, he would have done it by now? I suspect he's using the weapon to maintain power and control over his daughter and granddaughter. To bend them to his will.

Hastily, Benson grabs Sasha firmly by the shoulders and throws her to the hard unforgiving ground. He hauls her on to her back and uses the strength in his legs to straddle her and pin her arms against her body. His brutish hands grasp her neck, pushing down

The Lost Soul

and he doesn't appear bothered that the gun has fallen to the ground beside her head. Benson's recklessness is a clear indicator that he plans to end his daughter's life today. Jesus, he is pushing his thumbs hard into her throat trying to strangle her. Sasha's screams send ice-cold chills down my spine.

Fuck.

Steph's urgent voice shouts again to Benson, 'That's enough, Benson. Let Sasha go. You have nowhere to go.'

'I'd rather kill myself than let you take me in,' snarls Benson, as he raises his face to Steph. Sasha's panicked screams suddenly quieten as though she has run out of fight, then she makes one last effort to wriggle free. Her arms suddenly wrench free, and I see her father's face distort with anger as he tries to fight off his daughter's flailing arms. That's my girl. It's not in her to give in.

I can hear Zoe counting slowly to ten. 'What number are you at Zoe?' I turn to her briefly, whilst making my way to Sasha. 'Five,' she shouts, back.

'Good girl, nearly there. Count the last five numbers really slowly for me,' I call back.

Right. Let's finish this now. I pick up the pace and run the last few steps to the sparring couple. Spotting the gun on the grass, I kick it away direction and shout to Benson:

'Get your fucking hands off her!'

Throwing myself on top of him, I reach for his clothing, anything to pull him off her. I grasp his jacket and drag Benson off her, with all the strength I can muster. He's heavier, than I imagined,

The Lost Soul

but I don't stop until the poor excuse for a human being is thrown to his knees, a few feet away from Sasha. Stuart moves to Benson's side and helps me to drag him to his feet, while Jack checks out Sasha and helps her to her feet.

Sasha's face looks like she's boxed five rounds with Mike Tyson and will be imprinted on my mind forever. There are finger indentions and scratches on her neck, and her nose looks broken.

With shaking, bloody hands she pulls her grey cardigan, around herself in a protective gesture and wipes the tears from her eyes. She suddenly looks so small and vulnerable, as if the adrenaline that she had been using to keep her and her daughter safe, had now completely disappeared.

Pinning Benson's arms tightly behind his back, I wait for Steph to reach me with the cuffs. After what he has done to his family, he should be imprisoned somewhere cold and dark for the remainder of his miserable life. Deep down, there is also a part of me that wants revenge.

 He knows he's finished, there's no way back from this. The respectability, the nice home, the family, the wife, the career. Everything is gone. And it is all his own fault.

Steph reaches us and puts metal handcuffs on Benson. I watch as Steph reads him his rights, his face and nose are bloody, and his eyes remain cold and hard. A monster, through and through. What must it have been like to marry this man or to have been unfortunate enough to be his child? I really want to punch him, but the last time I did that, I became a cult vigilante on social media.

The Lost Soul

Sasha sways gently and Jack slides his arm around her waist to hold her steady, in turn, she leans against him, uses his strength to regain her own. I ignore the stab of jealousy that causes a dip in the pit of my stomach. Jealousy that believes it should be me holding her steady and giving her comfort.

I sense her brown bloodshot eyes looking for me and I hold her gaze for a moment before nodding grimly. Sasha, my fearless warrior woman leaves Jack and walks slowly, with her back straight and an air of confidence, to face her father. The monster who had abused her, abused her mother and kidnapped his own daughter and grandchild. She tilts her chin, defiantly and holds his gaze.

'You are a bully, a bastard and I fucking hate you,' she hisses, before swallowing spittle and spitting in his face. Then she walks off, with her head held high, to find her daughter.

I am about to walk away, but I simply can't leave it alone. My mind won't settle. Fuck it. So, facing the man with the hard eyes and chilling face, the one who has no scruples, I step right in his personal space. When we're nose to nose, I say:

'Strange how you always pick on someone smaller or physically weaker than yourself. In my mind, you're nothing but a sick coward.' I pull my fist back, see the panic in his eyes and punch him hard in the face.

Steph's eyes widen in horror. 'Nick!'

I ignore her, enjoying the sight of blood that is spreading across his dazed expression and remembering the way he cowered when he knew I was about to hit him. That's the thing with bullies, they are so used to being the instigator, they think they're invincible.

'That's for Sasha and for Zoe,' I tell him, feeling satisfied that I got my moment with Benson. It was so worth it. Turning, I walk away, to find my family. Zoe is being cradled like a baby in her mother's arms, and who can blame either of them. Their ordeal must have been terrifying.

My eyes seek out Sasha's brown ones, 'Are you okay?' I ask, stroking her cheek softly. She swallows and for a moment, I glimpse the exhaustion and strain behind her eyes, how the ordeal of being kidnapped with her young child, has taken its toll on her. So, I reach out and pull them both close.

'I counted to ten, but you hadn't got Mummy, so I counted again,' Zoe smiles through her tears, as I hold them tightly.

I stroke her head and smile at her sweet face, before leaning in to kiss her cheek. 'You did good, Zoe. Very good.'

There's a noise and I turn to see Benson, his hands are securely cuffed behind him, he begins to walk, but he's moving backwards. Bloody hell, I don't think he realises which direction he is going in.

'Stop!' I shout, as Steph, Stuart and Jack try to warn Benson what is coming next.

Benson turns around, he finally looks forward and sees that he's standing so very close to the edge of the reservoir. 'Bugger,' he says, looking back at the three people surrounding him. 'No way out,' he mutters.

The Lost Soul

'There is,' Steph pleads, putting her hand out, 'Don't do this.'

I turn Sasha and Zoe away, shield them from what I think is about to happen.

'No!' Sasha screams in horror. She hates her pathetic excuse for a father, but I'm sure she would never want him to do this. It's almost as though he wants her to have this last ugly memory of him. A bastard to the end.

'I'm not going to prison,' are his last words as he free falls, down into the deep, dark waters of the reservoir.

The echo of Sasha's anguished sobs spread across the desolate moorland, like the ghosts of the tragic Bronte siblings whose lives were taken much too soon, and all I can do is soothe her and hold her close.

Stuart shakes his head and puts a hand briefly on Steph's shoulder as they stand by the water's edge, looking for sign of life. Jack follows slowly, taking Steph's hand and lacing his fingers through hers, offering whatever comfort he can. We are all in shock.

For long moments, the three search for Benson. Steph turns to look at us and shakes her head.

Bloody hell. He never came back up.

When they finally reach us. Stuart is the first to speak.

'Can I have a word?' He says, his face grim. I nod, I think I know what's coming, and my heart slams in my chest.

This is the end of beginning.

The Lost Soul

Part 41: Sasha

I am holding Zoe tightly in my arms, on this chilly May morning. Nick is talking quietly to Stuart nearby. I can't make out what is being said, but I catch the words, 'I'm sorry.'

Nick nods, and with his head down and slumped shoulders, he walks my way. When he reaches me, and raises his face to mine, I know that something is drastically wrong. His face is pale, his eyes are half-closed and his lips are set in a grim line. When his eyes fully open and he looks at me, my heart misses a beat. There is a feeling of utter despair emanating from him.

After witnessing my father throw himself into the the reservoir, my nerves are on edge. I hated him, true, but he was still my father. Right or wrong. He had always been a strong influence in my life, he had provided a roof over my head and food in my belly as a child and influenced the way I wanted to live my life as I grew older; when I understood that I didn't have to live with fear and cruelty in my life. I knew that I deserved better.

How can I mourn someone as detestable as my father? I argued inwardly. How can I let this unpredictable and cruel man win? Because to do that, would make me the victim, and there is no way I'm taking that title.

The Lost Soul

No way in hell.

I would gladly have killed him with my bare hands, for what he had put my daughter through over the past sixteen hours. She is the innocent in all of this, she shouldn't have to pay for being my daughter. And, for that I'll never forgive him.

So, I guess, throwing himself into the reservoir was a fitting way to end his life, full of drama and angst. And totally his own choice.

At this point though, I am not sure how much more emotional torment I can take today. My thoughts turn to my mother, still in hospital, battered in body and spirit. Will she be relieved he's gone? Will she be upset? For the loss of a husband, the same way I am half-heartedly stricken by my father's death.

After all, she must have loved him at some point in her life. There would have been some good memories, wouldn't there? Who knows what goes on behind clothes doors, because often you are only able to see, what people allow you to see.

I lower Zoe to the ground, but don't let go of her hand. I need to keep her close. Jack and Steph, wait patiently by their car, waiting patiently for us to finish our conversations.

'Sasha,' Nick begins, his eyes glistening.

This is it. It feels very much like a goodbye.

'Don't say it, Nick. Don't bloody say it,' I dare him to utter the words that will tear us apart.

The Lost Soul

'I'm sorry, Sasha but I have to go,' he says, his voice husky with emotion. Glancing at his fisted hands, it appears that it is as hard for him to leave us, as it is for us to be left.

'No!' I argue. 'We can work this out,' I can hear my voice rising. I know I'm making a fool of myself, as tears blur my vision, but I can't bear it if he leaves. I have fallen in love with this gentle, loving, protective man. Not a young teenage love, like the one I had with Dylan, but a grown-up friendship, that simmered slowly into love. We are like two kindred spirits, finding each other through a never-ending storm.

'I'm sorry Sasha, maybe in another life, we would have had a chance,' he reaches out, begging for my understanding, for my forgiveness.

'Another life?' I ask harshly, as hot, tears fall down my cheeks. I take a step away from him, 'but this is the only life we have, don't we owe each other the chance to make this work?'

He brushes a hand over his face, shaking his head, 'I wish we could, but I have to move on. I have to move away. We can use this opportunity to make people think that I drowned too.' He looks at Stuart, standing beside us, now. His face solemn, his brows furrowed in sadness.

'I need to keep you and Zoe safe,' Nick's voice is strained, 'it's the only way. If something happened to either of you, because of me, I'd never forgive myself.'

Stuart steps forward, strokes Zoe's hair and admits, 'He's right, Sasha. I helped Jules because I thought it was the right thing to

The Lost Soul

do, but in doing that, I sentenced him to a lifetime of looking over his shoulder. That's no way for someone to live.'

Nick gently cups my sore face in his large hand. His forehead bends to touch mine. 'I'm sorry.' He whispers, as my tears continue to fall and my heart breaks. 'So, fucking sorry.'

He turns to Zoe and gives her a sad smile, 'I've got to go away for a while, Zoe. Give your mummy lots of cuddles, and don't let her hands get too wrinkled.' He aims for humour, so that my daughter has no idea what he is really doing. If he is anything like me, his heart is shattering into tiny pieces.

'Let's go,' he tells Stuart, quietly.

This has been a day of contrasts, a day of pain, fear, joy and love. And finally, a day of extreme loss.

As I stand on the rugged moorland by the reservoir, Zoe's hand in mine, the cold wind in my hair, the numbness takes hold, and the sun reflects my dark mood by moving behind the clouds.

And, then I remember, it's my birthday. Jesus. How unlucky am I?

I watch as he walks away from me in his thick navy zip-top sweatshirt and black jeans. His shoulders slump as he walks across the moors, with Stuart, back to the car. Each step taking him further away from me. I feel bereft and numb.

Damn, why can't I have the bloody fairy tale?

The Lost Soul

Part 42: Zoe

I wake up crying, and mummy rushes into my room, she sits on the side of my bed. She is making soft sounds to help settle me.

Wiping my wet tears from my face, I let mummy snuggle into me and stroke my hair. It always soothes me.

'Will the bad man come back?' I ask mummy, rubbing my finger up and down her arm.

'No, he won't.' Mummy says with a strong voice. He won't be able to hurt you again.'

'But.'

'No buts, darling,' Mummy strokes my face. 'They recovered his body, so there is no way he can come back.'

'Sometimes, I see him in my dreams,' I whisper, my eyelids beginning to droop.

'Me too,' she says quietly.

'Wish Nick was still here,' I tell her. It's a secret, I don't usually say his name because it makes mummy cry.

'Me too,' she whispers back, as sleep claims me.

The Lost Soul

The Lost Soul

Part 43: Sasha

There has been no contact.

Two weeks have passed, and I can't stop thinking about Nick. He said he had to go away, to keep Zoe and me safe. He told me it was for the best. The best for who? Don't I get a say in the decision?

Stuart called me the day after my father's death, to say that Nick was leaving the country, to start a new life. I want the best for him, I really do, I don't want him to be constantly worrying someone will recognise him or find out about his past.

The police interviewed me after Nick had left, and I gave them my statement. I explained about my father and what had happened after Zoe's birthday party. It seemed straightforward and there was no need to mention Nick's name. Steph, Jack, and I had put together a story, about what happened when my father jumped into the reservoir, which we all stuck to, and it also gave Nick a get out clause.

Mostly, I wanted Nick to be happy and to be free.

Steph had taken Zoe and me to the local hospital to be checked out, particularly my sore face. Thankfully, my nose wasn't broken. But the pain I have, isn't physical or to do with my face.

The Lost Soul

I must admit, that starting afresh, where nobody knows me, sounds very appealing at the moment too. A new beginning, where no one knows that my dad was a psychotic serial abuser. So, considering all things, Zoe and I are doing all right. We are just getting through each day, one step at a time. If I'm honest though, I'm struggling to settle back into daily life again and Zoe still has nightmares.

Telling mum about dad, and what he did to Zoe and me, was hard. She cried down the line, for a long time. She kept repeating how sorry she was for everything. How she wished things had been different, so that I could have had a happier life. Tears had rolled down my cheeks, and it was all I could do, not to scream down the phone, that my dad was a bastard, and deserved everything he got, after the way he had treated us.

The good news is that she is now recuperating at Shore House and starting the slow process of reclaiming her life. At least my mum will have a chance to move forward now, perhaps she will even find some peace and happiness. With Stuart and Jenny's support, she will have every chance to start over.

Which brings me full circle to me, and why I'm struggling. I can't change the way I feel about Nick. I can't turn my feelings for him off, as though they are water in a tap. I can't pretend that Nick wasn't attacked, and that Zoe and I weren't kidnapped and dragged to that godforsaken reservoir.

Nick and I had grown close, not just as friends, but had fallen for each other in a more intimate and emotional sense. We had a connection. Despite this, a part of me, is mad at him because he didn't choose me and Zoe, when I needed him to fight for us. I

The Lost Soul

just wanted to be that person for him, the one he couldn't live without.

I know I'm in love with him, and I'm pretty sure he feels the same way, but he left us, and walked away. My mind is constantly shifting gear, from despair over losing him, to thinking about what could have been. He could so easily have been the man of my dreams.

Zoe sits at the dining table, in her blue dress with pink flowers, her little purple stockinged legs swinging backwards and forwards.

'Mummy, I've done a picture for Nick,' do you think he'll like it?' she asks eagerly, 'I wish I could give it to him. Will he come back?'

Shaking my head, I quickly wipe away a stray tear.

Moving to her side, I put my hand on her shoulder, and look at the picture. She's drawn herself in the middle with long curly hair, and me and Nick are standing either side, holding her hands. We are all smiling. It's very basic and we all have matchstick bodies, arms and legs, but the colours and facial expressions are great.

'This is wonderful, baby,' my voice is husky with emotion.

Smiling, I stroke her cheek. 'He will love it Zoe, we all look so happy.' Tears form in my eyes, and I use the sleeve of my dark red woollen dress to wipe away the rogue ones that reach my cheeks.

The Lost Soul

As I lower myself into the chair next to Zoe, and watch her choose a pink felt tipped pen, I can't help but wonder what the future holds for us now. Do I continue to work here and manage Greystones, with Vi looking after Zoe? Taking small steps until Zoe is at school full-time? Zoe's voice breaks into my thoughts, 'are you all right mummy?'

I force myself to smile, my daughter should not be worrying about me. I am the parent here.

'Of course, I am sweetie,' I reassure her, putting my arm around her small shoulders and squeezing them gently, 'I just feel a bit tired.' I kiss her soft cheek.

At some point in my life, I am going to have to make decisions that will impact on our journey together, important ones. Do I go left or right? Do I stay safe or spread my wings? Asking myself important questions, such as is he worth it? Do I trust him? And, despite his history, despite everything, I know I do.

However, trusting and loving someone, particularly in certain circumstances may not be enough. Sometimes, you have to know when to let go. Oh, bloody hell, I am spinning in circles again. It boils down to two things. Do I love him? Is he worth fighting for?

The grey mist in my mind clears, as I glance at Zoe's drawing of the three of us. And suddenly, there is nothing but clear blue skies, and everything becomes clear. I know what to do.

I make a decision.

Picking up my phone, I find Stuart's name and press call. He answers on the third ring. 'It's Sasha,' I say, 'I need your help.'

The Lost Soul

***

New staff have been brought in to cover my shifts, and Zoe's nursery have been alerted that we are moving away. Jenny arranges new passports because we're going to need new names.

So here I am, two weeks later, arriving on the beautiful Greek island of Corfu, with a five-year-old daughter and three suitcases, hot and tired. We take a taxi, loving the luscious green scenery, the winding roads and the amazing views of the landscape and sea. Eventually, on a gently sloping road, we arrive outside the gates of a large beautiful white walled villa in an affluent area, to the north-east of the island, called Kassiopi. I am still clutching the address on the handwritten note that Jenny has given me.

I reach out and unclasp Zoe's seatbelt. She's wearing a pink jersey dress decorated with small, white spots, on her back is a small Peppa Pig rucksack and clasped tightly in her little hands is Baby Annabell. Inside the rucksack is the folded drawing for Nick, which I proudly took a photo of, because she has attempted to write his name; 'to Nik, I ms u. Zoe. x'

My heart swelled with love when my daughter asked me to help her write the words. Opening the taxi door, I step outside into the heat of the midday sun. 'Zoe,' I murmur, gesturing with a hand, as she nods and climbs across the seat to follow me. The driver steps out of the car, opens the boot, takes out my three suitcases, and shows me on his fingers, to let me know the fare.

I'm wearing a light white cardigan over a simple emerald-green knee length dress and sandals. I reach into my purse, that sits

The Lost Soul

snugly inside my small brown crossover bag, and give him the money, telling him to keep the change.

As the taxi pulls away, I take Zoe's hand and press the silver buzzer on the wall beside the gate. I press three times and there is no answer. Damn, this isn't what I was expecting. This is not how I pictured our reunion. My stomach plummets with disappointment.

'Mummy, I need a wee,' Zoe says in a low voice. This is all I need, I wipe my warm forehead with my free hand, trying to ignore the rising panic in the pit of my stomach. Looking left down the winding tree lined street, I hope that Nick will materialise, like he does in my dreams, I'm gutted to see that the only sign of life is a young couple, walking hand in hand along the pavement.

A warm breeze blows across my arms, and my heart strums, when I hear a deep gasp from behind me. Slowly, I turn to my right and hold my breath. About ten yards away, just emerging from a corner, is the familiar sight of the man I love.

Panic sets in, what if he doesn't want me, or us? What if I imagined everything that has happened between us? Take a leap of faith, I tell myself.

'Nick! Nick! It's Nick, Mummy.' Zoe shouts, pulling on my hand. Without asking, she unclasps her hand from mine, drops Baby Annabell and runs to Nick.

He takes my breath away, in his white T-shirt, brown knee-length shorts and flip flops, but I stand firm. Watching him. Waiting. He

The Lost Soul

thought he was alone in this world, a nomad wandering from place to place, determined to hide from his past.

But he was wrong.

He's not alone. Anymore.

Our eyes meet and I smile. The shock on his face is priceless, but he quickly regains his composure, a huge smile spreads across his beautiful face, as he stoops to pick up Zoe and twirls her around.

'Zoe! What a great surprise!' he laughs at her giggles, holding her tight and kissing her cheek. 'I've missed you.'

'Missed you too,' Zoe's little hands grasp the sides of his face. 'I did you a picture. It's in Peppa.'

'We can get it in a moment,' I interrupt gently, picking up the discarded doll and walking slowly towards them. Watching the tender scene, it fills my heart with a joy I can't explain. That's the moment I know I've made the right decision, in coming here.

Carefully, Nick lowers Zoe to the ground, and faces me. His blue eyes are bright, but I can see he's apprehensive, see the bob of his throat as he swallows.

'Hi,' I say with a smile, reaching out to put my hand over his heart.

At my touch he closes his eyes and puts his hand over mine. When he opens his eyes, his face breaks into the biggest smile, lighting up my world.

'I can't believe you're here,' he says quietly.

The Lost Soul

'Where else would we be? We need to be, where you are. It doesn't matter where that is,' I say. And, then I mouth the word, 'home,' and before I take my next breath, I'm in his arms and he's kissing me as though we've been apart forever.

'Mummy, I really need a wee,' Zoe's voice sings in the background, bringing us back to reality.

Yes, I got the fairytale.

The Lost Soul

Part 44: Epilogue – Jules (two weeks later)

'On the BBC Leeds and West Yorkshire News tonight, Jules Walker the man arrested for the murder of Ray Delossi in Oxfordshire, six months ago, is believed to be dead. He was witnessed arguing with a man at Ponden Reservoir, near Stanbury, West Yorkshire yesterday afternoon. During the altercation, both men fell in the reservoir, which is fifty feet deep. Both appeared to get into difficulty, however, only one body has been recovered. The body has been identified as Oxfordshire MP, Lewis Benson. The local police diving team continue to search for Walker's body.

'Benson, was wanted by the police in connection with a vicious assault on his wife, and for kidnapping his estranged daughter and young granddaughter at gunpoint, in Haworth, West Yorkshire. Police arrived on the scene as Walker pulled the woman and her daughter, from Benson, kicking the gun to safety, before both engaged in a fight, resulting in them falling into the reservoir. It appears that the would-be vigilante saved the day again.'

'Jules' a soft voice calls, as I stare at the screen of my laptop.

Sasha comes into the open plan living and dining room and puts a gentle hand on my shoulder, 'I know you're worried that this isn't

The Lost Soul

over, but I think it is, you need to stop watching that YouTube news bulletin,' she says in quiet voice.

I place my large hand over hers and hold it there. She looks beautiful in a red thin strapped summer dress which rests just above the knee. Her skin has turned a golden brown in the two weeks that they've been here, on the island. The finger marks around her throat, and the bruising on her nose and cheek, courtesy of her father, have faded now.

I think back to that day six weeks ago, at Ponden reservoir, near Haworth. As if it were yesterday, I see Stuart, Jack Steph and myself running to Lewis Benson who is dragging Sasha and a crying Zoe slowly over the moor to the deep water. Sometimes, I wake up at night, panicking that I don't reach them in time, that I failed them, but thankfully, the nightmares are becoming less frequent. I need to let the baggage go, all of it.

It's time to move on.

Closing the laptop, I make a mental note that I will not watch the bulletin again. If there are problems, I'm sure that Stuart and Jenny will be in touch, but for now, I need to enjoy life. I put the laptop on the oak dining table, stand up and take Sasha's hand. When we reach the brown leather sofa I flop down and pull her gently onto my lap.

My heart lifts when she chuckles, and I reach out and tuck a stray curl around her ear. 'Have I told you how beautiful you are today?' I whisper into her ear. I hear her sharp intake of breath at my touch, I'll never get tired of seeing her reaction to me.

The Lost Soul

'Yes,' she whispers back, as my shoulders tense. 'You told me you loved me in bed, last night when you were sleeping,' she smiles, cupping the side of my face.

I feel my cheeks warm, at her honesty, I cannot believe I said that while I was sleeping. It makes me wonder what else I say when I'm not awake.

'Well, I do Sasha. You are beautiful and I bloody love you,' I kiss her cheek softly, my voice is husky with emotion, 'so very much. I never expected to find you, or thought I deserved you, but here you are. You and Zoe have filled the hole within my soul and made my heartbeat again.'

Her eyes lock onto mine, her brown ones holding my blue ones. With the help of Stuart and Jenny, we've got new identities. According to our passports, my name is now Julian Wakefield and Sasha's new name is Sasha Wakefield. We're supposed to be married, something which I plan to rectify in a few months, and exchange the cheap sapphire and gold engagement ring I gave her last week, for something more substantial, when things have settled down.

The villa, Casa Alina - Alina meaning light in Greek, is beautiful both inside and out. Stuart and Jenny purchased it as a holiday home five years ago. Casa Alina sits in the hills of the affluent north-east coast of the island, near the newly redeveloped fishing village of Kassiopi. It's a stunning five-bedroomed villa with a gated entrance, and a huge blue tiled walk-in pool, which has delighted Zoe.

The Lost Soul

The villa is modern with a nautical theme throughout, which I think may be connected to Jenny and Stuart's charity, The Lighthouse. There are several blue and white lighthouses tastefully dotted around the property.

Zoe runs into the room, I don't want her to catch her mummy sitting on my knee, so I shuffle my hand underneath Sasha and swivel her so that she's sitting beside me. I catch Sasha's eyes and she smiles a silent thank you, I can't believe how lucky I am, to have them both here, with me.

I still have to pinch myself, that Sasha chose to be with me, that I am worthy of her and Zoe. I will be forever grateful that I'm part of their small family unit. For a long time, I felt like everything I touched turned to ashes in my fingers. For a long time, I believed that I didn't deserve to be happy, particularly after I killed Ray Delossi. I was lost and didn't think I'd ever find the place where I was meant to be.

But now I've found it. Somehow, despite everything, I've found where I fit in. It's not a place, it's a feeling, and Sasha and Zoe, are that feeling. They are my home. For a long time, I was trying to exist in this harsh world, without expectations, without happiness. Now the tide has turned, and I finally have something to look forward to, to love and cherish.

Zoe's skin is tinted by the sun, and she wiggles from side to side in her pink and blue Peppa Pig swimming costume, complete with uninflated, orange-coloured arm bands which she has pushed onto her small skinny arms. I think coming here to Corfu has helped her to forget her ordeal and to concentrate on the here and now.

The Lost Soul

'Mummy, can we go to the pool now?' She pleads touching her mother's legs. Zoe is under strict instructions that she is not allowed near the pool unless she has an adult with her. We need to keep her safe. I stroke Sasha's neck lightly, I can't help but grin, I love this life.

In the realistic sense, we are living a normal life, doing everyday things that new couples do. Last week we took the plunge and decided to share a bed. It was getting harder to pretend that we didn't feel that way about each other, we knew it was just a matter of time. We had needed to let things settle, after what happened with her father.

'Right, girls,' I push myself to a standing position and reach down to take Sasha's hands. I look at my watch, it's 10 o'clock, and we need to be back here for 2pm. 'Pool time! I just need to change into my trunks.'

'Jules!' Zoe suddenly says. 'I like your new name, it suits you,' she smiles. We told her that Nick was my middle name, and that I wanted to use my first name of Jules again for a while.

'Jules', Zoe puts her small hand on my arm, 'Can I jump into the pool on my own?'

Sasha looks at me, shocked. I'm teaching Zoe how to swim, and I'd like her to gain confidence, under supervision.

'We'll see,' Sasha cuts in, her brows drawn together. She's worried about the whole drowning thing.

The Lost Soul

I check my watch, 'time for a few hours in the pool, a quick lunch and for us to be smartly dressed for the wedding at 2pm,' I tell them both, feeling very organised.

It's Jack and Steph's wedding day.

'What is smartly?' Zoe asks. This child is full of questions.

'I'll tell you about it when we get in the pool,' I call, as I walk to the bedroom.

'C'mon,' I hear Sasha tell her daughter. 'Let's leave these arm bands here, Jules can blow them up, while we get the towels.' Sasha mutters that I might not have enough puff to do both bands and they suddenly burst into giggles.

'I heard that!' I shout back, with a lightness to my voice. Dropping my grey knee length shorts to the floor, I collect the navy swim trunks from my drawer and pull them on. I feel lighter in myself than I've felt in a long time. Like the younger me, the one before Blip died, before Ray Delossi. Dare I even say I'm happy now, would you believe that? Sasha did that, she helped me to learn to live again. Her touch brought me back to life.

I hear their laughter, and I can't help but smile, I seem to do a lot of that these days. I love listening to their chatter, watching their natural, loving relationship. The domestic bliss of family life, with its highs and lows and easy dose of reality.

***

'Look, what I can do Jules!' Zoe's excited voice squeaks in my ear. She's splashing her arms and twirling herself around in circles at the same time. 'Swish, swish.' I smile, resting my feet on the bottom of the pool, and flicking water gently at her, while my shoulders heat up in the Grecian sun.

'Well done, Zoe,' I smile. 'You are getting so confident. How do you feel about taking your arm bands off for a while and practicing swimming without them?'

'Yes, Jules. Please, can I?' she smiles with excitement. 'You won't let go of me, will you?' she asks throwing her arms around my neck.

I look across at Sasha, who is reading her kindle on the sunbed, 'as long as you don't let go of her.'

I nod. I'll never let go of either of them.

***

At 2pm we are suitably dressed up, and ready to watch Jack and Steph's wedding. I'm relatively smart in a white shirt, open at the neck and dark grey trousers. Sasha looks gorgeous in a white knee length, short sleeved jersey dress, with pale red poppies on it and Zoe leans into me, sitting in between us both. She's wearing a white dress with pink hearts on and a plastic silver tiara. She has a princess Barbie doll in her hand.

We sit on the large brown leather sofa, facing my laptop, which is stacked on a couple of books on the oak coffee table, I rest my arm over the back of the sofa on Sasha's shoulder.

'Can you see them?' Jenny's voice is quiet as it comes through the speaker on my laptop. Steph comes into view, walking down the aisle of the Oxford registrar office, clutching Stuart's arm.

The Lost Soul

'Yes, she looks great,' Sasha's voice answers. Steph is wearing an ivory lace, twenties style knee length dress. She looks beautiful. It's still hard to think of her as Steph, rather than DI Rutland, but it becomes easier as time goes by.

Ben, Steph's son by Ray Delossi, stands beside almost head-to-head with Jack, he's tall, like his mum. Both look smart in charcoal-coloured suits, each with a red tie and an ivy lapel flower to match Steph's dress.

I glance across at Sasha and find her eyes are already watching me. She smiles and mouths, 'I love you.' I mouth the same back, and let my fingers caress the soft skin of her neck.

Ben is beaming, and I can't help but think of Zoe as Jack touches his shoulder, when it's time to put the rings on their fingers, gently coaching him through the process of being the Best Man at his mum's wedding.

'She looks like a princess,' Zoe's voice is serious, in awe, her eyes are glued to the screen.

'She does,' Sasha says, reaching up to put her hand over my fingers.

The couple turn to walk back, and I hear Jenny sniffle. 'Beautiful,' she whispers, as they walk closer and the newlyweds, wave at the camera. It feels as though they're waving to us. A man's soulful voice begins to sing John Lennon's song, Imagine, and there is nothing but the feeling of joy, love and happiness. The exact ingredients for a wedding.

The Lost Soul

'That'll be us, one day Sasha,' I say quietly, mesmerised with the happy couple.

Jenny turns the camera to face us. 'That was just beautiful,' she says. 'Sending you all lots of love. Live, be happy. Don't look back.' She blows us a kiss, before disconnecting the feed.

Sasha stands up, wipes her eyes. I love that about her, never afraid to show her feelings.

'Well, when that day comes,' she smiles, as Zoe plays with her princess doll, 'I'll be right here.' She reaches down and leans into me for a quick kiss.

As we break away, I push off the sofa to a standing position, so that I'm facing her. I cup her cheek, cherishing the warm softness of her skin.

'Mummy! Jules!' Zoe's voice breaks through our moment.

'Yes, sweetie,' Sasha answers, as we both look at her.

'Can I be a princess when you get married?'

What can you say to that? My vision blurs for a moment. I love this little girl. I would die for her.

'Oh, I think that can be arranged,' I tell her, reaching down to scoop her up and bring her into our arms.

'You are already my little princess,' Sasha strokes her daughter's hair.

'Our little princess,' I correct, smiling at Zoe, loving these two people with every bone in my body.

The Lost Soul

Through the dark days, the times when I felt so alone, even hated myself. I never dared hope to feel again, to find a way to live my life. What I did to Ray Delossi will always haunt me, as will, what he did to Blip. But I need to take a leaf out of Jenny's book, remember her words of advice, especially when the dark days threaten.

Life. At its simplest. Live, be happy. Don't look back.

It's the only way.

The Lost Soul

Acknowledgments

Jules Walker has played on my mind since the moment he disappeared from the police car at the end of my second book, The Ghost Chaser. Several ideas came to mind before a plan began to form. Giving Jules a second chance felt like the right way to go.

It's been strange writing this book during Covid, and I would be lying if I said that the new 'normal' we now find ourselves living, hasn't affected how I write. It makes me more thoughtful and appreciative of life in general. Particularly, as I write this, that I have an imminent new grandchild on the way, to join my two beautiful little ones. It reminds me of the importance of enjoying family life, and of making time to re-charge and chill, doing something that makes us feel good, perhaps reading a good book.

Thanks, as always to my wonderfully willing team of pre-readers who read first drafts and give essential feedback. Denise, Julia, Wendy and Lisa. You are such an important part of this process, for without feedback you are unable to get a true reflection of your book and where it is going.

To my editor, Lisa – who reads the end product and polishes it like a pair of new shoes! Thank you for your constructive feedback and for the wonderful job that you do with edits. It's important to note, at this point that sometimes what I see in my head, is not always clear in print. I am so lucky that you are on this journey with me.

My social media friends and family, including the lovely Heather, Rose, and Alison, not to mention the great Happy Gardens FB group, have given much needed support and the odd boost, particularly when I took on the roles of District Councillor, Vaccination Lead and had a knee replacement, earlier in the year. Goodness, did that all happen in 2021?

The hubby should be mentioned. He fits his heavy workload around my books, dipping in and out when I need help and getting them publish-ready for Amazon. My rock.

Of course, I couldn't finish without saying a big heartfelt thank you to everyone who reads my books and to those also, who take the time to write a review on Amazon. That's the place that monitors interest, so the more reviews, the more my books pick up interest.

Thank you all.

AJ Warren (Andrea) x

Read on for reviews of my previous books

The Lost Soul

What readers say about my books

The Lamp-post Shakers

'Fantastic read. Really enjoyed it!

Very well written and kept me gripped to keep reading more.

Look forward to reading the next novel!'

Donna

The Ghost Chaser

'A really good follow up book. Lovely location and great story.'

Steph

The Box

'Another excellent read, the third in the Lighthouse Series! If you want a good read, these are the books for you!'

Beryl

The Lost Soul

‘

Printed in Great Britain
by Amazon